"Moriarty has produced another gripping, satirical hit . . . While the momentum of who actually died drives *Big Little Lies* forward, its can't-put-downability comes from its darker subplots . . . Read to the end."
—Oprah.com

"[Moriarty] is a fantastically nimble writer, so sure-footed that the book leaps between dark and light seamlessly; even the big reveal in the final pages feels earned and genuinely shocking."
—*Entertainment Weekly*

"Written with a light, snappy hand that belies the complex, sometimes risky circumstances in which [Moriarty's] women are placed."
—*USA Today*

"Ms. Moriarty's long-parched fans have something new to dig into . . . *Big Little Lies* [may have] even more staying power than *The Husband's Secret*."
—*The New York Times*

"*Big Little Lies* tolls a warning bell about the big little lies we tell in order to survive. It takes a powerful stand against domestic violence even as it makes us laugh at the adults whose silly costume party seems more reminiscent of a middle-school dance."
—*The Washington Post*

"Irresistible . . . Moriarty's sly humor and razor-sharp insights will keep you turning the pages."
—*People*

"Funny and thrilling, page-turning but with emotional depth, *Big Little Lies* is a terrific follow-up to *The Husband's Secret*."
—*Booklist* (starred review)

"Moriarty demonstrates an excellent talent for exposing the dark, seedy side of the otherwise 'perfect' family unit . . . Highly recommended."
—*Library Journal* (starred review)

TITLES BY LIANE MORIARTY

Truly Madly Guilty

Big Little Lies

The Husband's Secret

The Hypnotist's Love Story

What Alice Forgot

The Last Anniversary

Three Wishes

Big Little Lies

LIANE MORIARTY

BERKLEY

New York

BERKLEY
An imprint of Penguin Random House LLC
1745 Broadway, New York, NY 10019

Copyright © 2014 by Liane Moriarty
"Readers Guide" copyright © 2014 by Penguin Random House LLC
Penguin Random House supports copyright. Copyright fuels creativity, encourages diverse
voices, promotes free speech, and creates a vibrant culture. Thank you for buying an authorized
edition of this book and for complying with copyright laws by not reproducing, scanning, or
distributing any part of it in any form without permission. You are supporting writers and
allowing Penguin Random House to continue to publish books for every reader.

BERKLEY and the BERKLEY & B colophon are registered trademarks of
Penguin Random House LLC.

Cover art © 2019 Home Box Office, Inc. All Rights Reserved.
HBO® is a service mark of Home Box Office, Inc.

Berkley trade paperback tie-in edition ISBN: 9780399587191

The Library of Congress has cataloged the G. P. Putnam's Sons hardcover edition as follows:

Moriarty, Liane.
Big little lies / Liane Moriarty.—First American Edition.
pages   cm
ISBN 978-0-399-16706-5
1. Female friendship—Fiction.   2. Parenting—Fiction.   3. Women—Fiction   I. Title.
PR9619.4.M67B54   2015
823'.92—dc23
2015019201

G. P. Putnam's Sons hardcover edition / July 2014
Berkley trade paperback edition / August 2015
Berkley premium tie-in edition / February 2017
Berkley trade paperback tie-in edition / February 2017

Printed in the United States of America
17   19   21   23   24   22   20   18   16

With love to Margaret

You hit me, you hit me, now you have to kiss me.

—SCHOOL YARD CHANT

Pirriwee Public School

. . . where we live and learn by the sea!

Pirriwee Public is a BULLY-FREE ZONE!

We do *not* bully.

We do not *accept* being bullied.

We *never* keep bullying a secret.

We have the *courage* to speak up if we see
our friends bullied.

We say NO to bullies!

1.

That doesn't sound like a school trivia night," said Mrs. Patty Ponder to Marie Antoinette. "That sounds like a riot."

The cat didn't respond. She was dozing on the couch and found school trivia nights to be trivial.

"Not interested, eh? Let them eat cake! Is that what you're thinking? They do eat a lot of cake, don't they? All those cake stalls. Goodness me. Although I don't think any of the mothers ever actually eat them. They're all so sleek and skinny, aren't they? Like you."

Marie Antoinette sneered at the compliment. The "let them eat cake" thing had grown old a long time ago, and she'd recently heard one of Mrs. Ponder's grandchildren say it was meant to be "let them eat brioche" and also that Marie Antoinette never said it in the first place.

Mrs. Ponder picked up her television remote and turned down the volume on *Dancing with the Stars*. She'd turned it up loud earlier because of the sound of the heavy rain, but the downpour had eased now.

She could hear people shouting. Angry hollers crashed through the quiet, cold night air. It was somehow hurtful for Mrs. Ponder to hear, as if all that rage were directed at her. (Mrs. Ponder had grown up with an angry mother.)

"Goodness me. Do you think they're arguing over the capital of Guatemala? Do you know the capital of Guatemala? No? I don't either. We should Google it. Don't sneer at me."

Marie Antoinette sniffed.

"Let's go see what's going on," said Mrs. Ponder briskly. She was feeling nervous and therefore behaving briskly in front of the cat, the same way she'd once done with her children when her husband was away and there were strange noises in the night.

Mrs. Ponder heaved herself up with the help of her walker. Marie Antoinette slid her slippery body comfortingly in between Mrs. Ponder's legs (she wasn't falling for the brisk act) as she pushed the walker down the hallway to the back of the house.

Her sewing room looked straight out onto the school yard of Pirriwee Public.

"Mum, are you mad? You can't live this close to a primary school," her daughter had said when she was first looking at buying the house.

But Mrs. Ponder loved to hear the crazy babble of children's voices at intervals throughout the day, and she no longer drove, so she couldn't care less that the street was jammed with those giant, truck-like cars they all drove these days, with women in big sunglasses leaning across their steering wheels to call out terribly urgent information about Harriett's ballet and Charlie's speech therapy.

Mothers took their mothering so seriously now. Their frantic little faces. Their busy little bottoms strutting into the school in their tight gym gear. Ponytails swinging. Eyes fixed on the mobile phones held in the palms of their hands like compasses. It made Mrs. Ponder laugh. Fondly though. Her three daughters, although older, were exactly the same. And they were all so pretty.

"How are you this morning?" she always called out if she was on the front porch with a cup of tea or watering the front garden as they went by.

"Busy, Mrs. Ponder! Frantic!" they always called back, trotting along, yanking their children's arms. They were pleasant and friendly and just a touch condescending because they couldn't help it. She was so old! They were so busy!

The fathers, and there were more and more of them doing the school run these days, were different. They rarely hurried, strolling past with a measured casualness. No big deal. All under control. That was the message. Mrs Ponder chuckled fondly at them too.

But now it seemed the Pirriwee Public parents were misbehaving. She got to the window and pushed aside the lace curtain. The school had recently paid for a window guard after a cricket ball had smashed the glass and nearly knocked out Marie Antoinette. (A group of Year 3 boys had given her a hand-painted apology card, which she kept on her fridge.)

There was a two-story sandstone building on the other side of the playground with an event room on the second level and a big balcony with ocean views. Mrs. Ponder had been there for a few functions: a talk by a local historian, a lunch hosted by the Friends of the Library. It was quite a beautiful room. Sometimes ex-students had their wedding receptions there. That's where they'd be having the school trivia night. They were raising funds for SMART Boards, whatever they were. Mrs. Ponder had been invited as a matter of course. Her proximity to the school gave her a funny sort of honorary status, even though she'd never had a child or grandchild attend. She'd said no thank you to the school trivia night invitation. She thought school events without the children in attendance were pointless.

The children had their weekly school assembly in the same room. Each Friday morning, Mrs. Ponder set herself up in the sewing room with a cup of English Breakfast and a ginger-nut biscuit. The sound of the children singing floating down from the second floor of the building always made her weep. She'd never believed in God, except when she heard children singing.

There was no singing now.

Mrs. Ponder could hear a lot of bad language. She wasn't a prude about bad language—her eldest daughter swore like a trooper—but it was upsetting and disconcerting to hear someone maniacally screaming that particular four-letter word in a place that was normally filled with childish laughter and shouts.

"Are you all drunk?" she said.

Her rain-splattered window was at eye level with the entrance doors to the building, and suddenly people began to spill out. Security lights illuminated the paved area around the entrance like a stage set for a play. Clouds of mist added to the effect.

It was a strange sight.

The parents at Pirriwee Public had a baffling fondness for costume parties. It wasn't enough that they should have an ordinary trivia night; she knew from the invitation that some bright spark had decided to make it an "Audrey and Elvis" trivia night, which meant that the women all had to dress up as Audrey Hepburn and the men had to dress up as Elvis Presley. (That was another reason Mrs. Ponder had turned down the invitation. She'd always abhorred costume parties.) It seemed that the most popular rendition of Audrey Hepburn was the *Breakfast at Tiffany's* look. All the women were wearing long black dresses, white gloves and pearl chokers. Meanwhile, the men had mostly chosen to pay tribute to the Elvis of the latter years. They were all wearing shiny white jumpsuits, glittery gemstones and plunging necklines. The women looked lovely. The poor men looked perfectly ridiculous.

As Mrs. Ponder watched, one Elvis punched another across the jaw. He staggered back into an Audrey. Two Elvises grabbed him from behind and pulled him away. An Audrey buried her face in her hands and turned aside, as though she couldn't bear to watch. Someone shouted, "Stop this!"

Indeed. What would your beautiful children think?

"Should I call the police?" wondered Mrs. Ponder out loud, but then she heard the wail of a siren in the distance, at the same time as a woman on the balcony began to scream and scream.

> **Gabrielle:** It wasn't like it was just the mothers, you know. It wouldn't have happened without the dads. I guess it *started* with the mothers. We were the main players, so to speak. The mums. I can't stand the word "mum." It's a frumpy word. "Mom" is better. With an *o*. It sounds skinnier. We should change to the American spelling. I have body-image issues, by the way. Who doesn't, right?

> **Bonnie:** It was all just a terrible misunderstanding. People's feelings got hurt, and then everything just spiraled out of control. The way it does. All conflict can be traced back to someone's feelings getting hurt, don't you think? Divorce. World wars. Legal action. Well, maybe not every legal action. Can I offer you an herbal tea?

> **Stu:** I'll tell you exactly why it happened: *Women don't let things go.* Not saying the blokes don't share part of the

blame. But if the girls hadn't gotten their knickers in a knot . . . And that might sound sexist, but it's not, it's just a fact of life. Ask any man—not some new-age, artsy-fartsy, I-wear-moisturizer type, I mean a real man—ask a real man, then he'll tell you that women are like the Olympic athletes of grudges. You should see my wife in action. And she's not even the worst of them.

Miss Barnes: Helicopter parents. Before I started at Pirriwee Public, I thought it was an exaggeration, this thing about parents being overly involved with their kids. I mean, my mum and dad loved me, they were, like, *interested* in me when I was growing up in the nineties, but they weren't, like, *obsessed* with me.

Mrs. Lipmann: It's a tragedy, and deeply regrettable, and we're all trying to move forward. I have no further comment.

Carol: I blame the Erotic Book Club. But that's just me.

Jonathan: There was nothing erotic about the Erotic Book Club, I'll tell you that for free.

Jackie: You know what? I see this as a feminist issue.

Harper: Who said it was a feminist issue? What the heck? I'll tell you what started it: the *incident* at the kindergarten orientation day.

Graeme: My understanding was that it all goes back to the stay-at-home mums battling it out with the career mums. What do they call it? The Mummy Wars. My wife wasn't involved. She doesn't have time for that sort of thing.

Thea: You journalists are just loving the French-nanny angle. I heard someone on the radio today talking about the "French maid," which Juliette was certainly not. Renata had a housekeeper as well. Lucky for some. I have four children, and no staff to help out! Of course, I don't have a problem *per se* with working mothers, I just wonder why they bothered having children in the first place.

Melissa: You know what I think got everyone all hot and bothered? The head lice. Oh my gosh, don't let me get started on the head lice.

Samantha: The head lice? What did that have to do with anything? Who told you that? I bet it was Melissa, right? That poor girl suffered post-traumatic stress disorder after her kids kept getting reinfected. Sorry. It's not funny. It's not funny at all.

Detective-Sergeant Adrian Quinlan: Let me be clear: This is not a circus. This is a murder investigation.

2.

Six Months Before the Trivia Night

F orty. Madeline Martha Mackenzie was forty years old today. "I am forty," she said out loud as she drove. She drew the word out in slow motion, like a sound effect. *"Fooorty."*

She caught the eye of her daughter in the rearview mirror. Chloe grinned and imitated her mother. "I am five. *Fiiiive.*"

"Forty!" trilled Madeline like an opera singer. "Tra la la la!"

"Five!" trilled Chloe.

Madeline tried a rap version, beating out the rhythm on the steering wheel. "I'm forty, yeah, forty—"

"That's enough now, Mummy," said Chloe firmly.

"Sorry," said Madeline.

She was taking Chloe to her kindergarten—"Let's Get Kindy Ready!"—orientation. Not that Chloe required any orientation before starting school next January. She was already very firmly oriented at Pirriwee Public. At this morning's drop-off Chloe had been busy taking charge of her brother, Fred, who was two years older but often seemed younger. "Fred, you forgot to put your book bag in the basket! That's it. In there. Good boy."

Fred had obediently dropped his book bag in the appropriate basket before running off to put Jackson in a headlock. Madeline had pretended not to see the headlock. Jackson probably deserved it. Jackson's mother, Renata, hadn't seen it either, because she was deep in conversation with Harper, both of them frowning earnestly over the stress of educating their gifted children. Renata and Harper attended the same weekly support group for parents of gifted children. Madeline imagined them all sitting in a circle, wringing their hands while their eyes shone with secret pride.

While Chloe was busy bossing the other children around at orientation (her gift was bossiness, she was going to run a corporation one day), Madeline was going to have coffee and cake with her friend Celeste. Celeste's twin boys were starting school next year too, so they'd be running amuck at orientation. (Their gift was shouting. Madeline had a headache after five minutes in their company.) Celeste always bought exquisite and very expensive birthday presents, so that would be nice. After that, Madeline was going to drop Chloe off with her mother-in-law, and then have lunch with some friends before they all rushed off for school pickup. The sun was shining. She was wearing her gorgeous new Dolce & Gabbana stilettos (bought online, thirty percent off). It was going to be a lovely, lovely day.

"Let the Festival of Madeline begin!" her husband, Ed, had said this morning when he brought her coffee in bed. Madeline was famous for her fondness of birthdays and celebrations of all kinds. Any excuse for champagne.

Still. Forty.

As she drove the familiar route to the school, she considered her magnificent new age. Forty. She could still feel "forty" the way it felt when she was fifteen. Such a colorless age. Marooned in the middle of your life. Nothing would matter all that much when you were forty. You wouldn't have real feelings when you were forty, because you'd be safely cushioned by your frumpy forty-ness.

Forty-year-old woman found dead. Oh dear.

Twenty-year-old woman found dead. Tragedy! Sadness! Find that murderer!

Madeline had recently been forced to do a minor shift in her head when she heard something on the news about a woman dying in her forties. *But, wait, that could be me! That would be sad! People would be sad if I was dead! Devastated, even. So there, age-obsessed world. I might be forty, but I am cherished.*

On the other hand, it was probably perfectly natural to feel sadder over the death of a twenty-year-old than a forty-year-old. The forty-year-old had enjoyed twenty years more of life. That's why, if there was a gunman on the loose, Madeline would feel obligated to throw her middle-aged self in front of the twenty-year-old. Take a bullet for youth. It was only fair.

Well, she would, if she could be sure it was a nice young person. Not one of those insufferable ones, like the child driving the little blue Mitsubishi in front of Madeline. She wasn't even bothering to hide the fact that she was using her mobile phone while she drove, probably *texting* or updating her Facebook status.

See! This kid wouldn't have even noticed the loose gunman! She would have been staring vacantly at her phone, while Madeline sacrificed her life for her! It was infuriating.

The little car appeared to be jammed with young people. At least three in the back, their heads bobbing about, hands gesticulating. Was that somebody's foot waving about? It was a tragedy waiting to happen. They all needed to concentrate. Just last week, Madeline had been having a quick coffee after her ShockWave class and was reading a story in the paper about how all the young people were killing themselves by sending texts while they drove. *On my way. Nearly there!* These were their last foolish (and often misspelled) words. Madeline had cried over the picture of one teenager's grief-stricken mother, absurdly holding up her daughter's mobile phone to the camera as a warning to readers.

"Silly little idiots," she said out loud as the car weaved dangerously into the next lane.

"Who is an idiot?" said her daughter from the backseat.

"The girl driving the car in front of me is an idiot because she's driving her car and using her phone at the same time," said Madeline.

"Like when you need to call Daddy when we're running late?" said Chloe.

"I only did that one time!" protested Madeline. "And I was very careful and very quick! And I'm *forty* years old!"

"Today," said Chloe knowledgeably. "You're forty years old today."

"Yes! Also, I made a quick call, I didn't send a text! You have to take your eyes off the road to text. Texting while driving is illegal and naughty, and you must promise to never ever do it when you're a teenager."

Her voice quivered at the thought of Chloe being a teenager and driving a car.

"But you're allowed to make a quick phone call?" checked Chloe.

"No! That's illegal too," said Madeline.

"So that means you broke the law," said Chloe with satisfaction. "Like a *robber*."

Chloe was currently in love with the idea of robbers. She

was definitely going to date bad boys one day. Bad boys on motorcycles.

"Stick with the nice boys, Chloe!" said Madeline after a moment. "Like Daddy. Bad boys don't bring you coffee in bed, I'll tell you that for free."

"What are you babbling on about, woman?" sighed Chloe. She'd picked this phrase up from her father and imitated his weary tone perfectly. They'd made the mistake of laughing the first time she did it, so she'd kept it up, and said it just often enough, and with perfect timing, so that they couldn't help but keep laughing.

This time Madeline managed not to laugh. Chloe currently trod a very fine line between adorable and obnoxious. Madeline probably trod the same line herself.

Madeline pulled up behind the little blue Mitsubishi at a red light. The young driver was *still* looking at her mobile phone. Madeline banged on her car horn. She saw the driver glance in her rearview mirror, while all her passengers craned around to look.

"Put down your phone!" she yelled. She mimicked texting by jabbing her finger in her palm. "It's illegal! It's dangerous!"

The girl stuck her finger up in the classic up-yours gesture.

"Right!" Madeline pulled on her emergency brake and put on her hazard lights.

"What are you doing?" said Chloe.

Madeline undid her seat belt and threw open the car door.

"But we've got to go to orientation!" said Chloe in a panic. "We'll be late! Oh, *calamity*!"

"Oh, calamity" was a line from a children's book that they used to read to Fred when he was little. The whole family said it now. Even Madeline's parents had picked it up, and some of Madeline's friends. It was a very contagious phrase.

"It's all right," said Madeline. "This will only take a second. I'm saving young lives."

She stalked up to the girl's car on her new stilettos and banged on the window.

The window slid down, and the driver metamorphosed from a shadowy silhouette into a real young girl with white skin, sparkly nose ring and badly applied, clumpy mascara. She looked up at Madeline with a mixture of aggression and fear. "What is your *problem?*" Her mobile phone was still held casually in her left hand.

"Put down that phone! You could kill yourself and your friends!" Madeline used the exact same tone she used on Chloe when she was being extremely naughty. She reached in the car, grabbed the phone and tossed it to the openmouthed girl in the passenger seat. "OK? Just stop it!"

She could hear their gales of laughter as she walked back to her SUV. She didn't care. She felt pleasantly stimulated. A car pulled up behind hers. Madeline smiled, lifted her hand apologetically and hurried back to be in her car before the lights changed.

Her ankle turned. One second it was doing what an ankle was meant to do, and the next it was flipping out at a sickeningly wrong angle. She fell heavily on one side. Oh, calamity.

That was almost certainly the moment the story began.

With the ungainly flip of an ankle.

3.

Jane pulled up at a red light behind a big shiny SUV with its hazard lights blinking and watched a dark-haired woman hurry along the side of the road back to it. She wore a floaty, blue summer dress and high strappy heels, and she waved apologetically, charmingly at Jane. The morning sun caught one of the woman's earrings, and it shone as if she'd been touched by something celestial.

A glittery girl. Older than Jane but definitely still glittery. All her life Jane had watched girls like that with scientific interest. Maybe a little awe. Maybe a little envy. They weren't necessarily the prettiest, but they decorated themselves so affectionately, like Christmas trees, with dangling earrings, jangling bangles and delicate, pointless scarves. They touched your arm a lot when they spoke. Jane's best friend at school had been a glittery girl. Jane had a weakness for them.

Then the woman fell, as if something had been pulled out from underneath her.

"Ouch," said Jane, and she looked away fast to save the woman's dignity.

"Did you hurt yourself, Mummy?" asked Ziggy from the backseat. He was always very worried about her hurting herself.

"No," said Jane. "That lady over there hurt herself. She tripped."

She waited for the woman to get up and get back in her car, but she was still on the ground. She'd tipped back her head to the sky, and her face had that compressed look of someone in great pain. The traffic light turned green, and a little blue Mitsubishi that had been in front of the SUV zoomed off with a squeal of tires.

Jane put her signal on to drive around the car. They were on their way to Ziggy's orientation day at the new school, and she had no idea where she was going. She and Ziggy were both nervous and pretending not to be. She wanted to get there in plenty of time.

"Is the lady OK?" said Ziggy.

Jane felt that strange lurch she sometimes experienced when she got distracted by her life, and then something (it was often Ziggy) made her remember just in time the appropriate way for a nice, ordinary, well-mannered grown-up to behave.

If it weren't for Ziggy she would have driven off. She would have been so focused on her goal of getting him to his kindergarten orientation that she would have *left a woman sitting on the road, writhing in pain*.

"I'll just check on her," said Jane, as if that were her intention all along. She flicked on her own hazard lights and opened the car door, aware as she did of a selfish sense of resistance. *You are an inconvenience, glittery lady!*

"Are you all right?" she called.

"I'm fine!" The woman tried to sit up straighter and whimpered, her hand on her ankle. "Ow. Shit. I've rolled my ankle, that's all. I'm such an *idiot*. I got out of the car to go tell the girl in front of me to stop texting. Serves me right for behaving like a school prefect."

Jane crouched down next to her. The woman had shoulder-length, well-cut dark hair and the faintest sprinkle of freckles across her nose. There was something aesthetically pleasing about those freckles, like a childhood memory of summer, and they were very nicely complemented by the fine lines around her eyes and the absurd swinging earrings.

Jane's resistance vanished entirely.

She liked this woman. She wanted to help her.

(Although, what did that say? If the woman had been a toothless, warty-nosed crone she would have continued to feel resentful? The injustice of it. The cruelty of it. She was going to be nicer to this woman because she liked her freckles.)

The woman's dress had an intricately embroidered cutout pattern of flowers all along the neckline. Jane could see tanned freckly skin through the petals.

"We need to get some ice on it straightaway," said Jane. She knew about ankle injuries from her netball days and she could see this woman's ankle was already beginning to swell. "And keep it elevated." She chewed her lip and looked about hopefully for someone else. She had no idea how to handle the logistics of making this actually happen.

"It's my birthday," said the woman sadly. "My fortieth."

"Happy birthday," said Jane. It was sort of cute that a woman of *forty* would even bother to mention that it was her birthday.

She looked at the woman's strappy shoes. Her toenails were painted a lustrous turquoise. The stiletto heels were as thin as toothpicks and perilously high.

"No wonder you did your ankle," said Jane. "No one could walk in those shoes!"

"I know, but aren't they gorgeous?" The woman turned her

foot at an angle to admire them. "Ouch! *Fuck*, that hurts. Sorry. Excuse my language."

"Mummy!" A little girl with dark curly hair, wearing a sparkling tiara, stuck her head out the window of the car. "What are you doing? Get up! We'll be late!"

Glittery mother. Glittery daughter.

"Thanks for the sympathy, darling!" said the woman. She smiled ruefully at Jane. "We're on our way to her kindergarten orientation. She's very excited."

"At Pirriwee Public?" said Jane. She was astonished. "But that's where I'm going. My son, Ziggy, is starting school next year. We're moving here in December." It didn't seem possible that she and this woman could have anything in common, or that their lives could intersect in any way.

"Ziggy! Like Ziggy Stardust? What a great name!" said the woman. "I'm Madeline, by the way. Madeline Martha Mackenzie. I always mention the Martha for some reason. Don't ask mc why." She held out her hand.

"Jane," said Jane. "Jane no-middle-name Chapman."

Gabrielle: The school ended up split in two. It was, like, I don't know, a civil war. You were either on Team Madeline or Team Renata.

Bonnie: No, no, that's awful. That never happened. There were no *sides*. We're a very close-knit community. There was too much alcohol. Also, it was a full moon. Everyone goes a little crazy when it's a full moon. I'm serious. It's an actual verifiable phenomenon.

Samantha: Was it a full moon? It was pouring rain, I know that. My hair was all boofy.

Mrs. Lipmann: That's ridiculous and highly defamatory. I have no further comment.

Carol: I know I keep harping on about the Erotic Book Club, but I'm sure something happened at one of their little quote-unquote meetings.

Harper: Listen, I *cried* when we learned Emily was gifted. I thought, *Here we go again!* I'd been through it all before with Sophia, so I knew what I was in for! Renata was in the same boat. *Two* gifted children. Nobody understands the stress. Renata was worried about how Amabella would settle in at school, whether she'd get enough stimulation and so on. So when that child with the ridiculous name, that Ziggy, did what he did, and it was only the orientation morning! Well, she was understandably very distressed. That's what started it all.

4.

J ane had brought along a book to read in the car while Ziggy was doing his kindergarten orientation, but instead she accompanied Madeline Martha Mackenzie (it sounded like the name of a feisty little girl in a children's book) to a beachside café called Blue Blues.

The café was a funny little misshapen building, almost like a cave, right on the boardwalk next to Pirriwee Beach. Madeline hobbled along in bare feet, leaning heavily and unselfconsciously on Jane's shoulder as if they were old friends. It felt intimate. She could smell Madeline's perfume, something citrusy and delicious. Jane hadn't been touched much by other grown-ups in the last five years.

As soon as they opened the door of the café, a youngish man came out from behind the counter, his arms outstretched. He was dressed all in black, with curly blond surfer hair and a stud in the side of his nose. "Madeline! What's happened to you?"

"I am gravely injured, Tom," said Madeline. "And it's my *birthday*."

"Oh, calamity," said Tom. He winked at Jane.

While Tom settled Madeline in a corner booth, bringing her ice wrapped in a tea towel and propping her leg up on a chair with a cushion, Jane took in the café. It was "completely charming," as her mother would have said. The bright blue uneven walls were lined with rickety shelves filled with secondhand books. The timber floorboards shone gold in the morning light, and Jane breathed in a heady mix of coffee, baking, the sea and old books. The front of the café was all open glass, and the seating was arranged so that wherever you sat you faced the beach, as if you were there to watch the sea perform a show. As Jane looked around her, she felt that dissatisfied feeling she often experienced when she was somewhere new and lovely. She couldn't quite articulate it except with the words *If only I were here.* This little beachside café was so exquisite, she longed to really be there—except, of course, she *was* there, so it didn't make sense.

"Jane? What can I get you?" said Madeline. "I'm buying you coffee and treats to thank you for everything!" She turned to the fussing barista. "Tom! This is Jane! She's my knight in shining armor. My knight-ess."

Jane had driven Madeline and her daughter to the school, after first nervously parking Madeline's massive car in a side street. She'd taken a spare booster seat from the back of Madeline's car for Chloe and put it in the back of her own little Honda, next to Ziggy.

It had been a project. A tiny crisis overcome.

It was a sad indictment of Jane's mundane life that she'd found the whole incident just a little bit thrilling.

Ziggy too had been wide-eyed and self-conscious at the novelty of having another child in the backseat with him, especially one as effervescent and charismatic as Chloe. The little girl had chatted nonstop the whole way, explaining everything Ziggy needed to know about the school, and who the teachers would be, and how they had to wash their hands before they went into the classroom, with just *one* paper towel, and where they sat to have their lunch, and how you weren't allowed peanut butter, because some people had allergies and could *die*, and she already had her lunch box, and it had Dora the Explorer on it, and what did Ziggy's lunch box have on it?

"Buzz Lightyear," Ziggy had answered promptly, politely, and completely untruthfully, as Jane hadn't bought his lunch box yet, and they hadn't even discussed the need for a lunch box. He was in day care three days a week at the moment, and meals were provided. Packing a lunch box was going to be new for Jane.

When they got to the school, Madeline had stayed in the car while Jane took the children in. Actually, Chloe had taken them in, marching along in front of them, tiara gleaming in the sunlight. At one point Ziggy and Jane had exchanged looks as if to say, *Who are these marvelous people?*

Jane had been mildly nervous about Ziggy's orientation morning and conscious of the fact that she would need to hide her nerves from Ziggy, because he was prone to anxiety. It had felt like she was starting a new job: her job as a primary school mother. There would be rules and paperwork and procedures to learn.

However, walking into school with Chloe was like arriving with a golden ticket. Two other mothers immediately accosted them, "Chloe! Where's your mum?" Then they introduced themselves to Jane, and Jane had a story to tell about Madeline's ankle, and next thing, the kindergarten teacher, Miss Barnes, wanted to hear, and Jane found herself the center of attention, which was quite pleasant, to be honest.

The school itself was beautiful, perched at the end of the headland, so that the blue of the distant ocean seemed to be constantly sparkling in Jane's peripheral vision. The classrooms were in long, low sandstone buildings and the leafy-treed playground seemed to be full of enchanting secret spots to encourage the imagination: cubbyholes in between trees, sheltered pathways, even a tiny, child-sized maze.

When she'd left, Ziggy had been walking into a classroom hand in hand with Chloe, his little face flushed and happy, and Jane had walked outside to her car, feeling flushed and happy herself, and there was Madeline in the passenger seat, waving and smiling delightedly, as if Jane were her great friend, and Jane had felt a lessening of something, a loosening.

Now she sat next to Madeline in Blue Blues and waited for her coffee to arrive, watching the water and feeling the sunshine on her face.

Maybe moving here was going to be the beginning of something, or the end, which would be even better.

"My friend Celeste will be here soon," said Madeline. "You might have seen her at the school, dropping off her boys. Two little blond ruffians. She's tall, blond, beautiful and flustered."

"I don't think so," said Jane. "What's she got to be flustered about if she's tall, blond and beautiful?"

"Exactly," said Madeline, as if that answered the question. "She's got this equally gorgeous, rich husband too. They still hold hands. *And* he's nice. He buys *me* presents. Honestly, I have no idea why I stay friends with her." She looked at her watch. "Oh, she's hopeless. Always late! Anyway, I'll interrogate you while we wait." She leaned forward and gave her full attention to Jane. "Are you new to the peninsula? I don't know your face at all. With kids the same age you'd think we would have run into each other at GymbaROO or story hour or whatever."

"We're moving here in December," said Jane. "We live in Newtown at the moment, but I decided it might be nice to live near the beach for a while. It was just on a whim, I guess."

The phrase "on a whim" came to her out of nowhere, and both pleased and embarrassed her.

She tried to make it a whimsical story, as if she were indeed a whimsical girl. She told Madeline that one day a few months back she'd taken Ziggy for a trip to the beach, seen the rental sign outside a block of apartments and thought, *Why not live near the beach?*

It wasn't a lie, after all. Not exactly.

A day at the beach, she'd kept telling herself, over and over, as she drove down that long swooping road, as if someone were listening in on her thoughts, questioning her motives.

Pirriwee Beach was one of the top ten most beautiful beaches in the world! She'd seen that somewhere. Her son deserved to see one of the top ten most beautiful beaches in the world. Her *beautiful, extraordinary* son. She kept looking at him in the rearview mirror, her heart aching.

She didn't tell Madeline that, as they'd walked hand in hand back to the car, sandy and sticky, the word "help" screamed silently in her head, as if she were begging for something: a solution, a cure, a reprieve. A reprieve from what? A cure for what? A solution for what? Her breathing had become shallow. She'd felt beads of sweat at her hairline.

Then she'd seen the sign. Their lease at their Newtown apartment was up. The two-bedroom unit was in an ugly, soulless, redbrick block of apartments, but it was only a five-minute walk to the beach. "What if we moved right here?" she'd said to Ziggy, and his eyes had lit up, and all at once it had seemed like the apartment was exactly the solution to whatever was wrong with her. A sea change, people called it. Why shouldn't she and Ziggy have a sea change?

She didn't tell Madeline that she'd been taking six-month leases in different rental apartments across Sydney ever since Ziggy was a baby, trying to find a life that worked. She didn't tell her that, maybe the whole time, she'd been circling closer and closer to Pirriwee Beach.

And she didn't tell Madeline that, when she'd walked out of the real estate office after signing the lease, she'd noticed for the first time the sort of people who lived on the peninsula—golden-skinned and beach-haired, the sort of people who surfed before breakfast, who took pride in their bodies—and she'd thought of her own pasty white legs beneath her jeans, and then she'd thought of how her parents would feel so nervous driving along that winding peninsula road, her dad's knuckles white on the steering wheel, except they'd still do it, without complaint, and all at once Jane had been convinced that she'd just made a truly reprehensible mistake. But it was too late.

"So here I am," she finished lamely.

"You're going to love it here," Madeline enthused. She adjusted the ice on her ankle and winced. "Ow. Do you surf? What about your husband? Or your partner, I should say. Or boyfriend? Girlfriend? I am open to all possibilities."

"No husband," Jane said. "No partner. It's just me. I'm a single mum."

"*Are* you?" said Madeline, as if Jane had just announced something rather daring and wonderful.

"I am." Jane smiled foolishly.

"Well, you know, people always like to forget this, but *I* was a single mother," said Madeline. She lifted her chin, as if she were addressing a crowd of people who disagreed with her. "My ex-husband walked out on me when my older daughter, Abigail, was a baby. She's fourteen. I was quite young too, like you. Only twenty-six. Although I thought I was over the hill. It was hard. Being a single mother is *hard*."

"Well, I have my mum and——"

"Oh, sure, sure. I'm not saying I didn't have support. I had my parents to help me too. But my God, there were some nights, when Abigail was sick, or when I got sick, or worse, when we both got sick, and . . . Anyway." Madeline stopped and shrugged. "My ex is remarried now to someone else. They have a little girl about the same age as Chloe, and Nathan has become father of the year. Men often do when they get a second chance. Abigail thinks her dad is wonderful. I'm the only one left holding a grudge. They say it's good to let your grudges go, but I don't know, I'm quite fond of my grudge. I tend it like a little pet."

"I'm not really into forgiveness either," said Jane.

Madeline grinned and pointed her teaspoon at her. "Good for you. Never forgive. Never forget. That's my motto."

Jane couldn't tell how much she was joking.

"So what about Ziggy's dad?" continued Madeline. "Is he in the picture at all?"

Jane didn't flinch. She'd had five years to get good at it. She felt herself becoming very still.

"No. We weren't actually together." She delivered her line perfectly. "I didn't even know his name. It was a . . ." Stop. Pause. Look away as if unable to make eye contact. "Sort of a . . . one-off."

"You mean a one-night stand?" said Madeline immediately,

sympathetically, and Jane almost laughed out loud with the surprise of it. Most people, especially of Madeline's age, reacted with
a delicate, slightly distasteful expression that said, *I get it and I'm
cool with it, but I now place you in a different category of person.* Jane
was never offended by their distaste. She found it distasteful too.
She just wanted that particular topic of conversation closed off for
good, and most of the time that's exactly what happened. Ziggy
was Ziggy. There was no dad. Move right along.

"Why don't you just say you split up with the father?" her
mother had asked in the early days.

"Lies get complicated, Mum," said Jane. Her mother had no
experience with lies. "This way we just close the conversation
down."

"I remember one-night stands," said Madeline wistfully. "The
things I did in the nineties. Lordy me. I hope Chloe never finds
out. Oh, calamity. Was yours fun?"

It took Jane a second to comprehend the question. She was
asking *if her one-night stand was fun.*

For a moment Jane was back in that glass bubble of an elevator
as it slid silently up the center of the hotel. His hand around the
neck of the champagne bottle. The other hand on her lower back,
pulling her forward. They were both laughing so hard. Deep
creases around his eyes. She was weak with laughter and desire.
Expensive smells.

Jane cleared her throat.

"I guess it was fun," she said.

"Sorry," said Madeline. "I was being frivolous. It was because
I was thinking of my own frivolous youth. Or maybe because
you're so young and I'm so old, and I'm trying to be cool. How
old are you? Do you mind my asking?"

"Twenty-four," said Jane.

"Twenty-four," breathed Madeline. "I'm forty today. I told you that already, didn't I? You probably think you'll never be forty, right?"

"Well, I *hope* I'll be forty," said Jane. She'd noticed before how middle-aged women were obsessed with the topic of age, always laughing about it, moaning about it, going on and on about it, as if the process of aging were a tricky puzzle they were trying to solve. Why were they so mystified by it? Jane's mother's friends seemed to literally have no other topic of conversation, or they didn't when they spoke to Jane. "Oh, you're so young and beautiful, Jane." (When she clearly wasn't; it was like they thought one followed the other: If you were young, you were automatically beautiful!) "Oh, you're so young, Jane, you'll be able to fix my phone/computer/camera." (When in fact a lot of her mother's friends were more technologically savvy than Jane.) "Oh, you're so young, Jane, you have so much energy." (When she was so tired, so very, very tired.)

"And listen, how do you support yourself?" said Madeline worriedly, sitting up straight, as if this were a problem she needed to solve right this minute. "Do you work?"

Jane nodded at her. "I work for myself as a freelance book-keeper. I've got a good client base now, lots of small businesses. I'm fast. So I turn the work over fast. It pays the rent."

"Clever girl," said Madeline approvingly. "I supported myself too when Abigail was little. For the most part anyway. Every now and then Nathan would rouse himself to send a check. It was hard, but it was also sort of satisfying, in a fuck-you kind of way. You know what I mean."

"Sure," said Jane. Jane's life as a single mother wasn't making

a fuck-you point to anyone. Or at least not in the way that Madeline meant.

"You'll definitely be one of the younger kindergarten mums,"
mused Madeline. She took a sip of her coffee and grinned wickedly. "You're even younger than my ex-husband's delightful new
wife. Promise me you won't make friends with her, will you? I got
you first."

"I'm sure I won't even meet her," said Jane, confused.

"Oh, you will," grimaced Madeline. "Her daughter is starting
kindergarten at the same time as Chloe. Can you imagine?"

Jane couldn't imagine.

"The kindy mums will all have coffee, and there will be my
ex-husband's wife sitting across the table, sipping her herbal tea.
Don't worry, there won't be any punch-ups. Unfortunately it's all
very boring and amicable and terribly grown-up. Bonnie even
kisses me hello. She's into yoga and chakras and all that shit. You
know how you're meant to hate your wicked stepmother? My
daughter *adores* her. Bonnie is so 'calm,' you see. The opposite of
me. She speaks in one of those soft . . . low . . . melodious voices
that make you want to punch a wall."

Jane laughed at Madeline's imitation of a low, melodious voice.

"You probably will make friends with Bonnie," said Madeline. "She's impossible to hate. I'm very good at hating people,
and even I find it difficult. I really have to put my heart and soul
into it."

She shifted the ice again on her ankle.

"When Bonnie hears I've hurt my ankle, she'll bring me a
meal. She just loves any excuse to bring me a home-cooked meal.
Probably because Nathan told her I'm a terrible cook, so she
wants to make a point. Although the worst thing about Bonnie is

that she's probably not actually making a point. She's just freakishly nice. I'd love to throw her meals straight in the bin, but they're too damned delicious. My husband and children would kill me."

Madeline's expression changed. She beamed and waved. "Oh! She's here at last! Celeste! Over here! Come and see what I've done!"

Jane looked up and her heart sank.

It shouldn't matter. She knew it shouldn't matter. But the fact was that some people were so unacceptably, hurtfully beautiful, it made you feel ashamed. Your inferiority was right there on display for the world to see. *This* was what a woman was meant to look like. Exactly this. She was right, and Jane was wrong.

You're a very fat, ugly little girl, a voice said insistently in her ear with hot, fetid breath.

She shuddered and tried to smile at the horribly beautiful woman walking toward them.

> **Thea:** I assume you've heard by now that Bonnie is married to Madeline's ex-husband, Nathan? So that was complicated. You might want to explore that. I'm not telling you how to do your job, of course.

> **Bonnie:** That had absolutely *nothing* to do with *anything*. Our relationship was completely amicable. Just this morning I left a vegetarian lasagna on their doorstep for her poor husband.

> **Gabrielle:** I was new to the school. I didn't know a soul. "Oh, we're such a caring school," the principal told me. Blah, blah, blah. Let me tell you, the first

thing I thought when I walked into that playground on that kindergarten orientation day was *cliquey*. Cliquey, cliquey, cliquey. I'm not surprised someone ended up dead. Oh, all right. I guess that's overstating it. I was a little surprised.

5.

Celeste pushed open the glass door of Blue Blues and saw Madeline straightaway. She was sharing a table with a small, thin young girl wearing a blue denim skirt and a plain white V-necked T-shirt. Celeste didn't recognize the girl. She felt an instant, sharp sense of disappointment. "Just the two of us," Madeline had said.

Celeste readjusted her expectations of the morning. She took a deep breath. Recently, she'd noticed something strange happening when she talked to people in groups. She couldn't quite remember how to *be*. She'd find herself thinking: *Did I just laugh too loudly? Did I forget to laugh? Did I just repeat myself?*

For some reason when it was just her and Madeline, it was OK. It was because she'd known Madeline for such a long time. Her personality felt intact when it was just the two of them.

Maybe she needed a tonic. That's what her grandmother would have said. What was a tonic?

She weaved through the tables toward them. They hadn't noticed her yet. They were deep in conversation. She could see the girl's profile clearly. She was too young to be a school mother. She must be a nanny or an au pair. Probably an au pair. Maybe European? With not much English? That would explain the slightly stiff, strained way she was sitting, as though she needed to concentrate. Of course, maybe she had nothing to do with the school at all. Madeline traveled with ease through dozens of overlapping social circles, making both lifelong friends and lifetime enemies along the way; probably more of the latter. Madeline thrived on conflict and was never happier than when she was outraged.

Madeline saw Celeste and her face lit up. One of the nicest things about Madeline was the way her face transformed when she saw you, as if there were no one else in the world she'd rather see.

"Hello, birthday girl!" Celeste called out.

Madeline's companion swung around in her chair. She had brown hair scraped back painfully hard from the forehead, like she was in the military or the police force.

"What happened to you, Madeline?" said Celeste as she got close enough to see Madeline's leg propped up on the chair. She smiled politely at the girl, and the girl seemed to shrink away, as if Celeste had sneered, not smiled. (Oh, God, she *had* smiled at her, hadn't she?)

"This is Jane," said Madeline. "She saved me from the side of the road after I twisted my ankle trying to save young lives. Jane, this is Celeste."

"Hi," said Jane. There was something naked and raw about Jane's face, like it had just been scrubbed too hard. She was chewing gum with tiny movements of her jaw, as if it were a secret.

"Jane is a new kindergarten mother," said Madeline as Celeste sat down. "Like you. So it's my responsibility to bring you both up-to-date with everything you need to know about school politics at Pirriwee Public. It's a minefield, girls. A minefield, I tell you."

"School politics?" Jane frowned and used two hands to pull hard on her ponytail so it was even tighter still. "I won't get involved in any school politics."

"Me either," agreed Celeste.

Jane would always remember how she recklessly tempted fate that day. "I won't get involved in any school politics," she'd said, and someone up there had overheard and hadn't liked her attitude. Far too confident. "We'll see about that," they'd said, and then sat back and had a good old laugh at her expense.

Celeste's birthday gift was a set of Waterford crystal champagne glasses.

"Oh my God, I love them. They're absolutely gorgeous," said Madeline. She carefully took one out of the box and held it up to the light, admiring the intricate design, rows of tiny moons. "They must have cost you a small fortune."

She almost said, *Thank God you're so rich, darling,* but she stopped herself in time. She would have said it if it were just the two of them, but presumably Jane, a young single mother, was not well off, and of course, it was impolite to talk about money in company. She did actually know that. (She said this defensively to her husband in her head, because he was the one who was always reminding her of the social norms she insisted on flouting.)

Why did they all have to tread so very delicately around Celeste's money? It was like wealth was an embarrassing medical condition. It was the same with Celeste's beauty. Strangers gave Celeste the same furtive looks they gave to people with missing limbs, and if Madeline ever mentioned Celeste's looks, Celeste responded with something like shame. "Shhh," she'd say, looking around fearfully in case someone overheard. Everyone wanted to be rich and beautiful, but the truly rich and beautiful had to pretend they were just the same as everyone else. Oh, it was a funny old world.

"So, school politics, girls," Madeline said as she carefully replaced the glass in the box. "We'll start at the top with the Blond Bobs."

"The Blond Bobs?" Celeste squinted, as if there were going to be a test afterward.

"The Blond Bobs rule the school. If you want to be on the PTA, you have to have a blond bob," said Madeline. She demonstrated the required haircut with her hand. "It's like a bylaw."

Jane chortled, a dry little chuckle, and Madeline found herself desperate to make her laugh again.

"It shouldn't be peroxide blond, obviously; it should be expensive blond, and then you get it cut in that sort of 'mum' haircut, where it's like a helmet."

"You're being mean." Celeste tapped her lightly on the arm.

"I'm not!" protested Madeline. "I love that hairstyle! I told Lucy Ponder when I'm ready to run for the PTA she can give me the approved blond bob." She said to Jane, "Lucy Ponder is a local hairdresser, and she's the daughter of the lady who lives in the house overlooking the school playground. Everyone is connected to everyone in Pirriwee."

"Really?" said Jane. A flash of something both hopeful and fearful crossed her face, and she glanced quickly over her shoulder.

"It's OK, we're safe, no Blond Bobs in sight," said Madeline.

"So are the Blond Bobs nice?" asked Celeste. "Or should we steer clear?"

"Well, they mean well," said Madeline. "They mean very, very well. They're like . . . Hmmm, what *are* they like?" She tapped her fingers on the table, trying to think of the right way to describe the Blond Bobs. "They're like mum prefects. They feel very strongly about their roles as school mums. It's like their religion. They're fundamentalist mothers."

"You're exaggerating," said Celeste.

"Of course I am," agreed Madeline.

"Are any of the kindergarten mothers Blond Bobs?" asked Jane.

"Let's see now," said Madeline. "Oh yes, Harper. She's your quintessential Blond Bob. She's on the PTA *and* she has a horrendously gifted daughter with a mild nut allergy. So she's part of the Zeitgeist, lucky girl."

"Come on now, Madeline, there's nothing lucky about having a child with a nut allergy," said Celeste.

"I know," said Madeline. She knew she was getting too show-offy in her desire to make Jane laugh. "I'm teasing. Let's see. Who else? There's Carol Quigley. She's sort of a wannabe Blond Bob; she's not quite blond enough. She's not actually on the PTA yet, but she's doing her bit for the school by keeping it clean. She's obsessed with cleanliness. She runs in and out of the classroom with a bottle of spray-and-wipe."

"She does not," said Celeste.

"She does!"

"What about dads?" Jane opened a packet of chewing gum and slipped another piece into her mouth like illegal contraband. She appeared to be obsessed with gum, although you couldn't really see her chewing it. She didn't quite meet Madeline's eye as she asked the question. Was she hoping to meet a single dad perhaps?

"Well, I've heard on the grapevine we've got at least one stay-at-home dad in kindergarten this year," said Madeline. "His wife is some hotshot in the corporate world. Jackie Somebody. She's the CEO of a bank, I think."

"Not Jackie Montgomery," said Celeste.

"That's it."

"Goodness," murmured Celeste.

"We'll probably never see her. It's hard for the mums working full-time. Who else works full-time? Oh. Renata. Renata is in one of those finance jobs—equities or, I don't know, stock options? Is that a thing? Or maybe she's an analyst. I think that's it. She analyzes stuff. Every time I ask her to explain her job, I forget to listen. Her children are geniuses too. Obviously."

"So Renata is a Blond Bob?" said Jane.

"No, no. She's a career woman. She has a full-time nanny. I think she just imported a new one from France. She likes European stuff. Renata doesn't have time to help at the school. She has board meetings to attend. Whenever you talk to her she's just been to a board meeting, or she's on her way back from a board meeting, or she's preparing for a board meeting. I mean, how often do these boards have to meet?"

"Well, it depends on—" began Celeste.

"It was a rhetorical question," interrupted Madeline. "My point is she can't go more than five minutes before she mentions a board meeting, just like Thea Cunningham can't go more than five minutes without mentioning she has four children. She's a kindergarten mother too, by the way. She has four children. She can't get over it. Um, do I sound bitchy?"

"Yes," said Celeste.

"Sorry," said Madeline. She did feel a bit guilty. "I was trying to be entertaining. Blame my ankle. Quite seriously, it's a very lovely school and everyone is very lovely and we're all going to have a lovely, lovely time and make lovely, lovely new friends."

Jane chortled and did her discreet gum-chewing thing. She seemed to be drinking coffee and chewing gum at the same time. It was peculiar.

"So, these 'gifted and talented' children," asked Jane. "Are the children tested or something?"

"There's a whole identification process," said Madeline. "And they get special programs and 'opportunities.' They stay in the same class, but they're given more difficult assignments, I guess, and sometimes they're pulled out for separate sessions with a specialist teacher. Look, obviously you don't want your child being bored in class, waiting for everyone else to catch up. I *do* understand that. I just get a little . . . well, for example, last year I had a little conflict with Renata."

"Madeline *loves* conflict," said Celeste to Jane.

"Renata somehow found time in between board meetings to ask the teachers to organize an exclusive little excursion just for the gifted kids. It was to see a play. Well, come on now, you don't have to be bloody gifted to enjoy *theater*. I'm the marketing manager at the Pirriwee Peninsula Theatre, you see, so that's how I got wind of it."

"She won of course," grinned Celeste.

"Of course I won," said Madeline. "I got a special group discount and all the kids went and I got half-price champagne at interval for all the parents and we had a great time."

"Oh! Speaking of which!" said Celeste. "I nearly forgot to give you your champagne! Did I— Oh, yes, here it is." She rummaged through her voluminous straw basket in her typically breathless way and handed over a bottle of Bollinger. "Can't give you champagne glasses without champagne."

"Let's have some now!" Madeline lifted the bottle by the neck, suddenly inspired.

"No, no," said Celeste. "Are you crazy? It's too early for drinking. We have to pick the kids up in two hours. And it's not chilled."

"Champagne *breakfast*!" said Madeline. "It's all in the way you package it. We'll have champagne and orange juice. Half a glass each! Over two hours. Jane? Are you in?"

"I guess I could have a *sip*," said Jane. "I'm a cheap drunk."

"I bet you are, because you weigh about ten kilos," said Madeline. "We'll get on well. I love cheap drunks. More for me."

"Madeline," said Celeste. "Keep it for another time."

"But it's the Festival of Madeline," said Madeline sadly. "And I'm injured."

Celeste rolled her eyes. "Pass me a glass."

> **Thea:** Jane was tipsy when she picked up Ziggy from orientation. So, you know, it just paints a certain type of picture, doesn't it? Young single mother drinking first thing in the morning. Chewing gum too. Not a good first impression. That's all I'm saying.

> **Bonnie:** For heaven's sake, nobody was drunk! They had a champagne breakfast at Blue Blues for Madeline's fortieth. They were just a little giggly. That's what I heard, anyway; we actually couldn't make orientation day because we were doing a family healing retreat in Byron Bay. It was an incredible spiritual experience. Would you like the website address?

Harper: You knew from the very first day that Madeline, Celeste, and Jane were a little threesome. They arrived with their arms around one another like twelve-year-olds. Renata and I didn't get invited to their little soiree, even though we'd known Madeline since all our boys were in kindergarten together, but as I said to Renata that night, when we were having the most divine degustation menu at Remy's (that was *before* the rest of Sydney discovered it by the way), I really didn't care less.

Samantha: I was working. Stu took Lily to orientation. He mentioned some of the mothers had just come from a champagne breakfast. I said, "Right. What are their names? They sound like my sort of people."

Jonathan: I missed all that. Stu and I were talking about cricket.

Melissa: You didn't hear this from me, but *apparently* Madeline Mackenzie got so drunk that morning, she fell over and sprained her ankle.

Graeme: I think you're barking up the wrong tree there. I don't see how an ill-advised champagne breakfast could have led to murder and mayhem, do you?

Champagne is never a mistake. That had always been Madeline's mantra.

But afterward, Madeline did wonder if just this once it might have been a tiny error of judgment. Not because they were drunk.

They weren't. It was because when the three of them walked into the school, laughing together (Madeline had decided she didn't want to stay in the car and miss seeing Chloe come out, so she hopped in, hanging on to their elbows), they trailed behind them the unmistakable scent of *party*.

People never like missing out on a party.

6.

Jane was not drunk when she arrived back at the school to pick up Ziggy. She had had three mouthfuls of that champagne at the most.

But she was feeling euphoric. There had been something about the pop of the champagne cork, the naughtiness of it, the unexpectedness of the whole morning, those beautiful long fragile glasses catching the sunlight, the surfy-looking barista bringing over three exquisite little cupcakes with candles, the smell of the ocean, the feeling that she was maybe making new friends with these women who were somehow so different from any of her other friends: older, wealthier, more sophisticated.

"You'll make new friends when Ziggy starts school!" her mother had kept telling her, excitedly and irritatingly, and Jane had to make a big effort not to roll her eyes and behave like a sulky, nervous teenager starting at a new high school. Jane's mother had three best friends whom she had met twenty-five years ago when Jane's older brother, Dane, started kindergarten. They all went out for coffee on that first morning and had been inseparable ever since.

"I don't need new friends," Jane had told her mother.

"Yes you do. You need to be friends with other mothers," her mother said. "You support one another! You understand what you're going through." But Jane had tried that with Mothers Group and failed. She just couldn't relate to those bright, chatty women and their bubbly conversations about husbands who weren't "stepping up" and renovations that weren't finished before the baby was born and that hilarious time they were so busy and tired *they left the house without putting on any makeup!* (Jane, who was wearing no makeup at the time, and never wore makeup, had kept her face blank and benign, while she inwardly shouted: *What the* fuck?)

And yet, strangely, she related to Madeline and Celeste, even though they really had nothing in common except for the fact that their children were starting kindergarten, and even though Jane was pretty sure that Madeline would never leave the house without makeup either, but she felt already that she and Celeste (who also didn't wear makeup; luckily, her beauty was shocking enough without improvement) could tease Madeline about this, and she'd laugh and tease them back, as if they were already established friends.

So Jane wasn't ready for what happened.

She wasn't on alert. She was too busy getting to know Pirriwee Public (everything so cute and compact; it made life seem so manageable), enjoying the sunshine and the still novel smell of the sea. Jane felt filled with pleasure at the thought of Ziggy's school days. For the first time since he was born, the responsibility of being in charge of Ziggy's childhood weighed lightly on her. Her new apartment was walking distance from the school. They would walk to school each day, past the beach and up the tree-lined hill.

At her own suburban primary school she'd had views of a six-lane highway and the scent of barbecued chicken from the shop next door. There had been no cleverly designed, shady little play areas with charming, colorful tile mosaics of grinning dolphins and whales. There were certainly no murals of underwater sea scenes or stone sculptures of tortoises in the middle of sandpits.

"This school is so cute," she said to Madeline as she and Celeste helped Madeline hop along to a seat. "It's *magical.*"

"I know. Last year's school trivia night raised money to redo the school yard," said Madeline. "The Blond Bobs know how to fund-raise. The theme was 'dead celebrities.' It was great fun. Hey, are you any good at trivia, Jane?"

"I'm excellent at trivia," said Jane. "Trivia and jigsaws are my two areas of expertise."

"Jigsaws?" said Madeline. "I'd rather stick pins in my eyes."

She sat down on a blue painted wooden bench built around the tree trunk of a Moreton Bay Fig and put her ankle up. A crowd of other parents soon formed around them, and Madeline held court, introducing Jane and Celeste to the mothers with older children she already knew and telling everyone the story of how she twisted her ankle saving young lives.

"Typical Madeline," a woman called Carol said to Jane. She was a soft-looking woman wearing a puffy-sleeved floral sundress and a big straw sun hat. She looked like she was off to a white clapboard church in *Little House on the Prairie*. (Carol? Wasn't she the one Madeline said liked to clean? Clean Carol.)

"Madeline just loves a fight," said Carol. "She'll take on anyone. Our sons play soccer together, and last year she got in an argument with this giant dad. All the husbands were hiding, and Madeline was standing this close to him, poking her finger into his chest like this, not giving an inch. It's a wonder she didn't get herself killed."

"Oh, him! The *under-seven age coordinator*." Madeline spat the words "under-seven age coordinator" as if they were "serial killer." "I shall loathe that man until the day I die!"

Meanwhile Celeste stood off slightly to the side, chatting in that ruffled, hesitant way of hers, which Jane was already beginning to recognize as characteristic of Celeste.

"What did you say your son's name was again?" Carol asked Jane.

"Ziggy," said Jane.

"Ziggy," repeated Carol uncertainly. "Is that an ethnic sort of a name?"

"Hello, there, I'm *Renata*!" A woman with a crisp gray symmetrical haircut and intense brown eyes behind stylish black-framed spectacles appeared in front of Jane, hand outstretched. It was like being accosted by a politician. She said her name with strange emphasis, as if Jane had been expecting her.

"Hello! I'm Jane. How are you?" Jane tried to match her enthusiasm. She wondered if this was the school principal.

A well-dressed, blond woman, who Jane thought probably qualified as one of Madeline's Blond Bobs, bustled over with a yellow envelope in her hand. "Renata," she said, ignoring Jane. "I've got that education report we were talking about at dinner—"

"Just give me a moment, Harper," said Renata with a touch of impatience. She turned back to Jane. "Jane, nice to meet you! I'm Amabella's mum, and I have Jackson in Year 2. That's *Amabella*, by the way, not *Anna*bella. It's French. We didn't make it up."

Harper continued to hover at Renata's shoulder, nodding along respectfully as Renata spoke, like those people who stand behind politicians at press conferences.

"Well, I just wanted to introduce you to Amabella and Jack-

son's nanny, who also happens to be French! *Quelle coïncidence!*
This is Juliette." Renata indicated a petite girl with short red hair
and an oddly arresting face, dominated by a huge, luscious-lipped
mouth. She looked like a very pretty alien.

"Pleased to meet you." The nanny held out a limp hand. She
had a strong French accent and looked bored out of her mind.

"You too," said Jane.

"I always think it's nice for the nannies to get to know each
other." Renata looked brightly between the two of them. "A little
support group, shall we say! What nationality are you?"

"She's not a nanny, Renata," said Madeline from the bench,
her voice brimming with laughter.

"Well, au pair, then," said Renata impatiently.

"Renata, listen to me, she's a *mother*," said Madeline. "She's
just young. You know, like we used to be."

Renata glanced uneasily at Jane, as if she suspected a practical
joke, but before Jane had a chance to say anything (she felt like she
should apologize), someone said, "Here they come!" and all the
parents surged forward as a pretty, blond, dimpled teacher who
looked like she'd been cast for the role of kindergarten teacher
ushered the children out from a classroom.

Two little fair-headed boys charged out first like they'd been
shot from a gun and headed straight for Celeste. "Oof," grunted
Celeste as two little fair heads rammed her stomach. "I quite liked
the idea of twins until I met Celeste's little demons," Madeline
had told Jane when they were having their champagne and orange
juice, while Celeste smiled distractedly, apparently unoffended.

Chloe sauntered out of the classroom with her arms linked
with two other little princess-like girls. Jane anxiously scanned
the children for Ziggy. Had Chloe dumped him? There he was.

He was one of the last to come out, but he looked happy. Jane gave him an *OK?* thumbs-up signal, and Ziggy lifted both thumbs up and grinned.

There was a sudden commotion. Everyone stopped to look.

It was a little curly-haired girl. The last one to come out of the classroom. She was sobbing, her shoulders hunched, clutching her neck.

"Aww," breathed the mothers, because she looked so pitiful and brave and her hair was so pretty.

Jane watched Renata hurry over, followed at a more relaxed pace by her odd-looking nanny. The mother, the nanny and the pretty, blond teacher all bent down to the little girl's height to listen to her.

"Mummy!" Ziggy ran to Jane, and she scooped him up.

It seemed like ages since she'd seen him, as if they'd both been on journeys to exotic far-off lands. She buried her nose in his hair. "How was it? Was it fun?"

Before he could answer, the teacher called out, "Could all the parents and children listen up for a moment? We've had such a lovely morning, but we just need to have a little chat about something. It's a little bit serious."

The teacher's dimples quivered in her cheeks, as if she were trying to put them away for a more appropriate time.

Jane let Ziggy slide back down to his feet.

"What's going on?" said someone.

"Something happened to Amabella, I think," said another mother.

"Oh, God," said someone else quietly. "Watch Renata get on the warpath."

"Now, someone just hurt Annabella—I'm sorry, *Amabella*—

and I want whomever it was to come over and apologize, because we don't hurt our friends at school, do we?" said the teacher in her teacher voice. "And if we do, we always say sorry, because that's what big kindergarten children do."

There was silence. The children either stared blankly at the teacher or swayed back and forth, looking at their feet. Some of them buried their faces against their mothers' skirts.

One of Celeste's twin boys tugged on her shirt. "I'm hungry!"

Madeline hobbled over from her seat under the tree and stood next to Jane. "What's the holdup?" She looked around her. "I don't even know where Chloe is."

"Who was it, Amabella?" said Renata to the little girl. "Who hurt you?"

The little girl said something inaudible.

"Was it an accident, maybe, Amabella?" said the teacher desperately.

"It wasn't an accident, for heaven's sake," snapped Renata. Her face was aflame with righteous rage. "Someone tried to choke her. I can see marks on her neck. I think she's going to have bruises."

"Good Lord," said Madeline.

Jane watched the teacher squat down at the little girl's level, her arm around her shoulders, her mouth close to her ear.

"Did you see what happened?" Jane asked Ziggy. He shook his head vigorously.

The teacher stood back up and fiddled with her earring as she faced the parents. "Apparently one of the boys . . . um, well. My problem is that the children obviously don't know one another's names yet, so Amabella can't tell me exactly which little boy—"

"We're not going to let this go!" interrupted Renata.

"Absolutely not!" agreed her hovering blond friend. *Harper,* thought Jane, trying to get all the names straight. *Hovering Harper.*

The teacher took a deep breath. "No. We won't let it go. I wonder if I could ask all the children . . . well, actually, maybe just the boys, to come over here for just a moment."

The parents pushed their sons forward with gentle shoves between the shoulder blades.

"Over you go," said Jane to Ziggy.

He grabbed hold of her hand and looked up at her pleadingly. "I'm ready to go home now."

"It's OK," said Jane. "It's just for a moment."

He wandered over and stood beside a boy who looked like a giant next to Ziggy. He was about a head taller than her son, with black curly hair and big strong shoulders. He looked like a little gangster.

The boys formed a straggling line in front of the teacher. There were about fifteen, of all shapes and sizes. Celeste's fair-haired twins stood at the end; one of them was running a Matchbox car over his brother's head, while the other one swatted it away like a fly.

"It's like a police lineup," said Madeline.

Someone snickered. "Stop it, Madeline."

"They should all face forward, then turn to the side to show their profiles," continued Madeline. To Celeste she said, "If it's one of your boys, Celeste, she won't be able to tell the difference. We'll have to do DNA testing. Wait—do identical twins have the same DNA?"

"You can laugh, Madeline; your child isn't a suspect," said another mother.

"They've got the same DNA but different fingerprints," said Celeste.

"Right, then, we'll have to dust for fingerprints," said Madeline.

"Shhhh," said Jane, trying not to laugh. She felt so desperately sorry for the mother of the child who was about to be publicly humiliated.

The little girl called Amabella held on to her mother's hand. The redheaded nanny folded her arms and took a step back.

Amabella surveyed the line of boys.

"It was him," she said immediately. She pointed at the little gangster kid. "He tried to choke me."

I knew it, thought Jane.

But then for some reason the teacher was putting her hand on Ziggy's shoulder, and the little girl was nodding, and Ziggy was shaking his head. "It wasn't me!"

"Yes, it was," said the little girl.

Detective-Sergeant Adrian Quinlan: A post-mortem is currently being undertaken to ascertain cause of death, but at this stage I can confirm the victim suffered right-rib fractures, a shattered pelvis, fractured base of skull, right foot and lower vertebrae.

7.

Oh, calamity, thought Madeline.

Wonderful. She'd just made friends with the mother of a little thug. He'd seemed so cute and sweet in the car. Thank God he hadn't tried to choke Chloe. That would have been awkward. Also, Chloe would have knocked him out with a right hook.

"Ziggy would *never* . . ." said Jane.

Her face had gone completely white. She looked horrified. Madeline saw the other parents take tiny steps back, forming a circle of space around Jane.

"It's all right." Madeline put a comforting hand on Jane's arm. "They're children! They're not civilized yet!"

"Excuse me." Jane stepped past two other mothers and into the middle of the little crowd, like she was stepping onto a stage. She put her hand on Ziggy's shoulder. Madeline's heart broke for them both. Jane seemed young enough to be her own daughter. In fact Jane reminded her a little of Abigail: that same prickliness and shy, dry humor.

"Oh dear," fretted Celeste next to Madeline. "This is awful."

"I didn't do anything," said Ziggy in a clear voice.

"Ziggy, we just need you to say sorry to Amabella, that's all," said Miss Barnes. Bec Barnes had taught Fred when he was in kindergarten. It had been her first year out of teachers college. She was good, but still very young and a bit too anxious to please the parents, which was absolutely fine when the parent was Madeline, but not when Renata Klein was the parent, and out for revenge. Although to be fair, any parent would want an apology if another child tried to choke theirs. (It probably hadn't helped that Madeline had made Renata look silly for thinking Jane was the nanny. Renata didn't like to look silly. Her children were geniuses, after all. She had a reputation to uphold. Board meetings to attend.)

Jane looked at Amabella. "Sweetheart, are you sure it was *this* boy who hurt you?"

"Could you say sorry to Amabella, please? You really hurt her quite badly," said Renata to Ziggy. She was speaking nicely, but firmly. "Then we can all go home."

"But it wasn't me," said Ziggy. He spoke very clearly and precisely and looked Renata straight in the eye.

Madeline took her sunglasses off and chewed on the stem. Maybe it *wasn't* him? Could Amabella have gotten it wrong? But she was gifted! She was actually quite a lovely little girl too. She'd been on playdates with Chloe and was very easygoing and let Chloe boss her about, taking the supporting role in whatever game they were playing.

"Don't lie," Renata snapped at Ziggy. She'd dropped her well-bred, "I'm still nice to other people's kids even when they hurt mine" demeanor. "All you need to do is say sorry."

Madeline saw Jane's body react instantly, instinctively, like the sudden rear of a snake or pounce of an animal. Her back straightened. Her chin lifted. "Ziggy doesn't lie."

"Well, I can assure you *Amabella* is telling the truth."

The little audience became very still. Even the other children were quiet, except for Celeste's twins, who were chasing each other around the playground, yelling something about ninjas.

"OK, so we seem to have reached a stalemate here." Miss Barnes clearly didn't know what in the world to do. She was twenty-four years old, for heaven's sake.

Chloe reappeared at Madeline's side, breathing hard from her exertions on the monkey bars. "I need a swim," she announced.

"Shhh," said Madeline.

Chloe sighed. "*May* I have a swim, *please*, Mummy?"

"Just shhhh."

Madeline's ankle ached. This was not turning out to be a very good fortieth birthday, thank you very much. So much for the Festival of Madeline. She really needed to sit back down. Instead she limped into the middle of the action.

"Renata," she said. "You know how children can be—"

Renata swung her head to glare at Madeline. "The child needs to take responsibility for his actions. He needs to see there are *consequences*. He can't go around choking other children and pretend he didn't do it! Anyway, what's this got to do with you, Madeline? Mind your own beeswax."

Madeline bristled. She was only trying to help! And "mind your own beeswax" was such a profoundly geeky thing to say. Ever since the conflict over the theater excursion for the gifted and talented children last year, she and Renata had been tetchy with each other, even though they were ostensibly still friends.

Madeline actually liked Renata, but right from the beginning there had been something competitive about their relationship. "See, I'm just the sort of person who would be bored out of my *mind* if I had to be a full-time mother," Renata would say confidentially to Madeline, and that wasn't meant to be offensive because Madeline *wasn't* actually a full-time mother, she worked part-time, but still, there was always the implication that Renata was the smart one, the one who needed more mental stimulation, because she had a *career* while Madeline had a *job*.

It didn't help that Renata's older son Jackson was famous at school for winning chess tournaments, while Madeline's son Fred was famous for being the only student in the history of Pirriwee Public brave enough to climb the giant Moreton Bay Fig tree and then leap the impossible distance onto the roof of the music room to retrieve thirty-four tennis balls. (The Fire Brigade had to be called to rescue him. Fred's street cred at school was sky-high.)

"It doesn't matter, Mummy." Amabella looked up at her mother with eyes still teary. Madeline could see the red finger marks around the poor child's neck.

"It does matter," said Renata. She turned to Jane. "Please make your child apologize."

"Renata," said Madeline.

"Stay *out* of it, Madeline."

"Yes, I don't think we should get involved, Madeline," said Harper, who was predictably nearby and spent her life agreeing with Renata.

"I'm sorry, but I just can't make him apologize for something he says he didn't do," said Jane.

"Your child is lying," said Renata. Her eyes flashed behind her glasses.

"I don't think he is," said Jane. She lifted her chin.

"I just want to go home now, *please*, Mummy," said Amabella. She began to sob in earnest. Renata's weird-looking new French nanny, who had been silent the whole time, picked her up, and

Amabella wrapped her legs around her waist and buried her face in her neck. A vein pulsed in Renata's forehead. Her hands clenched and unclenched.

"This is completely . . . unacceptable," Renata said to poor distraught Miss Barnes, who was probably wondering why they hadn't covered situations like this at teachers college.

Renata leaned down so that her face was only inches away from Ziggy. "If you ever touch my little girl like that again, you will be in big trouble."

"Hey!" said Jane.

Renata ignored her. She straightened and spoke to the nanny. "Let's go, Juliette."

They marched off through the playground, while all the parents pretended to be busy tending to their children.

Ziggy watched them go. He looked up at his mother, scratched the side of his nose and said, "I don't think I want to come to school anymore."

> **Samantha:** All the parents have to go down to the police station and make a statement. I haven't had my turn yet. I feel quite sick about it. They'll probably think I'm guilty. Seriously, I feel guilty when a police car pulls up next to me at the traffic lights.

8.

Five Months Before the Trivia Night

The reindeers ate the carrots!"

Madeline opened her eyes in the early morning light to see a half-eaten carrot shoved in front of her eyes by Chloe. Ed, who was snoring gently next to her, had taken a lot of time and care last night, gnawing on the carrots to make the most authentic-looking reindeer bites. Chloe was sitting comfortably astride Madeline's stomach in her pajamas, hair like a mop, big grin, wide-awake shiny eyes.

Madeline rubbed her own eyes and looked at the clock. Six a.m. Probably the best they could hope for.

"Do you think Santa Claus left Fred a potato?" said Chloe hopefully. "Because he's been pretty naughty this year!"

Madeline had told her children that if they were naughty, Santa Claus might leave them a wrapped-up potato, and they would always wonder what the wonderful gift was that the potato replaced. It was Chloe's dearest wish for Christmas that her brother would receive a potato. It would probably please her more than the dollhouse under the tree. Madeline had seriously considered wrapping up potatoes for both of them. It would be such an incentive for good behavior throughout the next year. "Remember the potato," she could say. But Ed wouldn't let her. He was too damned nice.

"Is your brother up yet?" she said to Chloe.

"I'll wake him!" shouted Chloe, and before Madeline could stop her she was gone, pounding down the hallway.

Ed stirred. "It's not morning time, is it? It couldn't be morning time."

"Deck the halls with something and holly!" sang Madeline. "Tra la la la la, la la la la!"

"I'll pay you a thousand dollars if you stop that sound right now," said Ed. He put his pillow over his face. For a very nice man, he was surprisingly cruel about her singing.

"You don't have a thousand dollars," said Madeline, and she launched into "Silent Night."

Her mobile phone beeped with a text message, and Madeline picked it up from the bedside table while still singing.

It was Abigail. It was Abigail's year to spend Christmas Eve and morning with her father, Bonnie and her half sister. Skye, who was born three months after Chloe, was a fair-haired, fey little girl who followed Abigail around like an adoring puppy. She also looked a lot like Abigail had when she was a child, which made Madeline feel uneasy, and sometimes teary, as though something precious had been stolen from her. It was clear that Abigail preferred Skye to Chloe and Fred, who refused to idolize her, and Madeline often found herself thinking, *But, Abigail, Chloe and Fred are your* real *brother and sister, you should love them more!* which was not technically true. Madeline could not quite believe that all three had equal footing as Abigail's half siblings.

She read the text: *Merry Christmas, Mum. Dad, Bonnie, Skye and me all here at the shelter from 5:30 a.m.! I've already peeled forty potatoes! It's a beautiful experience being able to contribute like this. Feel so blessed. Love, Abigail.*

"She's never peeled a freaking potato in her life," muttered Madeline as she texted back: *That's wonderful, darling. Merry XMAS to you too, see you soon, xxx!*

She put the phone down on the bedside table with a bang, suddenly exhausted, and tried her best to restrain the little eruption of fury behind her eyes.

Feel so blessed . . . A beautiful experience.

This from a fourteen-year-old who whined if she was asked to set the table. Her daughter was starting to sound just like Bonnie.

"Bleh," she said out loud.

Bonnie had arranged for the whole family to volunteer at a homeless shelter on Christmas morning. "I just hate all that crass *commercialism* of Christmas, don't you?" she'd told Madeline last week, when they'd run into each other in the shops. Madeline had been doing Christmas shopping, and her wrists were looped with dozens of plastic shopping bags. Fred and Chloe were both eating lollipops, their lips a garish red. Meanwhile Bonnie was carrying a tiny bonsai tree in a pot, and Skye was walking along next to her eating a *pear*. ("A fucking pear," Madeline had told Celeste later. For some reason she couldn't get over the pear.)

How in the world had Bonnie managed to get Madeline's ex-husband out of bed at that time of morning to go to work in a homeless shelter? Nathan wouldn't get up before eight a.m. in the ten years they'd been together. Bonnie must give him organic blow jobs.

"Abigail is having a 'beautiful experience' with Bonnie at the homeless shelter," Madeline said to Ed.

Ed took his pillow off his face.

"That's revolting," he said.

"I know," said Madeline. This is why she loved him.

"Coffee," he said sympathetically. "I'll get you coffee."

"PRESENTS!" shouted Chloe and Fred from down the hallway.

Chloe and Fred couldn't get enough of the crass commercialism of Christmas.

> **Harper:** Can you imagine how strange it must have been for Madeline to have her ex-husband's child in the same kindergarten class as her own child? I remember Renata and I talked about it over brunch. We were quite concerned how it would affect the classroom dynamics. Of course, Bonnie loved to pretend it was all so nice and amicable. "Oh, we all have Christmas lunch together." Spare me. I *saw* them at the trivia night. I saw Bonnie *throw* her drink all over Madeline!

9.

It was just becoming light when Celeste woke up on Christmas morning. Perry was sound asleep, and there was no sound from the adjoining room where the boys were sleeping. They'd been almost demented with excitement about Santa Claus finding them in Canada (letters had been sent to Santa informing him of the change of address), and with their body clocks all confused, she and Perry had had terrible trouble getting them off to sleep. The boys were sharing a king-size bed, and they'd kept wrestling in that hysterical way they sometimes did, where laughter skidded into tears and then back again into laughter, and Perry had shouted from the next room, "Go to sleep, boys!" and all of a sudden there was silence, and when Celeste had checked in a few seconds later they were both lying flat on their backs, arms and legs spread, as if exhaustion had simultaneously knocked them out cold.

"Come and look at this," she'd said to Perry, and he'd come in and stood next to her, and they'd watched them sleep for a few minutes before grinning at each other and tiptoeing out to have a drink to celebrate Christmas Eve.

Now Celeste slid out from underneath the feathery quilt and walked to the window overlooking the frozen lake. She put her hand flat against the glass. It felt cold, but the room was warm. There was a giant Christmas tree in the center of the lake, glowing with red and green lights. Snowflakes fell softly. It was all so beautiful she felt like she could taste it. When she looked back on this holiday, she'd remember its flavor: full and fruity, like the mulled wine they'd had earlier.

Today, after the boys had opened their presents and they'd eaten a room service breakfast (pancakes with maple syrup!), they'd go out to play in the snow. They'd build a snowman. Perry had booked them a sleigh ride. Perry would post pictures of them all frolicking in the snow on Facebook. He'd write something like: *The boys have their first white Christmas!* He loved Facebook. Everyone teased him about it. Big, successful banker posting photos on Facebook, writing cheery comments about his wife's friends' recipe posts.

Celeste looked back at the bed where Perry was sleeping. He always slept with a tiny perplexed frown, as if his dreams puzzled him.

As soon as he woke he'd be desperate to give Celeste his gift. He loved giving presents. The first time she knew she wanted to marry him was when she saw the anticipation on his face, watching his mother open a birthday present he'd bought for her. "Do you like it?" he'd burst out as soon she tore the paper, and his family had all laughed at him for sounding like a big kid.

She wouldn't need to fake her pleasure. Whatever he chose would be perfect. She'd always prided herself on her ability to choose thoughtful gifts, but Perry outdid her. On his last overseas trip he'd found the most ridiculously tizzy pink crystal champagne stopper. "I took one look and thought *Madeline*," he'd said. Madeline had loved it of course.

Today would be perfect in every way. The Facebook photos

wouldn't lie. So much joy. Her life had so much joy. That was an actual verifiable fact.

There really was no need to leave him until the boys finished high school.

That would be the right time to leave. On the day they finished their last exams. "Put down your pens," the exam supervisors would say. That's when Celeste would put down her marriage.

Perry opened his eyes.

"Merry Christmas!" smiled Celeste.

> **Gabrielle:** Everyone thinks Celeste and Perry have the perfect marriage, but I'm not sure about that. I walked by them, sitting in their car parked on the side of the road on the trivia night. Celeste looked gorgeous, of course. I've personally witnessed her eating carbs like there's no tomorrow, so don't tell me there's any justice in this world. They were both staring straight ahead, not looking at each other, all dressed up in their costumes, not saying a word.

10.

Jane woke to the sound of people shouting "Happy Christmas!" from the street below her apartment window. She sat up in bed and tugged at her T-shirt; it was damp with sweat. She'd been dreaming. A bad one. She'd been lying flat on her back while Ziggy stood next to her, in his shortie pajamas, smiling down at her, one foot on her throat.

"Get off, Ziggy, I can't breathe!" she'd been trying to say, but he'd stopped smiling and was studying her with benign interest, as if he were performing a scientific experiment.

She put her hand to her neck and took big gulps of air.

It was just a dream. Dreams mean nothing.

Ziggy was in bed with her. His warm back pressed against her. She turned around to face him and put a fingertip to the soft, fragile skin just above his cheekbone.

He went to bed each night in his own bed and woke up each morning in with her. Neither of them ever remembered how he got there. Maybe it's magic, they decided. "Maybe a good witch carries me in each night," Ziggy said, wide-eyed but with a bit of a grin, because he only half believed in all that kind of stuff.

"He'll just stop one day," Jane's mother said whenever Jane

mentioned that Ziggy still came into her bed each night. "He won't be still doing it when he's fifteen."

There was a new freckle on Ziggy's nose Jane hadn't noticed before. He had three freckles on his nose now. They formed the shape of a sail.

One day a woman would lie in bed next to Ziggy and study his sleeping face. There would be tiny black dots of whiskers across his upper lip. Instead of those skinny little boy shoulders, he'd have a broad chest. What sort of man would he be?

"He's going to be a gentle, *lovely* man, just like Poppy," her mother would say adamantly, as if she knew this for an absolute fact.

Jane's mother believed Ziggy was her own beloved father, reincarnated. Or she pretended to believe this, anyway. Nobody could really tell how serious she was. Poppy had died six months before Ziggy was born, right when Jane's mother had been halfway through reading a book about a little boy who was supposedly a reincarnated World War II fighter pilot. The idea that her grandson might actually be her dad had gotten stuck in her head. It had helped with her grieving.

And of course, there was no son-in-law to offend with talk that his son was actually his wife's grandfather.

Jane didn't exactly encourage the reincarnation talk, but she didn't discourage it either. Maybe Ziggy *was* Poppy. Sometimes she could discern a faint hint of Poppy in Ziggy's face, especially when he was concentrating. He got the same puckered forehead.

Her mother had been furious when Jane called to tell her what had happened at the orientation day.

"That's outrageous! Ziggy would *never* choke another child! That child has never harmed a fly. He's just like Poppy. Remember how

Poppy couldn't bear to swat a fly? Your grandma would be dancing about, yelling, 'Kill it, Stan! Kill the damned thing!'"

There had been silence then, which meant that Jane's mother had been felled by an attack of the giggles. She was a silent giggler.

Jane had waited it out, until her mother finally got back on the phone and said shakily, "Oh, that did me good! Laughter is wonderful for the digestion. Now, where were we? Oh yes! Ziggy! That little *brat*! Not Ziggy, of course, the little girl. Why would she accuse our darling Ziggy?"

"I don't know," said Jane. "But the thing is, she didn't seem like a brat. The mother was sort of awful, but her daughter seemed nice. Not a brat."

She could hear the uncertainty in her voice, and her mother heard it too.

"But darling, you can't possibly think Ziggy really tried to *choke* another child?"

"Of course not," Jane had said, and changed the subject.

She readjusted her pillow and wriggled into a more comfortable position. Maybe she could go back to sleep. "Ziggy will have you up at the crack of dawn," her mother had said, but Ziggy didn't seem overly excited about Christmas this year, and Jane wondered if she'd failed him in some way. She often experienced an uneasy sense that she was somehow faking a life for him, giving him a pretend childhood. She tried her best to create little rituals and family traditions for birthdays and holidays. "Let's put your stocking out now!" But where? They'd moved too often for there to be a regular spot. The end of his bed? The door handle? She floundered about, and her voice became high and strained. There was something fraudulent about it. The rituals weren't real like they were in other families where there was a mum and a dad and at least one sibling. Sometimes she felt like Ziggy might be just going along with it for her sake, and that he could see right through her, and he knew he was being shortchanged.

She watched the rise and fall of his chest.

He was so beautiful. There was no way he hurt that little girl and lied about it.

But all sleeping children were beautiful. Even really horrible children probably looked beautiful when they slept. How could she know for sure that he hadn't done it? Did anyone really know their child? Your child was a little stranger, constantly changing, disappearing and reintroducing himself to you. New personality traits could appear overnight.

And then there was . . .

Don't think about it. Don't think about it.

The memory fluttered like a trapped moth in her mind.

It had been trying so hard to escape ever since the little girl had pointed at Ziggy. The pressure on Jane's chest. Terror rising, flooding her mind. A scream trapped in her throat.

The bruises were black, purple and red.

"She's going to have bruises!" the child's mother had said.

No, no, no.

Ziggy was Ziggy. He could not. He would not. She knew her child.

He stirred. His blue-veined eyelids twitched.

"Guess what day it is," said Jane.

"Christmas!" shouted Ziggy.

He sat up so fast, the side of his head slammed violently against Jane's nose and she fell back against the pillow, tears streaming.

Thea: I always thought there was something not quite right about that child. That Ziggy. Something funny about his eyes. Boys need a male role model. I'm sorry, but it's a fact.

Stu: Bloody hell, there was a lot of fuss about that Ziggy kid. I didn't know what to believe.

11.

D o you fly as high as this plane, Daddy?" asked Josh. They were about seven hours into their flight from Vancouver back home to Sydney. So far so good. No arguments. They'd put the boys on either side of them in separate window seats and Celeste and Perry were in adjacent aisle seats.

"Nope. Remember I told you? I have to fly really low to avoid radar detection," said Perry.

"Oh yeah." Josh turned his face back to the window.

"Why do you have to avoid radar detection?" asked Celeste.

Perry shook his head and shared a tolerant "women!" grin with Max, who was sitting on the other side of Celeste and had leaned over to listen to the conversation. "It's obvious isn't it, Max?"

"It's top secret, Mummy," Max told her kindly. "No one *knows* that Daddy can fly."

"Oh, of course," said Celeste. "Sorry. Silly of me."

"See, if I got caught, they'd probably want to run a whole *battery* of tests on me," said Perry. "Find out just how I developed these superpowers, then they'd want to recruit me for the Air Force, I'd have to go on secret missions."

"Yeah, and we don't want that," said Celeste. "Daddy already travels enough."

Perry reached across the aisle and put his hand over hers in silent apology.

"You can't really fly," said Max.

Perry raised his eyebrows, widened his eyes and gave a little shrug. "Can't I?"

"I don't *think* so," said Max uncertainly.

Perry winked at Celeste over Max's head. He'd been telling the twins for years that he had secret flying abilities, going into ridiculous detail about how he'd discovered his secret powers when he was fifteen, which was the age when they'd probably learn to fly too, assuming they'd inherited his powers and eaten enough broccoli. The boys could never tell if he was serious or not.

"I was flying when I skied over that big jump yesterday," said Max. He used his hand to demonstrate his trajectory. "Whoosh!"

"Yeah, you were flying," said Perry. "You nearly gave Daddy a heart attack."

Max chuckled.

Perry linked his hands in front of him and stretched out his back. "Ow. I'm still stiff from trying to keep up with you lot. You're all too fast."

Celeste studied him. He looked good: tanned and relaxed from the last five days, skiing and sledding. This was the problem. She was still hopelessly, helplessly attracted to him.

"What?" Perry glanced at her.

"Nothing."

"Good holiday, eh?"

"It was a great holiday," said Celeste with feeling. "Magical."

"I think this is going to be a good year for us," said Perry. He held her eyes. "Don't you? With the boys starting school, hopefully you'll get a bit more time to yourself, and I'm . . ." He stopped, and ran his thumb across his armrest as if he were doing some sort of quality-control test. Then he looked up at her. "I'm going to do everything in my power to make this a good year for us." He smiled self-consciously.

He did this sometimes. He said or did something that made her feel as besotted with him as she'd been that very first year after they'd met at that boring business lunch, where she'd first truly understood those four words: *swept off my feet*.

Celeste felt a sense of peace wash over her. A flight steward was coming down the aisle, offering chocolate chip cookies baked on board the plane. The aroma was delicious. Maybe it was going to be a really good year for them.

Perhaps she *could* stay. It was always such a glorious relief when she allowed herself to believe she could stay.

"Let's go down to the beach when we get home," said Perry. "We'll build a big sand castle. Snowman one day. Sand castle the next. Gosh you kids have a good life."

"Yep," Josh yawned, and stretched out luxuriously in his business-class seat. "It's pretty good."

> **Melissa:** I remember I saw Celeste and Perry and the twins down on the beach during the school holidays. I said to my husband, "I think that's one of the new kindergarten mums." His eyes nearly popped out of his head. Celeste and Perry were all loving and laughing and helping their kids make this really elaborate sand castle. It was kind of sickening, to be honest. Like, even their *sand castles* were better than ours.

12.

Detective-Sergeant Adrian Quinlan: We're looking at all angles, all possible motives.

Samantha: So we're, like, seriously using the word . . . "*murder*"?

Four Months Before the Trivia Night

I want to have a playdate with Ziggy," announced Chloe one warm summer night early in the new year.

"All right," said Madeline. Her eyes were on her older daughter. Abigail had taken an age cutting up her steak into tiny precise squares, and now she was pushing the little squares back and forth, as if she were arranging them into some sort of complicated mosaic. She hadn't put a single piece in her mouth.

Ed said quietly to Madeline, "Wasn't Ziggy the one who . . . you know?" He put his hands to his throat and made his eyes bulge.

"What are you doing, Daddy?" Chloe giggled fondly. "Daft Daddy."

"You should have a playdate with Skye." Abigail put down her fork and spoke to Chloe. "She's very excited about being in the same class as you."

"That's nice, isn't it?" said Madeline in the strained, sugary tone she knew she used whenever her ex-husband's daughter came up in conversation. "Isn't that *nice*."

Ed spluttered on his wine, and Madeline gave him a dark look.

"Skye is sort of like *my* sister, isn't she, Mummy?" said Chloe now. Unlike her mother, she'd been thrilled to learn she was going to be in the same kindergarten class as Skye, and she'd asked this question about forty thousand times.

"No, Skye is *Abigail's* half sister," said Madeline with saint-like patience.

"But I'm Abigail's sister too!" said Chloe. "So that means Skye and I must be sisters! We could be twins, like Josh and Max!"

"Speaking of which, have you seen Celeste since they got back from Canada?" asked Ed. "Those photos Perry put on Facebook were amazing. *We* should have a white Christmas one day. When we win the lottery."

"Brrrr," said Madeline. "They looked cold."

"I'd be an *awesome* snowboarder," said Fred dreamily.

Madeline shuddered. Fred was her little adrenaline junkie. If something could be climbed he climbed it. She could no longer bear to watch him skateboard. At just seven, he flipped and spun and hurled his skinny body through the air like a kid twice his age. Whenever she saw those cool, laid-back dudes interviewed on TV about their latest BASE-jumping/rock-climbing/how-can-we-do-our-best-to-kill-ourselves adventure, she thought, *There's Fred*. He even looked the part with his scruffy, too-long surfer-boy hair.

"You need a haircut," she said.

Fred wrinkled his freckled nose in disgust. "I don't!"

"I'll call Ziggy's mum," said Madeline to Chloe, "and arrange a playdate."

She'd actually been meaning to call Jane since before Christmas, but work had gotten busy, and they'd been away up the coast in between Christmas and New Year's. Poor Jane didn't know anyone in the area, and she'd seemed so devastated that day after that awful incident at orientation.

"Madeline, are you sure that's a good idea?" said Ed quietly. "He sounds like he might be a bit rough."

"Well, we don't know for sure," said Madeline.

"But you said Amabella Klein pointed him out in a lineup."

"Innocent people have been picked out of police lineups before," said Madeline to Ed.

"If that kid lays a finger on Chloe—" began Ed.

"Oh, for heaven's sake," said Madeline. "Chloe can look after herself!" She looked at Abigail's plate. "Why aren't you eating?"

"We like Renata and Geoff," said Ed. "So if their daughter says this kid, this Ziggy, hurt her, then we should be supportive. What sort of a name is Ziggy, anyway?"

"We don't like Renata and Geoff that much," said Madeline. "Abigail, *eat!*"

"Don't we?" said Ed. "I thought I liked Geoff."

"You tolerate him," said Madeline. "He's the bird-watcher, Ed, not the golfer."

"Is he?" Ed looked disappointed. "Are you sure?"

"You're thinking of Gareth Hajek."

"Am I?" Ed frowned.

"Yep," said Madeline. "Chloe, stop waving your fork around. Fred nearly lost an eye just then. Are you sick, Abigail? Is that why you're not eating?"

Abigail laid down her knife and fork. "I think I'm going vegan," she said grandly.

Bonnie was a vegan.

"Over my dead body you are," said Madeline.

Or over somebody's dead body, anyway.

Thea: You know that Madeline has a fourteen-year-old daughter, Abigail, from her previous marriage? I feel so sorry for children from broken homes, don't you? I'm just so glad I can offer my children a stable environment. I'm sure Madeline and Bonnie were fighting about Abigail at the trivia night.

Harper: I actually heard Madeline say, "I'm going to kill someone before the night is out." I assumed it was something to do with Bonnie. Not that I'm pointing fingers, of course.

Bonnie: Yes, Abigail is my stepdaughter, and it's absolutely true that Abigail had a few, well, issues, just typical teenage girl issues, but Madeline and I were working together as a team to help her. Can you smell lemon myrtle? I'm trying this new incense for the first time. It's good for stress. Take a deep breath. That's it. You look like you need a little stress relief, if you don't mind my saying.

13.

I t was one of those days. It had been a while. Not since well
before Christmas. Celeste's mouth was dry and hollow. Her
head throbbed gently. She followed the boys and Perry through
the school yard with her body held stiffly, carefully, as if she were
a tall fragile glass in danger of spilling.

She was hyperaware of everything: the warm air against her
bare arms, the straps of her sandals in between her toes, the edges
of the leaves of the Moreton Bay Fig tree, each sharply delineated
against the blue of the sky. It was similar to that intense way you
felt when you were newly in love, or newly pregnant, or driving a
car on your own for the very first time. Everything felt significant.

"Do you and Ed fight?" she'd asked Madeline once.

"Like cats and dogs," Madeline had said cheerfully.

Celeste could somehow tell she was talking about something
else entirely.

"Can we show Daddy the monkey bars first?" cried Max.

School started back in two weeks, but the uniform shop was
open for two hours this morning so parents could get what they
needed for the new year. Perry had the day off, and after they
picked up the boys' uniforms they were going around the point to
take the boys snorkeling.

"Sure," said Celeste to Max. He ran off, and as she watched

him go she realized it wasn't Max. It was Josh. She was losing her grip. She thought she was concentrating too hard when she wasn't concentrating enough.

Perry ran his fingertip down her arm and she shivered.

"You OK?" he asked. He lifted his sunglasses so she could see his eyes. The whites were very white. Her eyes were always bloodshot the morning after an argument, but Perry's eyes were always clear and shining.

"Fine." She smiled at him.

He smiled back and pulled her to him. "You look beautiful in that dress," he said in her ear.

This was the way they always behaved with each other the day after: tender and tremulous, as if they'd been through something terrible together, like a natural disaster, as if they'd barely escaped with their lives.

"Daddy!" shrieked Josh. "Come and watch us!"

"Coming!" cried Perry. He banged his fists against his chest like a gorilla and ran after them with his back hunched and his arms swinging, making gorilla noises. The boys went crazy with delighted terror and ran off.

It was just a bad fight, she told herself. *All couples fight.*

The previous night the boys had stayed overnight at Perry's mother's place. "Have a romantic dinner without these little ruffians," she'd said.

It had started over the computer.

She'd been double-checking the opening times for the uniform shop when the computer said something about a "catastrophic error." "Perry!" she'd called from the office, "there's something wrong with the computer!" and a tiny part of her warned: *No, don't tell him. What if he can't fix it?*

Stupid, stupid, stupid. She should have known better. But it was too late. He came into the office, smiling.

"Step aside, woman," he'd said.

He was the one who was good with computers. He liked being able to solve problems for her, and if he could have fixed it then, everything would have been fine.

But he couldn't fix it.

The minutes passed. She could see by the set of his shoulders that it wasn't going well.

"Don't worry about it," she said. "Leave it."

"I can do it," he said. He moved the mouse back and forth. "I know what the problem is; I just need to . . . *Damn* it."

He swore again. Softly at first, and then louder. His voice became like a blow. She winced each time.

And as his fury rose, a kind of matching fury rose within her, because she could already see exactly how the night was going to proceed, and how it could have proceeded if she hadn't made such a "catastrophic error."

The seafood platter she'd prepared would sit there uneaten. The pavlova would slide straight from the tray into the bin. All that time and effort and money wasted. She hated waste. It made her feel sick.

So when she said, "Please, Perry, just *leave* it," there was frustration in her voice. That was her fault. Maybe if she'd spoken nicely. Been more patient. Said nothing.

He swiveled the chair to face her. His eyes were already shiny with rage. Too late. He was gone. It was all over, red rover.

And yet *she didn't retreat*. She refused to retreat. She kept fighting right to the end because of the injustice of it, the ridiculousness of it. *I asked him to help fix the computer. It should not be like this,* a part of her continued to inwardly rage, even as the yelling began and her heart pounded and her muscles tensed in readiness. *It's not fair. It's not right.*

It was even worse than usual because the boys weren't at home. They didn't have to keep their voices down, to hiss at each other behind closed doors. The house was too big for the neighbors to hear them shout. It was almost like they both relished the opportunity to fight without boundaries.

Celeste walked down toward the monkey bars. They were in a cool, shady bottom corner of the playground. The boys would love playing here when they started school.

Perry was doing chin-ups on the monkey bars while the boys counted. His shoulders moved gracefully. He had to hold his legs up high because the monkey bars were so low to the ground. He'd always been athletic.

Was there some sick, damaged part of Celeste that actually *liked* living like this and wanted this shameful, dirty marriage? That's how she thought of it. As if she and Perry engaged in some sort of strange, disgusting and perverted sexual practice.

And sex was part of it.

There was always sex afterward. When it was all over. At about five a.m. Fierce, angry sex, with tears that slid onto each other's faces and tender apologies and the words murmured over and over: *Never again, I swear on my life, never again, this has to stop, we have to stop this, we should get help, never again.*

"Come on," she said to the boys. "Let's get to the uniform shop before it closes."

Perry dropped easily to the ground and grabbed a twin under each arm. "Gotcha!"

Did she love him as much as she hated him? Did she hate him as much as she loved him?

"We should try another counselor," she'd said to him early this morning.

"You're right," he'd said, as if it were an actual possibility. "When I get back. We'll talk about it then."

He was going away the next day. Vienna. It was a "summit" his firm was sponsoring. He would be delivering the keynote address on something terribly complex and global. There would be a lot of acronyms and incomprehensible jargon, and he'd stand there with a little pointer, making a red dot of light zip about on the PowerPoint presentation prepared by his executive assistant.

Perry was away often. He sometimes felt like an aberration in her life. A visitor. Her real life took place when he wasn't there. What happened never mattered all that much because he was always about to leave, the next day or the next week.

Two years ago, they'd gone to a counselor. Celeste had been buoyant with hope, but as soon as she saw the cheap vinyl couch and the counselor's eager, earnest face, she knew it was a mistake. She watched Perry weigh up his superior intelligence and social standing relative to the counselor and knew that this would be their first and last visit.

They never told her the truth. They talked about how Perry found it frustrating that Celeste didn't get up early enough and was always running late. Celeste said that sometimes "Perry lost his temper."

How could they admit to a stranger what went on in their marriage? The shame of it. The ugliness of their behavior. They were a fine-looking couple. People had been telling them that for years. They were admired and envied. They had all the privileges in the world. Overseas travel. A beautiful home. It was ungracious and ungrateful of them to behave the way they did.

"Just stop it," that nice eager woman would have surely said, disgusted and disapproving.

Celeste didn't want to tell her either. She wanted her to guess. *She wanted her to ask the right question.* But she never did.

After they left the counselor's office, they were both so exhilarated to be out of there, their performance over, that they went to a hotel bar in the middle of the afternoon and had a drink, and flirted with each other, and they couldn't keep their hands off each other. Halfway through his drink, Perry suddenly stood, took her hand and led her to the reception desk. They literally "got a room." Ha ha. So funny, so sexy. It was as though the counselor really had fixed everything. Because after all, how many married couples did *that*? Afterward she felt seedy and sexy and disheveled and filled with despair.

"So where's the uniform shop?" said Perry as they walked back up into the school's main quadrangle.

"I don't know," said Celeste. *How should I know? Why should I know?*

"The uniform shop, did you say? It's over here."

Celeste turned around. It was that intense little woman with the glasses from the orientation day. The one whose daughter said Ziggy tried to choke her. The curly-haired little girl was with her.

"I'm Renata," said the woman. "I met you at the orientation day last year. You're friends with Madeline Mackenzie, aren't you? Amabella, stop that. What are you doing?" The little girl was holding on to her mother's white shirt and shyly twisting her body behind her mother's. "Come and say hello. These are some of the boys who will be in your class. They're *identical twins*. Isn't that so interesting?" She looked at Perry, who had deposited the boys at his feet. "How in the world do you ever tell them apart?"

Perry held out his hand. "Perry," he said. "We can't tell them apart either. No idea which is which."

Renata pumped Perry's hand enthusiastically. Women always took to Perry. It was that Tom Cruise, white-toothed smile and the way he gave them his full attention.

"Very pleased to meet you. Here to get the boys their uniforms, are you? Exciting! Amabella was going to come with her nanny, but then my board meeting finished early so I decided to come myself."

Perry nodded along, as if this were all very fascinating.

Renata lowered her voice. "Amabella has become a little anxious ever since the incident at the school. Did your wife tell you? A little boy tried to choke her on the orientation day. She had bruises on her neck. A little boy called *Ziggy*. We seriously considered reporting it to the police."

"That's terrible," said Perry. "Jesus. Your poor little girl."

"Da-ad," said Max, pulling on his father's hand. "Hurry up!"

"Actually, I'm sorry," said Renata, looking brightly at Celeste. "I might have put my foot in it! Didn't you and Madeline have some sort of little birthday party with that boy's mother? Jane? Was that her name? A very young girl. I mistook her for an au pair. You might all be best friends, for all I know! I hear you were all drinking champagne! In the morning!"

"Ziggy?" frowned Perry. "We don't know anyone with a kid called Ziggy, do we?"

Celeste cleared her throat. "I met Jane for the first time that day," she said to Renata. "She gave Madeline a lift after she hurt her ankle. She was . . . well, she seemed very nice."

She didn't particularly want to be aligned with the mother of a bully, but on the other hand she'd liked Jane, and the poor girl had looked quite sick when Renata's daughter pointed out Ziggy.

"She's deluded, that's what she is," said Renata. "She absolutely refused to accept that her precious child did what he did. I've told Amabella to stay well away from this Ziggy. If I were you I'd tell your boys to steer clear too."

"Probably a good idea," said Perry. "We don't want them getting in with a bad crowd from day one." His tone was light and humorous, as if he weren't really taking any of it seriously, although, knowing Perry, the lightness was probably a cover. He had a particular paranoia about bullying because of his own experiences as a child. He was like a secret service guy when it came to his boys, his eyes darting about suspiciously, monitoring the park or the playground for rough kids or savage dogs or pedophiles posing as grandfathers.

Celeste opened her mouth. "Um," she said. *They're five. Is this a bit over the top?*

But then again, there was something about Ziggy. She'd only seen him briefly at the school, and she couldn't put her finger on exactly what it was about his face, but there was something about him that made her feel off-balance, something that filled her with mistrust. (But he was a beautiful little five-year-old boy, just like her boys! How could she feel like that about a five-year-old?)

"Mum! Come on!" Josh yanked on Celeste's arm.

She clutched at her tender right shoulder. "Ow!" For a moment the pain was so sharp, she fought nausea.

"Are you all right?" said Renata.

"Celeste?" said Perry. She could see the shameful recognition in his eyes. He knew exactly why it had hurt so much. There would be an exquisite piece of jewelry in his bag when he returned from Vienna. Another piece for her collection. She would never wear it, and he would never ask why.

For a moment Celeste couldn't speak. Big blocky words filled her mouth. She imagined letting them spill out.

My husband hits me, Renata. Never on the face of course. He's far too classy for that. Does yours hit you?

And if he does, and this is the question that really interests me: Do you hit back?

"I'm fine," she said.

14.

I 've invited Jane and Ziggy over for a playdate next week." Madeline was on the phone to Celeste as soon as she hung up from Jane. "I think you and the boys should come too. In case we run out of things to say."

"Right," said Celeste. "Thanks so much. A playdate with the little boy who—"

"Yes, yes," said Madeline. "The little strangler. But you know, our kids aren't exactly shrinking violets."

"I actually met the victim's mother yesterday when we were getting the boys' uniforms," said Celeste. "Renata. She's telling her daughter to avoid having anything to do with Ziggy and she suggested I tell my boys the same."

Madeline's hand tightened on the phone. "She had no right to tell you that!"

"I think she was just concerned—"

"You can't blacklist a child before he's even started school!"

"Well, I don't know, you can sort of understand, from her point of view. I mean, if that happened to Chloe, I mean, I guess . . ."

Madeline pressed the phone to her ear as Celeste's voice drifted. Ever since Madeline had first met her, Celeste had had this habit. She'd be chatting perfectly normally, and then she'd suddenly be floating off with the fairies.

That's how they'd met in the first place, because Celeste had been dreaming. Their kids were in swimming class together as toddlers. Chloe and the twins had stood on a little platform at the edge of the swimming pool while the teacher gave each child a turn practicing their dog paddle and floating. Madeline had noticed the gorgeous-looking mother watching the class, but they'd never bothered to talk to each other. Madeline was normally busy keeping an eye on Fred, who was four at the time and a handful. On this particular day, Fred had been happily distracted with ice cream, and Madeline was watching Chloe have her turn floating like a starfish when she noticed there was only one twin boy standing on the platform.

"Hey!" shouted Madeline at the teacher. *"Hey!"*

She looked for the beautiful mother. She was standing off to the side, staring off into the distance. "Your little boy!" she screamed. People turned their heads in slow motion. The pool supervisor was nowhere to be seen.

"For fuck's sake," said Madeline, and she jumped straight into the water, fully dressed, stilettos and all, and pulled Max from the bottom of the pool, choking and spluttering.

Madeline had yelled at everyone in sight, while Celeste hugged her two wet boys to her and sobbed crazy, grateful thanks. The swim school had been both obsequiously apologetic and appallingly evasive. The child wasn't in danger, but they were sorry it appeared that way and they would most certainly review their procedures.

They both pulled their children out of the swim school, and Celeste, who was an ex-lawyer, wrote them a letter demanding compensation for Madeline's ruined shoes, her dry-clean-only dress and of course a refund of all their fees.

So they became friends. And Madeline understood when Celeste first introduced her to Perry and it became clear that she'd only told her husband that they'd met through swimming lessons. It wasn't always necessary to tell your husband the whole story.

Now Madeline changed the subject.

"Has Perry gone away to wherever he's going this time?" she asked.

Celeste's voice was suddenly crisp and clear again. "Vienna. Yes. He'll be gone for three weeks."

"Missing him already?" said Madeline. Joke.

There was a pause.

"You still there?" asked Madeline

"I like having toast for dinner," said Celeste.

"Oh yes, I have yogurt and chocolate biscuits for dinner whenever Ed goes away," said Madeline. "Good Lord, why do I look so tired?"

She was making the phone call while sitting on the bed in the office/spare room where she always folded laundry, and she'd just caught sight of her reflection in the mirrored wardrobe on one side of the wall. She got off the bed and walked over to the mirror, the phone still held to her ear.

"Maybe because you are tired," suggested Celeste.

Madeline pressed a fingertip beneath her eye. "I had a great night's sleep!" she said. "Every day I think, 'Gosh, you look a bit tired today,' and it's just recently occurred to me that it's not that I'm tired, it's that *this is the way I look now.*"

"Cucumbers? Isn't that what you do to reduce puffiness?" said Celeste idly. Madeline knew that Celeste was spectacularly disinterested in a whole chunk of life that Madeline relished: clothes, skin care, makeup, perfume, jewelry, accessories. Sometimes Madeline looked at Celeste with her long red-gold hair pulled back any-old-how and she longed to grab her and *play with her* like she was one of Chloe's Barbie dolls.

"I am mourning the loss of my youth," she told Celeste.

Celeste snorted.

"I know I wasn't that beautiful to begin with—"

"You're still beautiful," said Celeste.

Madeline made a face at herself in the mirror and turned away. She didn't want to admit, even to herself, just how much the aging of her face really did genuinely depress her. She wanted to be above such superficial concerns. She wanted to be depressed about the state of the world, not the crumpling and creasing of her skin. Each time she saw evidence of the natural aging of her body, she felt irrationally ashamed, as if she weren't trying hard enough. Meanwhile, Ed got sexier each year that went by as the lines around his eyes deepened and his hair grayed.

She sat back down on the spare bed and began folding clothes.

"Bonnie came to pick up Abigail today," she told Celeste. "She came to the door and she looked like, I don't know, a *Swedish fruit picker*, with this red-and-white-checked scarf on her head, and Abigail ran out of the house. She *ran*. As if she couldn't wait to get away from her old hag of a mother."

"Ah," said Celeste. "Now I get it."

"Sometimes I feel like I'm losing Abigail. I feel her drifting, and I want to grab her and say, 'Abigail, he left you too. He walked out on both of us.' But I have to be the grown-up. And the awful thing is, I think she is actually happier when she's with their stupid family, meditating and eating chickpeas."

"Surely not," said Celeste.

"I know, right? I hate chickpeas."

"Really? I quite like chickpeas. They're good for you too."

"Shut up. So are you bringing the boys over to play with Ziggy? I feel like that poor little Jane is going to need some friends this year. Let's be her friends and look after her."

"Of course we'll come," said Celeste. "I'll bring chickpeas."

Mrs. Lipmann: No. The school has not had a trivia night end in bloodshed before. I find that question offensive and inflammatory.

15.

I want to live in a double-decker house like this," said Ziggy as they walked up the driveway to Madeline's house.

"Do you?" said Jane. She adjusted her bag in the crook of her arm. In her other arm she carried a plastic container of freshly baked banana muffins.

You want a life like this? I'd quite like a life like this too.

"Hold this for a moment, will you?" She handed Ziggy the container so she could take another two pieces of gum out of her bag, studying the house as she did. It was an ordinary two-story, cream-brick family house. A bit ramshackle-looking. The grass needed a mow. Two double kayaks hung above the car in the garage. Boogie boards and surfboards leaned against the walls. Beach towels hung over the balcony. A child's bike had been abandoned on the front lawn.

There wasn't anything all that special about this house. It was similar to Jane's family home, although Jane's home was smaller and tidier, and they were an hour's drive from the beach, so there wasn't all the evidence of the beach activities, but it had the same casual, simple, suburban feel.

This was childhood.

It was so simple. Ziggy wasn't asking for too much. He deserved a life like this. If Jane hadn't gone out that night, if she hadn't drunk that third tequila slammer, if she'd said no thank you when he'd slid onto the seat next to hers, if she'd stayed home and finished her law degree and gotten a job and a husband and a mortgage and done it all the proper way, then maybe one day she would have lived in a family house and been a proper person living a proper life.

But then Ziggy wouldn't have been Ziggy. And maybe she wouldn't have had any children at all. She remembered the doctor, his sad frown, just a year before she got pregnant. "Jane, you need to understand, it's going to be very difficult, if not impossible, for you to conceive."

"Ziggy! Ziggy, Ziggy, Ziggy!" The front door flew open and Chloe, in a fairy dress and gum boots, came running out and dragged Ziggy off by the hand. "You're here to play with me, OK? Not my brother Fred."

Madeline appeared behind her, wearing a red-and-white polka-dotted 1950s-style dress with a full skirt. Her hair was pulled up in a swinging ponytail.

"Jane! Happy New Year! How are you? It's so lovely to see you. Look, my ankle is all healed! Although you'll be pleased to see I'm wearing flat shoes."

She stood on one foot and twirled her ankle, showing off a sparkly red ballet shoe.

"They're like Dorothy's ruby slippers," said Jane, handing Madeline the muffins.

"Exactly, don't you love them?" said Madeline. She unpeeled the lid of the container. "Good Lord. Don't tell me you *baked* these?"

"I did," said Jane. She could hear Ziggy's laughter from somewhere upstairs. Her heart lifted at the sound.

"Look at you, with freshly baked muffins, and I'm the one dressed like a 1950s housewife," said Madeline. "I love the idea of baking, but then I can't seem to make it a reality, I never seem to have all the ingredients. How do you manage to have all that flour and sugar and, I don't know, vanilla extract?"

"Well," said Jane, "I buy them. From this place called a supermarket."

"I suppose you make a list," said Madeline. "And then you remember to take the list with you."

Jane saw that Madeline's feelings about Jane's baking were similar to Jane's feelings about Madeline's accessories: confused admiration for an exotic behavior.

"Celeste and the boys are coming today. She'll hoover up those muffins of yours. Tea or coffee? We'd better not have champagne every time we meet, although I could be convinced. Got anything to celebrate?"

Madeline led her into a big combined kitchen and living area.

"Nothing to celebrate," said Jane. "Just ordinary tea would be great."

"So how did the move go?" asked Madeline. "We were away up the coast when you were moving, otherwise I would have offered Ed to help you. I'm always offering him up as a mover. He loves it."

"Seriously?"

"No, no. He hates it. He gets so cross with me. He says, 'I'm not an appliance you can loan out!'" She put on a deep voice to imitate her husband as she switched the kettle on, her ponytail swinging. "But you know, he pays money to lift weights at the gym, so why not lift a few boxes for free? Have a seat. Sorry about the mess."

Jane sat down at a long timber table covered with the detritus of family life: ballerina stickers, a novel facedown, sunscreen, keys, some sort of electronic toy, an airplane made out of Legos.

"My family helped me move," said Jane. "There are a lot of stairs. Everyone was kind of mad at me, but they're the ones who never let me pay for movers."

("If I'm lugging this freakin' refrigerator back *down* these stairs in six months' time, then I'll——" her brother had said.)

"Milk? Sugar?" asked Madeline as she dunked tea bags.

"Neither, just black. Um, I saw one of those kindergarten mothers this morning," Jane told Madeline. She wanted to bring up the subject of the orientation day while Ziggy wasn't in the room. "At the gas station. I think she pretended not to see me."

She didn't think it. She knew it. The woman had snapped her head in the other direction so fast, it was like she'd been slapped.

"Oh, really?" Madeline sounded amused. She helped herself to a muffin. "Which one? Do you remember her name?"

"Harper," said Jane. "I'm pretty sure it was Harper. I remember I called her Hovering Harper to myself because she seemed to hover about Renata all the time. She's one of your Blond Bobs, I think, with a long droopy face. Kind of like a basset hound."

Madeline chortled. "That's Harper exactly. Yes, she's very good friends with Renata, and she's bizarrely proud about it, as if Renata is some sort of celebrity. She always needs to let you know that she and Renata see each other socially. 'Oh, we all had a *marvelous* night at some *marvelous* restaurant.'" She took a bite of her muffin.

"I guess that's why Harper doesn't want to know me then," said Jane. "Because of what happened——"

"Jane," interrupted Madeline. "This muffin is . . . *magnificent*."

Jane smiled at Madeline's amazed face. There was a crumb on her nose.

"Thanks, I can give you the recipe if you—"

"Oh, Lord, I don't want the recipe, I just want the *muffins*." Madeline took a big sip of her tea. "You know what? Where's my phone? I'm going to text Harper right now and demand to know why she pretended not to see my new muffin-baking friend today."

"Don't you dare!" said Jane. Madeline, she realized, was one of those slightly dangerous people who jumped right in defending their friends and stirred up far bigger waves than the first tiny ripple.

"Well, I won't have it," said Madeline. "If those women give you a hard time over what happened at orientation, I'll be furious. It could happen to anyone."

"I *would* have made Ziggy apologize," said Jane. She needed to make it clear to Madeline that she was the sort of mother who made her child say sorry. "I believed him when he said he didn't do it."

"Of course you did," said Madeline. "I'm sure he didn't do it. He seems like a gentle child."

"I'm one hundred percent positive," said Jane. "Well, I'm ninety-nine percent positive. I'm . . ."

She stopped and swallowed because she was suddenly feeling an overwhelming desire to explain her doubts to Madeline. To tell her exactly what that 1 percent of doubt represented. To just . . . say it. To turn it into a story she'd never shared with anyone. To package it up into an incident with a beginning, a middle and an end.

It was a beautiful, warm spring night in October. Jasmine in the air. I had terrible hay fever. Scratchy throat. Itchy eyes.

She could just talk without thinking about it, without feeling it, until the story was done.

And then perhaps Madeline would say in her definite, don't-argue manner: *Oh, you mustn't worry about that, Jane. That's of no consequence! Ziggy is exactly who you think he is. You are his mother. You know him.*

But what if she did the opposite? If the doubt Jane was feeling right now was reflected even for an instant on Madeline's face, then what? It would be the worst betrayal of Ziggy.

"Oh, Abigail! Come have a muffin with us!" Madeline looked up as a teenage girl came into the kitchen. "Jane, this is my daughter Abigail." A false note had crept into Madeline's voice. She put down her muffin and fiddled with one of her earrings. "Abigail?" she said again. "This is Jane!"

Jane turned in her chair. "Hi, Abigail," she said to the teenage girl, who was standing very still and straight, her hands clasped in front of her as if she were taking part in a religious ceremony.

"Hello," said Abigail, and she smiled at Jane, a sudden flash of unexpected warmth. It was Madeline's brilliant smile, but apart from that you would never have picked them for mother and daughter. Abigail's coloring was darker and her features were sharper. Her hair hung down her back in that ratty, just-got-out-of-bed look and she wore a shapeless sack-like brown dress over black leggings. Intricate henna markings extended from her hands all the way up her forearms. Her only jewelry was a silver skull hanging from a black shoelace around her neck.

"Dad is picking me up," said Abigail.

"What? No he's not," said Madeline.

"Yeah, I'm going to stay there tonight because I've got that thing tomorrow with Louisa and we have to be there early, and it's closer from Dad's place."

"It's ten minutes closer at the most," protested Madeline.

"But it's just easier going from Dad and Bonnie's place," said Abigail. "We can get out the door faster. We won't be sitting waiting in the car while Fred looks for his shoes or Chloe runs back inside to get a different Barbie doll or whatever."

"I suppose Skye never has to go back inside for her Barbie doll," said Madeline.

"Bonnie would never let Skye play with Barbie dolls in a million years," said Abigail with a roll of her eyes, as if that would be obvious to anyone. "I mean, you really shouldn't let Chloe play with them, Mum; they're, like, badly unfeminist, and they give her unrealistic body-shape expectations."

"Yes, well, the ship has sailed when it comes to Chloe and Barbie." Madeline gave Jane a rueful smile.

There was a beep of a horn from outside.

"That's him," said Abigail.

"You already *called* him?" said Madeline. Color rose in her cheeks. "You arranged this without asking me?"

"I asked Dad," said Abigail. She came around the side of the table and gave Madeline a kiss on the cheek. "Bye, Mum."

"Nice to meet you." Abigail smiled at Jane. You couldn't help but like her.

"Abigail Marie!" Madeline stood up from the table. "This is unacceptable. You don't just get to choose where you're going to spend the night."

Abigail stopped. She turned around.

"Why not?" she said. "Why should you and Dad get to choose who *gets the next turn of me*?" Jane could again see a resemblance to Madeline in the way Abigail quivered with rage. "As if I'm something you *own*. Like I'm your car and you get to share me."

"It's not like that," began Madeline.

"It *is* like that," said Abigail.

There was another beep of the horn from outside.

"What's going on?" A middle-aged man strolled into the kitchen, wearing a wet suit rolled down to his waist, revealing a broad, very hairy chest. He was with a little boy who was dressed exactly the same way, except his chest was skinny and hairless. He said to Abigail, "Your dad is out front."

"I *know* that," said Abigail. She looked at the man's hairy chest. "You should not walk around like that in public. It's disgusting."

"What? Showing off my fine physique?" The man banged a proud fist against his chest and smiled at Jane. She smiled back uneasily.

"Revolting," said Abigail. "I'm going."

"We'll talk more about this later!" said Madeline.

"Whatever."

"Don't you *whatever* me!" called out Madeline. The front door slammed.

"Mummy, I am starved to *death*," said the little boy.

"Have a muffin," said Madeline gloomily. She sank back down into her chair. "Jane, this is my husband, Ed, and my son, Fred. Ed, Fred. Easy to remember."

"Because they rhyme," clarified Fred.

"Gidday," said Ed. He shook Jane's hand. "Sorry about the 'disgusting' sight of me. Fred and I have been surfing." He sat down next to Madeline and put his arm around her. "Abigail giving you grief?"

Madeline pressed her face against his shoulder. "You're like a wet, salty dog."

"These are *good*." Fred took a gigantic bite from his muffin while simultaneously snaking out his hand and taking a second one. Jane would bring extra next time.

"Mummy! We neeeeeed you!" Chloe called from down the hallway.

"I'm going to go ride my skateboard." Fred took a third muffin.

"Helmet," said Madeline and Ed at the same time.

"Mummy!" Chloe shouted.

"Coming!" said Madeline. "Talk to Jane, Ed."

She went off down the hallway.

Jane prepared herself to carry the conversation, but Ed grinned easily at her, took a muffin and settled back in his chair. "So you're Ziggy's mum. How'd you come up with the name Ziggy?"

"My brother suggested it," said Jane. "He's a big Bob Marley fan and I guess Bob Marley called his son Ziggy." She paused, remembering the miraculous weight of her new baby in her arms, his solemn eyes. "I liked that it was kind of out-there. My name is so dull. Plain Jane and all that."

"Jane is a beautiful, classic name," said Ed very definitely, making her fall in love with him just a little. "In point of *fact*, I had 'Jane' on my list when we were naming Chloe, but I got overruled, and I'd already won on 'Fred.'"

Jane's eyes were caught by a wedding photo on the wall: Madeline wearing a champagne-colored tulle dress, sitting on Ed's lap, both of them had their eyes screwed shut with helpless laughter.

"How did you and Madeline meet?" she asked to make conversation.

Ed brightened. It was obviously a story he liked to tell.

"I lived across the street from her when we were kids," he said. "Madeline lived next door to a big Lebanese family. They had six sons: big strapping boys. I was terrified of them. They used to play cricket in the street, and sometimes Madeline would join in. She'd come trotting out, half the size of these big lumps, and she'd have ribbons in her hair and those shiny bangles, well *you* know what she's like, the girliest girl you'd ever seen, but my God, she could play cricket."

He put down his muffin and stood up to demonstrate. "So out she'd come, flick, flick of the hair, flounce, flounce of the dress, and she'd take the bat, and next thing, WHAM!" He slammed an imaginary cricket bat. "And those boys would fall to their knees, clutching their heads."

"Are you telling the cricket story again?" Madeline returned from Chloe's bedroom.

"That's when I fell in love with her," said Ed. "Truly, madly, deeply. Watching from my bedroom window."

"I didn't even know he existed," said Madeline airily.

"Nope, she didn't. So we grow up and leave home, and I hear from my mum that Madeline has married some wanker," said Ed.

"Shhh." Madeline slapped his arm.

"Then, years later, I go to this barbecue for a friend's thirtieth birthday. There's a cricket game in the backyard, and who's out there batting in her stilettos, all blinged up, exactly the same, but little Madeline from across the road. My heart just about stopped."

"That's a very romantic story," said Jane.

"I nearly didn't go to that barbecue," said Ed. Jane saw that his eyes were shiny, even though he must have told this story a hundred times before.

"And I nearly didn't go either," said Madeline. "I had to cancel a pedicure, and I would normally *never* cancel a pedicure."

They smiled at each other.

Jane looked away. She picked up her mug of tea and took a sip even though it was all gone. The doorbell rang.

"That will be Celeste," said Madeline.

Great, thought Jane, continuing to pretend-sip her empty mug of tea. *Now I'll be in the presence of both great love and great beauty.*

All around her was color: rich, vibrant color. She was the only colorless thing in this whole house.

> **Miss Barnes:** Obviously parents form their own social groups *outside* of school. The conflict at the trivia night might not necessarily have anything to do with what was going on at Pirriwee Public. I just thought I should point that out.

> **Thea:** Yes, well, Miss Barnes would say that, wouldn't she?

16.

"What did you think of Jane?" Madeline asked Ed that night in the bathroom as he cleaned his teeth and she used her fingertip to apply an eye-wateringly expensive dab of eye cream to her "fine lines and wrinkles." (She had a marketing degree, for heaven's sake. She knew she'd just blown her money buying a jar of hope.) "Ed?"

"I'm cleaning my teeth, give me a moment." He rinsed his mouth out, spat and tapped his toothbrush on the side of the basin. *Tap, tap, tap.* Always three definite, decisive taps, as if the toothbrush were a hammer or wrench. Sometimes, if she'd been drinking champagne, she could get weak from laughter just watching Ed tap his toothbrush on the basin.

"Jane looks about twelve years old to me," said Ed. "*Abigail* seems older than her. I can't get my head around her being a fellow parent." He pointed his toothbrush at her and grinned. "But she'll be our secret weapon at this year's trivia night. She'll know the answers to all the Gen Y questions."

"I reckon I might know more pop culture stuff than Jane," said Madeline. "I get the feeling she's not your typical twenty-four-year-old. She seems almost old-fashioned in some ways, like someone from my mother's generation."

She examined her face, sighed and put her jar of hope back on the shelf.

"She can't be that old-fashioned," said Ed. "You said she got pregnant after a one-night stand."

"She went ahead and *had* the baby," said Madeline. "That's sort of old-fashioned."

"But then she should have left him on the church doorstep," said Ed. "In a wicked basket."

"A what?"

"A wicker basket. That's a word, isn't it? Wicker?"

"I thought you said a *wicked* basket."

"I did. I was covering up my mistake. Hey, what's with all the *gum*? She was chewing it all day."

"I know. It's like she's addicted."

He turned off the bathroom light. They both went to opposite sides of the bed, snapped on their bedside lamps and pulled back the cover in a smooth, practiced, synchronized move that proved, depending on Madeline's mood, that they either had the perfect marriage or that they were stuck in a middle-class suburban rut and they needed to sell the house and go traveling around India.

"I'd quite like to give Jane a makeover," mused Madeline as Ed found his page in his book. He was a big fan of Patricia Cornwell murder mysteries. "The way she pulls back her hair like that. All flat on her head. She needs some volume."

"Volume," murmured Ed. "Absolutely. That's what she needs. I was thinking the same thing." He flipped a page.

"We need to help find her a boyfriend," said Madeline.

"You'd better get on that," said Ed.

"I'd quite like to give Celeste a makeover too," said Madeline.

"I know that sounds strange. Obviously she looks beautiful no matter what."

"Celeste? Beautiful?" said Ed. "Can't say I've noticed."

"Ha, ha." Madeline picked up her book and put it straight down again. "They seem so different, Jane and Celeste, but I feel like they're also sort of similar. I can't quite work out how."

Ed put down his own book. "I can tell you how they're similar."

"Can you now?"

"They're both damaged," said Ed.

"Damaged?" said Madeline. "How are they damaged?"

"Don't know," said Ed. "I just recognize damaged girls. I used to date them. I can spot a crazy chick a mile off."

"So was I damaged too?" asked Madeline. "Is that what attracted you?"

"Nope," said Ed. He picked up his book again. "You weren't damaged."

"Yes I was!" protested Madeline. She wanted to be interesting and damaged too. "I was heartbroken when you met me."

"There's a difference between heartbroken and damaged," said Ed. "You were sad and hurt. Maybe your heart was broken, but *you* weren't broken. Now, be quiet, because I think I'm falling for a red herring here, and I'm not falling for it, Ms. Cornwell, no I'm not."

"Mmmm," said Madeline. "Well, *Jane* might be damaged, but I don't see what Celeste has got to be damaged about. She's beautiful and rich and happily married and she doesn't have an ex-husband stealing her daughter away from her."

"He's not trying to steal her away," said Ed, his eyes back on his book. "This is just Abigail being a teenager. Teenagers are crazy. You know that."

Madeline picked up her own book.

She thought of Jane and Ziggy walking off hand in hand down the driveway as they left that afternoon. Ziggy was telling Jane something, one little hand gesticulating wildly, and Jane had her head tipped to one side, listening, her other hand holding out the car keys to open her car. Madeline heard her say, "I know! Let's go to that place where we got those yummy tacos!"

Watching them brought back a flood of memories from the years when she was a single mother. For five years it had been just her and Abigail. They'd lived in a little two-bedroom flat above an Italian restaurant. They ate a lot of takeout pasta and free garlic bread. (Madeline had put on seven kilos.) They were the Mackenzie girls in unit nine. She'd changed Abigail's name back to her maiden name (and she refused to change it again when she married Ed. A woman could only change her surname so many times before it got ridiculous). She couldn't stand having Abigail walk around with her father's surname when Nathan chose to spend his Christmas lying on a beach in Bali with a trashy little hairdresser. A hairdresser who, by the way, didn't even have good hair: black roots and split ends.

"I always thought that Nathan's punishment for walking out on us would be that Abigail wouldn't love him the way she loved me," she said to Ed. "I used to say it to myself all the time. 'Abigail won't want Nathan walking her down the aisle. He'll pay the price,' I thought. But you know what? He's not paying for his sins. Now he's got Bonnie, who is nicer and younger and prettier than me, he's got a brand-new daughter who can write out the whole alphabet, and now he's getting Abigail too! He got away with it all. He hasn't got a single regret."

She was surprised to hear her voice crack. She thought she

was just angry, but now she knew she was hurt. Abigail had infuriated her before. She'd frustrated and annoyed her. But this was the first time she'd hurt her.

"She's meant to love *me* best," she said childishly, and she tried to laugh, because it was a joke, except that she was deadly serious. "I thought she loved me best."

Ed put his book back down and put his arm around her. "Do you want me to kill the bastard? Bump him off? I could frame Bonnie for it."

"Yes please," said Madeline into his shoulder. "That would be lovely."

> **Detective-Sergeant Adrian Quinlan:** We haven't made any arrests at this stage. I can say that we do believe we have probably already spoken to the person or persons involved.

> **Stu:** I don't think anyone, including the police, have got the faintest idea about who did what.

17.

Gabrielle: I thought there might have been a certain, I don't know, etiquette about handing out party invitations. I thought what happened on that first day of kindergarten was kind of inappropriate.

5

S mile, Ziggy, smile!"

Ziggy finally smiled at the exact same moment that Jane's father yawned. Jane clicked the shutter and then checked the photo on the screen of her digital camera. Ziggy and her mum were both smiling beautifully, while her dad was captured mid-yawn: mouth agape, eyes scrunched. He was tired because he'd had to get up so early to make it all the way to the peninsula from Granville to see his grandson on his first day of school. Jane's parents had always gone to bed late and gotten up late, and these days anything that required them leaving the house before nine a.m. was a tremendous effort. Her father had taken early retirement from his job in the public service last year, and since then, he and Jane's mother had been staying up late doing their puzzles until three or four in the morning. "Our parents are turning into vampires," Jane's brother had said to her. "Jigsaw-playing vampires."

"Would you like my husband to take a photo of all of you together?" said a woman standing nearby. "I'd offer to take it myself, but technology and I are not friends."

Jane looked up. The woman wore a full-length paisley skirt with a black singlet. Her wrists seemed to be adorned with twine, and she wore her hair in one long single plait. There was a tattoo of a Chinese symbol on her shoulder. She looked a bit out of place next to all the other parents in their casual beachwear, gym gear or business clothes. Her husband seemed a good deal older than her and was wearing a T-shirt and shorts: standard middle-aged-dad gear. He was holding the hand of a tiny, mouse-like little girl with long scraggly hair, whose uniform looked like it was three sizes too big for her.

I bet you're Bonnie, thought Jane suddenly, remembering how Madeline had described her ex-husband's wife, at the same time as the woman said, "I'm Bonnie, and this is my husband, Nathan, and my little girl, Skye."

"Thanks so much," said Jane, handing over the camera to Madeline's ex-husband. She went to stand with her parents and Ziggy.

"Say cheese and biscuits!" Nathan held up the camera.

"Huh?" said Ziggy.

"Coffee," yawned Jane's mother.

Nathan took the photo. "There you go!"

He handed back the camera, just as another little curly-haired girl marched straight up to his daughter. Jane felt sick. She recognized her immediately. It was the girl who had accused Ziggy of trying to choke her. Amabella. Jane looked around. Where was the angry mother?

"What is your name?" said Amabella importantly to Skye. She was carrying a large pile of pale pink envelopes.

"Skye," whispered the little girl. She was so painfully shy, it hurt to watch her try to squeeze the words out.

Amabella flipped through her envelopes. "Skye, Skye, Skye."

"Goodness, can you read all those names already?" asked Jane's mother.

"I've actually been reading since I was three," said Amabella politely. She continued to flip. "Skye!" She handed over a pink envelope. "This is an invitation to my fifth birthday. It's an *A* party, because my name starts with *A*."

"Already reading before they start school!" said Jane's dad chummily to Nathan. "Top of the class already! Must have had tutoring, do you reckon?"

"Well, not to blow our own trumpet or anything, but Skye here is already reading quite well too," said Nathan. "And we don't believe in tutoring, do we, Bon?"

"We prefer to let Skye's growth happen organically," said Bonnie.

"Organic, eh?" said Jane's dad. He furrowed his brow. "Like fruit?"

Amabella turned to Ziggy. "What's your—" She froze. An expression of pure panic crossed her face. She clutched the pink envelopes tight to her chest as if to prevent Ziggy from stealing one and, without saying a word, she turned on her heel and ran off.

"Goodness. What was that all about?" said Jane's mother.

"Oh, that was the kid who said I hurt her," said Ziggy matter-of-factly. "But I never did, Grandma."

Jane looked around the playground. Everywhere she looked she could see children in brand-new, too-big school uniforms.

Every single one was holding a pale pink envelope.

Harper: Look, nobody in that school knew Renata better than me. We were very close. I can tell you for a fact, she was not trying to make a point that day.

Samantha: Oh my God, of *course* she was making a point.

18.

Madeline was being assaulted by a vicious bout of PMS on Chloe's first day of school. She was fighting back, but to no avail. *I choose my mood,* she told herself as she stood in the kitchen, tossing back evening primrose capsules like Valium. (She knew it was no use, you were meant to take them regularly, but she had to try something, even though the stupid things were probably just a waste of money.) She was furious with the bad timing. She would have liked to have found a way to blame someone, ideally her ex-husband, but she couldn't find a way to make Nathan responsible for her menstrual cycle. No doubt Bonnie danced in the moonlight to deal with the ebbs and flows of womanhood.

PMS was still a relatively new experience for Madeline. Another jolly part of the aging process. She'd never really believed in it before. Then, as she hit her late thirties, her body said, *OK, you don't believe in PMS? I'll show you PMS. Get a load of this, bitch.*

Now, for one day every month, she had to fake everything: her basic humanity, her love for her children, her love for Ed. She'd once been appalled to hear of women claiming PMS as a defense for murder. Now she understood. She could happily murder someone today! In fact, she felt like there should be some sort of recognition for her remarkable strength of character that she didn't.

All the way to school she did deep-breathing exercises to help calm her mood. Thankfully Fred and Chloe weren't fighting in the backseat. Ed hummed to himself as he drove, which was kind of unbearable (the unnecessary, relentless *cheerfulness* of the man), but at least he was wearing a clean shirt and hadn't insisted on wearing the too-small white polo shirt with the tomato sauce stain he thought was invisible. PMS would not win today. PMS would not ruin this milestone.

They found a legal parking spot straightaway. The children actually got out of the car the first time they were asked.

"Happy New Year, Mrs. Ponder!" she called out as they walked past the little white weatherboard cottage next to the school, where plump, white-haired Mrs. Ponder sat on her fold-out chair with a cup of tea and the newspaper.

"Morning!" called Mrs. Ponder eagerly.

"Keep walking, keep walking," Madeline hissed at Ed as he started to slow his pace. He loved a good long chat with Mrs. Ponder (she'd been a nurse in Singapore during the war), or with anyone really, particularly if they were over the age of seventy.

"Chloe's first day of school!" Ed called out. "Big day!"

"Ah, bless," said Mrs. Ponder.

They kept walking.

Madeline had her mood under control, like a rabid dog on a tight leash.

The school yard was filled with chatting parents and shouting children. The parents stood still while the children ran helter-skelter around them, like marbles skidding about a pinball machine. There were the new kindergarten parents smiling brightly and nervily. There were the Year 6 mums in their animated, unbreakable little circles, secure in their positions as queens of the school. There were the Blond Bobs caressing their freshly cut blond bobs.

Ah, it was lovely. The sea breeze. The children's bright little faces—and, oh for fuck's sake, there was her ex-husband.

It wasn't like she hadn't known he'd be there, but it was outrageous that he looked so comfortable in *Madeline's* school yard, so pleased with himself, so ordinary and dad-ly. And worse, he was taking a photo of Jane and Ziggy (they belonged to Madeline!) and a pleasant-looking couple who didn't seem much older than Madeline, but who she knew must be Jane's parents. He was a terrible photographer too. *Don't rely on Nathan to capture a memory for you. Don't rely on Nathan for anything.*

"There's Abigail's dad," said Fred. "I didn't see his car out front." Nathan drove a canary-yellow Lexus. Poor Fred would have quite liked a father who cared about cars. Ed didn't even know the difference between models.

"That's my half sister!" Chloe pointed at Nathan and Bonnie's daughter. Skye's school uniform was gigantic on her, and with her big sad eyes and long, fair, wavy, wispy hair, she looked like a sad little waif from a production of *Les Misérables*. Madeline could already see what was going to happen. Chloe was going to adopt Skye. Skye was exactly the sort of shy little girl Madeline would have taken under her wing when she was at school. Chloe would ask Skye to come over for playdates so she could play with her hair.

Just at that moment, Skye blinked rapidly as a strand of her hair fell in her eyes, and Madeline blanched. The child blinked *just like Abigail* used to blink when her hair fell in her eyes. That was a piece of Madeline's child, Madeline's past and Madeline's heart. There should be a law against ex-husbands procreating.

"For the millionth time, Chloe," she hissed, "Skye is Abigail's half sister, not yours!"

"Deep breaths," said Ed. "Deeeep breaths."

Nathan handed the camera back to Jane and strolled toward them. He'd grown out his hair recently. It was thick and gray and flip-flopping about on his forehead as if he were a middle-aged, Australian Hugh Grant. Madeline suspected he'd grown it deliberately to one-up Ed, who was almost completely bald now.

"Maddie," he said. He was the only person in the world to call her Maddie. Once, that had been a source of great pleasure; now it was a source of profound irritation. "Ed, mate! And little, hmmm . . . It's your first day at school too, isn't it?" Nathan could never be bothered to remember Madeline's children's names. He held up his palm for a high five with Fred. "Gidday, champ." Fred betrayed her by high-fiving him back.

Nathan kissed Madeline on the cheek and shook Ed's hand enthusiastically. He took an ostentatious relish in the civility of his dealings with his ex-wife and family.

"Na*than*," intoned Ed. He had a particular way of saying Nathan's name, a deepening and drawling of his voice and an emphasis on the second syllable. It always made Nathan frown slightly, never quite sure if he was being laughed at or not. But today it wasn't enough to save Madeline's mood.

"Big day, big day," said Nathan. "You two are old hands, but this is a first for us! I'm not ashamed to say I got a bit teary when I saw Skye in her school uniform."

Madeline couldn't help herself. "Skye is not your first child to start school, Nathan," she said.

Nathan flushed. She'd broken their unspoken no-hard-feelings rule. But for God's sake. Only a saint could let that one go. Abigail had been at school for two months before Nathan had noticed. He'd called up in the middle of the day for a chat. "She's at school," Madeline had told him. *"School?"* he'd spluttered. "She's not old enough for school, is she?"

"Speaking of Abigail, Maddie, are you OK if we swap weekends this week?" said Nathan. "We're going to see Bonnie's mother down at Bowral on Saturday, and Abigail hates to miss seeing her."

Bonnie materialized by his side, smiling beatifically. She was always smiling beatifically. Madeline suspected drugs.

"My mother and Abigail have such a special connection," she said to Madeline, as if this would be news that Madeline would welcome.

This was the thing: Who would want their daughter having a "special connection" with their ex-husband's wife's mother? Only Bonnie could think that you would want to hear that, and yet, you couldn't complain, could you? You couldn't even think, *Shut up, bitch*, because Bonnie was not a bitch. So all Madeline could do was just stand there and nod and *take it*, while her mood snarled and snapped and strained at the leash.

"Sure," she said. "No problem."

"Daddy!" Skye pulled on Nathan's shirt, and he lifted her up onto his hip while Bonnie gazed tenderly at them both.

"I'm so sorry, Maddie, but I'm just not cut out for this." That's what Nathan had said when Abigail was three weeks old, a fretful baby, who, since she'd been home from the hospital, had never slept longer than thirty-two minutes. Madeline had yawned, "Me either." She didn't think he meant it *literally*. An hour later, she'd watched in stunned amazement as he'd packed his clothes into his long red cricket bag and his eyes had rested briefly on the baby, as if she belonged to someone else, and he'd left. She would never

ever forgive or forget that cursory glance he gave his beautiful baby daughter. And now that daughter was a teenager, who made her own lunch and caught the bus to high school all on her own and called out over her shoulder as she left, "Don't forget I'm staying at Dad's place tonight!"

"Hi, Madeline," said Jane.

Jane was once again wearing a plain V-necked white T-shirt (did she own no other sort of shirt?), the same blue denim skirt and thongs. Her hair was pulled back in that painfully tight ponytail, and of course she was doing her clandestine gum-chewing. Her simplicity was somehow a relief to Madeline's mood, as if Jane were what she needed to feel better, in the same way that you longed for plain dry toast after you'd been ill.

"Jane," she said warmly. "How are you? I see you met my delightful ex-husband here and his family."

"Ho, ho, ho," said Nathan, presumably sounding like Santa Claus because he didn't know how else to respond to the "delightful ex-husband" barb.

Madeline felt Ed's hand rest on her shoulder, a warning that she was skating too close to the line of incivility.

"I did," said Jane. Her face gave nothing away. "These are my parents, Di and Bill."

"Hello! Your grandson is just beautiful." Madeline shrugged off Ed and shook hands with Jane's parents, who were somehow *lovely*, you could just tell by looking at them.

"We actually think Ziggy is my own darling father reincarnated," sparkled Jane's mother.

"No we don't," said Jane's dad. He looked at Chloe, who was pulling at Madeline's dress. "And this must be your little one, eh?"

Chloe handed a pink envelope to Madeline. "Can you keep

this, Mummy? It's an invitation to Amabella's party. You have to come dressed as something starting with *A*. I'm going to dress up as a princess." She ran off.

"Apparently poor little Ziggy isn't invited to that party," Jane's mother said in a lowered voice.

"Mum," said Jane. "Leave it."

"What? She shouldn't be handing out invitations in the playground unless she's asking the whole class," said Madeline.

She scanned the playground for Renata and saw Celeste walk in through the school gates, late as usual, holding hands with the twins, looking impossibly gorgeous. It was as though another species had turned up at school. Madeline saw one of the Year 2 dads catch sight of Celeste and do a comical double take and nearly trip over a schoolbag.

And there was Renata, bustling straight for Celeste and handing her two pink envelopes.

"I'm going to kill her," said Madeline.

> **Mrs. Lipmann:** Look, I'd rather not say anything further. We deserve to be left in peace. A parent is dead. The entire school community is grieving.
>
> **Gabrielle:** Hmmm, I wouldn't say the *entire* school community is grieving. That might be a stretch.

Celeste saw the man trip while he was checking her out.

Maybe she should have an affair. It might make something happen, push her marriage over the cliff it had been inexorably creeping toward for so many years.

But the thought of being with any other man besides Perry filled her with a heavy, listless sensation. She'd be so bored. She was not interested in other men. Perry made her feel alive. If she left him, she'd be single and celibate and bored forever. It wasn't fair. He ruined her.

"You're holding my hand too tight," said Josh.

"Yeah, Mummy," said Max.

She loosened her grip.

"Sorry, boys," she said.

It hadn't been a good morning. First, there was something cataclysmically wrong with one of Josh's socks that could not be rectified with any amount of adjusting. Then Max couldn't find a very specific little Lego man with a very specific yellow hat that he required right at that very minute.

They'd both wailed and wailed for Daddy. They didn't care that he was on the other side of the world. They wanted him. Celeste wanted Perry too. He would have fixed Josh's sock. He would have found Max's Lego man. She'd always known that she was going to struggle with the school-morning routine. She and the boys were late sleepers and generally out-of-sorts in the morning, whereas Perry woke up happy and energetic. If he'd been here this morning, they would have been early for their first day at school. There would have been laughter in the car, not silence, interspersed by pitiful shudders from the boys.

She'd given them lollipops in the end. They were still sucking on them as she got them out of the car, and she'd seen one of the kindergarten mothers she recognized from the orientation day walk by and smile sweetly at the boys, while flicking Celeste a "bad mother" look.

"There's Chloe and Ziggy!" said Josh.

"Let's go kill them!" said Max.

"Boys, don't talk like that!" said Celeste. Good God. What would people think?

"Just pretend-killing, Mummy," said Josh kindly. "Chloe and Ziggy like it!"

"Celeste! It is Celeste, isn't it?" A woman appeared in front of her as the boys ran off. "I met you and your husband at the uniform shop a few weeks ago." She touched her chest. "Renata. I'm Amabella's mum."

"Of course! Hi, Renata," said Celeste.

"Perry couldn't make it today?" Renata looked around hopefully.

"He's in Vienna," said Celeste. "He travels a lot for work."

"I'm sure he *does*," said Renata knowingly. "I thought I recognized him the other day and so I Googled him when I got back home, and that's when it clicked! *The* Perry White! I've actually seen your husband speak a few times. I'm in the funds-management world myself!"

Great. A Perry groupie. Celeste often wondered what the Perry groupies would think if they were to see him doing the things he did.

"I've got some invitations for the boys to Amabella's fifth-birthday party." Renata handed her two pink envelopes. "Of course, you and Perry are most welcome to come along. Nice way for all the parents to start getting to know one another!"

"Lovely." Celeste took the envelopes and put them in her bag.

"Good morning, ladies!" It was Madeline, wearing one of her beautiful signature dresses. She had two spots of color high on her cheeks and a dangerous glitter in her eyes. "Thank you for Chloe's invitation to Amabella's party."

"Oh dear, is Amabella handing them out?" Renata frowned and patted at her handbag. "Oh dear. She must have taken them from my handbag. I *did* mean to hand them discreetly to the parents."

"Yes, because it looks like you're inviting the whole class except for one little boy."

"I assume you're talking about Ziggy, the child who left bruises on my daughter's neck," said Renata. "He didn't make it onto the invitation list. Surprise, surprise."

"Come on now, Renata," said Madeline. "You can't do this."

"So sue me." Renata shot Celeste a glinting, mischievous look, as if they were in on a joke together.

Celeste took a breath. She didn't want to be involved. "I might just—"

"I'm *so* sorry, Renata," interrupted Madeline with a queenly look of apology. "But Chloe won't be able to make it to the party."

"What a pity," Renata said. She pulled hard on the diagonal strap of her handbag, as if she were adjusting body armor. "You know what? I think I might terminate this conversation before I say something I regret." She nodded at Celeste. "Nice to see you again."

Madeline watched her go. She seemed invigorated.

"This is war, Celeste," she said happily. "War, I tell you!"

"Oh, Madeline," sighed Celeste.

Harper: I know we all like to put Celeste on a pedestal but I don't think she always made the best nutritional choices for her children. I saw the twins eating *lollipops for breakfast* on their first day of school!

Samantha: Parents do tend to judge each other. I don't know why. Maybe because none of us really know what we're doing? And I guess that can sometimes lead to conflict. Just not normally on this sort of scale.

Jackie: I, for one, don't have the time to be judging other parents. Or the interest. My children are only one part of my life.

Detective-Sergeant Adrian Quinlan: In addition to the murder investigation, we expect to be charging multiple parents with assault. We're deeply disappointed and quite shocked to see a group of parents behaving this way.

19.

O h, Madeline," sighed Ed.

He parked the car, pulled the keys from the ignition and turned to look at her. "You can't make Chloe miss her friend's party just because Ziggy isn't invited. That's crazy."

They'd driven straight from the school down to the beach to have a quick coffee at Blue Blues with Jane and her parents. It had been Jane's mother who had suggested it, and it had seemed so important to her that Madeline, who had an overly ambitious list of things to achieve on the kids' first day at school, felt she couldn't say no.

"No it's not," said Madeline, although she was already feeling the first twinges of regret. When Chloe heard she was missing Amabella's *A* party there would be hell to pay. Amabella's last birthday party had been insane: jumping castle, a magician *and* a disco.

"I'm in a very bad mood today," she told Ed.

"Really?" said Ed. "I would never have noticed."

"I miss the children," said Madeline. The backseat of the car felt so empty and silent. Her eyes filled with tears.

Ed guffawed. "You're kidding, right?"

"My baby has started school," wept Madeline. Chloe had marched straight into the classroom, walking right alongside Miss

Barnes, as if she were a fellow teacher, chatting the whole way, probably making a few suggestions for changes to the curriculum.

"Yep," said Ed. "And not a moment too soon. I think those were the words you used yesterday on the phone to your mother."

"And I had to stand there in the school yard, making polite conversation with my ex-bloody-husband!" Madeline's mood flipped from teary back to angry.

"Yeah, I don't know if I'd use the word *polite*," said Ed.

"It's hard enough being a single mother," said Madeline.

"Um. What?" said Ed.

"Jane! I'm talking about Jane, of course. I remember Abigail's first day of school. I felt like a freak. It felt like everyone was so disgustingly *married*. All the parents were in perfect little pairs. I never felt so alone." Madeline thought of her ex-husband today, looking comfortably about the school yard. Nathan had no clue as to what it had been like for Madeline for all those years she'd brought Abigail up on her own. He wouldn't deny it. Oh no. If she were to scream at him, "It was hard! It was so hard!" he'd wince and look so sad and so sorry, but no matter how hard he tried, *he would never really get it.*

She was filled with impotent rage. There was nowhere to aim it except straight at Renata. "So just imagine how Jane feels when her child is the *only one* not invited to a party. Imagine it."

"I know," said Ed. "Although I guess after what happened, you can sort of see it from Renata's point of view—"

"No you can't!" cried Madeline.

"Jesus. Sorry. No. Of course I can't." Ed looked in the rearview mirror. "Oh, look, here's your poor little friend pulled up behind us. Let's go eat cake with her. That will fix things."

He undid his seat belt.

"If you're not asking every child in the class, you don't hand out the invitations on the playground," said Madeline. "Every mother knows that. It's a *law of the land*."

"I could talk about this subject all day long," said Ed. "I really could. There is nothing else I want to talk about today other than Amabella's fifth-birthday party."

"Shut up," said Madeline.

"I thought we didn't say 'shut up' in our house."

"Fuck off, then," said Madeline.

Ed grinned. He put a hand to the side of her face. "You'll feel better tomorrow. You always feel better tomorrow."

"I know, I know." Madeline took a deep breath and opened the car door to see Jane's mother fling herself out of Jane's car and hurry along the sidewalk toward her, slinging her handbag over her shoulder and smiling frantically. "Hi! Hi there! Madeline, will you just walk along the beach with me for a bit while the others order our coffee?"

"Mum." Jane walked behind with her father. "You've *seen* the beach. You don't even like the beach!"

You didn't have to be gifted and talented to see that Jane's mother wanted to talk alone with Madeline.

"Of course I will . . . Di." The name came to her like a gift.

"I'll come too then," sighed Jane.

"No, no, you go into the café and help your dad get settled and order something nice for me," said Di.

"Yes, because I'm such a doddering old senior citizen." Jane's father put on a quavering old man's voice and clutched Jane's arm. "Help me, darling daughter."

"Off you go," said Di firmly.

Madeline watched Jane struggle with whether or not to insist, before giving a tiny shrug and giving up.

"Don't take too long," she said to her mother. "Or your coffee will get cold."

"Get me a double-shot espresso and the chocolate mud cake with cream," said Madeline to Ed.

Ed gave her a thumbs-up and led Jane and her father into Blue Blues, while Madeline reached down and slipped off her shoes. Jane's mother did the same.

"Did your husband take the day off work for Chloe's first day at school?" asked Di as they walked across the sand toward the water. "Oh, goodness, the glare!" She was wearing sunglasses, but she shielded her eyes with the back of her hand.

"He's a journalist for the local paper," said Madeline. "He's got very flexible hours, and he works from home a lot."

"That must be nice. Or is it? Does he get under your feet?" Di picked her way unsteadily across the sand. "Sometimes I send Bill off to buy me something at the supermarket I don't really need, just to give myself a little breather."

"It works pretty well for us," said Madeline. "I work three days a week for the Pirriwee Peninsula Theatre Company, so Ed can pick the kids up when I'm working. We're not making a fortune but, you know, we both love our jobs, so we're happy."

My God, why was she talking about money? It was like she was defending their choice of lifestyles. (And to be honest, they didn't love their jobs *that* much.) Was it because she sometimes felt like her whole life was in competition with high-flying career women like Renata? Or was it just because money was on her mind because of that shocking electricity bill she'd opened this morning? The truth was that although they weren't wealthy, they were certainly not struggling, and thanks to Madeline's savvy on-line shopping skills, even her wardrobe didn't need to suffer.

"Ah, yes, money. They say it doesn't buy happiness, but I don't know about that." Di pushed her hair out of her eyes and looked around the beach. "It is a very pretty beach. We're not really beach people, and obviously no one wants to see *this* in a bikini!" She made a face of pure loathing and gestured at her perfectly ordinary body, which Madeline judged to be about the same size as her own.

"I don't see why not," said Madeline. She had no patience for this sort of talk. It drove her to distraction the way women wanted to bond over self-hatred.

"But it will be nice for Jane and Ziggy, living near the beach, I think, I guess, and ah, you know, I just wanted to really thank you, Madeline, for taking Jane under your wing the way you have." She took her sunglasses off and looked directly at Madeline. Her eyes were pale blue, and she was wearing a frosted pink eye shadow, which wasn't quite working for her, although Madeline approved of the effort.

"Well, of course," said Madeline. "It's hard when you move to a new area and you don't know anyone."

"Yes, and Jane has moved so *often* in the last few years. Ever since she had Ziggy, she can't seem to stay put, or find a nice circle of friends, and she'd kill me for saying this, it's just, I'm not sure what's really going on with her."

She stopped, looked back over her shoulder at the café and compressed her lips.

"It's hard when they stop telling you things, isn't it?" said Madeline after a moment. "I have a teenage daughter. From a previous relationship." She always felt compelled to clarify this when she spoke about Abigail, and then felt obscurely guilty for doing so. It was like she was separating Abigail out somehow, putting her into a different category. "I don't know why I was so shocked when Abigail stopped telling me things. That's what all teenagers do, right? But she was such an open little girl. Of course, Jane isn't a teenager."

It was like she'd given Di permission to speak freely. She turned to Madeline enthusiastically. "I know! She's twenty-four, a grown-up! But they never seem like grown-ups. Her dad tells me I'm worrying over nothing. It's true that Jane is doing a beautiful job bringing up Ziggy, and she supports herself, won't take a cent from us! I slip money into her pockets like a pickpocket. Or the opposite of a pickpocket. But she's changed. Something has changed. I can't put my finger on it. It's like this deep unhappiness that she tries to hide. I don't know if it's depression or drugs or an eating disorder or what. She got so painfully thin! She used to be quite voluptuous."

"Well," said Madeline, thinking, *If it's an eating disorder, you probably gave it to her.*

"Why am I telling you this?" said Di. "You won't want to be her friend anymore! You'll think she's a drug addict! She's not a drug addict! She only has three out of the ten top signs of drug addiction. Or four at the most. You can't believe what you read on the Internet, anyway."

Madeline laughed, and Di laughed too.

"Sometimes I feel like waving my hand in front of her eyes and saying, 'Jane, Jane, are you still in there?'"

"I'm pretty sure she's—"

"She hasn't had a boyfriend since before Ziggy was born. She broke up with this boy. Zach. We all loved Zach, gorgeous boy, and Jane was very upset over the breakup, *very* upset, but gosh, that was what, six years ago now? She couldn't still be grieving over Zach, could she? He wasn't *that* good-looking!"

"I don't know," said Madeline. She wondered wistfully if her coffee was sitting on the table up at Blue Blues getting cold.

"Next thing she's pregnant, and supposedly Zach isn't the father, although we did always wonder about that, but she was absolutely adamant that Zach was *not* the father. She said it over and over again. A one-night stand, she said. No way of contacting the father. Well, you know, she was halfway through her arts-law degree, it wasn't ideal, but everything happens for a reason, don't you think?"

"Absolutely," said Madeline, who did not believe that at all.

"She'd been told by a doctor that she was likely to have a lot of trouble falling pregnant naturally, so it just seemed like it was meant to be. And then my darling dad died while Jane was pregnant and that's why it seemed like his soul might have come back in—"

"*Mu-um!* Madeline!"

Jane's mother startled, and they both turned away from the sea to see Jane standing on the boardwalk outside Blue Blues, waving frantically. "Your coffee is ready!"

"Coming!" called Madeline.

"I'm sorry," said Di as they walked back up from the beach. "I talk too much. Can you please forget everything I said? It's just that when I saw poor little Ziggy didn't get asked to that child's birthday party, I felt like crying. I'm so emotional these days, and then we had to get up so early today, I'm feeling quite light-headed. I didn't used to be, I used to be quite hard-hearted. It's my age, I'm fifty-eight. My friends are the same, we went out for lunch the other day, we've been friends since our children started kindergarten! We were all talking about how we feel like fifteen-year-olds, weeping at the drop of a hat."

Madeline stopped walking. "Di," she said.

Di turned to her nervously, as if she were about to be told off. "Yes?"

"I'll keep an eye on Jane," she said. "I promise."

> **Gabrielle:** See, part of the problem was that Madeline sort of *adopted* Jane. She was like a crazy, protective big sister. If you ever said anything even mildly critical of her Jane, you'd have Madeline snarling at you like a rabid dog.

20.

It was eleven a.m. on the first day of Ziggy's school life.

Had he already had his morning tea by now? Was he eating his apple and his cheese and crackers? His tiny box of raisins? Jane's heart twisted at the thought of him carefully opening his new lunch box. Where would he sit? Who would he talk to? She hoped Chloe and the twins were playing with him, but they could just as easily be ignoring him. It wasn't like one of the twins would stroll up to Ziggy, hand outstretched, and say, "Why, hello! Ziggy, isn't it? We met a few weeks back at a playdate. How have you been?"

She stood up from the dining room table where she was working and stretched her arms high above her head. He'd be fine. Every child went to school. They survived. They learned the rules of life.

She went into the tiny kitchen of her new apartment to switch the kettle on for a cup of tea she didn't especially feel like. It was just an excuse to take a break from the accounts of Perfect Pete's Plumbing. Pete might be a perfect plumber, but he wasn't that great at keeping his paperwork in order. Every quarter she received a shoe box filled with an odd assortment of scrunched, smudged, strange-smelling paperwork: invoices, credit card bills and receipts, most of which were not claimable. She could just imagine Pete emptying out his pockets, scooping up all the receipts from the console of his car in one meaty hand, stomping around his house, grabbing every piece of paper he could find before stuffing the lot into the shoe box with a gusty sigh of relief. Job done.

She went back to the dining room table and picked up the next receipt. Perfect Pete's wife had just spent $335 at the beautician, where she had enjoyed the "classic facial," "deluxe pedicure" and a bikini-line wax. So that was nice for Perfect Pete's wife. Next was an unsigned permission note for a school excursion to Taronga Zoo last year. On the back of the permission note, a child had written in purple crayon: "I HATE TOM!!!!!"

Jane studied the permission note.

I will/will not be able to attend the excursion as a parent helper.

Perfect Pete's wife had already circled "will not." Too busy getting her bikini line done.

She crumpled the receipt and permission slip in her hand and walked back into the kitchen.

She could be a parent helper if Ziggy ever went on an excursion. After all, that was why she'd originally decided to become a bookkeeper so she could be "flexible" for Ziggy, and "balance motherhood and career," even though she always felt foolish and fraudulent when she said things like that, as if she weren't really a mother, as if her whole life were a fake.

It would be fun to go on a school excursion again. She could still remember the excitement. The treats on the bus. Jane could secretly observe Ziggy interact with the other children. Make sure he was normal.

Of course he was normal.

She thought again, as she had been all morning, of the pale

pink envelopes. So many of them! It didn't matter that he wasn't invited to the party. He was too little to feel hurt, and none of the children knew one another yet anyway. It was silly to even think about it.

But the truth was, she felt deeply hurt on his behalf, and somehow responsible, as if she'd messed up. She'd been so ready to forget all about the incident on orientation day, and now it was back at the forefront of her mind again.

The kettle boiled.

If Ziggy really had hurt Amabella, and if he did something like that again, he would never get invited to any parties. The teachers would call Jane in for a meeting. She would have to take him to see a child psychologist.

She would have to say out loud all her secret terrors about Ziggy.

Her hand shook as she poured the hot water into the mug.

"If Ziggy isn't invited, then Chloe isn't going," Madeline had said at coffee this morning.

"Please don't do that," Jane had said. "You're going to make things worse."

But Madeline just raised her eyebrows and shrugged. "I've already told Renata."

Jane had been horrified. Great. Now Renata would have even more reason to dislike her. Jane would have an *enemy*. The last time she had had anything close to an enemy, she was in primary school herself. It had never crossed her mind that sending your child to school would be like going back to school yourself.

Perhaps she should have made him apologize that day, and apologized herself. "I'm so sorry," she could have said to Renata.

"I'm terribly sorry. He's never done anything like this before. I will make sure it never happens again."

But it was no use. Ziggy said he didn't do it. She couldn't have reacted any other way.

She took the cup of tea to the dining room table, sat back down at her computer and unwrapped a new piece of gum.

Right. Well, she would volunteer for anything on offer at the school. Apparently parental involvement was good for your child's education (although she'd always suspected that was propaganda put out by the schools). She would try to make friends with other mothers, apart from Madeline and Celeste, and if she ran into Renata she would be polite and friendly.

"This will all blow over in a week," her father had said at coffee this morning when they were discussing the party.

"Or it will all blow up," said Madeline's husband, Ed. "Now that my wife is involved."

Jane's mother had laughed as if she'd known Madeline and her propensities for years. (What had they been talking about for so long on the beach? Jane inwardly squirmed at the thought of her mother revealing every concern she had about Jane's life: *She can't seem to get a boyfriend! She's so skinny! She won't get a good haircut!*)

Madeline had fiddled with a heavy silver bracelet around her wrist. "Kaboom!" she'd said suddenly, and swirled her hands in opposite directions to indicate an explosion, her eyes wide. Jane had laughed, even while she thought, *Great. I've made friends with a crazy lady.*

The only reason Jane had had an enemy in primary school was because it was decreed to be so by a pretty, charismatic girl called Emily Berry, who always wore red ladybug hair clips in her hair.

Was Madeline the forty-year-old version of Emily Berry? Champagne instead of lemonade. Bright red lipstick instead of strawberry-flavored lip gloss. The sort of girl who merrily stirred up trouble for you and you still loved her.

Jane shook her head to clear it. This was ridiculous. She was a grown-up. She was not going to end up in the principal's office like she had when she was ten. (Emily had sat up on the chair next to her, kicking her legs, chewing gum and grinning over at Jane whenever the principal looked the other way, as if it were all a great lark.)

Right. Focus.

She picked up the next document from Pete the Plumber's shoe box and held it carefully with her fingertips. It was greasy to touch. This was an invoice from a wholesale plumbing supplier. *Well done, Pete. This actually relates to your business.*

She rested her hands on the keyboard. *Come on. Ready, set, go.* In order for the data-inputting side of her job to be both profitable and bearable she had to work fast. The first time an accountant gave her a job, he'd told her it was about six to eight hours' work. She'd done it in four, charged him for six. Since her first job she'd gotten even faster. It was like playing a computer game, seeing if she could get to a higher level each time.

It wasn't her dream job, but she did quite enjoy the satisfaction of transforming a messy pile of paperwork into neat rows of figures. She loved calling up her clients, who were now mostly small-business people like Pete, and telling them she'd found a new deduction. Best of all, she was proud of the fact that she'd supported herself and Ziggy for the last five years without having to ask her parents for money, even if it had meant that she sometimes worked well into the night while he slept.

This was not the career she'd dreamed of as an ambitious seventeen-year-old, but now it was hard to remember ever feeling innocent and audacious enough to dream of a certain type of life, as if you got to choose how things turned out.

A seagull squawked, and for a moment she was confused by the sound.

Well, she'd chosen *this*. She'd chosen to live by the beach, as if she had as much right as anyone else. She could reward herself for two hours' work with a walk on the beach. A walk on the beach in the middle of the day. She could go back to Blue Blues, buy a coffee to go and then take an arty photo of it sitting on a fence with the sea in the background and post it on Facebook with a comment: *Work break! How lucky am I?* People would write, *Jealous!*

If she packaged the perfect Facebook life, maybe she would start to believe it herself.

Or she could even post, *Mad as hell!! Ziggy the only one in the class not invited to a birthday party!! Grrrrr.* And everyone would write comforting things, like, *WTF?* and *Awwww. Poor little Ziggy!*

She could shrink her fears down into innocuous little status updates that drifted away on the news feeds of her friends.

Then she and Ziggy would be normal people. Maybe she'd even go on a date. Keep Mum happy.

She picked up her mobile phone and read the text her friend Anna had sent yesterday.

Remember Greg? My cousin u met when we were like 15?! He's moved to Syd. Wants your number to ask u for a drink! OK? No pressure! (He's pretty hot now. Got my genes!! Ha ha.) x

Right.

She remembered Greg. He'd been shy. Short. Reddish hair. He'd made a lame joke that no one got, and then when everyone said, "What? What?" he'd said, "Don't worry about it!" That had stuck in her head because she'd felt sorry for him.

Why not?

She could handle a drink with Greg.

It was time. Ziggy was in school. She lived by the beach.

She sent back the text: *OK x.*

She took a sip of her tea and put her hands on the keyboard.

It was her body that reacted. She wasn't even thinking about the text. She was thinking about Pete the Plumber's receipt for wastes and plugs.

A violent swoop of nausea made her fold in two, her forehead resting against the table. She pressed her palm across her mouth. Blood rushed from her head. She could smell that scent. She could swear it was real, that it was actually here in the apartment.

Sometimes, if Ziggy's mood changed too fast, without warning, from happy to angry, she could smell it on him.

She half straightened, gagging, and picked up her phone. She texted Anna with shaky fingers: *Don't give it to him! Changed my mind!*

The text came back almost instantly.

Too late. ☺

Thea: I heard Jane had a quote-unquote fling with one of the fathers. I've no idea which one. Except I know it wasn't my husband!

Bonnie: She did not.

Carol: You know there was a *man* in their Erotic Book Club? Not my husband, thank goodness. He only reads *Golf Australia.*

Jonathan: Yes, I was the man in the so-called Erotic Book Club, except that was just a joke. It was a book club. A perfectly ordinary book club.

Melissa: Didn't Jane have an affair with the stay-at-home dad?

Gabrielle: It wasn't Jane who had the affair! I always thought she was born-again. Flat shoes, no jewelry, no makeup. But good body! Not an ounce of fat. She was the skinniest mother in the school. God, I'm hungry. Have you tried the 5:2 diet? This is my fast day. I am dying of starvation.

21.

Celeste arrived early for school pickup. She ached for her twins' compact little bodies, and for that all too brief moment when their hands curled, suffocatingly, possessively, around her neck and she kissed their hot, hard, fragrant little heads before they squirmed away. But she knew she would probably be yelling at them within fifteen minutes. They'd be tired and crazy. She couldn't get them to sleep until nine p.m. last night. Much too late. Bad mother. "Just go to sleep!" she'd ended up shrieking. She always had trouble getting them to bed at a reasonable hour, except when Perry was at home. They listened to Perry.

He was a good dad. A good husband too. Most of the time.

"You need a bedtime routine," her brother had said on the phone from Auckland today, and Celeste had said, "Oh, what a revolutionary idea! I would never have thought of it!"

If parents had children who were good sleepers, they assumed this was due to their good parenting, not good luck. They followed the rules, and the rules had been proven to work. Celeste must therefore not be following the rules. And you could never prove it to them! They would die smug in their beds.

"Hi, Celeste."

Celeste startled. "Jane!" She pressed a hand to her chest. As usual, she'd been dreaming and hadn't heard footsteps. It bugged her the way she kept jumping like a lunatic when people appeared.

"Sorry," said Jane. "I didn't mean to creep up on you."

"How was your day?" asked Celeste. "Did you get lots of work done?"

She knew that Jane supported herself doing bookkeeping work. Celeste imagined her sitting at a tidy desk in her small bare apartment (she hadn't been there, but she knew the block of plain redbrick apartments on Beaumont Street down by the beach, and she assumed inside would be unadorned, like Jane. No fuss. No knickknacks). The simplicity of her life seemed so compelling. Just Jane and Ziggy. One sweet (putting aside the strange choking incident, of course), quiet, dark-haired child. No fights. Life would be calm and uncomplicated.

"I got a bit done," said Jane. Her mouth made tiny little mouse-like movements as she chewed gum. "I had coffee this morning with my parents and Madeline and Ed. Then the day sort of disappeared."

"The day goes so fast," agreed Celeste, although hers had dragged.

"Are you going back to work now that the kids are at school?" asked Jane. "What did you do before the twins?"

"I was a lawyer," said Celeste. *I was someone else.*

"Huh. I was meant to be a lawyer," said Jane. There was something wry and sad in her voice that Celeste couldn't quite interpret.

They turned down the grassy laneway that led past a little white weatherboard house that almost seemed to be part of the school.

"I wasn't really enjoying it," said Celeste. Was this true? She had hated the stress. She ran late every day. But didn't she once love some aspects of it? The careful untangling of a legal issue. Like math, but with words.

"I couldn't go back to practicing law," said Celeste. "Not with the boys. Sometimes I think I might do teaching. Teach legal studies. But I'm not sure that really appeals either." She had lost her nerve for work, like she'd lost her nerve for skiing.

Jane was silent. She was probably thinking that Celeste was a spoiled trophy wife.

"I'm lucky," said Celeste. "I don't have to work. Perry is . . . well, he's a hedge fund manager."

Now she sounded show-offy, when she'd meant to sound grateful. Conversations with women about work could be so fraught. If Madeline had been there, she would have said, "Perry earns a shitload, so Celeste can live a life of leisure." And then she would have done a typical Madeline about-face and said something about how bringing up twin boys wasn't exactly a life of leisure and that Celeste probably worked harder than Perry.

Perry liked Madeline. "Feisty," he called her.

"I have to start doing some sort of exercise routine while Ziggy is at school," said Jane. "I'm so unfit. I get breathless going up a tiny slope. It's terrible. Everyone around here is so fit and healthy."

"I'm not," said Celeste. "I do no exercise at all. Madeline is always after me to go to the gym with her. She's crazy for those classes, but I hate gyms."

"Me too," said Jane with a grimace. "Big sweaty men."

"We should go walking together when the kids are at school," said Celeste. "Around the headland."

Jane gave her a quick, shy, surprised grin. "I'd love that."

Harper: You know how Jane and Celeste were supposedly great friends? Well, obviously it wasn't all roses,
because I did overhear something at the trivia night,
quite by accident. It must have been only minutes before it happened. I was going out on the balcony to get
some fresh air—well, to have a cigarette, if you must
know, because I had a number of things on my mind—
anyway, Jane and Celeste were out there, and Celeste
was saying, "I'm sorry. I'm just so, so sorry."

It was about an hour before school pickup when Samira, Madeline's boss at the Pirriwee Theatre, called to discuss marketing for
the new production of *King Lear.* Just before she hung up (finally!
Madeline didn't get paid for the time she spent on these phone
calls, and if her boss offered to pay, she'd have said no, but still, it
would have been nice to have had the opportunity to graciously
refuse), Samira mentioned that she had a "whole stack" of compli-
mentary front-row Disney On Ice tickets if Madeline wanted
them.

"When for?" asked Madeline, looking at her wall calendar.

"Um, let's see. Saturday, February twenty-eighth, two p.m."

The box on the calendar was empty, but there was something familiar about the date. Madeline reached for her handbag
and pulled out the pink envelope that Chloe had given her that
morning.

Amabella's *A* party was at two p.m., Saturday, February 28.

Madeline smiled. "I'd love them."

Thea: The invitations for Amabella's party went out *first.*
And then next thing, that very same afternoon, Mad-

eline is handing out free tickets for Disney On Ice, like she's Lady Muck.

Samantha: Those tickets cost a fortune, and Lily was so desperate to go. I didn't realize it was the same day as Amabella's party, but then again, Lily didn't know Amabella from a bar of soap, so I felt bad, but not that bad.

Jonathan: I always said the best part of being a stay-at-home dad was leaving behind all the office politics. Then first day of school I get caught up in some war between these two women!

Bonnie: We went to Amabella's party. I think Madeline forgot to offer us one of the Disney tickets. I'm sure it was just an oversight.

Detective-Sergeant Adrian Quinlan: We're talking to parents about *everything* that went on at that school. I can assure you it wouldn't be the first time that a dispute over a seemingly inconsequential matter led to violence.

22.

Three Months Before the Trivia Night

Celeste and Perry sat on the couch, drinking red wine, eating Lindt chocolate balls and watching their third episode in a row of *The Walking Dead*. The boys were sound asleep. The house was quiet, except for the crunch of footsteps coming from the television. The main character was creeping through the forest, his knife drawn. A zombie appeared from behind a tree, her face black and rotting, her teeth snapping, making that guttural sound that zombies apparently make. Celeste and Perry both jumped and screamed. Perry spilled some of his red wine.

He dabbed at the splash of wine on his T-shirt. "That scared the life out of me."

The man on the screen drove his knife through the zombie's skull.

"Gotcha!" said Celeste.

"Pause it while I get us a refill," said Perry.

Celeste picked up the remote and paused the DVD. "This is even better than last season."

"I know," said Perry. "Although I think it gives me bad dreams."

He brought over the bottle of wine from the sideboard.

"Are we going to some kid's birthday party tomorrow?" he asked as he refilled her glass. "I ran into Mark Whittaker at Catalinas today and he seemed to think we were going. He said the mother mentioned we were invited. Renata somebody. Actually, did I meet a Renata that day when I went to the school with you?"

"You did," said Celeste. "We were invited to Amabella's party. But we're not going."

She wasn't concentrating. That was the problem. She didn't have time to prepare. She was enjoying the wine, chocolate and zombies. Perry had only gotten back less than a week ago. He was always so loving and chipper after a trip, especially if he'd left the country. It somehow cleansed him. His face always seemed smoother, his eyes brighter. The layers of frustration would take weeks to build up again. The children had been in feral little moods tonight. "Mummy gets a rest tonight," Perry told the boys earlier, and he'd done the whole bath, teeth, story routine on his own, while she sat on the couch, reading her book and drinking a Perry Surprise. It was a cocktail he'd invented years ago. It tasted of chocolate and cream and strawberries and cinnamon, and every woman he ever prepared it for went crazy over it. "I'll give you my children in return for that recipe," Madeline had once told Perry.

Perry filled his own glass. "Why aren't we going?"

"I'm taking the boys to Disney On Ice. Madeline got free tickets, and a group of us are going." Celeste broke off another piece of chocolate. She'd texted her apologies to Renata and hadn't heard back. As the nanny did most of the school pickups and drop-offs, Celeste hadn't run into her since the first day of school. She knew she was aligning herself with Madeline and Jane by saying no, but, well, she *was* aligned with Madeline and Jane. And this was a fifth-birthday party. This was not a matter of life or death.

"So I'm not welcome at this Disney thing?" said Perry. He

sipped his wine. She felt it then. In her stomach. A tiny squeeze. But his tone was casual. Humorous. If she trod carefully, she might still save the night.

She put down the chocolate. "Sorry," she said. "I thought you'd appreciate a bit of alone time. You can go to the gym."

Perry stood above her with the wine bottle still in his hand. He smiled. "I've been away for three weeks. I'm away again next Friday. Why would I need alone time?"

He didn't sound or look angry, but she could feel something in the atmosphere, like an electrical charge before a storm. The hairs on her arms stood up.

"I'm sorry," she said. "I didn't think."

"You sick of me already?" He looked hurt. He *was* hurt. She'd been thoughtless. She should have known better. Perry was always looking for evidence that she didn't really love him. It was like he expected it, and then he was angry when he believed himself proven right.

She went to stand up from the couch, but that would turn it into a confrontation. Sometimes, if she behaved normally, she could gently nudge them back on track. Instead, she looked up at him. "The boys don't even know this little girl. And I hardly ever take them to see live shows. It just seemed like this was the better option."

"Well, why *don't* you take them to live shows?" said Perry. "We don't need free tickets! Why didn't you tell Madeline to give the tickets to someone who would really appreciate them?"

"I don't know. It wasn't about money, really."

She hadn't thought of that. She was depriving some other mother of a free ticket. She should have thought of the fact that Perry would be back and he'd want to spend time with the boys,

but he was away so often, she was used to making social arrange-
ments that suited her.

"I'm sorry," she said calmly. She was sorry, but it was fruitless,
because he would never believe her. "I probably should have chosen the party." She stood up. "I'm going to take my contacts out.
My eyes are itchy."

She went to walk past him. He grabbed her upper arm. His
fingers dug into the flesh.

"Hey," she said. "That hurts."

It was part of the game that her initial reaction was always one
of outrage and surprise, as if this had never happened before, as if
he maybe didn't know what he was doing.

He gripped harder.

"Don't," she said. "Perry. Just don't."

The pain ignited her anger. The anger was always there: a res-
ervoir of flammable fuel. She heard her voice turn high and hysterical. A shrieking shrewish woman.

"Perry, this is not a big deal! Don't turn everything into a big
deal."

Because now it was no longer about the party. Now it was
about every other time. His hand tightened further. It looked like
he was making a decision: exactly how much to hurt her.

It hurt, but not that much.

He shoved her, just hard enough so that she staggered back
clumsily.

Then he took a step back and lifted his chin, breathing heavily
through his nostrils, his arms hanging loosely by his sides. He
waited to see what she'd do next.

There were so many options.

Sometimes she tried to respond like an adult. "That is unacceptable."

Sometimes she yelled.

Sometimes she walked away.

Sometimes she fought back. She punched and kicked him the way she'd once punched and kicked her older brother. For a few moments he would let her, as if it were what he wanted, as if it were what he needed, before he grabbed her wrists. She wasn't the only one who woke up the next day with bruises. She'd seen them on Perry's body. She was as bad as he was. As sick as he was. "I don't care who started it!" she always said to the children.

None of the options were effective.

"I will leave you if you ever do that again," she said after the first time, and she was deadly serious, my God she was serious. She knew exactly how she was meant to behave in a situation like this. The boys were only eight months old. Perry cried. She cried. He promised. He swore on his children's lives. He was heartbroken. He bought her the first piece of jewelry she would never wear.

A week after the twins had their second birthday, it happened again. Worse than the first time. She was devastated. The marriage was over. She was going to leave. There was no doubt at all. But that very night, both boys woke up with terrible coughs. It was croup. The next day Josh got so sick, their GP said, "I'm calling an ambulance." Josh was in intensive care for three nights. The tender purple bruises on Celeste's left hip were laughably irrelevant when a doctor stood in front of her saying gently, "We think we should intubate."

All she'd wanted was for Josh to be OK. And then he *was* OK, sitting up in his bed, demanding *The Wiggles* and his brother in a voice still husky from that awful tube. She and Perry were euphoric with relief, and a few days after they brought Josh home from the hospital, Perry left for Hong Kong, and the moment for dramatic action had passed.

And the unassailable fact that underlay all her indecisiveness was this: She loved Perry. She was still *in* love with him. She still had a crush on him. He made her happy and made her laugh. She still enjoyed talking with him, watching TV with him, lying in bed with him on cold, rainy mornings. She still wanted him.

But each time she didn't leave, she gave him tacit permission to do it again. She knew this. She was an educated woman with choices, places to go, family and friends who would gather around, lawyers who would represent her. She could go back to work and support herself. She wasn't frightened that he'd kill her if she tried to leave. She wasn't frightened that he'd take the children away from her.

One of the school mums, Gabrielle, often chatted with Celeste in the playground after school while her son and Celeste's boys played ninjas. "I'm starting a new diet tomorrow," she'd told Celeste yesterday. "I probably won't stick to it, and then I'll be all filled with self-loathing." She looked Celeste up and down and said, "You've got no idea what I'm talking about, do you, skinny minny?" *Actually I do,* Celeste thought. *I know exactly what you mean.*

Now she pressed her hand to her upper arm and battled the desire to cry. She wouldn't be able to wear that sleeveless dress tomorrow now.

"I don't know why . . ." She stopped. *I don't know why I stay. I don't know why I deserve this. I don't know why you do this, why we do this, why this keeps happening.*

"Celeste," he said hoarsely, and she could see the violence draining from his body. The DVD started again. Perry picked up the remote and turned off the television.

"Oh God. I'm so sorry." His face sagged with regret.

It was over now. There would be no further recriminations about the party. In fact, the very opposite. He'd be tender and solicitous. For the next few days up until he left for his trip, no woman would be more cherished than Celeste. Part of her would enjoy it: the tremulous, teary, righteous feeling of being wronged.

She let her hand drop from her arm.

It could have been so much worse. He rarely hit her face. She'd never broken a limb or needed stitches. Her bruises could always be kept secret with a turtleneck or sleeves or long pants. He would never lay a finger on the children. The boys never saw. It could be worse. Oh, so much worse. She'd read the articles about proper domestic violence victims. That was terrible. That was real. What Perry did didn't count. It was small stuff, which made it all the more humiliating, because it was so . . . tacky. So childish and trite.

He didn't cheat on her. He didn't gamble. He didn't drink to excess. He didn't ignore her, like the way her father had ignored her mother. That would be the worst. To be ignored. To not be seen.

Perry's rage was an illness. A mental illness. She saw the way it took hold of him, how he tried his best to resist. When he was in the throes of it, his eyes became red and glassy, as if he were drugged. The things he said didn't even make sense. It wasn't him. The rage wasn't him. Would she leave him if he got a brain tumor and the tumor affected his personality? Of course she wouldn't.

This was just a glitch in an otherwise perfect relationship. Every relationship had its glitches. Its ups, its downs. It was like motherhood. Every morning the boys climbed into bed with her for a cuddle, and at first it was heavenly, and then, after about ten minutes or so, they started fighting, and it was terrible. Her boys were gorgeous little darlings. Her boys were feral little animals.

She would never leave Perry any more than she could leave the boys.

Perry held out his arms. "Celeste?"

She turned her head, took a step away, but there was no one else there to comfort her. There was only him. The real him. She stepped forward and laid her head against his chest.

> **Samantha:** I'll never forget the moment when Perry and Celeste walked into the trivia night. There was like this ripple across the room. Everyone just stopped and stared.

23.

"Isn't this FANTASTIC!" cried Madeline to Chloe as they took their really very excellent seats in front of the giant ice rink. "You can feel the cold from the ice! Brrr! Oh! Can you hear the music? I wonder where the princesses—"

Chloe had reached over and placed one hand gently over her mother's mouth. "Shhh."

Madeline knew she was talking too much because she was feeling anxious and ever so slightly guilty. Today needed to be stupendous to make it worth the rift she'd created between herself and Renata. Eight kindergarten children, who would otherwise be attending Amabella's party, were here watching Disney On Ice because of Madeline.

Madeline looked past Chloe at Ziggy, who was nursing a giant stuffed toy on his lap. *Ziggy* was the reason they were here today, she reminded herself. Poor Ziggy wouldn't have been at the party. Dear little fatherless Ziggy. Who was possibly a secret psychopathic bully . . . but still!

"Are you taking care of Harry the Hippo this weekend, Ziggy?" she said brightly. Harry the Hippo was the class toy. Every weekend it went home with a different child, along with a scrapbook that had to be returned with a little story about the weekend, accompanied by photos.

Ziggy nodded mutely. A child of few words.

Jane leaned forward, discreetly chewing gum as always. "It's quite stressful having Harry to stay. We have to give Harry a good time. Last weekend he went on a roller coaster— Ow!" Jane recoiled as one of the twins, who was sitting next to her and fighting his brother, elbowed her in the back of the head.

"Josh!" said Celeste sharply. "Max! Just stop it!"

Madeline wondered if Celeste was OK today. She looked pale and tired, with purplish shadows under her eyes, although on Celeste they looked like an artful makeup effect that everyone should try.

The lights in the auditorium began to dim, and then went to black. Chloe clutched Madeline's arm. The music began to pound, so loud that Madeline could feel the vibrations. The ice rink filled with an array of colorful, swooping, whirling Disney characters. Madeline looked down the row of seats at her guests, their profiles illuminated by the blazing spotlights on the ice. Every child was looking straight ahead, little backs straight, enthralled by the spectacle in front of them, and every parent had turned to look at their child's profile, enchanted by their enchantment.

Except for Celeste, who had dropped her head and pressed her hand to her forehead.

I have to leave him. Sometimes, when she was thinking about something else, the thought came into her head with the shock and the force of a flying fist. *My husband hits me.*

God almighty, what was wrong with her? All that insane rationalizing. A *glitch*, for God's sake. Of course she had to leave. Today! Right now! As soon as they got home from the show she would pack her bags.

But the boys would be so tired and grumpy.

.   .   .

I t was fantastic," said Jane to her mother, who had called up to
ask how Disney On Ice went. "Ziggy loved it. He says he wants
to learn how to ice-skate."

"Your grandfather loved to ice-skate!" said her mother trium-
phantly.

"There you go," said Jane, not bothering to tell her mother
that every single child had announced after the show that they
now wanted to learn how to ice-skate. Not just those with past
lives.

"Well, and you'll never guess who I ran into at the shops
today," said her mother. "Ruth Sullivan!"

"Did you?" said Jane, wondering if this was the real reason for
the call. Ruth was her ex-boyfriend's mother.

"How's Zach?" she asked dutifully as she unwrapped a new
piece of gum.

"Fine," said her mother. "He's, er, well he's engaged, darling."

"Is he?" said Jane. She slipped the gum in her mouth and chewed,
wondering how she felt about that, but there was something else
distracting her now, a tiny possibility of a tiny catastrophe. She
began walking around their messy apartment, picking up cushions
and discarded clothes.

"I wasn't sure I should tell you," said her mother. "I know it
was a long time ago, but he did break your heart."

"He didn't break my heart," said Jane vaguely.

He did break her heart, but he broke it so gently, so respectfully and regretfully, the way a nice, well-brought-up nineteen-
year-old boy did break your heart when he wanted to go on a
Contiki tour of Europe, and sleep with lots of girls.

When she thought about Zach now it was like remembering an old school friend, someone she would hug with genuine teary tenderness if they met at their school reunion, and then not see again until the next reunion.

Jane got down on her knees and looked under the couch.

"Ruth asked about Ziggy," said her mother meaningfully.

"Did she?" said Jane.

"I showed her the photo of Ziggy on his first day of school, and I was watching her face, and she didn't say anything, thank goodness, but I just *knew* what she was thinking, because I have to say, Ziggy's face in that photo does look a *teeny* bit like—"

"Mum! Ziggy looks nothing like Zach," said Jane, getting back to her feet.

She hated it when she caught herself deconstructing Ziggy's beautiful face, looking for a familiar feature: the lips, the nose, the eyes. Sometimes she thought she'd see something, a flash of something out of the corner of her eye, and then she'd die a little, before quickly reassembling Ziggy into Ziggy.

"Oh, I know!" said her mother. "Nothing at all like Zach!"

"And Zach is not Ziggy's father."

"Oh, I know that, darling. Goodness. I know that. You would have told me."

"More to the point, I would have told *Zach*."

Zach had phoned her after Ziggy was born. "Is there something you need to tell me, Jane?" he'd said in a tight, bright voice. "Nope," Jane had told him, and she'd heard his tiny exhalation of relief.

"Well, I know *that*," said her mother. She quickly changed the subject. "Tell me. Did you get some good photos with the class toy? Your father is e-mailing you this wonderful place where you can get them printed off for . . . How much is it, Bill? How much? No, Jane's photos! For that thing she has to do for Ziggy!"

"Mum," interrupted Jane. She walked into the kitchen and picked up Ziggy's backpack where it lay on the floor. She held it upside down. Nothing fell out. "It's fine, Mum. I know where to get the photos done."

Her mother ignored her. "Bill! Listen to me! You said there was a website . . ." Her voice faded.

Jane walked into Ziggy's bedroom, where he was sitting on the floor playing with his Legos. She lifted up his bedclothes and shook them.

"He's going to e-mail you the details," said her mother.

"Wonderful," said Jane distractedly. "I've got to go, Mum. I'll call you tomorrow."

She hung up. Her heart pounded. She pressed the palm of her hand to her forehead. No. Surely not. She could not have been so stupid.

Ziggy looked up at her curiously.

Jane said, "I think we've got a problem."

There was silence when Madeline picked up the phone.

"Hello?" said Madeline again. "Who is it?"

She could hear someone crying and saying something incoherent.

"Jane?" Madeline suddenly recognized the voice. "What's the matter? What is it?"

"It's *nothing*," said Jane. She sniffed. "Nobody died. It's sort of *funny*, really. It's *hilarious* that I'm crying over this."

"What happened?"

"It's just . . . Oh, what will those other mothers think of me *now*?" Jane's voice quavered.

"Who cares what they think!" said Madeline.

"I care!" said Jane.

"Jane. Just tell me. What is it? What happened?"

"We've lost him," sobbed Jane.

"Lost who? You've lost Ziggy?" Madeline felt the panic rise. She was obsessed with losing her own children, and quickly confirmed their respective locations: Chloe in bed, Fred doing his reading with Ed, Abigail staying at her dad's place (yet again).

"We left him sitting on the seat. I remember actually thinking what a disaster it would be if we left him behind. I actually *thought* that, but then Josh got his nosebleed and we all got distracted. I've left a message on the lost-property number, but he wasn't labeled or anything . . ."

"Jane. You're not making any sense."

"Harry the Hippo! We've *lost* Harry the Hippo!"

Thea: That's the thing about these Gen Y kids. They're careless. Harry the Hippo had been with the school for over ten years. That cheap synthetic toy she replaced it with smelled just terrible. Made in China. The hippo's face wasn't even friendly.

Harper: Look, it wasn't so much that she lost Harry the Hippo, but that she put photos in the scrapbook of the little exclusive group who went to Disney On Ice. So all the kids get to see that, and the poor little tots are thinking, *Why wasn't I invited?* As I said to Renata, that was just thoughtless.

Samantha: Yes, and you know what's really shocking? Those were *the last photos ever taken of Harry the Hippo.* Harry the Heritage-Listed Hippo. Harry the . . . Sorry, it's not funny. It's not funny at all.

Gabrielle: Oh my God, the *fuss* when poor Jane lost the class toy, and everyone is pretending it's not a big deal, but clearly it *is* a big deal, and I'm thinking, "Can you people get a life?" Hey, do I look thinner than when we last met? I've lost three kilos.

24.

Two Months Before the Trivia Night

GOOOOO GREEEEEN!" cried Madeline as she sprayed green hair spray into Chloe's hair for the athletics carnival.

Chloe and Fred were "Dolphins" and their house color was green, which was fortunate because Madeline looked good in green. When Abigail had been at her old primary school, her house color was unflattering yellow.

"That stuff is so bad for the ozone layer," said Abigail.

"Really?" Madeline held the spray can aloft. "Didn't we fix that?"

"Mum, you can't fix the hole in the ozone layer!" Abigail rolled her eyes with contempt as she ate her homemade, preservative-free, flaxseed-and-whatever-the-hell-else-was-in-it muesli. These days whenever she came home from her father's place, she got out of his car, weighed down with food, as if she'd been provisioned for a trip to the wilderness.

"I didn't mean we fixed the whole ozone layer, I meant the thing with aerosol cans. The, umm, the something-or-others." Madeline held up the hair-spray can and frowned at it, trying to read the writing on the side, but the type was too small. Madeline had once had a boyfriend who thought she was cute and stupid, and it was true, she was cute and stupid the whole time she was with him. Living with a teenage daughter was exactly the same.

"The CFCs," said Ed. "Aerosol cans don't have CFCs anymore."

"Whatever," said Abigail.

"The twins think their mum is going to win the mothers race today," said Chloe as Madeline began to French-braid her green hair. "But I told them you were a trillion times faster."

Madeline laughed. She couldn't imagine Celeste running in a race. She'd probably run in the wrong direction, or not even notice the starter gun had gone off. She was always so distracted.

"Bonnie will probably win," said Abigail. "She's a really fast runner."

"*Bonnie?*" said Madeline.

"Ahem," warned Ed.

"What?" snapped Abigail. "Why shouldn't she be fast?"

"I just thought she was more into yoga and things like that. Non-cardio things," said Madeline. She returned to Chloe's hair.

"She's fast. I've seen her in a race with Dad at the beach, and Bonnie is, like, *much* younger than you, Mum."

Ed chuckled. "You're a brave girl, Abigail."

Madeline laughed. "One day, Abigail, when you're thirty, I'm going to repeat back to you some of the things you've said to me over the past year—"

Abigail threw down her spoon. "I'm just saying don't get upset if you don't win!"

"Yes, yes, OK, thank you," said Madeline soothingly. She and Ed had laughed at Abigail, when she hadn't meant to be funny, and she didn't quite understand why it was funny, so she now felt embarrassed, and therefore enraged.

"I mean, I don't know why you feel so competitive with her," said Abigail viciously. "It's not like *you* want to be married to Dad anymore, do you, so what's your problem?"

"Abigail," said Ed. "I don't like your tone. Speak nicely to your mother."

Madeline shook her head slightly at Ed.

"God!" Abigail pushed away her breakfast bowl and stood up.

Oh, calamity, thought Madeline. *There goes the morning.* Chloe swiveled her head away from Madeline's hands so she could watch her sister.

"I can't even speak now!" Abigail's whole body trembled. "I can't even be myself in my own home! I can't relax!"

Madeline was reminded of Abigail's first-ever tantrum, when she was nearly three. Madeline had thought that she was never going to have a tantrum, all due to her good parenting. So it had been such a shock to see Abigail's little body whipped about by violent emotion. (She'd wanted to keep eating a chocolate frog she'd dropped on the supermarket floor. Madeline should just have let the poor kid eat it.)

"Abigail, there's no need to be so dramatic. Just calm down," said Ed.

Madeline thought, *Thank you, darling, because that always works, doesn't it, telling a woman to calm down.*

"Mu-uuum! I can only find one shoe!" hollered Fred from down the hallway.

"Just a minute, Fred!" called back Madeline.

Abigail shook her head slowly, as if truly flabbergasted by the outrageous treatment she was forced to endure.

"You know what, Mum?" she said without looking at Madeline. "I was going to tell you this later, but I'll tell you now."

"MU-UM!" yelled Fred.

"Mummy is busy!" screeched Chloe.

"Look under your bed!" shouted Ed.

Madeline's ears rang. "What is it, Abigail?"

"I've decided I want to live full-time with Dad and Bonnie."

"What did you say?" said Madeline, but she'd heard.

She'd feared it for so long, and everyone kept saying, *No, no, that would never happen. Abigail would never do that. She needs her mother.* But Madeline had known for months it was coming. She knew it would happen. She wanted to scream at Ed: *Why did you tell her to calm down?*

"I just feel it's better for me," said Abigail. "Spiritually." She'd stopped trembling now and calmly took her bowl from the table over to the sink. Lately she'd begun walking the same way Bonnie walked, back ballet-dancer straight, eyes on some spiritual point on the horizon.

Chloe's face crumpled. "I don't want Abigail to live with her dad!" Tears spilled copiously. The color on the green lightning shapes on her cheeks began to run.

"MU-UM!" shouted Fred. The neighbors would think he was being murdered.

Ed dropped his forehead into his hand.

"If that's what you really want," said Madeline. Abigail turned from the sink and met her eyes, and for a moment it was just the two of them, like it was for all those years. Madeline and Abigail. The Mackenzie girls. When life was quiet and simple. They used to eat breakfast in bed together before school, side by side, pillows behind their backs, their books on their laps. Madeline held her gaze. *Remember, Abigail? Remember us?*

Abigail turned away. "That's what I want."

Stu: I was there at the athletics carnival. The mothers race was fucking hilarious. Excuse my French. But some of

those women—you'd think it was the Olympics.
Seriously.

Samantha: Oh rubbish. Ignore my husband. Nobody was
taking it seriously. I was laughing so hard, I got a stitch.

Nathan was at the carnival. Madeline couldn't believe it when
she ran into him outside the sausage sizzle stall, hand in hand
with Skye. This morning of all mornings.

Not many dads came to the athletics carnival, unless they
were stay-at-home dads or their children were especially sporty,
but here was Madeline's ex-husband taking the time off work to
be there, wearing a striped polo shirt and shorts, baseball cap and
sunglasses, the quintessential Good Daddy uniform.

"So . . . this is a first for you!" said Madeline. She saw there
was a whistle around his neck. He was volunteering, for God's
sake. He was being involved. *Ed* was the sort of dad who volun-
teered at the school, but he was on deadline today. Nathan was
pretending to be Ed. He was pretending to be a good man, and
everyone was falling for it.

"Sure is!" beamed Nathan, and then his grin faded as presumably it crossed his mind that his firstborn daughter must have
taken part in athletics carnivals when she was in primary school
too. Of course, these days, he was at all of Abigail's events. Abigail wasn't sporty, but she played the violin, and Nathan and Bonnie were at every concert without fail, beaming and clapping, as
if they'd been there all along, as if they'd driven her to those violin lessons in Petersham where you could never get a parking
spot, as if they'd helped pay for all those lessons that Madeline

couldn't afford as a single mother with an ex-husband who didn't contribute a single cent.

And *now she was choosing him.*

"Has Abigail spoken to you about . . ." Nathan winced a little, as if he were referring to a delicate health issue.

"About living with you?" said Madeline. "She has. Just this morning, actually."

The hurt felt physical. Like the start of a bad flu. Like betrayal.

He looked at her. "Is that . . ."

"Fine with me," said Madeline. She would not give him the satisfaction.

"We'll have to work out the money," said Nathan.

He paid child support for Abigail now that he was a good person. Paid it on time. Without complaint, and neither of them ever referred to the first ten years of Abigail's life, when apparently it hadn't cost anything to feed or clothe her.

"So you mean I'll have to pay you child support now?" said Madeline.

Nathan looked shocked. "Oh, no I didn't mean *that*—"

"But you're right. It's only fair if she's living at your place most of the time," said Madeline.

"Obviously, I would never take your money, Maddie," he interrupted. "Not when I . . . when I didn't . . . when I wasn't able to . . . when all those years—" He grimaced. "Look, I'm *aware* that I wasn't the best father when Abigail was little. I should never have mentioned money. Things are just a bit tight for us at the moment."

"Maybe you should sell your flashy sports car," said Madeline.

"Yeah," said Nathan. He looked mortified. "I should. You're right. Although it's not actually worth as much as you . . . Anyway."

Skye gazed up at her father with big worried eyes, and she did that rapid blinking thing again that Abigail used to do. Madeline saw Nathan smile fiercely at the little girl and squeeze her hand. She'd shamed him. She'd shamed him while he stood hand in hand with his waif-like daughter.

Ex-husbands should live in different suburbs. They should send their children to different schools. There should be legislation to prevent this. You were not meant to deal with complicated feelings of betrayal and hurt and guilt at your kids' athletics carnivals. Feelings like this should not be brought out in public.

"Why did you have to move here, Nathan?" she sighed.

"What?" said Nathan.

"Madeline! Time for the Kindy Mums Race! You up for it?" It was the kindergarten teacher, Miss Barnes, hair up in a high ponytail, skin glowing like an American cheerleader. She looked fresh and fecund. A delicious ripe piece of fruit. Even riper than Bonnie. Her eyelids didn't sag. Nothing sagged. Everything in her bright young life was clear and simple and perky. Nathan took his sunglasses off to see her better, visibly cheered just by the sight of her. Ed would have been the same.

"Bring it on, Miss Barnes," said Madeline.

Detective-Sergeant Adrian Quinlan: We're looking at the victim's relationships with every parent who attended the trivia night.

Harper: Yes, as a matter of fact, I do have certain theories.

Stu: Theories? I've got nothing. Nothing but a hangover.

25.

The kindergarten mothers gathered in a ragged, giggly line at the start line of their race. The sunlight reflected off their sunglasses. The sky was a giant blue shell. The sea glinted sapphire on the horizon. Jane smiled at the other mothers. The other mothers smiled back at her. It was all very nice. Very sociable. "I'm sure it's all in your head," Jane's mother had told her. "Everyone will have forgotten that silly mix-up on orientation day."

Jane had been trying so hard to fit into the school community. She did canteen duty every two weeks. Every Monday morning she and another parent volunteer helped out Miss Barnes by listening to the children practice their reading. She made polite chitchat at drop-off and pickup. She invited children over for playdates.

But Jane still felt that something was not right. It was there in the slight turn of a head, the smiles that didn't reach the eyes, the gentle waft of judgment.

This was not a big deal, she kept telling herself. This was little stuff. There was no need for the sense of dread. This world of lunch boxes and library bags, grazed knees and grubby little faces, was in no way connected to the ugliness of that warm spring night and the bright downlight like a staring eye in the ceiling, the pressure on her throat, the whispered words worming their way into her brain. *Stop thinking about it. Stop thinking about it.*

Now Jane waved at Ziggy, who was sitting on the bleachers near the sidelines with the kindergarten kids under the watchful eye of Miss Barnes.

"You know I'm not going to win, right?" she'd said to him this morning at breakfast. Some of these mothers had personal trainers. One of them *was* a personal trainer.

"On your marks, mums!" said Jonathan, the nice stay-at-home dad who had gone with them to Disney On Ice.

"How many meters is this, anyway?" said Harper.

"That finish line looks like it's a *long* way away," said Gabrielle. "Let's all go have coffee instead."

"Is that Renata and Celeste holding the finishing tape?" said Samantha. "How did they get out of this?"

"I think Renata said that she—"

"Renata has shin splints," interrupted Harper. "Very painful apparently."

"We should all stretch, girls," said Bonnie, who was dressed like she was about to teach a yoga class, a yellow singlet top sliding off one shoulder as she languidly lifted one ankle and pulled it up behind her leg.

"Oh, by the way, Jess?" said Audrey or Andrea. Jane could never remember her name. She stepped right up close to Jane and spoke in a low, confidential voice, as if she were about to reveal a deep, dark secret. Jane had gotten used to it by now. The other day she stepped up close, lowered her voice and said, "Is it library day today?"

"It's Jane," said Jane. (She could hardly be offended.)

"Sorry," said Andrea or Audrey. "Listen. Are you for or against?"

"For or against what?" said Jane.

"Ladies!" cried Jonathan.

"Cupcakes," said Audrey or Andrea. "For or against?"

"She's for," said Madeline. "Fun police."

"Madeline, let her speak for herself," said Audrey or Andrea. "She looks very health-conscious to me."

Madeline rolled her eyes.

"Um, well, I *like* cupcakes?" said Jane.

"We're doing a petition to ban parents from sending in cupcakes for the whole class on their kids' birthdays," said Andrea or Audrey. "There's an obesity crisis, and every second day the children are having sugary treats."

"What I don't get is why this school is so obsessed with *petitions*," said Madeline irritably. "It's so adversarial. Why can't you just make a suggestion?"

"Ladies, *please!*" Jonathan held up his starter gun.

"Where's Jackie today, Jonathan?" asked Gabrielle. The mothers were all mildly obsessed with Jonathan's wife, ever since she'd been interviewed on the business segment of the evening news a few nights back, sounding terrifyingly precise and clever about a corporate takeover and putting the journalist in his place. Also, Jonathan was very good-looking in a George Clooney–esque way, so constant references to his wife were necessary to show that they hadn't noticed this and weren't flirting with him.

"She's in Melbourne," said Jonathan. "Stop talking to me. On your *marks!*"

The women moved to the start line.

"Bonnie looks so professional," commented Samantha as Bonnie crouched down into a starting position.

"I hardly ever run these days," said Bonnie. "It's so violent on the joints."

Jane saw Madeline glance over at Bonnie and dig the toe of her sneaker firmly into the grass.

"Enough with the chitchat, ladies!" roared Jonathan.

"I love it when you're masterful, Jonathan," said Samantha.

"Get set!"

"This is quite nerve-racking," said Audrey or Andrea to Jane. "How do the poor kids cope with the—"

The gun cracked.

> **Thea:** I do have my own ideas about what might have happened but I'd rather not speak ill of the dead. As I say to my four daughters, "If you can't say anything nice, don't say anything at all."

26.

Celeste could feel the pressure of Renata's grip at the other end of the finishing tape, and she tried to match it with her own, except that she kept forgetting to concentrate on where she was and what she was doing.

"How's Perry?" called out Renata. "In the country at the moment?"

Whenever Renata made an appearance at school or school events, she made an amusing point of not talking to Jane or Madeline (Madeline loved it, poor Jane not so much), but she always talked to Celeste, in a defensive, prickly way, as though Celeste were an old friend who had wronged her but she was choosing to be mature and rise above it.

"He's great," called back Celeste.

Last night it had been over Legos. The boys had left their Legos everywhere. She should have made them pick them up. Perry was right. It was just easier to do it herself after they were asleep, rather than do battle with them. The whining. The drama. She just didn't have the resilience last night to go through it. Lazy parenting. She was a bad mother.

"You're turning them into spoiled brats," Perry had said.

"They're only five," Celeste had said. She was sitting on the couch folding laundry. "They get tired after school."

"I don't want to live in a pigsty," said Perry. He kicked at the Legos on the floor.

"So pick them up yourself," said Celeste tiredly.

There. Right there. She brought it on herself. Every time.

Perry just looked at her. Then he got down on his hands and knees and carefully picked up every piece of Lego from the carpet and put it in the big green box. She'd kept folding, watching him. Was he really going to just pick it all up?

He stood and carried the box over to where she sat. "It's pretty simple. Either get the kids to pick it up, or pick it up yourself, or pay for a fucking housekeeper."

In one swift move he up-ended the entire box of Legos over her head in a noisy, violent torrent.

The shock and humiliation made her gasp.

She stood up, grabbed a handful of Legos from her lap and threw them straight at his face.

See there? Again. Celeste at fault. She behaved like a child. It was almost laughable. Slapstick. Two grown-ups throwing things at each other.

He slapped her across the face with the back of his hand.

He never punched her. He would never do anything so un-couth. She staggered back, and her knee banged against the edge of the glass coffee table. She regained her balance and flew at him with her hands like claws. He shoved her away from him with disgust.

Well, why not? Her behavior was disgusting.

He went to bed then, and she cleaned up all the Legos and threw their uneaten dinner in the bin.

Her lip was bruised and tender this morning, like she was about to get a cold sore. It wasn't enough for anyone to comment upon. Her knee had banged against the side of the coffee table, and it was stiff and painful. Not too bad. Not much at all, really.

This morning Perry had been cheerful, whistling while he boiled eggs for the boys.

"What happened to your neck, Daddy?" said Josh.

There was a long, thin, red scratch down the side of his neck where Celeste must have scratched him.

"My neck?" Perry had put his hand over the scratch and glanced over at Celeste with laughter in his eyes. It was the sort of humorous, secret look that parents share when their children say something innocent and cute about Santa Claus or sex. As if what happened last night were a normal part of married life.

"It's nothing, mate," he'd said to Josh. "I wasn't looking where I was going and I walked into a tree."

Celeste couldn't get the expression on Perry's face out of her mind. He thought it was funny. He genuinely thought it was funny, and of no particular consequence.

Celeste pressed a finger to her tender lip.

Was it normal?

Perry would say, "No, we're not normal. We're not Mr. and Mrs. Average, mediocre people in mediocre relationships. We're different. We're special. We love each other more. Everything is more intense for us. We have better sex."

The starter gun cracked the air, startling her.

"Here they come!" said Renata.

Fourteen women ran straight at them as if they were chasing thieves, arms pumping, chests thrust forward, chins jutting, some of them laughing but most looking deadly serious. The children shouted and hollered. Celeste tried to look for the boys, but she couldn't see them.

"I can't run in the mothers race after all," she'd told them this morning. "I fell down the stairs after you went to bed last night."

"Awwww," said Max, but it was an automatic whine. He didn't seem to really care.

"You should be more careful," Josh had said quietly, without looking at her.

"I should," Celeste had agreed. She really should.

Bonnie and Madeline led the pack. They pulled in front. It was neck and neck. *Go Madeline,* thought Celeste. *Go, go, go—YES!* Their chests hit the finishing tape. Definitely Madeline.

B onnie by a nose!" shouted Renata.

"No, no, I'm sure Madeline was first," said Bonnie to Renata. Bonnie didn't seem to have exerted herself at all. The color on her cheeks was just a little higher than usual.

"No, no, it was you, Bonnie," said Madeline breathlessly, although she knew she'd won because she kept Bonnie in her peripheral vision. She bent over, hands on her knees, trying to catch her breath. There was a stinging sensation on her cheekbone where her necklace had whipped across it.

"I'm pretty sure it was Madeline," said Celeste.

"Definitely Bonnie," interrupted Renata, and Madeline nearly laughed out loud. *So your vendetta has come to this now, Renata? Not letting me win the mothers race?*

"I'm sure it was Madeline," said Bonnie.

"I'm sure it was Bonnie," countered Madeline.

"Oh, for heaven's sake, let's call it a tie," said a Year 6 mother, a Blond Bob in charge of handing out the ribbons.

Madeline straightened. "Absolutely not. Bonnie is the winner."

She plucked the blue winner's ribbon from the Year 6 mother's hand and pressed it into Bonnie's palm, folding her fingers over it, as if she were entrusting one of the children with a two-dollar coin. "You beat me, Bonnie." She met Bonnie's pale blue eyes and saw understanding register. "You beat me fair and square."

> **Samantha:** Madeline won. We were all killing ourselves laughing when Renata insisted it was Bonnie. But do I think that led to a *murder*? No, I do not.

> **Harper:** I came in third, if anyone is interested.

> **Melissa:** Technically, *Juliette* came third. You know, Renata's nanny? But Harper was all, "A twenty-one-year-old nanny doesn't count!" And then, of course, these days, we all like to pretend Juliette never existed.

27.

Samantha: Listen, you need to get your head around the demographics of this place. So first of all you've got your blue collars—tradies, we call them. We've got a *lot* of tradies in Pirriwee. Like my Stu. Salt of the earth. Or salt of the sea, because they all surf, of course. Most of the tradies grew up here and never left. Then you've got your alternative types. Your dippy hippies. And in the last ten years or so, all these wealthy execs and banker wankers have moved in and built massive McMansions up on the cliffs. But! There's only one primary school for all our kids! So at school events you've got a plumber, a banker and a crystal healer standing around trying to make conversation. It's hilarious. No wonder we had a riot.

Celeste arrived home from the athletics carnival to find her house cleaners' car parked out front. When she turned the key in the front door, the vacuum cleaner was roaring upstairs.

She went into the kitchen to make herself a cup of tea. The cleaners came once a week on a Friday morning. They charged two hundred dollars and did a beautiful, sparkling job.

Celeste's mother had gasped when she'd heard how much Celeste spent on cleaning. "Darling, I'll come and help you once a week," she'd said. "You can save the money for something else."

Her mother could not grasp the scale of Perry's wealth. When she first visited the big house with the sweeping beach views, she'd walked around with the polite, strained expression of a tourist watching a confronting cultural demonstration. She'd finally agreed it was very "airy." For her, two hundred dollars was a scandalous amount of money to spend on something that you could—should—do yourself. She would be horrified if she could see Celeste right now, *sitting down*, while other people cleaned her house. Celeste's mother had never sat down. She'd come home from working night shift at the hospital, walk straight into the kitchen and make the family a cooked breakfast, while Celeste's dad read the paper and Celeste and her brother fought.

Good God, the fights Celeste had had with her brother. He'd hit her. She'd always hit him back.

Maybe if she hadn't grown up with a big brother, if she hadn't grown up with that tough Aussie tomboy mentality: If a boy hits you, you hit him right back! Perhaps if she'd wept softly and prettily the first time that Perry had hit her, then maybe it wouldn't keep happening.

The vacuum cleaner stopped, and she heard a man's voice, followed by a roar of raucous laughter. Her cleaners were a young married Korean couple. They normally worked in complete silence when Celeste was in the house, so they mustn't have heard her come in. They only showed her their professional faces. She felt irrationally hurt, as if she wanted to be their friend. *Let's all laugh and chat while you clean my house!*

There were running footsteps above her head and a peal of girlish laughter.

Stop having fun in my house. Clean.

Celeste drank her tea. The mug stung her sore lip.

She felt jealous of her cleaners.

Here she sat, in her big house, sulking.

.   She put down her tea, took her AmEx card out of her wallet and opened her laptop. She logged on to the World Vision website and clicked through photos of children available for sponsorship: products on a shelf for rich white women like her. She already sponsored three children, and she tried to get the boys interested. "Look! Here's little Blessing from Zimbabwe. She has to walk miles for fresh water. You just have to walk to the tap." "Why doesn't she just get some money from the ATM?" said Josh. It was Perry who answered, who patiently explained, who talked to the children about gratitude and helping those less fortunate than themselves.

Celeste sponsored another four children.

Writing letters and birthday cards to them all would take hours.

Ungrateful bitch.

Deserve to be hit. Deserve it.

She pinched the flesh on her upper thighs until it brought tears to her eyes. There would be new bruises tomorrow. Bruises she'd given herself. She liked to watch them change, deepening, darkening and then slowly fading. It was a hobby. An interest of hers. Nice to have an interest.

She was losing her mind.

She trawled through charity websites representing all the pain and suffering the world has to offer: cancer, rare genetic disorders, poverty, human rights abuse, natural disasters. She gave and gave and gave. Within twenty minutes she'd donated twenty thousand dollars of Perry's money. It gave her no satisfaction, no pride or pleasure. It sickened her. She made charitable donations while a young girl got down on her hands and knees and scrubbed the grubby corners of her shower stall.

Clean your own house, then! Sack the cleaners. But that wouldn't help them either, would it? Give more money to charity! Give until it hurts.

She spent another five thousand dollars.

Would that hurt their financial situation? She didn't actually know. Perry took care of the money. It was his area of expertise, after all. He didn't hide it from her. She knew that he would happily go through all their accounts and investment portfolios with her, if she so wished, but the thought of knowing the exact figures gave her vertigo.

"I opened the electricity bill today and I just wanted to cry," Madeline had said the other day, and Celeste had wanted to offer to pay it for her, but of course, Madeline didn't want her charity. She and Ed were perfectly comfortable. It was just that there were so many different levels of "comfortable," and at Celeste's level no electricity bill could make her cry. Anyway, you couldn't just hand money over to your friends. You could pick up lunch or coffee whenever you could, but even then you had to be careful not to offend, to not do it so often that it looked like you were showing off, as if the money were part of her, when in fact the money was Perry's, it had nothing to do with her, it was just random luck, like the way she looked. It wasn't a decision she'd made.

Once, when she'd been at uni, she'd been in a great mood, and she'd bounced into her tutorial and sat next to a girl called Linda.

"Morning!" she'd said.

An expression of comical dismay crossed Linda's face.

"Oh, Celeste," she'd moaned. "I just can't handle you today. Not when I'm feeling like shit and you waltz in here looking like . . . you know, like *that*." She waved her hand at Celeste's face, as if at something disgusting.

The girls around them had exploded with joyous laughter, as if something hilarious and subversive had finally been said out loud. They laughed and laughed, and Celeste had smiled stiffly, idiotically, because how could you possibly respond to that? It felt like a slap, but she had to respond like it was a compliment. You had to be grateful. *Don't ever look too happy,* she told herself. *It's aggravating.*

Grateful, grateful, grateful.

The vacuum cleaner started again upstairs.

Perry had never, in all their years together, made a comment on how she chose to spend their (his) money, except to remind her occasionally, mildly, humorously, that she could spend more if she liked. "You know we can afford to get you a new one," he'd said once when he came upon her in the laundry, scrubbing furiously at a stain on the collar of a silk shirt.

"I like this one," she'd said.

(The stain was blood.)

Once she stopped working, her relationship to money had changed. She used it the same way she'd use someone else's bathroom: carefully and politely. She knew that in the eyes of the law and society (supposedly) she was contributing to their lives by running the house and bringing up the boys, but she still never spent Perry's money in the same way she'd once spent her own.

She'd certainly never spent twenty-five thousand dollars in one afternoon. Would he comment? Would he be angry? Was that why she'd done it? Sometimes, on the days when she could feel his rage simmering, when she knew it was only a matter of time, when she could smell it in the air, she'd deliberately provoke him. She'd *make* it happen, so it was done.

Even when she was giving to charity, was it really just another step in the sick dance of their marriage?

It wasn't like it was unprecedented. They went to charity balls and Perry would bid twenty, thirty, forty thousand dollars with the unsmiling nod of a head. But that wasn't about giving, so much as winning. "I'll never be outbid," he told her once.

He *was* generous with his money. If he ever discovered that a family member or friend was in need, he discreetly wrote a check or did a direct transfer, waving away thanks, changing the subject, seemingly embarrassed by the ease with which he could solve someone else's financial crisis.

The doorbell rang, and she went to answer it.

"Mrs. White?" A stocky, bearded man handed her a giant bouquet of flowers.

"Thank you," said Celeste.

"Someone is a lucky lady!" said the man, as if he'd never seen a woman receive such an impressive arrangement.

"I sure am!"

The sweet heavy scent tickled her nose. Once, she'd loved to receive flowers. Now it was like being handed a series of tasks: Find the vase. Cut the stems. Arrange them like so.

Ungrateful bitch.

She read the tiny card.

I love you. I'm sorry. Perry.

Written in the florist's handwriting. It was always so strange to see Perry's words transcribed by someone else. Did the florist wonder what Perry had done? What husbandly transgression he had committed last night? Coming home late?

She carried the flowers toward the kitchen. The bouquet was shaking, she noticed, shivering as if it were cold. She tightened her grip on the stems. She could throw them against the wall, but it would be so unsatisfying. They would flop ineffectually to the ground. There would be drifts of sodden petals across the carpet. She'd have to scrabble around on the floor for them before the cleaners came downstairs.

For God's sake, Celeste. You know what you have to do.

She remembered the year she turned twenty-five: the year she appeared in court for the first time, the year she bought her first car and invested in the stock market for the first time, the year she played competitive squash every Saturday. She had great triceps and a loud laugh.

That was the year she met Perry.

Motherhood and marriage had made her a soft, spongy version of the girl she used to be.

She laid the flowers down carefully on the dining room table and went back to her laptop.

She typed the words "marriage counselor" into Google.

Then she stopped. Backspace, backspace, backspace. No. Been there, done that. This wasn't about housework and hurt feelings. She needed to talk to someone who knew that people behaved like this; someone who would ask the right questions.

She could feel her cheeks burn as she typed in the two shameful words.

"Domestic." "Violence."

28.

There are harder things than this, thought Madeline as she folded a pair of white skinny jeans and added them to the half-packed open suitcase on Abigail's bed.

Madeline had no right to the feelings she was experiencing. Their magnitude embarrassed her. They were wildly disproportionate to the situation at hand.

So, Abigail wanted to live with her father and she wasn't being all that nice about it. But she was fourteen. Fourteen-year-olds were not known for their empathy.

Madeline kept thinking she was fine about it. She was over it. No big deal. She was busy. Other things to do. And then it would hit her again, like a blow to the abdomen. She'd find herself taking short shallow breaths as if she were in labor. (Twenty-seven hours with Abigail. Nathan and the midwife joked about football while Madeline died. Well, she didn't die, but she remembered thinking that this sort of pain could only end in death, and the last words she'd hear would be about Manly's chances of winning the premiership.)

She lifted one of Abigail's tops from the laundry basket. It was a pale peachy color, and it didn't suit Abigail's coloring, but she loved it. It was hand-wash only. Bonnie could do that now. Or maybe the new upgraded version of Nathan did laundry now. Nathan Version 2.0. Stays with his wife. Volunteers at homeless shelters. Hand-washes.

He was coming over later today with his brother's truck to pick up Abigail's bed.

Last night Abigail had asked Madeline if she could please take her bed to Nathan's house. It was a beautiful four-poster canopy bed that Madeline and Ed had given Abigail for her fourteenth birthday. It had been worth every exorbitant cent to see the ecstasy on Abigail's face when she first saw it. She'd actually danced with joy. It was like remembering another person.

"Your bed stays here," Ed said.

"It's her bed," Madeline said. "I don't mind if she takes it." She said it to hurt Abigail, to hurt her back, to show that she didn't care that Abigail was moving out, that she would now come to visit on weekends, but her real life, her real home would be somewhere else. But Abigail wasn't hurt at all. She was just pleased she was getting the bed.

"Hey," said Ed from the bedroom door.

"Hey," said Madeline.

"Abigail should be packing her own clothes," said Ed. "Surely she's old enough."

Maybe she was, but Madeline did all the laundry in the house. She knew where things were in the wash, dry, fold, put-away assembly line, so it made sense for Madeline to do it. Ever since Ed had first met Abigail, he'd always expected just a little too much of her. How many times had she heard those exact words? "Surely she's old enough." He didn't know children of Abigail's age, and it seemed to Madeline that he always shot just a little too high. It was different with Fred and Chloe, because he'd been there from the beginning. He knew and understood them in a way he never really knew and understood Abigail. Of course, he was fond of her, and he was a good, attentive stepdad, a tricky role he'd taken on immediately without complaint (two months after they began dating, Ed went with Abigail to a Father's Day morning tea at school; Abigail had adored him back then), and maybe they would have had a great relationship except that Nathan the prodigal father had returned at the worst time, when Abigail was eleven. Too old to be managed. Too young to understand or control her feelings. She changed overnight. It was as though she thought showing Ed even just basic courtesy was a betrayal of her father. Ed had an old-fashioned authoritarian streak that didn't respond well to disrespect, and it certainly compared unfavorably to Nathan's let's-have-a-laugh persona.

"Do you think it's my fault?" said Ed.

Madeline looked up. "What?"

"That Abigail is moving in with her dad?" He looked distressed, uncertain. "Was I too hard on her?"

"Of course not," she said, although she did think it was partly his fault, but what was the point in saying that? "I think Bonnie is the real attraction," she said.

"Do you ever wonder if Bonnie has had electric-shock treatment?" mused Ed.

"There is a kind of *blankness* about her," agreed Madeline.

Ed came in and ran his hand over one of the posts of Abigail's bed. "I had a hell of a job putting this together," he said. "Do you think Nathan will be able to manage it?"

Madeline snorted.

"Maybe I should offer to help," said Ed. He was serious. He couldn't bear to think of a DIY job being done badly.

"Don't you dare," said Madeline. "Shouldn't you be gone? Don't you have an interview?"

"Yeah, I do." Ed bent to kiss her.

"Someone interesting?"

"It's Pirriwee Peninsula's oldest book club," said Ed. "They've been meeting once a month for forty years."

"I should start a book club," said Madeline.

Harper: I will say this for Madeline: She invited all the parents to join her book club, including Renata and me. I already belong to a book club, so I declined, which is probably just as well. Renata and I always enjoyed quality literature, not those lightweight, derivative bestsellers. Pure fluff! Each to their own, of course.

Samantha: The whole Erotic Book Club started as a joke. It was actually my fault. I was doing canteen duty with Madeline and I said something to her about a raunchy scene in the book she'd chosen. It wasn't even that raunchy, to be honest, I was just having a laugh, but then Madeline says, "Oh, did I forget to mention it was an erotic book club?" So we all started calling it the Erotic Book Club, and the more people like Harper and Carol clutched their pearls, the worse Madeline got.

Bonnie: I teach a yoga class on Thursday nights, otherwise I would have loved to have joined Madeline's book club.

29.

One Month Before the Trivia Night

I have to take in my family tree tomorrow," said Ziggy.

"No, that's next week," said Jane.

She was sitting on the bathroom floor, leaning against the wall while Ziggy had a bath. Steam and the scent of strawberry bubble bath filled the air. He loved to wallow in deep, very hot bubble baths. "Hotter, Mummy, hotter!" he was always demanding while his skin turned so red, Jane was worried she was scalding him. "More bubbles!" Then he played long, complicated games through the bubbles, incorporating erupting volcanoes, Jedi knights, ninjas and scolding mothers.

"We need special cardboard for the family tree," said Ziggy.

"Yes, we'll get some on the weekend," said Jane. She grinned at him. He'd molded the bubbles on his head into a Mohawk. "You look funny."

"No, I look supercool," said Ziggy. He went back to his game. "Kapow! Kapow! Ow! Stop that right now! Watch out, Yoda! Where's your lightsaber? Say please, Yoda! Here it is!"

Water splashed and bubbles flew.

Jane returned to the book Madeline had chosen for their first book club meeting. "I picked something with lots of sex, drugs and murder," Madeline had said, "so we have a lively discussion. Ideally there should be an argument."

The book was set in the 1920s. It was good. Jane had somehow gotten out of the habit of reading for pleasure. Reading a
novel was like returning to a once-beloved holiday destination.

Right now she was in the middle of a sex scene. She flipped
the page.

"I'll punch you in the face, Darth Vader!" cried Ziggy.

"Don't say 'punch you in the face,'" said Jane without looking
up. "That's not nice." She kept reading. A cloud of strawberry-
scented bubbles floated onto the page of her book. She pushed it
away with her finger. She was feeling something: a tiny pinpoint
of feeling. She shifted slightly on the bathroom tiles. No. Surely
not. From a book? From two nicely written paragraphs? But yes.
She was. She was ever so slightly aroused.

It was a revelation that after all this time she could still feel
something so basic, so biological, so pleasant.

For a moment she saw the staring eye in the ceiling and her
throat tightened, but then her nostrils twitched with a sudden
flare of anger. *I refuse,* she said to the memory. *I refuse you today,
because guess what, I have other memories of sex. I have lots of memories
of an ordinary boyfriend and an ordinary bed, where the sheets weren't
that crisp and there were no staring eyes in the ceiling and there wasn't
that muffled, draped silence, there was music and ordinariness and natural light and he thought I was pretty, you bastard, he thought I was pretty,
and I was pretty, and how dare you, how dare you, how dare you?*

"Mummy?" said Ziggy.

"Yes?" she said. She felt a crazed, angry kind of happiness, as if
someone were daring her not to be.

"I need that spoon that's shaped sort of like this." He drew a
semicircle in the air. He wanted the egg slicer.

"Oh, Ziggy, that's enough kitchen stuff in the bath," she said, but she was already putting her book down and standing up to go and get it for him.

"Thank you, Mummy," said Ziggy angelically, and she looked down at his big green eyes with the tiny droplets of water beaded on his eyelashes and she said, "I love you so much, Ziggy."

"I need that spoon pretty fast," said Ziggy.

"OK," she said.

She turned to leave the bathroom, and Ziggy said, "Do you think Miss Barnes will be mad at me for not bringing in my family tree project?"

"Darling, it's next week," said Jane. She went into the kitchen and read out loud from the notice stuck to the fridge by a magnet. "'All the children will have a chance to talk about their family trees when they bring in their projects on Friday, March twenty-four'—oh, calamity."

He was right. The family tree was due tomorrow. She'd had it in her head that it was due the same Friday as her dad's birthday dinner, but then Dad's dinner had been moved until a week later because her brother was going away with a new girlfriend. It was all bloody Dane's fault.

No. It was her fault. She only had one child. She had a diary. It shouldn't be that hard. They'd have to do it now. Right now. She couldn't send him to school without his project. He'd be calling attention to himself, and he hated it when that happened. If it were Madeline's Chloe, she couldn't care less. She'd giggle and shrug and look cute. Chloe liked being the center of attention, but all poor Ziggy wanted was to blend in to the crowd, just like Jane, but for some reason the opposite kept happening.

"Let the water out of the bath, Ziggy!" she called. "We have to do that project now!"

"I need the special spoon!" called back Ziggy.

"There's no time!" shrieked Jane. "Let the water out now!"

Cardboard. They needed a large sheet of cardboard. Where would they get that from at this time of night? It was past seven. All the shops would be closed.

Madeline. She'd have some spare cardboard. They could drive around to her place and Ziggy could stay in the car in his pajamas while Jane rushed in and got it.

She texted Madeline: *Crisis! Forgot family tree project!!!!!!!!!! (Idiot!) Do you have spare sheet of cardboard! If so, can I drive around and pick it up?*

She pulled the instruction sheet off the fridge.

The family tree project was designed to give the child "a sense of their personal heritage and the heritage of others, while reflecting on the people who are important in their lives now and in the past." The child had to draw a tree and put a photo of themselves in the middle, then include photos and names of family members, ideally dating back to at least two generations, including siblings, aunties, uncles, grandparents and "if possible great-grandparents or even great-great-grandparents!"

There was a big underlined note down at the bottom.

NOTE TO PARENTS: OBVIOUSLY YOUR CHILD WILL NEED YOUR HELP, BUT PLEASE MAKE SURE THEY HAVE CONTRIBUTED TO THIS PROJECT! I WANT TO SEE <u>THEIR</u> WORK, NOT <u>YOURS</u>! ☺ Miss (Rebecca) Barnes

It shouldn't take that long. She already had all the photos ready. She'd been feeling so smug about not leaving that until the last minute. Her mother had gotten prints done of photos from the family albums. There was even one of Ziggy's great-great-grandfather on Jane's dad's side, taken in 1915 just a few short months before he died on the battlefield in France. All Jane had to do was get Ziggy to draw the tree and write out at least some of the names.

Except it was already past his bedtime. She'd let him stay far too long in the bath. He was ready for story and bed. He'd be moaning and yawning and sliding off his chair, and she'd have to beg and bribe and cajole, and the whole process would be excruciating.

This was silly. She should just put him to bed. It was ridiculous to make a five-year-old stay up late to do a school project.

Maybe she could just give him the day off tomorrow? A sickie? But he loved Fridays. FAB Fridays. That's what Miss Barnes called them. Also, Jane really needed him to go to school tomorrow so she could work. She had three deadlines to meet.

Do it in the morning before school? Ha. Yeah, right. She could barely get him to put his shoes on in the morning. Both of them were useless in the mornings.

Deep breaths. Deep breaths.

Who knew that kindergarten could be so stressful? Oh, this was funny! This was so funny. She just couldn't seem to make herself laugh.

Her mobile phone was silent. She picked it up and looked at it. Nothing. Madeline normally answered texts immediately. She'd probably had enough of Jane lurching from crisis to crisis.

"Mummy! I need my spoon!" cried Ziggy.

Her phone rang. She snatched it up.

"Madeline?"

"No, love, it's Pete." It was Pete the Plumber. Jane's heart sank. "Listen, love——"

"I know! I'm so sorry! I haven't done the pay yet. I'll do it tonight."

How could she have forgotten? She always did the pay slips for Pete by lunchtime on a Thursday, so he could pay his "boys" on Friday.

"No worries," said Pete. "See ya, love."

He hung up. Not one for small talk.

"Mummy!"

"Ziggy!" Jane marched into the bathroom. "It's time to let the water out! We've got to do your family tree project!"

Ziggy lay stretched out on his back, his hands nonchalantly crossed behind his head like a sunbather on a beach of bubbles. "You said we didn't have to take it in tomorrow."

"We do! I was right, you were wrong! I mean, you were right, I was wrong! We have to do it right now! Quick! Let's get into your pajamas!"

She reached into the warm bathwater and wrenched out the plug, knowing as she did that she was making a mistake.

"No!" shouted Ziggy, enraged. He liked pulling the plug out himself. "I'll do it!"

"I gave you enough chances," said Jane in her sternest, firmest voice. "It's time to get out. Don't make a fuss."

The water roared. Ziggy roared. "*Mean* Mummy! I do it! You let me do it! No, no."

He threw himself forward to grab for the plug so he could put it back in and pull it back out again. Jane held the plug up high out of his grasp. "We don't have time for that!"

Ziggy stood up in the bathwater, his skinny, slippery little body covered in bubbles and his face contorted in demented rage. He grabbed for the plug, slipped, and Jane had to grab his arm hard to stop him from falling and probably knocking himself out.

"You HURT me!" screamed Ziggy.

Ziggy's near fall had made Jane's heart lurch, and now she was furious with him.

"QUIT YELLING!" she yelled.

She grabbed a towel from the rail and wrapped it around him, lifting him straight out of the bath, kicking and screaming. She carried him into his bedroom and laid him with elaborate care on the bed because she was terrified she might throw him against the wall.

He screamed and thrashed back on the bed. Spittle frothed over his lips. "I HATE YOU!" he screamed.

The neighbors must be close to calling the police.

"Stop it," she said in a reasonable, grown-up voice. "You are behaving like a baby."

"I want a different Mummy!" shouted Ziggy. His foot rammed her stomach, nearly winding her.

Her self-control slipped from her grasp. "STOP IT! STOP IT! STOP IT!" She screamed like a madwoman. It felt good, as if she deserved this.

Ziggy stopped instantly. He scuttled back against the headboard, looking up at her in terror. He curled up in a little naked ball, his face squashed into his pillow, sobbing piteously.

"Ziggy," she said. She put her hand on his knobbly spine and he jerked away from her. She felt sick with guilt. "I'm sorry for yelling like that," she said. She draped the bath towel back over his naked body. *I'm sorry for wanting to throw you against the wall.*

He flipped over and launched himself at her, clinging to her like a koala, his arms around her neck, his legs around her waist, his wet, snotty face buried in her neck.

"It's OK," she said. "Everything is OK." She retrieved the towel from the bed and wrapped it back around him. "Quick. Let's get you into your pj's before you get cold."

"There's someone buzzing," said Ziggy.

"What?" said Jane.

Ziggy lifted his head from her shoulder, his face alert and inquisitive. "Hear it?"

Someone was buzzing the security door for their apartment.

Jane carried him out into the living room.

"Who is it?" said Ziggy. He was thrilled. There were still tears on his cheeks but his eyes were bright and clear. He'd moved on as if that whole terrible incident had never taken place.

"I don't know," said Jane. Was it someone complaining about the noise? The police? The child protection authorities coming to take him away?

She picked up the security phone. "Hello?"

"It's me! Let me in! It's chilly."

"Madeline?" She buzzed her in, put Ziggy down and went to open the front door of the apartment.

"Is Chloe here too?" Ziggy bounced about excitedly, the towel slipping off his shoulders.

"Chloe is probably in bed, like you should be." Jane looked down the stairwell.

"Good evening!" Madeline beamed radiantly up at her as she

click-clacked up the stairs in a watermelon-colored cardigan, jeans and high-heeled, pointy-toed boots.

"Hello?" said Jane.

"Brought you some cardboard." Madeline held up a neatly rolled cylinder of yellow cardboard like a baton.

Jane burst into tears.

30.

It's nothing! I was happy for an excuse to get out of the house," said Madeline over the top of Jane's teary gratitude. "Now, quick sticks, let's get you dressed, Ziggy, and we'll knock this project over."

Other people's problems always seemed so surmountable, and other people's children so much more biddable, thought Madeline as Ziggy trotted off. While Jane collected the family photos, Madeline looked around Jane's small, neat apartment, reminded of the two-bedroom apartment she and Abigail used to share.

She was romanticizing those days, she knew it. She wasn't remembering the constant money worries or the loneliness of those nights when Abigail was asleep and there was nothing good on TV.

Abigail had been living with Nathan and Bonnie now for two weeks, and it seemed it was all going perfectly well for everyone except Madeline. Tonight, when Jane's text had come through, the little children were asleep, Ed was working on a story and Madeline had just sat down to watch *America's Next Top Model*. "Abigail!" she'd called out as she switched it on, before she remembered the empty bedroom, the four-poster bed replaced by a sofa bed for Abigail to use when she came for weekends, and Madeline didn't know how to be with her daughter anymore, because she felt like she'd been fired from her position as mother.

She and Abigail normally watched *America's Next Top Model* to-gether, eating marshmallows and making catty remarks about the contestants, but now Abigail was happily living in a TV-free house. Bonnie didn't "believe" in television. Instead, they all sat around and *listened to classical music and talked* after dinner.

"Rubbish," scoffed Ed when he heard this.

"Apparently it's true," Madeline said. Of course, now when Abigail came to "visit," all she wanted to do was lie on the couch and gorge on television, and because Madeline was now the treat-giving parent, she let her. (If she'd spent a week just listening to classical music and talking, she'd want to watch TV too.)

Bonnie's whole life was a slap across Madeline's face. (A gentle slap, more of a condescending, kindly pat, because Bonnie would never do anything violent.) That's why it was so nice to be able to help Jane out, to be the calm one, with answers and solutions.

"I can't find glue to paste on the photos," said Jane worriedly as they laid everything out on the table.

"Got it." Madeline pulled a pencil case out of her handbag and selected a black marker for Ziggy. "Let's see you draw a great big tree, Ziggy."

It was all going well until Ziggy said, "We have to put my father's name on it. Miss Barnes said it doesn't matter if we don't have a photo, we just put the person's name."

"Well, you know that you don't have a dad, Ziggy," said Jane calmly. She'd told Madeline that she'd always tried to be as honest as possible with Ziggy about his father. "But you're lucky, because you've got Uncle Dane, and Grandpa, and Great-uncle Jimmy." She held up photos of smiling men like a winning hand of cards. "*And* we've even got this amazing photo of your great-great-grand-father, who was a soldier!"

"Yes, but I still have to write my dad's name down in that box," said Ziggy. "You draw a line from me to my mummy and my daddy. That's the way you do it."

He pointed at the example of a family tree that Miss Barnes had included, demonstrating a perfect unbroken nuclear family, with mum, dad and two siblings.

Miss Barnes really needs to rethink this project, thought Madeline. She'd had enough trouble herself when she was helping Chloe with hers. There had been the tricky matter of whether a line should be drawn from Abigail's picture to Ed. "You'll have to put in a photo of Abigail's *real* dad," Fred had said helpfully, looking over their shoulders. "And his car?"

"No we don't," Madeline had said.

"It doesn't have to be exactly like the one Miss Barnes gave you," Madeline said to Ziggy. "Everyone's project will be different. That's just an example."

"Yes, but you have to write down your mother's *and* your father's name," said Ziggy. "What's my dad's name? Just say it, Mummy. Just spell it. I don't know how to spell it. I'll get in trouble if I don't write down his name."

Children did this. They sensed when there was something controversial or sensitive and they pushed and pushed like tiny prosecutors.

Poor Jane had gone very still.

"Sweetheart," she said carefully, her eyes on Ziggy, "I've told you this story so many times. Your dad would have loved you if he'd known you, but I'm so sorry, I don't know his name, and I know that's not fair—"

"But you have to write a *name* there! Miss Barnes said!" There was a familiar note of hysteria in his voice. Overtired five-year-olds needed to be handled like explosive devices.

"I don't *know* his name!" said Jane, and Madeline recognized the gritted-teeth note in her voice too, because there was something in your children that could bring out the child in yourself. Nothing and nobody could aggravate you the way your child could aggravate you.

"Oh, Ziggy, darling, see, this happens *all* the time," said Madeline. For God's sake. It probably did. There were plenty of single mothers in the area. Madeline was going to have a word with Miss Barnes tomorrow to ensure that she stopped assigning this ridiculous project. Why try to slot fractured families into neat little boxes in this day and age?

"This is what you do. You write 'Ziggy's dad.' You know how to write 'Ziggy,' don't you? Of course you do, that's it."

To her relief, Ziggy obeyed, writing his name with his tongue out the side of his mouth to help him concentrate. "What neat writing!" encouraged Madeline feverishly. She didn't want to give him time to think. "You are a much neater writer than my Chloe. And that's it! You're done! Your mum and I will stick down the rest of the photos while you're asleep. Now. Story time! Right? And I'm wondering, could *I* read you a story? Would that be OK? I'd love to see your favorite book."

Ziggy nodded dumbly, seemingly overwhelmed by her torrent of chatter. He stood up, his little shoulders drooping.

"Good night, Ziggy," said Jane.

"Good night, Mummy," said Ziggy. They kissed each other good night like warring spouses, their eyes not meeting, and then Ziggy took Madeline's hand and allowed her to lead him off to his bedroom.

In less than ten minutes she was back out in the living room. Jane looked up. She was carefully pasting the last photo onto the family tree.

"Out like a light," said Madeline. "He actually fell asleep while I was reading, like a child in a movie. I didn't know children really did that."

"I'm so sorry," said Jane. "You shouldn't have to come over here and put another child to bed, but I am so grateful to you, because I didn't want to get into a conversation with him just before bed about that, and——"

"Shhhh." Madeline sat down next to her and put her hand on her arm. "It was nothing. I know what it's like. Kindergarten is stressful. They get so tired."

"He's never been like that before," said Jane. "About his father. I mean, I always knew it might be an issue one day, but I thought it wouldn't be until he was thirteen or something. I thought I'd have time to work out exactly what to say. Mum and Dad always said stick to the truth, but you know, the truth isn't always . . . it's not always . . . well, it's not always that——"

"Palatable," offered Madeline.

"Yes," said Jane. She adjusted the corner of the photo she'd just glued down and surveyed the piece of cardboard. "He'll be the only one in the class without a picture in the box for his father."

"That's not the end of the world," said Madeline. She touched the photo of Jane's dad with Ziggy on his lap. "Plenty of lovely men in his life." She looked at Jane. "It's annoying that we don't have anyone with two mummies in the class. Or two daddies. When Abigail was at primary school in the Inner West, we had all sorts of families. We're a bit too white-bread here on the peninsula. We like to think we're terribly diverse, but it's only our bank accounts that vary."

"I do know his name," said Jane quietly.

"You mean Ziggy's father?" Madeline lowered her voice too.

"Yes," said Jane. "His name was Saxon Banks." Her mouth went a bit wonky when she said the words, as if she were trying to make unfamiliar sounds from a foreign language. "Sounds like a respectable name, doesn't it? A fine, upstanding citizen. Quite sexy too! Sexy Saxon." She shuddered.

"Did you ever try to get in touch with him?" asked Madeline. "To tell him about Ziggy?"

"I did not," said Jane. It was an oddly formal turn of phrase.

"And why did you not?" Madeline imitated her tone.

"Because Saxon Banks was not a very nice fellow," said Jane. She put on a silly, posh voice and held her chin high, but her eyes were bright. "He was not a nice chap at all."

Madeline returned to her normal voice. "Oh, Jane, what did that bastard do to you?"

31.

Jane couldn't believe she'd said his name out loud to Madeline. Saxon Banks. As if Saxon Banks were just another person.

"Do you want to tell me?" said Madeline. "You don't have to tell me."

She was obviously curious, but not in that avid way that Jane's friends had been the next day ("Spill, Jane, spill! Give us the dirt!"), and she was sympathetic, but her sympathy wasn't weighed down by maternal love, like it would be if it were Jane's mother hearing the story.

"It's not that big a deal, really," said Jane.

Madeline sat back in her chair. She took off the two hand-painted wooden bangles she was wearing on her wrist and placed them carefully on top of each other on the table in front of her. She pushed the family tree project to one side.

"OK," she said. She knew it was a big deal.

Jane cleared her throat. She took a piece of gum out of the packet on the table.

"We went to a bar," she said.

. . .

Z ach had broken up with her three weeks earlier.

It had been a great shock. Like a bucket of icy water thrown in the face. She thought they were on the path toward engagement rings and a mortgage.

Her heart was broken. It was definitely broken. But she knew it would heal. She was even relishing it a little, the way you could sometimes relish a head cold. She wallowed deliciously in her misery, crying for hours over photos of her and Zach, but then drying her tears and buying herself a new dress because she deserved it because her heart was broken. Everybody was so gratifyingly shocked and sympathetic. *You were such a great couple! He's crazy! He'll regret it!*

There was the feeling that it was a rite of passage. Part of her was already looking back on this time from afar. *The first time my heart was broken.* And part of her was kind of curious about what was going to happen next. Her life had been going one way, and now, just like that—wham!—it was heading off in another direction. Interesting! Maybe after she finished her degree she'd travel for a year, like Zach. Maybe she'd date an entirely different sort of guy. A grungy musician. A computer geek. A smorgasbord of boys awaited her.

"You need *vodka*!" her friend Gail had said. "You need *dancing*."

They went to a bar at a hotel in the city. Harbor views. It was a warm spring night. She had hay fever. Her eyes were itchy. Her throat was scratchy. Spring always brought hay fever, but also that sense of possibility, the possibility of an amazing summer.

There were some older men, maybe in their early thirties, at the table next to them. Executive types. They bought them drinks. Big, expensive, creamy cocktails. They chugged them back like milk shakes.

The men were from interstate, staying at the hotel. One of them took a shine to Jane.

"Saxon Banks," he said, taking her hand in his much larger one.

"You're Mr. Banks," Jane said to him. "The dad in *Mary Poppins*."

"I'm more like the chimney sweep," said Saxon. He held her eyes and sang softly, *"A sweep is as lucky, as lucky can be."*

It's not very hard for an older man with a black AmEx and a chiseled chin to make a tipsy nineteen-year-old swoon. Bit of eye contact. Sing softly. Hold a tune. There you go. Done deal.

"Go for it," Gail said in her ear. "Why not?"

She couldn't come up with a reason why not.

No wedding ring. There was probably a girlfriend back home, but it wasn't up to Jane to do a background check (was it?) and she wasn't about to begin a relationship with him. It was a one-night stand. She'd never had one before. She'd always hovered on the side of prudish. Now was the time to be young and free and a bit crazy. It was like being on holidays and deciding to give bungee jumping a go. And this would be such a *classy* one-night stand, in a five-star hotel, with a five-star man. There would be no regrets. Zach could go off on his tacky Contiki tour and grope the girls on the back of the bus.

Saxon was funny and sexy. They laughed and laughed as the glass bubble elevator slid up through the center of the hotel. Then the sudden muffled carpeted silence of the corridor. His room key sliding in and the instant, tiny green light of approval.

She wasn't too drunk. Just nicely drunk. Exhilarated. Why not? she kept telling herself. Why not try bungee jumping? Why not leap off the edge into nothing? Why not be a bit naughty? It was fun. It was funny. It was *living life*, the way Zach wanted to *live life* by going on a bus tour around Europe and climbing the Eiffel Tower.

He poured her a glass of champagne, and they drank together, looking at the view, and then he removed the champagne glass from her hand and placed it on the bedside table, and she felt like she was in a movie scene she'd seen a hundred times before, even while part of her laughed at his pretentious masterfulness.

He put his hand on the back of her head and pulled her to him, like someone executing a perfect dance move. He kissed her, one hand pressed firmly on her lower back. His aftershave smelled like money.

She was there to have sex with him. She did not change her mind. She did not say no. It was certainly not rape. She *helped* him take her clothes off. She giggled like an idiot. She lay in bed with him. There was just one point when their naked bodies were pressed together and she saw the strangeness of his hairy, unfamiliar chest and she felt a sudden desperate longing for the lovely familiarity of Zach's body and smell, but it was OK, she was perfectly prepared to see it through.

"Condom?" she murmured at the appropriate point, in the appropriate low throaty voice, and she thought he'd take care of that in the same smooth, discreet way he'd done everything else, with a better brand of condom than she'd ever used before, but that's when he'd put his hands around her neck and said, "Ever tried this?"

She could feel the hard clamp of his hands.

"It's fun. You'll like it. It's a rush. Like cocaine."

"No," she said. She grabbed at his hands to try to stop him. She could never bear the thought of not being able to breathe. She didn't even like swimming underwater.

He squeezed. His eyes were on hers. He grinned, as if he were tickling, not choking her.

He let go.

"I don't like that!" she gasped.

"Sorry," he said. "It can be an acquired taste. You just need to relax, Jane. Don't be so uptight. Come on."

"No. Please."

But he did it again. She could hear herself making disgusting, shameful gagging sounds. She thought she would vomit. Her body was covered in cold sweat.

"Still no?" He lifted his hands.

His eyes turned hard. Except maybe they'd been hard all along.

"Please don't. Please don't do that again."

"You're a boring little bitch, aren't you? Just want to be fucked. That's what you came here for, hey?"

He positioned her underneath him and shoved himself inside her as if he were operating some sort of basic machinery, and as he moved, he put his mouth close to her ear and he said things: an endless stream of casual cruelty that slid straight into her head and curled up, wormlike, in her brain.

"You're just a fat ugly little girl, aren't you? With your cheap jewelry and your trashy dress. Your breath is disgusting, by the way. Need to learn some dental hygiene. Jesus. Never had an original thought in your life, have you? Want a tip? You've got to respect yourself a bit more. Lose that weight. Join a gym, for fuck's sake. Stop the junk food. You'll never be beautiful, but at least you won't be fat."

She did not resist in any way. She stared at the downlight in the ceiling, blinking at her like a hateful eye, observing everything, seeing it all, agreeing with everything that he said. When he rolled off her, she didn't move. It was as though her body didn't belong to her anymore, as though she'd been anesthetized.

"Shall we watch TV?" he said, and he picked up the remote control and the television at the end of the bed came to life. It was one of the *Die Hard* movies. He flicked through channels while she put back on the dress that she'd loved. (She'd never spent that much money on a dress before.) She moved slowly and stiffly. It wouldn't be until days later that she would find bruises on her arms, her legs, her stomach and her neck. As she dressed, she didn't try to hide her body from him, because he was like a doctor who had operated on her and removed something appalling. Why try to hide her body when he already knew just how abhorrent it was?

"You off, then?" he said when she was dressed.

"Yes. Bye," she said. She sounded like a thick-witted twelve-year-old.

She could never understand why she felt the need to say "bye." Sometimes she thought she hated herself mostly for that. For her dopey, bovine "bye." Why? Why did she say that? It was a wonder she didn't say "thanks."

"See you!" It was like he was trying not to laugh. He found her laughable. Disgusting and laughable. She was disgusting and laughable.

She went back downstairs in the glass bubble elevator.

"Would you like a taxi?" said the concierge, and she knew he could barely contain his disgust: disheveled, fat, drunk, slutty girl on her way home.

After that, nothing ever seemed quite the same.

32.

O h, *Jane*."
    Madeline wanted to sweep Jane into her arms and onto
her lap and rock her back and forth as if she were Chloe.
She wanted to find that man and hit him, kick him, yell obsceni-
ties at him.

"I guess I should have taken the morning-after pill," said Jane.
"But I never even thought about it. I had bad endometriosis when
I was younger, and a doctor told me I'd have a lot of trouble getting pregnant. I can go for months without a period. When I finally realized I was pregnant, it was . . ."

She'd told her story in a low voice that Madeline had had to
strain to hear, but now she lowered it even further to almost a
whisper, her eyes on the hallway leading to Ziggy's bedroom.
"Much too late for an abortion. And then my grandfather died,
and that was a big shock to us all. And then I went a bit strange.
Depressed, maybe. I don't know. I left uni and moved back home,
and I just slept. For hours and hours. It was like I was sedated or
really jet-lagged. I couldn't bear to be awake."

"You were probably still in shock. Oh, Jane. I'm so sorry that
happened to you."

Jane shook her head as if she'd been given something she didn't deserve. "Well. It's not like I got raped in an alleyway. I have to take responsibility. It wasn't that big a deal."

"He assaulted you! He—"

Jane lifted a hand. "Lots of women have bad sexual experiences. That was mine. The lesson is: Don't go off with strange men you meet in bars."

"I can assure you I went off with my share of men I met in bars," said Madeline. She'd done it once or twice. It had never been like that. She would have poked his eyes out. "Do not for a moment think that you're in *any* way to blame, Jane."

Jane shook her head. "I know. But I do try to keep it in perspective. Some people do really like that erotic asphyxiation stuff." Madeline saw her put a hand unconsciously to her neck. "You might be into it, for all I know."

"Ed and I think it's erotic if we find ourselves in bed without a wriggling child in between us," said Madeline. "Jane, my darling girl, that wasn't sexual experimentation. What that man did to you was *not*—"

"Well, don't forget you heard the story from my perspective," interrupted Jane. "He might remember it differently." She shrugged. "He probably doesn't even remember it."

"And that was verbal abuse. Those things he said to you." Madeline felt the fury rise again. How could she fight this creep? How could she make him pay? "Those vile things."

When Jane had told her the story, she hadn't needed to try to think back to remember the exact words. She'd recited his insults in a dull monotone, as if she were reciting a poem or a prayer.

"Yes," said Jane. *"Fat ugly little girl."*

Madeline winced. "You are not."

"I was overweight," said Jane. "Some people would probably say I was fat. I was into food."

"A foodie," said Madeline.

"Nothing as sophisticated as that. I just loved all food, and I especially loved fattening food. Cakes. Chocolate. *Butter.* I just loved butter."

An expression of mild awe crossed her face, as if she couldn't quite believe she was describing herself.

"I'll show you a photo," she said to Madeline. She flicked through her phone. "My friend Em just posted this on Facebook for Throwback Thursday. It's me at her nineteenth birthday. Just a few months before . . . before I got pregnant."

She held up the phone for Madeline to see. There was Jane wearing a red sheath dress with a low neckline. She was standing in between two other girls of the same age, all three of them beaming at the camera. Jane looked like a different person: softer, uninhibited, much, much younger.

"You were *curvy*," said Madeline, handing back the phone. "Not fat. You look gorgeous in this photo."

"It's sort of interesting when you think about it," said Jane, glancing at the photo once before she flicked it off with her thumb. "Why did I feel so weirdly *violated* by those two words? More than anything else that he did to me, it was those two words that hurt. 'Fat.' 'Ugly.'"

She spat out the two words. Madeline wished she would stop saying them.

"I mean a fat, ugly *man* can still be funny and lovable and successful," continued Jane. "But it's like it's the most shameful thing for a woman to be."

"But you weren't, you're not——" began Madeline.

"Yes, OK, but so what if I was!" interrupted Jane. "What if I *was*! That's my point. What if I was a bit overweight and not especially pretty? Why is that so terrible? So disgusting? Why is that the end of the world?"

Madeline found herself without words. To be fat and ugly actually would be the end of the world for her.

"It's because a woman's entire self-worth rests on her looks," said Jane. "That's why. It's because we live in a beauty-obsessed society where the most important thing a woman can do is make herself attractive to men."

Madeline had never heard Jane speak this way before, so aggressively and fluently. Normally she was so diffident and self-deprecating, so ready to let someone else have the opinions.

"Is that really true?" said Madeline. For some reason she wanted to disagree. "Because you know I *often* feel secretly inferior to women like Renata and Jonathan's bloody hotshot wife. There they are, earning squillions and going to board meetings or whatever, and there's me, with my cute little part-time marketing job."

"Yes, but deep down you know that you win because you're prettier," said Jane.

"Well," said Madeline, "I don't know about that." She caught herself caressing her hair and dropped her hand.

"So that's why, if you're in bed with a man, and you're naked and vulnerable, and you're assuming that he finds you at least mildly attractive, and then he says something like that, well it's . . ." She gave Madeline a wry look. "It's kind of devastating." She paused. "And, Madeline, it infuriates me that I found it so devastating. It *infuriates* me that he had that power over me. I look in the mirror each day, and I think, 'I'm not overweight anymore,' but he's right, I'm still ugly. Intellectually I know I'm not ugly, I'm perfectly acceptable. But I feel ugly, because one man said it was so, and that made it so. It's pathetic."

"He was a prick," said Madeline helplessly. "He was just a stupid prick." It occurred to her that the more Jane expounded on ugliness, the more beautiful she looked, with her hair coming loose, her cheeks flushed and eyes shining. "You're beautiful," she began.

"No!" said Jane angrily. "I'm not! And that's OK that I'm not. We're not all beautiful, just like we're not all musical, and that's fine. And don't give me that inner beauty shining through crap either."

Madeline, who had been about to give her that inner beauty shining through crap, closed her mouth.

"I didn't mean to lose so much weight," said Jane. "It makes me angry that I lost weight, as if I were doing it for him, but I got all weird about food after that. Every time I went to eat it was like I could *see myself* eating. I could see myself the way he'd seen me: slovenly fat girl eating. And my throat would just . . ." She tapped a hand to her throat and swallowed. "Anyway! So it was quite effective! Like a gastric bypass. I should market it. The Saxon Banks Diet. One quick, only slightly painful session in a hotel room and there you go: lifelong eating disorder. Cost-effective!"

"Oh, Jane," said Madeline.

She thought of Jane's mother and her comment on the beach about "no one wants to see this in a bikini." It seemed to her that Jane's mother had probably helped lay the groundwork for Jane's mixed-up feelings about food. The media had done its bit, and women in general, with their willingness to feel bad about themselves, and then Saxon Banks had finished the job.

"Anyway," said Jane. "Sorry for that little tirade."

"Don't be sorry."

"Also, I don't have bad breath," said Jane. "I've checked with my dentist. Many times. But we'd been out for pizza beforehand. I had garlic breath."

So that was the reason for the gum obsession.

"Your breath smells like daisies," said Madeline. "I have an acute sense of smell."

"I think it was the shock of it more than anything," said Jane. "The way he changed. He seemed so nice, and I'd always thought I was a pretty good judge of character. After that, I felt like I couldn't really trust my own instincts."

"I'm not surprised," said Madeline. Could she have picked him? Would she have fallen for his *Mary Poppins* song?

"I don't regret it," said Jane. "Because I got Ziggy. My miracle baby. It was like I woke up when he was born. It was like he had nothing to do with that night. This beautiful tiny baby. It's only as he's started to turn into a little person with his own personality that it even occurred to me, that he might, that he might have, you know, inherited something from his . . . his father."

For the first time, her voice broke.

"Whenever Ziggy behaves in a way that seems out of character, I worry. Like on orientation day, when Amabella said he choked her. Of all the things to happen. *Choking.* I couldn't believe it. And sometimes I feel like I can see something in his eyes that reminds me of, of him, and I think, 'What if my beautiful Ziggy has a secret cruel streak? What if my son does that to a girl one day?'"

"Ziggy does not have a cruel streak," said Madeline. Her desperate need to comfort Jane cemented her belief in Ziggy's goodness. "He's a lovely, sweet boy. I'm sure your mother is right, he's your grandfather reincarnated."

Jane laughed. She picked up her mobile phone and looked at the time on the screen. "It's so late! You should go home to your family. I've kept you here this long, blathering on about myself."

"You weren't blathering."

Jane stood up. She stretched her arms high above her head so that her T-shirt rose and Madeline could see her skinny, white, vulnerable stomach. "Thank you so much for helping me get this damned project done."

"My pleasure." Madeline stood as well. She looked at where Ziggy had written "Ziggy's dad." "Will you ever tell him his name?"

"Oh, God, I don't know," said Jane. "Maybe when he's twenty-one, when he's old enough for me to tell him the whole truth and nothing but the truth."

"He might be dead," said Madeline hopefully. "Karma might have gotten him in the end. Have you ever Googled him?"

"No," said Jane. There was a complicated expression on her face. Madeline couldn't tell if it meant that she was lying or that even the thought of Googling him was too painful.

"*I'll* Google the awful creep," said Madeline. "What was his name again? Saxon Banks, right? I'll find him and then I'll put out a hit on him. There must be some kind of online murder-a-bastard service these days."

Jane didn't laugh. "Please don't Google him, Madeline. Please don't. I don't know why I hate the thought of your looking him up, but I just do."

"Of course I won't if you don't want me to, I was being flippant. Stupid. I shouldn't make light of it. Ignore me."

She held her arms out and gave Jane a hug.

To her surprise, Jane, who always presented a stiff cheek for a kiss, stepped forward and held her tightly.

"Thank you for bringing over the cardboard," she said.

Madeline patted Jane's clean-smelling hair. She'd nearly said, *You're welcome, my beautiful girl,* like she did to Chloe, but the word "beautiful" seemed so complicated and fraught right now. Instead she said, "You're welcome, my lovely girl."

33.

Are there any weapons in your house?" asked the counselor.

"Pardon?" said Celeste. "Did you say *weapons?*"

Her heart was still pounding from the fact that she was actually here, in this small yellow-walled room, with a row of cactus plants on the windowsill and colorful government-issued posters with hotline numbers on the walls, cheap office furniture on beautiful old floorboards. The counseling offices were in a federation cottage on the Pacific Highway on the Lower North Shore. The room she was in probably used to be a bedroom. Someone had once slept here, never dreaming that in the next century people would be sharing shameful secrets in this room.

When she'd gotten up this morning Celeste had been sure she wouldn't come. She intended to ring up and cancel as soon as she got the children to school, but then she'd found herself in the car, putting the address into the GPS, driving up the winding peninsula road, thinking the whole way that she would pull over in the next five minutes and call them up and say so sorry, but her car had broken down, she would reschedule another day. But she kept driving, as if she were in a dream or a trance, thinking of other things like what she'd cook for dinner, and then, before she knew it, she was pulling into the parking area behind the house and watching a woman coming out, puffing furiously on a cigarette as she opened the door of a banged-up old white car. A woman wearing jeans and a crop top, with tattoos like awful injuries all the way down her thin white arms.

She'd envisaged Perry's face. His amused, superior face. "You're not serious, are you? This is just so . . ."

So lowbrow. Yes, Perry. It was. A suburban counseling practice that specialized in domestic violence. It was listed on their website, along with depression and anxiety and eating disorders. There were two typos on the home page. She'd chosen it because it was far enough away from Pirriwee that she could be sure of not running into anyone she knew. Also, she hadn't really had any intention of turning up. She'd just wanted to make an appointment, to prove she wasn't a victim, to prove to some unseen presence that she was doing something about this.

"Our behavior is lowbrow, Perry," she'd said out loud in the silence of the car, and then she'd turned the key in the ignition and gone inside.

"Celeste?" prompted the counselor now.

The counselor *knew her name*. The counselor knew more about the truth of her life than anyone in the world besides Perry. She was in one of those naked nightmares, where you just had to keep walking through the crowded shopping center while everyone stared at your shameful, shocking nudity. She couldn't go back now. She had to see it through. She'd told her. She'd said it, very quickly, her eyes slightly off-center from the counselor's, pretending she was keeping eye contact. She'd spoken in a low, neutral voice, as if she were telling a doctor about a revolting symptom. It was part of being a grown-up, being a woman and a mother. You had to say uncomfortable things out loud. "I have this discharge." "I'm in a sort of violent relationship." "Sort of." Like a teenager hedging her words, distancing herself.

"Sorry. Did you just ask about *weapons?*" She recrossed her legs, smoothing the fabric of her dress across them. She'd deliberately chosen an especially beautiful dress that Perry had bought for her in Paris. She hadn't worn it before. She'd also put on makeup: foundation, powder, the whole kit and caboodle. She wanted to position herself, not as superior to other women, of *course* not, she didn't think that, not in a million years. But her situation was different from that woman in the parking lot. Celeste didn't need the phone number for a shelter. She just needed some strategies to fix her marriage. She needed tips. Ten top tips to stop my husband from hitting me. Ten top tips to stop my hitting him back.

"Yes, weapons. Are there any weapons in the house?" The counselor looked up from what must be a standard sort of checklist. *For God's sake,* thought Celeste. *Weapons!* Did she think Celeste lived in the sort of home where the husband kept an unlicensed gun under the bed?

"No weapons," said Celeste. "Although the twins have lightsabers." She noticed that she was putting on a well-bred private schoolgirl sort of voice and tried to stop it.

She wasn't a private schoolgirl. She'd married up.

The counselor laughed politely and noted something on the clipboard in front of her. Her name was Susi, which seemed to indicate a worrying lack of judgment. Why didn't she call herself Susan? "Susi" sounded like a pole dancer.

The other problem with Susi was that she appeared to be about twelve years old, and quite naturally, being twelve, she didn't know how to apply eyeliner properly. It was smudged around her eyes, giving her that raccoon look. How could this child give Celeste advice on her strange, complicated marriage? Celeste should be giving her advice on makeup and boys.

"Does your partner assault or mutilate the family pets?" said Susi blandly.

"*What?* No! Well, we don't have any pets, but he's not like that!" Celeste felt a surge of anger. Why had she subjected herself to this humiliation? She wanted to cry out, absurdly, *This dress is from Paris! My husband drives a Porsche! We are not like that!* "Perry would never hurt an animal," she said.

"But he hurts you," said Susi.

You don't know anything about me, thought Celeste sulkily, furiously. *You think I'm like the girl with the tattoos, and I am not, I am not.*

"Yes," said Celeste. "As I said, occasionally he, *we* become physically . . . violent." Her posh voice was back. "But as I tried to explain, I have to take my share of the blame."

"No one deserves to be abused, Mrs. White," said Susi.

They must teach them that line at counseling school.

"Yes," said Celeste. "Of course. I know that. I don't think I deserve it. But I'm not a victim. I hit him back. I throw things at him. So I'm just as bad as he is. Sometimes I start it. I mean, we're just in a very toxic relationship. We need techniques, we need *strategies* to help us . . . to make us stop. That's why I'm here."

Susi nodded slowly. "I understand. Do you think your husband is afraid of you, Mrs. White?"

"No," said Celeste. "Not in a physical sense. I think he's probably afraid I'll leave him."

"When these 'incidents' have taken place, have *you* ever been afraid?"

"Well, no. Well, sort of." She could see the point that Susi was trying to make. "Look, I know how violent some men can be, but with Perry and me, it's not that bad. It's bad! I know it's bad. I'm not delusional. But, see, I've never ended up in the hospital or anything like that. I don't need to go to a shelter or a refuge or whatever they're called. I have no doubt you see much, much worse cases than mine, but I'm fine. I'm perfectly fine."

"Have you ever been afraid that you might die?"

"Absolutely not," said Celeste immediately.

She stopped.

"Well, just once. It was just that my face . . . He had my face pressed into the corner of a couch."

She remembered the feeling of his hand on the back of her head. The angle of her face meant that her nose sort of folded in half, pinching her nostrils. She'd struggled frantically to free herself, like a pinned butterfly. "I don't think he realized what he was doing. But I did think, just for a moment, that I was going to suffocate."

"That must have been very frightening," said Susi without inflection.

"It was a bit." She paused. "I remember the dust. It was very dusty."

For a moment Celeste thought she might cry: huge, heaving, snotty sobs. There was a box of tissues sitting on the coffee table in between them for just that purpose. Her own mascara would run. She'd have raccoon eyes too, and Susi would think, *Not so upper class now, are you, lady?*

She pulled herself back from the brink of debasement and looked away from Susi. She studied her engagement ring.

"I packed a bag that time," she said. "But then . . . well, the boys were still so little. And I was so tired."

"On average, most victims will try to leave an abusive situation six or seven times before they finally leave permanently," said Susi. She chewed on the end of her pen. "What about your boys? Has your husband ever—"

"No!" said Celeste. A sudden terror took hold of her. Dear God. She was crazy coming here. They might report her to the Department of Community Services. They might take the children away.

She thought of the family tree projects the boys had taken in to school today. The carefully drawn lines connecting each of them to their twin, to her and to Perry. Their happy glossy faces.

"Perry has never ever laid a finger on the boys. He is a *wonderful* father. If I ever thought that the boys were in danger, I would leave; I would never, ever put them at risk." Her voice shook. "That's one of the reasons I haven't left, because he is so good with them. So patient! He's more patient with them than me. He adores them!"

"How do you think—" began Susi, but Celeste interrupted her. She needed her to understand how Perry felt about his children.

"We had so much trouble getting pregnant, or not getting pregnant. Staying pregnant. I had four miscarriages in a row. It was terrible."

It was like she and Perry had endured a two-year journey across stormy oceans and endless deserts. And then they'd reached the oasis. Twins! A natural pregnancy with twins! She'd seen the expression on the obstetrician's face when she found the second heartbeat. Twins. A high-risk pregnancy for someone with a history of recurrent miscarriage. The obstetrician was thinking, *No way*. But they made it all the way to thirty-two weeks.

"The boys were preemies. So there was all that going back and forth to the hospital for late-night feeds. We couldn't believe it when we finally got to bring them home. We just stood there in the nursery, staring at them, and then . . . well, then, those first few months were like a nightmare, really. They weren't good sleepers. Perry took three months off. He was wonderful. We got through it together."

"I see," said Susi.

But Celeste could tell she didn't see. She didn't understand that she and Perry were bound together forever by their experiences and their love for their sons. Breaking away from him would be like tearing flesh.

"How do you think the abuse impacts your sons?"

Celeste wished she would stop using the word "abuse."

"It doesn't impact them in any way," she said. "They have no idea. I mean, for the most part, we're just a very happy, ordinary, loving family. We can go for weeks, months even, without anything out of the ordinary."

Months was probably an exaggeration.

She was starting to feel claustrophobic in this tiny room. There wasn't enough air. She ran a fingertip across her brow, and it came back damp. What had she expected from this? Why had she come? She knew there were no answers. No strategies. No tips and techniques, for God's sake. Perry was Perry. There was no way out except to leave, and she would never leave while the children were little. She was going to leave when they were at university. She'd already decided that.

"What made you come here today, Mrs. White?" said Susi, as if she were reading her mind. "You said this has been going on since your children were babies. Has the violence been escalating recently?"

Celeste tried to remember why she'd made the appointment. It was the day of the athletics carnival.

It was something to do with the amused expression on Perry's face that morning when Josh asked him about the mark on his neck. And then she'd gone home after the carnival and felt envious of her cleaners because they were laughing. So she'd given twenty-five thousand dollars to charity. "Feeling philanthropic were you, darling?" Perry had said wryly a few weeks later when the credit card bill came in, but he'd made no further comment.

"No, it hasn't been escalating," she said to Susi. "I'm not sure why I finally made an appointment. Perry and I went to marriage counseling once, but it didn't . . . Well, nothing came of that. It's hard because he travels a lot for work. He'll be away again next week."

"Do you miss him when he's away?" said Susi. It seemed as though this wasn't a question on her clipboard, it was just something that she wanted to know.

"Yes," said Celeste. "And no."

"It's complicated," said Susi.

"It's complicated," agreed Celeste. "But all marriages are complicated, aren't they?"

"Yes," said Susi. She smiled. "And no." Her smile vanished. "Are you aware that a woman dies every week in Australia as a result of domestic violence, Mrs. White? Every week."

"He's not going to *kill* me," said Celeste. "It's not like that."

"Is it safe for you to go home today?"

"Of course," said Celeste. "I'm perfectly safe."

Susi raised her eyebrows.

"Our relationship is like a seesaw," explained Celeste. "First one person has the power, then the other. Each time Perry and I have a fight, especially if it gets physical, if I get hurt, then I get the power back. I'm on top."

She warmed to her theme. It was shameful sharing these things with Susi, but it was also a wonderful relief to be telling someone, to be explaining how it all worked, to be saying these secrets out loud.

"The more he hurts me, the higher I go and the longer I get to stay there. Then the weeks go by, and I can feel it shifting. He stops feeling so guilty and sorry. The bruises—I bruise easily—well, the bruises fade. Little things I do start to annoy him. He gets a bit irritable. I try to placate him. I start walking on eggshells, but at the same time I'm angry that I have to walk on eggshells, so sometimes I stop tiptoeing. I stomp on the eggshells. I *deliberately* aggravate him because I'm so angry with him, and with myself, for having to be careful. And then it happens again."

"So you've got the power right now," said Susi. "Because he hurt you recently."

"Yes," said Celeste. "I could actually do anything right now because he still feels so bad about what happened the last time. With the Legos. So right now everything is great. Better than great. That's the problem, see. It's so good right now, it's almost . . ."

She stopped.

"Worth it," finished Susi. "It's almost worth it."

Celeste met Susi's raccoon eyes. "Yes."

The blandness of Susi's gaze said nothing at all except, *Got it.* She wasn't being kind and maternal, and she wasn't reveling in the delicious superiority of her own kindness. She was just getting the job done. She was like that brisk, efficient lady at the bank or the telephone company who just wants to do her job and untangle that knotty problem for you.

They sat in silence for a moment. Outside the office door, Celeste could hear the murmur of voices, the ringing of a telephone and the distant sounds of traffic passing on the street outside. A sense of peace washed over her. The sweat on her face cooled. For five years, ever since it had begun, she'd been living her life with this secret shame draped so heavily over her shoulders, and for just a moment it lifted and she remembered the person she used to be. She still had no solution, no way out, but for just this moment she was sitting opposite someone who understood.

"He will hit you again," said Susi. That detached professionalism again. No pity. No judgment. It wasn't a question. She was stating a fact to move the conversation forward.

"Yes," said Celeste. "It will happen again. He'll hit me. I'll hit him."

It will rain again. I will get sick again. I will have bad days. But can't I enjoy the good times while they last?

But then why am I here at all?

"So what I'd like to talk about is coming up with a plan," said Susi. She flipped over a page on her clipboard.

"A plan," said Celeste.

"A plan," said Susi. "A plan for next time."

34.

ave you ever wanted to experiment with that, what's it called, erotic asphyxiation?" said Madeline to Ed as they lay in bed. He had his book. She had the iPad.

It was the night after she'd taken the cardboard over to Jane's place. She'd been thinking about Jane's story all day.

"Sure. I'm up for it. Let's give it a shot." Ed took off his glasses and put down his book, turning to her with enthusiasm.

"What? No! Are you kidding?" said Madeline. "Anyway, I don't want sex. I ate too much risotto for dinner."

"Right. Of course. Silly of me." Ed put his glasses back on.

"And people accidentally kill themselves doing that! They die all the time! It's a very dangerous practice, Ed."

Ed looked at her over the top of his glasses.

"I can't believe you wanted to choke me," said Madeline.

He shook his head. "I was just trying to show my willingness to accommodate." He glanced at her iPad. "Are you looking up ways to spice up our sex life or something?"

"Oh God no," said Madeline, with perhaps too much feeling.

Ed snorted.

She looked at the Wikipedia entry for erotic asphyxiation. "So apparently when the arteries on either side of the neck are compressed, you get a sudden loss of oxygen to the brain so you go into a semi-hallucinogenic state." She considered it. "I've noticed whenever I've got a head cold, I often feel quite amorous. That might be why."

"Madeline," said Ed. "You have never been amorous when you had a head cold."

"Really?" said Madeline. "Maybe I just forgot to mention it."

"Yeah, maybe you did." He went back to reading his book again. "I had a girlfriend who was into it."

"Seriously? Which one?"

"Well, maybe she wasn't theoretically a girlfriend. More like a random girl."

"And this random girl wanted you to . . ." Madeline put her hands around her own throat, stuck her tongue out the side of her mouth and made choking noises.

"Goddamn, that looks sexy when you do that," said Ed.

"Thanks." Madeline dropped her hands. "So did you do it?"

"Sort of halfheartedly," said Ed as he took off his glasses. He grinned to himself, remembering. "I was a bit drunk. I was having trouble following instructions. I remember she was disappointed with me, which I know you probably find impossible to fathom, but I didn't always thrill and delight—"

"Yes, yes." Madeline waved him quiet and looked back at her iPad.

"So why the sudden interest in erotic asphyxiation?" said Ed.

She told him Jane's story and watched the tiny muscles around his jaw flicker and his eyes narrow, the way they did when he heard a story on the news about a child being hurt.

"Bastard," he said finally.

"I know," said Madeline. "And he just gets away with it."

Ed shook his head. "Silly, silly girl." He sighed. "These sort of men just prey on—"

"Don't call her a silly girl!" Madeline sat up so fast, the iPad slipped off her legs. "That sounds like you're blaming her!"

Ed held up his hand as if to ward her off. "Of course I'm not. I just meant—"

"What if it were Abigail or Chloe?" cried Madeline.

"I actually *was* thinking of Abigail and Chloe," said Ed.

"So you'd blame them, would you? Would you say, 'You silly girl, you got what you deserved'?"

"Madeline," said Ed calmly.

Their arguments always went like this. The angrier Madeline got, the more freakishly calm Ed became, until he reached a point where he sounded like a hostage negotiator dealing with a lunatic and a ticking bomb. It was infuriating.

"You're *blaming the victim!*" She was thinking of Jane sitting in her cold, bare little apartment, the expressions that had crossed her face as she shared her sad, sordid little story, the *shame* she so obviously still felt all these years later. "I have to take responsibility," she'd said. "It wasn't that big a deal." She thought of the photo Jane had showed her. The open, carefree expression on her face. The red dress. Jane once wore bright colors! Jane once had cleavage! Now Jane dressed her bony body apologetically, humbly, like she wanted to disappear, like she was trying to be invisible, to make herself nothing. That man had done that to her.

"It's all fine and dandy for you to sleep with *random* women, but when a woman does, it's *silly*. That's a double standard!"

"Madeline," said Ed. "I was not blaming her."

He was still speaking in his I'm-the-grown-up-you're-the-crazy-one voice, but she could see a spark of anger in his eyes.

"You are! I can't believe you would say that!" The words bubbled out of her. "You're like those people who say, 'Oh, what did she expect? She was drinking at one o'clock in the morning, so of course she deserved to be raped by the whole football team!'"

"I am not!"

"You are so!"

Something changed in Ed's face. His face flushed. His voice rose.

"Let me tell you this, Madeline," he said. "If my daughter goes off one day with some wanker she's only just met in a hotel bar, I reserve the right to call her *silly!*"

It was stupid for them to be fighting about this. A rational part of her mind knew this. She knew that Ed didn't really blame Jane. She knew her husband was actually a better, nicer person than she was, and yet she couldn't forgive him for that "silly girl" comment. It somehow *represented* a terrible wrong. As a woman, Madeline was obliged to be angry with Ed on Jane's behalf, and for every other "silly girl," and for herself, because after all, it could have happened to her too, and even a soft little word like "silly" felt like a slap.

"I can't be in the same room as you right now." She hopped out of bed, taking the iPad with her.

"Be ridiculous, then," said Ed. He put his glasses back on. He was upset, but Madeline knew that he would read his book for twenty minutes, turn off the light and fall instantly asleep.

Madeline closed the door firmly (she would have preferred to slam it, but she didn't want the kids waking up) and marched down the stairs in the dark.

"Don't hurt your ankle on the stairs!" called out Ed from behind the door. He was already over it, thought Madeline.

She made herself a cup of chamomile tea and settled down on the couch. She hated chamomile tea, but it was supposedly soothing and calming and whatever, so she was always trying to make herself drink it. Bonnie only drank herbal tea, of course. According to Abigail, Nathan avoided caffeine now too. This was the problem with children and marriage breakups. You got all this information about your ex-husband that you would otherwise never know. She knew, for example, that Nathan called Bonnie his "bonnie Bon." Abigail had mentioned this in the kitchen one day. Ed, who had been standing behind her, silently stuck his finger down his throat, making Madeline laugh, but still, she could have done without hearing that. (Nathan had always been into alliteration; he used to call her his "mad Maddie"—not quite as romantic.) Why had Abigail felt the need to share those sorts of things? Ed thought it was deliberate, that she was trying to bait Madeline, to purposely hurt her, but Madeline didn't believe that Abigail was that malicious.

Ed always saw the worst in Abigail these days.

That's what was behind her sudden fury with him in the bedroom. It wasn't really anything to do with the "silly girl" comment. It was because she was still angry with Ed over Abigail moving in with Nathan and Bonnie, because the more time that passed, the more likely it seemed that it *was* Ed's fault. Maybe Abigail had been teetering on the edge of her decision, playing around with the idea but not really seriously considering it, and Ed's "calm down" comment had been just the shove she'd needed. Otherwise she'd still be here. It might have just been a passing phase. Teenagers did that. Their moods came and went.

Lately, Madeline's mind had been so filled with memories of the days when it was just her and Abigail that she sometimes had the strangest feeling that Ed, Fred and Chloe were interlopers. Who were these people? It was like they'd marched into Madeline and Abigail's life with all their noise and their stuff, their noisy computer games and their fighting, and they'd driven poor Abigail away.

She laughed at the thought of how outraged Fred and Chloe would be if they knew she dared question their existence, especially Chloe. "But where *was* I?" she always demanded when she looked at old photos of Madeline and Abigail. "Where was Daddy? Where was Fred?" "You were in my dreams," Madeline would say, and it was true. But they weren't in Abigail's dreams.

She sipped her tea and felt the anger slowly drain from her body. Nothing to do with the stupid tea.

Really it was that man's fault.

Mr. Banks. Saxon Banks.

An unusual name.

She rested her fingertips on the cool, smooth surface of the iPad.

"Don't Google him," Jane had begged, and Madeline had promised, so this was very wrong, but the desire to see the bastard was so irresistible. It was like when she read a story about a crime, she always wanted to see the offender, to study his or her face for signs of evil. (She could always find them.) And it was so easy, just a few keystrokes in that little rectangle, it was like her fingers were doing it without her permission and, while she was still deciding whether or not to break her promise, the search results were already on the screen in front of her, as if Google were an extension of her mind and she only had to think of it for it to happen.

She would just take a very, very quick look, she'd just skim it with her eyes, and then she'd close the page and delete all references to Saxon Banks from her search history. Jane would never know. It wasn't like Madeline could do anything about him. She wasn't going to plan some elaborate, satisfying revenge. (Although, already part of her mind had split off and was traveling down that path: Some sort of scam? To steal his money? To publicly humiliate or discredit him? There must be a way.)

She double-clicked, and one of those well-lit corporate head shots filled her screen. A property developer called Saxon Banks based in Melbourne. Was that him? A strong-jawed, classically handsome man with a pleased-with-himself smirk and eyes that seemed to look straight into Madeline's in a combative, bordering on aggressive way.

"You prick," said Madeline out loud. "You think you can do whatever you want to whomever you choose, don't you?"

What would she have done in Jane's situation? She couldn't imagine herself reacting the way Jane had. Madeline would have slapped him. She wouldn't have been undone by the words "fat" and "ugly," because her self-confidence about her looks was too high, even when she was nineteen—or especially when she was nineteen. She got to decide how she looked.

Perhaps this man specifically picked out girls who he knew would be vulnerable to his insults.

Or was this line of thought just another form of victim-blaming? *This wouldn't have happened to me. I would have fought. I wouldn't have stood for it. He wouldn't have shattered my self-respect.* Jane had been completely vulnerable at the time, naked, in his bed, silly girl.

Madeline caught herself. "Silly girl." She'd just thought exactly the same thing as Ed. She'd apologize in the morning. Well, she wouldn't apologize out loud, but she might make him a soft-boiled egg, and he'd get the message.

She studied the photo again. She couldn't see a resemblance to Ziggy. Or, actually, maybe she could? Perhaps a little around the eyes. She read the little biography next to his photo. Bachelor of this, masters of that, member of the Institute of whatever, blah, blah, blah. *In his spare time Saxon enjoys sailing, rock climbing and spending time with his wife and three young daughters.*

Madeline winced. Ziggy had three half sisters.

Madeline knew this now. She knew something she shouldn't know, and she couldn't un-know it. She knew something about Jane's own son that Jane herself didn't know. She hadn't just broken a promise, she'd violated Jane's privacy. She was a tacky little voyeur poking about the Internet, digging up photos of Ziggy's father. She'd been angered by what had happened to Jane, but part of her had almost relished the story, hadn't she? Hadn't she almost *enjoyed* feeling outraged over Jane's sad, sordid little sex story? Her sympathy came from the superior, comfy position of someone with a life in proper middle-class order: a husband, a home, a mortgage. Madeline was just like some of her mother's friends, who had been so excitedly sympathetic when Nathan left her and Abigail. They were sad and outraged for her, but in such a tut-tut-that's-oh-so-terrible way that left Madeline feeling brittle and defensive, even as she genuinely appreciated the home-cooked casseroles that were solemnly placed on her kitchen table.

Madeline stared into Saxon's face, and he seemed to stare back at her with knowing eyes, as if he knew every despicable thing there was to know about her. A wave of revulsion rushed over her, leaving her feeling clammy and shaky.

A scream sliced like a sword through the house's sleepy silence: "Mummy! Mummy, Mummy, Mummy!"

Madeline leapt to her feet, her heart hammering, even though she already knew it was just Chloe having another one of her nightmares.

"Coming! I'm coming!" she called as she ran down the hallway. She could fix this. She could so easily fix this, and it was such a relief, because Abigail didn't want or need her anymore, and there were evil people like Saxon Banks out there in the world waiting to hurt Madeline's children, in big ways and small ways, and there wasn't a damned thing she could do about it, but at least she could drag that monster out from under Chloe's bed and kill it with her bare hands.

35.

Miss Barnes: After that little drama on orientation day, I was steeling myself for a tough year, but it seemed to get off to a good start. They were a great bunch of kids, and the parents weren't being too annoying. Then about halfway through the first term it all fell apart.

Two Weeks Before the Trivia Night

atte and a muffin."

Jane looked up from her laptop, and then down again at the plate in front of her. There was an artful scribble of whipped cream on the plate next to the muffin. "Oh, thanks, Tom, but I didn't order—"

"I know. The muffin is on the house," said Tom. "I hear from Madeline that you're a baker. So I wanted to get your expert opinion on this new recipe I'm trying. Peach, macadamia nut and lime. Crazy stuff. The lime, I mean."

"I only bake muffins," said Jane. "I never eat them."

"Seriously?" Tom's face fell a little.

Jane said hurriedly, "But I'll make an exception today."

The weather had turned cold this week, a little practice session for winter, and Jane's apartment was chilly. That gray sliver of ocean she could see from her apartment window just made her feel colder still. It was like a memory of summers lost forever, as if she lived in a gray, brooding, postapocalyptic world. "God, Jane, that's a bit dramatic. Why don't you take your laptop and set yourself up at a table at Blue Blues?" Madeline had suggested. So Jane had started turning up each day with her laptop and files.

The café was filled with sun and light, and Tom had a wood-fire stove running. Jane gave a little exhalation of pleasure each time she stepped in the door. It was like she'd gotten on a plane and flown into an entirely different season compared with her miserable, damp apartment. She made sure that she was only there in between the morning rush and the afternoon rush so she didn't take up a paying table, and of course she ordered coffees and a small lunch throughout the day.

Tom the barista had begun to seem like a colleague, someone who shared the cubicle next to hers. He was good for a chat. They liked the same TV shows, some of the same music. (Music! She'd forgotten the existence of music, like she'd forgotten books.)

Tom grinned. "I'm turning into my grandma, aren't I? Force-feeding everyone. Just try one mouthful. Don't eat it all to be polite." Jane watched him go, and then averted her eyes when she realized she was enjoying looking at the breadth of his shoulders in his standard black T-shirt. She knew from Madeline that Tom was gay, and in the process of recovering from a badly broken heart. It was a cliché, but it also seemed to be so often true: Gay men had really good bodies.

Something had been happening over the last few weeks, ever since she'd read that sex scene in the bathroom. It was like her body, her rusty, abandoned body, was starting up again of its own accord, creaking back to life. She kept catching herself idly, accidentally looking at men, and at women too, but mainly men, not so much in a sexual way, but in a sensual, appreciative, aesthetic way.

It wasn't beautiful people like Celeste who were drawing Jane's eyes, but ordinary people and the beautiful ordinariness of their bodies. A tanned forearm with a tattoo of the sun reaching out across the counter at the service station. The back of an older man's neck in a queue at the supermarket. Calf muscles and collarbones. It was the strangest thing. She was reminded of her father, who years ago had an operation on his sinuses that returned the sense of smell he hadn't realized he'd lost. The simplest smells sent him into rhapsodies of delight. He kept sniffing Jane's mother's neck and saying dreamily, "I'd forgotten your mother's smell! I didn't know I'd forgotten it!"

It wasn't just the book.

It was telling Madeline about Saxon Banks. It was repeating those stupid little words he'd said. They needed to stay secret to keep their power. Now they were deflating the way a jumping castle sagged and wrinkled as the air hissed out.

Saxon Banks was a nasty person. There were nasty people in this world. Every child knew that. Your parents taught you to stay away from them. Ignore them. Walk away. Say, "No. I don't like that," in a loud, firm voice, and if they keep doing it, you go tell a teacher.

Even Saxon's insults had been school yard insults. *You smell. You're ugly.*

She'd always known that her reaction to that night had been too big, or perhaps too small. She hadn't ever cried. She hadn't told anyone. She'd swallowed it whole and pretended it meant nothing, and therefore it had come to mean everything.

Now it was like she wanted to keep talking about it. A few

days ago, when she and Celeste had their morning walk, she'd told her a shorter version of what she'd told Madeline. Celeste hadn't said all that much, except that she was sorry and that Madeline was absolutely right and Ziggy was nothing like his father. The next day, Celeste gave Jane a necklace in a red velvet bag. It was a fine silver chain with a blue gemstone. "That gemstone is called a lapis," said Celeste in her diffident way. "It's supposedly a gemstone that 'heals emotional wounds.' I don't really believe that stuff—but anyway, it's a pretty necklace."

Now Jane put a hand to the pendant.

New friends? Was that it? The sea air?

The regular exercise was probably helping too. She and Celeste were both getting fitter. They'd both been so happy when they noticed they didn't have to stop and catch their breath when they reached the top of the flight of stairs near the graveyard.

Yes, it was probably the exercise.

All she'd needed all this time was a brisk walk in the fresh air and a healing gemstone.

She dug her fork into the muffin and lifted it to her mouth. The walks with Celeste were also returning her appetite. If she didn't watch out, she'd get fat again. Her throat closed up on cue, and she replaced the fork. So, not quite cured. Still weird about food.

But she must not offend lovely Tom. She picked up her fork and took the tiniest bite. The muffin was light and fluffy, and she could taste all the ingredients that Tom had mentioned: macadamia, peach, lime. She closed her eyes and felt everything: the warmth of the café, the taste of the muffin, the by now familiar smell of coffee and secondhand books. She took another, bigger forkful and scraped up some of the cream.

"OK?" Tom leaned over a table close to hers, cleaning it with a cloth he took from his back pocket.

Jane lifted a hand to indicate her mouth was full. Tom took a book that a customer had left on the table and replaced it on one of the higher shelves. His black T-shirt lifted away from his jeans, and Jane saw a glimpse of his lower back. Just a perfectly ordinary lower back. Nothing particularly notable about it. His skin during the winter was the color of a weak latte. During the summer it was the color of hot chocolate.

"It's wonderful," she said.

"Mmmm?" Tom turned around. There were only the two of them in the café right now.

Jane pointed her fork at the muffin. "This is amazing. You should charge a premium." Her mobile rang. "Excuse me."

The name on the screen said SCHOOL. The school had only called her once before, when Ziggy had a sore throat.

"Ms. Chapman? This is Patricia Lipmann."

The school principal. Jane's stomach contracted.

"Mrs. Lipmann? Is everything all right?" She hated the craven note in her voice. Madeline spoke to Mrs. Lipmann with cheerful, condescending affection, as if she were a dotty old family butler.

"Yes, everything is fine, although I would like to arrange a meeting with you as a matter of some urgency if I could? Ideally today. Would around two p.m. suit you, just before pickup?"

"Of course. Is everything—"

"Lovely. I'll look forward to seeing you then."

Jane put down her phone. "Mrs. Lipmann wants a meeting with me."

Tom knew most of the kids, parents and teachers at the school.

He'd grown up in the area and attended the school himself back when Mrs. Lipmann was a lowly Year 3 teacher.

"I'm sure you don't have anything to worry about," he said. "Ziggy is a good kid. Maybe she wants to put Ziggy in a special class or something."

"Mmmm." Jane took another absentminded forkful of muffin. Ziggy wasn't "gifted and talented." Anyway, she already knew from the tone of Mrs. Lipmann's voice that this wasn't going to be good news.

> **Samantha:** Renata went off her head when the bullying started. Part of the problem was the nanny hadn't been communicating, so it had been going on for a while without her knowing. Of course we now know that Juliette had other things on her mind besides her job.

> **Miss Barnes:** What parents don't understand is that a child can be a bully one minute and a victim the next. They're so ready to label! Of course, I do see this was different. This was . . . bad.

> **Stu:** My dad taught me: A kid hits you, you hit him back. Simple. It's like everything these days. A trophy for every kid in the soccer game. A prize in every bloody layer of Hot Potato. We're bringing up a generation of wimps.

> **Thea:** Renata *must* surely have blamed herself. The hours she worked, she barely saw her children! My heart just goes out to those poor little mites. Apparently they're

not coping well at the moment. Not coping well at all. Their lives will never be the same again, will they?

Jackie: Nobody says anything about *Geoff* working long hours. Nobody asks if *Geoff* knew what was going on with Amabella. It's my understanding Renata had a higher-paid, more stressful job than Geoff, but nobody blamed Geoff for having a career, nobody said, "Oh, we don't see much of Geoff at the school, do we?" No! But if the stay-at-home mums see a dad do pickup, they think he deserves a gold medal. Take my husband. He has his own little entourage.

Jonathan: They're my friends, not my entourage. You have to excuse my wife. She's in the middle of a hostile takeover. That might be why she's coming across a bit hostile. I think the school has to take responsibility. Where were the teachers when all this bullying was going on?

36.

Renata Klein has discovered that her daughter, Amabella, has been the victim of systematic, secret bullying over the last month," said Mrs. Lipmann without preamble as soon as Jane sat down opposite her. "Unfortunately Amabella won't say exactly what has been going on or who is involved. However, Renata is convinced that Ziggy is responsible."

Jane gulped convulsively. It was strange that she still felt shocked, as though some crazily optimistic part of her really had believed that Ziggy was about to be put into some sort of special class for marvelous children.

"What sort of . . ." Jane's voice disappeared. She cleared her throat with difficulty. She felt as though she were playing a role for which she wasn't properly qualified. Her parents should be at this meeting. People of the same era as Mrs. Lipmann. "What sort of bullying?"

Mrs. Lipmann made a little face. She looked like a lady who lunched; a society wife with good clothes and an expensive skin care regime. Her voice had that crystal-clear *don't mess with me* quality that was very effective, apparently, even with the famously naughty Year 6 boys.

"Unfortunately we're a little short on details," said Mrs.

Lipmann. "Amabella does have some unexplained bruises and grazes, and a . . . bite mark, and she has only said that 'someone has been mean to her.'" She sighed and tapped perfectly manicured nails on the manila folder in her lap. "Look, if it weren't for the incident on the orientation day, I wouldn't have called you in until we had anything more definitive. Miss Barnes says that incident appeared to be a one-off. She has observed Ziggy closely, because of what happened, and she describes him as a delightful child, who is a joy to teach and appears to be very caring and kind in his interactions with the other children."

The unexpected kindness of those words from Miss Barnes made Jane want to weep.

"Now, obviously we have a zero tolerance policy for bullying at Pirriwee Public. Zero. But in the rare cases where we do find cases of bullying, I want you to know that we believe we have a duty of care both to the victim and to the bully. So if we do find that Ziggy has been bullying Amabella, our focus won't be on punishing him, but on ensuring the behavior stops, obviously, immediately, and then on getting to the bottom of *why* he is behaving this way. He's a five-year-old boy, after all. Some experts say a five-year-old is incapable of bullying."

Mrs. Lipmann smiled at Jane, and Jane smiled back warily. *But wait, he's a delightful child. He hasn't done this!*

"Apart from what happened on orientation day, have there ever been any other incidents of this sort of behavior? At day care? Preschool? In Ziggy's interactions with children outside the classroom?"

"No," said Jane. "Absolutely not. And he always . . . Well." She'd been about to say that Ziggy had always steadfastly denied

Amabella's accusation from orientation day, but perhaps that just confused the issue. Mrs. Lipmann would think he had a history of lying.

"So there is nothing out of the ordinary in Ziggy's past, his home life, his background, that you think we should know, that might be relevant?" Mrs. Lipmann looked at her expectantly, her face kind and warm, as if to let Jane know that nothing would shock her. "I understand that Ziggy's father is not involved with his upbringing, is that right?"

It always took Jane a moment when strangers casually referred to "Ziggy's father." "Father" was a word that Jane associated with love and security. She always thought first of her own father, as if that must be surely whom they meant. She had to do a little leap in her mind to a hotel room and a downlight.

Well, Mrs. Lipmann, is this relevant? All I know about Ziggy's father is that he was keen on erotic asphyxiation and humiliating women. He appeared to be charming and kind. He could sing Mary Poppins *songs. I thought he was delightful—in fact, you'd probably think he was delightful too—and yet, he was not who he appeared to be at all. I guess you could describe him as a bully. So that may be relevant. Also, just to give you the whole picture, there is the possibility that Ziggy is actually my dead grandfather, reincarnated. And Poppy was a very gentle soul. So I guess it depends on whether you believe in a hereditary tendency toward violence, or reincarnation.*

"I can't think of anything relevant," said Jane. "He has a lot of male role models—"

"Oh, yes, yes, I'm sure he does," said Mrs. Lipmann. "Goodness. Some children here have fathers who travel or work such long hours, they never see them at all. So I'm certainly not implying that Ziggy is missing out because he's growing up in a single-parent household. I'm just trying to get the whole picture."

"Have you asked him about this?" asked Jane. Her heart twisted at the thought of Ziggy's being questioned by the school principal without her there. He slept with a teddy bear. He sat on her lap and sucked his thumb when he got tired. It still seemed like a minor miracle to her that he could walk and talk and dress himself, and now here he was living this whole other life separate from her, with big, grown-up, scary dramas taking place.

"I have, and he denies it quite emphatically, so without Amabella's corroboration it really is very difficult to know where to go next—"

She was interrupted by a knock on the door of her office. The school secretary put her head in. She shot a wary look at Jane. "Er, I thought I should let you know, Mr. and Mrs. Klein are already here."

Mrs. Lipmann blanched. "But they're not due for another hour."

"My board meeting was rescheduled," said a familiar, strident voice. Renata appeared at the secretary's shoulder, clearly ready to barge on in. "So we just wondered if you could fit us in—" She caught sight of Jane and her face hardened. "Oh. I see."

Mrs. Lipmann shot Jane an anguished look of apology. Jane knew from Madeline that Geoff and Renata regularly donated ostentatious sums of money to the school. "At last year's school trivia night, we all had to sit there like grateful peasants while Mrs. Lipmann thanked the Kleins for paying for the entire school to be air-conditioned," Madeline had told her. Then she'd brightened as a thought struck her. "Maybe Celeste and Perry can take them on this year. They can all play 'I'm richer than you' together."

The school secretary wrung her hands. Mrs. Lipmann made a

point of having an "open door" policy for school parents and was flexible about people dropping in without an appointment. The secretary had no experience with a situation like this. "Is it possible you could come back another time?" she said pleadingly to Renata.

"Not really," said Renata. "Anyway, I assume we're all here to discuss the same topic, aren't we?"

Mrs. Lipmann hurried out from behind her desk. "Mrs. Klein, I really think it would be better—"

"This is fortuitous, in fact!" Renata strode past the secretary and straight into the office, followed by a pale, stocky, ginger-haired man in a suit and tie, who was presumably Geoff. Jane hadn't met him before. Most of the fathers were still strangers to her.

Jane got to her feet and held her arms protectively across her body, her hands clutching at her clothes as if they were about to be ripped off. The Kleins were about to expose her and lay her ugly, shameful secrets bare for all the other parents to see. Ziggy wasn't the result of nice, normal, loving sex. He was the result of the shameful actions of a young, silly, fat, ugly girl.

Ziggy was not right, and he was not right because Jane had let that man be his father. She knew it was illogical, because Ziggy wouldn't otherwise exist, but it felt logical, because Ziggy was always going to be her son, of course he was, how could she not be his mother? But he was meant to be born later, when Jane had found him a proper daddy and a proper life. If she'd done everything properly he wouldn't be marked by this terrible genetic stain. He wouldn't be behaving this way.

She thought of the first time she'd seen him. He was so upset to be born, screaming with his whole body, tiny limbs flailing as if he were falling, and her first thought was, *I'm so sorry, little baby. I'm so sorry for putting you through this.* The exquisitely painful feeling that flooded her body reminded her of grief—even though she would have called it "joy," it felt the same. She had thought the raging torrent of her love for this funny-looking, little red-faced creature would surely wash away the dirty little memory of that night. But the memory stayed, clinging to the walls of her mind like a slimy black leech.

"You need to get that son of yours under control." Renata stepped directly in front of Jane. Her finger stabbed at the air near Jane's chest. Her eyes were bloodshot behind her glasses. Her anger was so palpable and righteous in the face of Jane's doubts.

"Renata," remonstrated Geoff. He held out a hand to Jane. "Geoff Klein. Please excuse Renata. She's very upset."

Jane shook his hand. "Jane Chapman."

"All right, well perhaps then, if we *are* all here together, perhaps we could have a constructive chat," said Mrs. Lipmann with a tinkle of nerves in her cut-glass voice. "Can I offer anyone tea or coffee? Water?"

"I don't want *refreshments*," said Renata. Jane saw with something like sick fascination that Renata's entire body was trembling. She looked away. Seeing the evidence of Renata's raw emotions was like seeing her naked.

"*Renata.*" Geoff held his arm diagonally across his wife's body, as if she were about to step in front of a car.

"I'll tell you what I want," said Renata to Mrs. Lipmann. "I want her child to stay the hell away from my daughter."

37.

Madeline pulled open the sliding door from the backyard and saw Abigail sitting on the couch, looking at something on her laptop. "Hey there!" she said, and winced at the fake cheer in her voice.

She couldn't speak naturally to her own daughter. Now that Abigail only came on weekends, it felt like Madeline was the host and Abigail was an important guest. She felt like she had to offer her drinks and check on her comfort. It was *ridiculous*. Whenever Madeline caught herself behaving this way, she got so angry, she went too far the other way and brusquely demanded that Abigail perform some domestic chore, like hanging out a basket of washing. The worst part was that Abigail behaved exactly like the good-mannered guest that Madeline had brought her up to be and picked up the laundry basket without comment, and then Madeline was guilty and confused. How could she ask Abigail to hang out washing when Abigail didn't bring any washing home with her? It was like asking your guest to hang out your laundry. So then she'd rush out to help put the clothes on the line and make stilted chitchat while all the words she couldn't say poured through her head: *Just come back home, Abigail, come back home and stop this. He left us. He left you. You were my reward. Missing out on you was his punishment. How could you choose him?*

"Whatcha doing?" Madeline plonked herself on the couch next to Abigail and peered at the laptop screen. "Is that *America's Next Top Model?*"

She didn't know how to *be* around Abigail anymore. It reminded her of trying to be friends with an ex-boyfriend. That studied casualness of your interactions. The fragility of your feelings, the awareness that the little quirks of your personality were no longer so adorable; they might even be just plain annoying.

Madeline had always played up to her role in the family as the comically crazy mother. She got overly excited and overly angry about things. When the children wouldn't do as they were told, she huffed and she puffed. She sang silly songs while she stood at the pantry door: "Where, oh where, are the tinned tomatoes? Tomatoes, wherefore art thou?!" The kids and Ed loved making fun of her, teasing her about everything from her celebrity obsessions to her glittery eye shadow.

But now, when Abigail was visiting, Madeline felt like a parody of herself. She was determined not to pretend to be someone she wasn't. She was forty! It was too late to be changing her personality. But she kept seeing herself through Abigail's eyes and assuming that she was being compared unfavorably to Bonnie. Because she'd chosen Bonnie, hadn't she? Bonnie was the mother Abigail would prefer. It actually had nothing to do with Nathan. The mother set the tone of the household. Every secret fear that Madeline had ever had about her own flaws (she was obviously too quick to anger, often too quick to judge, overly interested in clothes, spent far too much money on shoes, thought she was cute and funny when perhaps she was just annoying and tacky) was now at the forefront of her mind. *Grow up,* she told herself. *Don't take this so personally. Your daughter still loves you. She's just chosen to live with her father. It's no big deal.* But every interaction with Abigail was a constant battle between "This is who I am, Abigail, take it or leave it" and "Be better, Madeline, be calmer, be kinder, be more like Bonnie."

"Did you see Eloise get kicked off last week?" asked Madeline. This is what she would normally say to Abigail, so this is what she said.

"I'm not looking at *America's Next Top Model*," sighed Abigail. "I'm looking at Amnesty International. I'm reading about the violation of human rights."

"Oh," said Madeline. "Goodness."

"Bonnie and her mum are both members of Amnesty International," said Abigail.

"Of course they are," murmured Madeline. *This must be how Jennifer Aniston feels,* thought Madeline, *whenever she hears about Angelina and Brad adopting another orphan or two.*

"What?"

"That's great," said Madeline. "I think Ed is too. We give a donation each year."

Oh, God, listen to yourself! Stop competing! Was it even true? Ed might have let his membership lapse.

She and Ed did their best to be good people. She bought raffle tickets for charity, gave money to street performers, and was *always* sponsoring annoying friends who were running yet another marathon for some worthy cause (even though the true cause was their own fitness). When the kids were older, she assumed she would do some sort of volunteer work like her own mother did. That was enough, wasn't it? For a busy working mother? How dare Bonnie make her question every choice she made?

According to Abigail, Bonnie had recently decided she wasn't having any more children (Madeline didn't ask why, although she wanted to know) and so she'd donated Skye's pram, stroller, cot, change table and baby clothes to a battered women's shelter. "Isn't that amazing, Mum?" Abigail had sighed. "Other people would just sell that stuff." Madeline had recently sold Chloe's old baby dresses on eBay. Then she'd gleefully spent the money on a new pair of half-price designer boots.

"So what are you reading about?" Was it good for a fourteen-year-old girl to be learning about the atrocities of the world? It was probably wonderful for her. Bonnie was giving Abigail a social conscience, while Madeline was just encouraging poor body image. She thought about what poor Jane had said about society being obsessed with beauty. She imagined Abigail going into a hotel room with a strange man and him treating her the way that man had treated Jane. Rage ballooned. She imagined grabbing him by the hair on the back of his head and smashing his face over and over against some sort of concrete surface until it was a bloody, pulpy mess. Good God. She watched too much violent TV.

"What are you reading about, Abigail?" she said again, and hated the irritable edge in her voice. Did she have PMS again? No. It wasn't the right time. She couldn't even blame that. She was just permanently bad-tempered these days.

Abigail sighed. She didn't lift her eyes from the screen. "Child marriage and sex slavery," she said.

"That's awful," said Madeline. She paused. "Maybe don't . . ."

She stopped. She wanted to say something like *Don't let it upset you*, which was a terrible thing to say, which was just the sort of thing a privileged, frivolous, white Western woman would say, a woman who took far too much genuine pleasure in a new pair of shoes or a bottle of perfume. What would Bonnie say? *Let us med-*

itate on this together, Abigail. Ohmmm. See? There was her superficiality again. Making fun of meditation. How did meditating hurt anyone?

"They should be playing with dolls," said Abigail. Her voice was thick with angry teariness. "Instead, they're working in brothels."

You *should be playing with dolls,* thought Madeline. *Or at least playing with makeup.*

She felt a surge of righteous anger with Nathan and Bonnie, because, actually, Abigail *was* too young and sensitive to know about human trafficking. Her feelings were too fierce and uncontrolled. She had inherited Madeline's unfortunate talent for instant outrage, but her heart was far softer than Madeline's had ever been. She had too much empathy (although, of course, all that excessive empathy was never directed at Madeline or Ed, or Chloe and Fred).

Madeline remembered when Abigail was only about five or six and so proud of her new ability to read. She'd found her sitting at the kitchen table, her lips moving as she carefully sounded out a headline on the front page of a newspaper with an expression of pure horror and disbelief. Madeline couldn't remember now what the article was about. Murder, death, disaster. No. Actually she did remember. It was a story about a child taken from her bed in the early eighties. Her body was never found. Abigail still believed in Santa Claus at that time. "It's not true," Madeline had told her quickly, snatching up the paper and vowing never to leave it anywhere accessible ever again. "It's all made-up."

Nathan didn't know about that, because Nathan wasn't there.

Chloe and Fred were such different creatures. So much more resilient. Her darling little tech-savvy, consumerist savages.

"I'm going to do something about this," said Abigail, scrolling down the screen.

"Really?" said Madeline. *Well, you're not going to Pakistan, if that's what you're thinking. You're staying right here and watching* America's Next Top Model, *young lady.* "What do you mean? A letter?" She brightened. She had a marketing degree. She could write a better letter than Bonnie ever could. "I could help you write a letter to our MP petitioning for an—"

"No," interrupted Abigail scornfully. "That achieves nothing. I've got an idea."

"What sort of idea?" asked Madeline.

Afterward she would wonder if Abigail might have answered her truthfully, if she could have put a stop to the madness before it even began, but there was a knock on the front door just then and Abigail snapped shut the laptop.

"That's Dad," she said, getting to her feet.

"But it's only four o'clock," protested Madeline. She stood up too. "I thought I was driving you back at five."

"We're going to Bonnie's mother's for dinner," said Abigail.

"Bonnie's mother," repeated Madeline.

"Don't make a drama of it, Mum."

"I didn't say a word. I didn't say, for example, that you haven't seen *my* mother in weeks."

"Grandma is too busy with her social life to even notice," Abigail said accurately.

"Abigail's dad is here!" yelled Fred from the front of the house, meaning, *Abigail's dad's car is here!*

"Gidday, mate!" Madeline heard Nathan say to Fred. Sometimes just the sound of Nathan's voice could evoke a wave of visceral memory: betrayal, resentment, rage and confusion. *He just left. He just walked out and left us, Abigail, and I couldn't believe it, I just could not believe it, and that night, you cried and cried, that endless new baby cry that—*

"Bye, Mum," said Abigail, and she leaned down to kiss her compassionately on the cheek, as if Madeline were an elderly aunt she'd been visiting and now, *phew*, it was time to get out of this musty place and go back home.

38.

Stu: I'll tell you something I do remember. I ran into Celeste White once. I was on the other side of Sydney doing a job and I had to go pick up some new taps because someone had stuffed up . . . anyhow, long story short, I'm walking through a Harvey Norman store where they had all the bedroom furniture on display, and there's Celeste White, lying flat on her back in the middle of a double bed, staring at the ceiling. I did a double take and then said, "Hello, love," and she jumped out of her skin. It was like I'd caught her robbing a bank. It just seemed strange. Why was she lying on a discount double bed so far from home? Gorgeous-looking woman, stunning, but always a bit . . . skittish, you know. Sad to think about it now. Very sad.

Are you the new tenant?"

Celeste jumped and nearly dropped the lamp she was carrying.

"Sorry, I didn't mean to startle you," said a plumpish, forty-ish woman in gym gear, emerging from the apartment across the corridor. She was accompanied by two little girls, who looked like they were twins about the same age as Josh and Max.

"I'm sort of the new tenant," said Celeste. "I mean, yes, I am. I'm not sure exactly when we're moving in. It might be a while."

This hadn't been part of the plan. Talking to people. That was much too real. This whole thing was *hypothetical*. It would probably never actually come to be. She was just toying with the idea of a new life. She was doing it to impress Susi. She wanted to go back to her next appointment with her "plan" all in place. Most women probably had to be nudged along for months. Most women probably came back to their next appointment having done nothing. Not Celeste. She always did her homework.

"I've taken a six-month lease on a flat," she planned to tell Susi, casually, briskly. "In McMahons Point. I could walk into North Sydney. I've got a friend who is a partner at a small law firm in North Sydney. She offered me a job about a year ago, and I turned it down, but I'm sure she could still find me something. Anyway, if that didn't work out, I could get a job in the city. It's just a short ferry ride."

"Wow," Susi would say. She'd raise her eyebrows. "Good job."

Top of the class for Celeste. What a good girl. What a well-behaved battered wife.

"I'm Rose," said the woman. "And this is Isabella and Daniella."

Was she serious? She called her children Isabella and Daniella?

The girls smiled politely at her. One of them even said, "Hello." Definitely twins with far better manners than Celeste's boys.

"I'm Celeste. Nice to meet you!" Celeste turned the key as fast as she could. "I'd better—"

"Do you have kids?" said Rose hopefully, and the little girls looked at her hopefully.

"Two boys," said Celeste. If she mentioned that she had twin boys, the amazing coincidence would create at least five more minutes of conversation she couldn't bear.

She pushed open the door with her shoulder.

"Let me know if you need anything!" said Rose.

"Thanks! See you soon." Celeste let the door go, and the two little girls begin to squabble over whose turn it was to push the button for the elevator. "Oh for God's sake, girls, must we do this every single time?" said their mother in what was obviously her normal voice, as opposed to the polite social voice she'd just used for Celeste.

As soon as the door closed there was complete silence, the mother's voice cut off midsentence. The acoustics were good.

There was a mirrored feature wall right next to the door that looked like it was left over from an ambitious decorating project in the seventies. The rest of the place was completely neutral: blank white walls, hard-wearing gray carpet. Your quintessential rental property. Perry owned rental properties that were probably just like this. Theoretically, Celeste owned them too, but she didn't even know where they were.

If they'd saved for an investment property together, just *one*, then she would have enjoyed that. She would have helped renovate it, picked out tiles, dealt with the real estate agent, said, "Oh yes, of course!" when the tenant asked for something to be fixed.

That was the level of wealth where she would have felt comfortable. The unimaginable depths of Perry's money sometimes made her feel nauseated. She saw it on the faces of people when they saw her house for the first time, the way their eyes traveled across the wide expanses, the soaring ceilings, the beautiful rooms set up like little museum displays of wealthy family life. Each time, she battled with equal parts pride and shame. She lived in a house where every single room silently screamed: *WE HAVE A LOT OF MONEY. PROBABLY MORE THAN YOU.*

Those beautiful rooms were just like Perry's constant Facebook posts: stylized representations of their life. Yes, they did sometimes sit on that gloriously comfortable-looking couch and put glasses of champagne on that coffee table and watch the sun set over the ocean. Yes, they did. And sometimes, often, it was glorious. But that was also the couch where Perry had once held her face squashed into the corner and she'd thought she might die. And that Facebook photo captioned *Fun day out with the kids* wasn't a lie because it *was* a fun day out with the kids, and anyway, they didn't have a photo of what happened after the kids were in bed that night. Celeste's nose bled too easily. It always had.

She carried the lamp into the main bedroom of the apartment. It was quite a small room. She'd get a double bed. She and Perry had a king-size bed, of course. But this room would be crammed even with a queen.

She placed the lamp on the floor. It was a colorful, mushroom-shaped art deco lamp. She'd bought it because she loved it and because it was a style Perry would hate; not that he would have stopped her having it if she really wanted it, but he would have winced every time he looked at it, the way she would have winced at some of the gloomy-looking modern art pieces he pointed out in galleries. So he didn't buy them.

Marriage was about compromise. "Honey, if you really like that girlie, antique look, I'll get you the real thing," he would have said tenderly. "This is just a cheap, tacky rip-off."

When he said things like that, she heard, *You're cheap and tacky.*

She would take her time setting up this place with cheap, tacky things that she liked. She went to open one of the blinds to let in some light. She ran her fingertip along the slightly dusty windowsill. The place was pretty clean, but next time she'd bring some cleaning stuff and get it spick-and-span.

Up until now, she had never been able to leave Perry because she couldn't imagine where she would go, how they would live. It was a mind-set. It seemed impossible. This way, she would have an entire life set up, awaiting activation. She would have beds made up for the boys. She would have the fridge stocked. She would have toys and clothes in the cupboard. She wouldn't even need to pack a bag. She would have an enrollment form filled out for the local school.

She would be ready.

The next time Perry hit her, she wouldn't hit him back, or cry, or lie on her bed. She would say, "I'm leaving right now."

She studied her knuckles.

Or she'd leave when he was out of the country. Maybe that would be better. She would tell him on the phone. "You must know we couldn't go on like this," she'd say. "When you come back we'll be gone."

It was impossible to imagine his reaction.

If she truly, actually left.

If she ended the relationship then the violence would stop too, because he would no longer have the right to hit her, just like he would no longer have the right to kiss her. Violence was a private part of their relationship, like sex. It would no longer be appropriate if she left him. She wouldn't belong to him in the same way. She'd get back his respect. Theirs would be an amicable relationship. He'd be a courteous but cold ex-husband. She knew already that the coldness would hurt her more than his fists ever had. He'd meet someone else. It would take him about five minutes.

She left the main bedroom and walked down the tiny corridor to the room that would be for the boys. There was just enough room for two single beds, side by side. She'd get them new quilt

covers. Make it look nice. She was breathing hard, trying to imagine their baffled little faces. Oh, God. Could she really do this to
them?

Susi thought that Perry would try to get sole custody of the
children, but she didn't know Perry. His anger flared like a blow-
torch and then died. (Unlike hers. Celeste was angrier than he
was. She held grudges. Perry didn't hold grudges, but Celeste
did. She was awful. She remembered it all. She remembered
every single time, every single word.) Susi had insisted that she
begin documenting the "abuse," as she called it. "Write everything down," she'd said. "Take photographs of your injuries. Keep
doctors' reports. It could be important in any court cases or custody hearings." "Sure," Celeste had said, but she had no intention
of doing so. How humiliating to see their behavior written down.
It would look like they were describing a children's fight. *I snapped
at him. He yelled at me. I yelled back. He pushed me. I hit him. I got a
bruise. He got a scratch.*

"He wouldn't try to take the children away from me," Celeste
had told Susi. "He'd do what was best for them."

"He might think it was best for the children to stay with him,"
Susi had told Celeste in her cool, matter-of-fact way. "Men like
your husband often do go for custody. They have the resources.
The money. The contacts. It's something you need to prepare for.
Your in-laws might get involved. Suddenly everyone will have an
opinion."

Her in-laws. Celeste felt a pulse of grief. She'd always loved
being part of Perry's big, extended family. She loved the fact that
there were so many of them: random aunties, hordes of cousins,
a trio of silver-haired, grumpy great-uncles. She loved the fact
that Perry didn't even need a list when he went duty-free shop-

ping for perfume. *Chanel Coco Mademoiselle for Auntie Anita, Issey Miyake for Auntie Evelyn,* he'd murmur to himself. She loved seeing Perry throw his arms around a favorite male cousin, tears in his eyes because they hadn't seen each other for so long. It seemed to prove something essentially good about her husband.

Right from day one, Perry's family had warmly welcomed Celeste, as if they sensed that her own small, self-effacing family didn't quite stack up next to theirs, and that they could give her something she'd never had, besides money. Perry and family offered abundance in everything.

When Celeste sat at the big, long table, eating Auntie Anita's spanakopita, watching Perry chat patiently with the grumpy great-uncles, while the twins ran wild with the other kids, a vision of Perry hitting her would flash in her head, and it would seem impossible, fantastical, absurd, even if it had happened the night before, and along with the disbelief would come shame, because she knew it must somehow be her fault, because this was a good, loving family and *she* was the outsider, and imagine how appalled they would be to see her hitting and scratching their beloved Perry.

No one in that big, laughing family would ever believe that Perry could be violent, and Celeste had no desire for them to know, because the Perry who bought perfumes for his aunties was not the Perry who lost his temper.

Susi didn't know Perry. She knew examples and case studies and statistics. She didn't know that Perry's temper was only one part of him, it wasn't all of him. He wasn't just a man who hit his wife. He was a man who read bedtime stories to his children and put on funny voices, who spoke kindly to waitresses. Perry wasn't a villain. He was a man who just sometimes behaved very badly.

Other women in this situation were afraid that their husbands would find them and kill them if they tried to leave, but Celeste was afraid she'd miss him. The pure pleasure of seeing the boys run to him when he returned from a trip, watching him drop his bags and get straight down on his knees, arms held wide. "I need to kiss Mummy now," he'd say.

This was not simple. This was just a very strange marriage.

She walked back through the apartment, ignoring the kitchen. It was small and poky. She didn't want to think about cooking in that kitchen. The boys whining: *I'm hungry! Me too!*

Instead she went back into the main bedroom and plugged the lamp into the electrical outlet. The electricity was still on. The colors of the lamp turned rich and vibrant. She sat back and admired it. She *loved* her funny-looking lamp.

After she moved in she would have Jane and Madeline over to visit. She would show them her lamp and they'd cram onto that tiny balcony and have afternoon tea.

If she left Pirriwee, she'd miss her morning walks around the headland with Jane. For the most part they'd walked in silence. It was like a shared meditation. If Madeline had walked with them, they would have all three talked the whole time, but it was a different dynamic when it was just Jane and Celeste.

Recently, they'd both began to tentatively open up. It was interesting how you could say things when you were walking that you might not otherwise have said with the pressure of eye contact across a table. Celeste thought of the morning when Jane had told her about Ziggy's biological father, the repulsive man who had more or less raped her. She shuddered.

At least sex with Perry had never been violent, even when it followed violence, even when it was part of their strange, intense game of making up, of forgiving and forgetting. It was always about love, and it was always very, very good. Before she met Perry, she had never felt as powerful an attraction to a man, and she knew she never would again. It wasn't possible. It was too specific to them.

She would miss sex. She would miss living near the beach. She would miss coffee with Madeline. She would miss staying up late and watching DVD series with Perry. She would miss Perry's family.

When you divorce someone, you divorce their whole family, Madeline had told her once. Madeline had been close to Nathan's older sister, but now they rarely saw each other. Celeste would have to give up Perry's family as well as everything else.

There was too much to miss, too much to sacrifice.

Well. This was just an exercise.

She didn't have to go through with any of it. It was all just a theoretical exercise to impress her counselor, who probably wouldn't be all that impressed, because in the end this was really just about money. Celeste wasn't showing any particular courage. She could afford to rent and furnish an apartment that she would probably never use, using money that her husband had earned. Most of Susi's clients probably had no access to money, whereas Celeste could withdraw large chunks of cash from different accounts without Perry even noticing, or if he did, she could easily make up an excuse. She could tell him a friend needed cash and he wouldn't blink. He'd offer to give more. He wasn't like those other men who kept their wives virtually imprisoned by restricting their movements, their access to money. Celeste was as free as a bird.

She looked around the room. No built-in wardrobe. She'd

have to buy a closet. How had she missed that at the inspection? The first time Madeline had seen Celeste's enormous walk-in wardrobe, her eyes had gotten shiny, as if she'd heard a piece of beautiful music or poetry. "This, right here, is my dream come true."

Celeste's life was another person's dream come true.

"No one deserves to live like this," Susi had said, but Susi hadn't seen the whole of their lives. She hadn't seen the expression on the boys' faces when Perry spun his crazy stories about early-morning flights across the ocean. "You can't really fly, Daddy. Can he fly, Mummy? Can he?" She hadn't seen Perry rap-dancing with his kids or slow-dancing with Celeste on their balcony, the moon sitting low in the sky, shining on the sea as if it were there just for them.

"It's almost worth it," she'd told Susi.

Perhaps it was even *fair*. A little violence was a bargain price for a life that would otherwise be just too sickeningly, lavishly, moonlit perfect.

So then what the hell was she doing here, secretly planning her escape route like a prisoner?

39.

Ziggy," said Jane.

They were on the beach, building a sand castle out of cold sand. The late afternoon sky hung low and heavy, and the wind whistled. It was mid-autumn, so tomorrow could easily be beautiful and sunny again, but today the beach was virtually deserted. Far in the distance, Jane could see someone walking a dog, and one lone surfer in a full-body wet suit was walking toward the water, his board under his arm. The ocean was angry, chucking wave after wave—boom!—on the beach. White water churned and bubbled as if it were boiling and spat up crazy fountains of spray into the air.

Ziggy hummed as he worked on the sand castle, patting it with a spade Jane's mother had bought him.

"I saw Mrs. Lipmann yesterday," she said. "And Amabella's mummy."

Ziggy looked up. He was wearing a gray beanie pulled down over his ears and covering his hair. His cheeks were flushed with the cold.

"Amabella says that someone in her class has been secretly hurting her when the teacher isn't looking," said Jane. "Pinching her. Even . . . biting her."

God. It was too awful to contemplate. No wonder Renata was out for blood.

Ziggy didn't say anything. He put down the spade and picked up a plastic rake.

"Amabella's mummy thinks it's you," said Jane.

She nearly said, *It's not you, is it?* but she stopped herself.

Instead she said, "Is it you, Ziggy?"

He ignored her. He kept his eyes on the sand, carefully raking straight lines.

"*Ziggy,*" said Jane.

He put down the rake and looked at her. His smooth little face was remote. His eyes looked off somewhere behind her head.

"I don't want to talk about it," he said.

40.

Samantha: Have you heard about the petition? That's when I knew things were getting out of hand.

Harper: I'm not ashamed to say that I started the petition. For heaven's sake, the school was doing nothing! Poor Renata was at her wit's end. You need to be able to send your child to school and know that she's in a safe environment.

Mrs. Lipmann: I most emphatically disagree. The school was not "doing nothing." We had an extremely comprehensive plan of action. And let me be clear: We actually had no evidence that Ziggy was the one doing the bullying.

Thea: I signed it. That poor little girl.

Jonathan: Of course I didn't sign it. That poor little boy.

Gabrielle: Don't tell anyone, but I think I *accidentally* signed it. I thought it was the petition about getting the council to put in a pedestrian crossing on Park Street.

One Week Before the Trivia Night

Welcome to the inaugural meeting of the Pirriwee Peninsula Erotic Book Club!" said Madeline as she opened her front door with a flourish. She'd already treated herself to half a glass of champagne.

As she'd been preparing for tonight she'd berated herself for starting a book club. It was just a distraction from her grief over Abigail moving out. Was *grief* too dramatic a word? Probably. But that's how it felt. It felt like she'd suffered a loss, but no one was bringing her flowers, so she'd busied herself with a book club, of all things. (Why didn't she just go shopping?) She'd ostentatiously invited *all* the kindergarten parents, and ten parents had said yes. Then she'd chosen a juicy, rollicking book she knew she'd enjoy, and given everyone heaps of time to read it, before realizing that *everyone* would have a turn choosing a book, and so she'd probably end up having to wade through some awful, worthy tomes. Oh well. She had plenty of experience not doing her homework. She'd wing it on those nights. Or she'd cheat and ask Celeste for a summary.

"Stop calling it the Erotic Book Club," said her first guest, Samantha, as she handed over a plate of brownies. "People are starting to talk. Carol is obsessed."

Samantha was small and wiry, a pocket-size version of an athlete. She ran marathons, but Madeline forgave her for this flaw because Samantha seemed to say exactly what she thought and she was also one of those people who were completely at the mercy of her own sense of humor. She could frequently be seen around the playground, clutching somebody's arm to help her stay upright while she laughed helplessly.

Madeline was also fond of Samantha because during the first week of school Chloe had fallen passionately in love with Samantha's daughter, Lily (a fellow feisty princess). Madeline's fear that Chloe would befriend Skye had therefore proven unfounded. Thank God. With Abigail's desertion, it would have been just too much to bear right now if Madeline had to then have her ex-husband's kid over for playdates.

"Am I the first to arrive?" asked Samantha. "I left home early because I was desperate to get away from my children. I said to Stu, 'I'll leave you to it, mate.'"

"You are." Madeline led her into the living room. "Come and have a drink."

"Jane is coming, right?" said Samantha.

"Yes, why?" Madeline stopped.

"I just wondered if she knew about this petition that's circulating."

"What petition?" Madeline's teeth began to grind. Jane had told her about the new accusations being made against Ziggy.

Apparently Amabella refused to confirm or deny that it was Ziggy who had been hurting her, and according to Jane, Ziggy behaved oddly when she confronted him about it. Jane didn't know if that was evidence of his guilt or something else. Yesterday she'd been to the doctor to get a referral to a psychologist, which was probably going to cost her the earth. "I just need to be sure," she'd told Madeline. "You know, because of his . . . because of his background."

Madeline had wondered if those three girls, Ziggy's half sisters, were bullies. Then she'd blushed, ashamed of her ill-begotten knowledge.

"It's a petition to have Ziggy suspended from the school," said Samantha with an apologetic grimace, as if she'd stepped on Madeline's toe.

"*What?* That's ridiculous! Renata can't possibly think people would be so small-minded as to sign it!"

"It wasn't Renata. I think it was Harper who started it," said Samantha. "I think they're quite good friends, right? I'm still getting my head around all the politics of the place."

"Harper is very good friends with Renata, as she's quite keen to let you know," said Madeline. "They bonded over their gifted children." She picked up her champagne glass and drained it.

"I mean, Amabella seems like a lovely little girl," said Samantha. "I hate to think of her being secretly bullied, but a *petition*? To get rid of a five-year-old? It's outrageous." She shook her head. "I suppose I don't know what I'd do if it were Lily in the same situation, but Ziggy seems so adorable with those big green eyes, and Lily says he's always nice to her. He helped her find her favorite marble or something. Are you going to give me a drink?"

"Sorry," said Madeline. She poured Samantha a drink. "That explains the strange phone call I just got from Thea. She said she was pulling out of the book club. It seemed a bit odd, because she'd been going on about how she wanted to join a book club, how she needed to 'do something for herself.' She was even making some nudge-nudge-wink-wink comments about the raunchy sex scenes in the book, which was, you know, unsettling. But then just ten minutes ago, she called and said she had 'too many commitments.'"

"She has four children, you know," said Samantha.

"Oh, yes, it's a logistical nightmare," said Madeline.

They laughed wickedly together.

"I'm thirsting to death!" called out Fred from his bedroom.

"Daddy will bring you a glass of water!" called back Madeline.

Samantha stopped laughing. "You know what Lily said to me today? She said, 'Am I allowed to play with Ziggy?' and I said, 'Of course you are,' and she said—" Samantha stopped. Her voice changed. "Hello, Chloe."

Chloe stood at the door, clutching her teddy bear.

"I thought you were asleep," said Madeline sternly, even as her heart melted as it always did at the sight of her children in their pajamas. Ed was meant to be on kid duty while she hosted book club. He'd read the book, but he didn't want to join the club. He said the idea of book clubs brought back horrible memories of pretentious classmates in English Lit. "If anyone uses the words 'marvelous imagery' or 'narrative arc,' slap them for me," he'd told her.

"I was, but Daddy's snoring woke me up," said Chloe.

Due to the recent monster infestation of her room, Chloe had developed a new habit where Mummy or Daddy had to lie down with her "just for a few minutes" before she fell asleep. The only problem was that Madeline or Ed inevitably fell asleep too, emerging from Chloe's room an hour or so later, dazed and blinking.

"Lily's daddy snores too," said Samantha to Chloe. "It sounds like a train pulling in."

"Were you talking about Ziggy?" said Chloe chattily to Samantha. "He was crying today because Oliver's dad said he had to stay far, far away from Ziggy because Ziggy is a bully."

"Oh for God's sake," said Madeline. "Oliver's daddy is a bully. You should see him at the PTA meetings."

"So I punched Oliver," said Chloe.

"What?" said Madeline.

"Just a little bit," said Chloe. She gazed angelically up at them and hugged her teddy. "It didn't hurt him that much."

The doorbell rang at the same time as Fred called out, "Just letting you know, I'm *still* waiting for my glass of water!" and Samantha grabbed hold of Madeline's arm as she swayed with helpless laughter.

41.

Jane found out about the petition ten minutes before she was due to leave for Madeline's first book club meeting. She was in the bathroom cleaning her teeth when her mobile rang and Ziggy answered it.

"I'll get her," she heard him say. There was a patter of footsteps and he appeared in the bathroom. "It's my *teacher*!" he said in an awestruck voice, shoving the phone at her.

"Just a sec," mumbled Jane, because her mouth was full of toothpaste and water. She held her toothbrush aloft, but Ziggy just pushed the phone into her hand and stepped back fast. "Ziggy!" She fumbled with the phone, nearly dropped it, and then held it up high as she gargled, spat, and wiped her mouth. What *now*? Ziggy had been quiet and introspective this afternoon after school, but he'd said that Amabella wasn't even at school today, so it couldn't be that. Oh God. Had he done something to somebody else?

"Hi, Miss Barnes. Rebecca," she said to Miss Barnes. She liked Rebecca Barnes. She knew they were around the same age (there had been much excitement among the kids about the fact that Miss Barnes was turning twenty-four), and even though they weren't exactly friends, she sometimes sensed an unspoken solidarity between the two of them, the natural affinity between two people of the same generation when surrounded by people who were older or younger.

"Hi, Jane," said Miss Barnes. "I'm sorry, I tried to pick a time when I thought Ziggy would be in bed, but before it got too late—"

"Oh, well, he's just about to go to bed, actually." Jane made shoo-shoo motions at Ziggy. He looked aghast and ran off to his bedroom, probably worried that he was about to get into trouble with his teacher for being up late. (When it came to school, Ziggy was such a little rule-follower, always so anxious to please Miss Barnes. That's why it was so impossible to conceive of him behaving so badly if there was even the slightest danger of being caught. Jane kept coming smack up against these walls of impossibility. Ziggy was just not the sort of kid who did things like this.)

"What's up?" said Jane.

"Do you want me to call back later?" asked Miss Barnes.

"No, it's OK. He's gone off to his room. Has something happened?" She heard the sharpness in her voice. She'd made an appointment to see a psychologist for the following week. It was a cancellation, she was lucky to get it. She'd told Ziggy over and over that he must not lay a finger on Amabella, or any of the other kids, but he just said in a monotone, "I know that, Mummy. I don't hurt anyone, Mummy," and then always, after a few moments, "I don't want to talk about it." What else could she do? Punish him for something she had no conclusive proof that he'd actually done?

"I just wondered if you knew about this petition that's circulating," said Miss Barnes. "I wanted you to hear about it from me."

"A petition?" said Jane.

"A petition calling for Ziggy's suspension," said Miss Barnes.

"I'm so sorry. I don't know which parents are behind it, but I just wanted you to know that I'm furious about it, and I know Mrs. Lipmann will be furious too, and it will obviously have no bearing on, well, on anything."

"You mean people are actually signing it?" said Jane. She grabbed the top of a chair and watched her knuckles turn white. "But we don't even know for sure——"

"I *know*," said Miss Barnes. "I know we don't! From what I've seen, Amabella and Ziggy are friends! So I'm completely baffled. I watch them like a hawk, I really do. Well, I try, but I've got twenty-eight kids, two with ADHD, one with learning difficulties, two gifted kids, at least four whose parents think they're gifted, and one who is so allergic I feel like I should have one hand on the EpiPen at all times and——" Miss Barnes's voice had become rapid and high-pitched, but she suddenly stopped midsentence and cleared her throat before lowering her voice. "Sorry, Jane, I should not be talking like this to you. It's unprofessional. I'm just really upset on your behalf—and on Ziggy's behalf."

"That's OK," said Jane. It was somehow comforting to hear the stress in her voice.

"I have a real soft spot for Ziggy," said Miss Barnes. "And, I have to say, I have a soft spot for Amabella too. They're both lovely kids. I mean, I feel like I have pretty good instincts when it comes to kids, so that's why this whole thing is just so strange, so odd."

"Yes," said Jane. "I don't know what to do."

"We'll handle it," said Miss Barnes. "I promise you we'll handle it."

It was perfectly obvious she didn't know what to do either.

After she hung up, Jane went into Ziggy's bedroom.

He was sitting cross-legged on his bed, his back up against the wall, tears sliding down his face.

"Is *nobody* allowed to play with me now?" he said.

Thea: You've probably heard that Jane was drunk at the trivia night. It's just not appropriate at a school event. Look, I know it must have been very upsetting when all that business was going on with Ziggy, but I kept asking myself, *Why doesn't she just pull him out of the school?* It's not like she had family ties in the area. She should just have moved back to the western suburbs where she grew up and probably would have, you know, fit in.

Gabrielle: We were "delightfully tipsy." I remember Madeline saying that. "I feel delightfully tipsy." Typical Madeline. Poor Madeline . . . Anyway. It was those cocktails. They must have had about a thousand calories in them.

Samantha: *Everyone* was drunk. It was actually a great night until it all went to shit.

42.

"Where is Perry this time?" asked Gwen as she settled down on Celeste's couch with her knitting.

Gwen had been babysitting for the boys since they were babies. She was a grandmother of twelve, with an enviably firm manner and a little stash of gold-wrapped chocolate coins in her handbag, which wouldn't be necessary tonight, as the boys were already sound asleep.

"Geneva," said Celeste. "Or, wait, is it Genova? I can't remember. He'll still be in the air right now. He left this morning."

Gwen studied her in a fascinated sort of way. "He leads an exotic life, doesn't he?"

"Yes," said Celeste. "I guess he does. I shouldn't be very late. It's a new book club, so I'm not sure—"

"Depends on the book!" said Gwen. "My book club just did the most interesting book. Now, what was it called? It was about . . . Now, what was it about? Nobody really liked it all that much, to be honest, but my friend Pip, she likes to serve a dish that sort of complements the book, so she made this marvelous fish curry, although it was quite spicy, so we were all a little, you know, *Pip!*" Gwen waved both hands in front of her mouth to indicate spiciness.

The only problem with Gwen was that it was sometimes hard

to get away. Perry could do it charmingly, but Celeste found it awkward.

"Well, I'd better be off." Celeste leaned down to pick up her phone, which was on the coffee table in front of Gwen.

"That's a nasty bruise!" said Gwen. "What have you done to yourself?"

Celeste pulled the sleeve of her silk shirt farther down her wrist.

"Tennis injury," she said. "My doubles partner and I both went for the same shot."

"Ow!" said Gwen. She looked up at Celeste steadily. There was silence for a moment.

"Well," said Celeste. "As I said, the boys shouldn't wake—"

"It might be time to find another tennis partner," said Gwen. There was a no-nonsense edge to her voice. The one Celeste had heard her use to astonishing effect when the boys were fighting.

"Well. It was my fault too," said Celeste.

"I bet it wasn't." Gwen held Celeste's eyes. It occurred to Celeste that in all the years she'd known Gwen, there had never been mention of a husband. Gwen seemed so completely self-contained, so chatty and busy, with all her talk of her friends and grandchildren; the idea of a husband seemed superfluous.

"I'd better go," said Celeste.

43.

Ziggy was still crying when the babysitter knocked on the door. He'd told Jane that three or four kids (she couldn't get the facts straight, he was almost incoherent) had said that they weren't allowed to play with him.

He sobbed into Jane's thigh and stomach, where his face was uncomfortably wedged, after she'd sat down on the bed next to him and he'd suddenly launched himself at her, nearly knocking her flat on her back. She could feel the hard pressure of his little nose and the wetness of his tears spreading over her jeans as he pushed his face against her leg in a painful corkscrewing motion, as if he could somehow bury himself in her.

"That must be Chelsea." Jane pulled at Ziggy's skinny shoulders, trying to dislodge him, but Ziggy didn't even pause for breath.

"They were running away from me," he sobbed. "Really fast! And I felt like playing *Star Wars*!"

Right, thought Jane. She wasn't going to book club. She couldn't possibly leave him in a state like this. Besides, what if there were parents there who had signed the petition? Or who had told their children to stay away from Ziggy?

"Just wait here." She grunted as she unpeeled his limp, heavy body from her legs. He looked at her with a red, snotty, wet face and then threw himself facedown on his pillow.

"I'm sorry. I have to cancel," Jane told Chelsea. "But I'll pay you anyway."

She didn't have anything smaller than a fifty-dollar note. "Oh, ah, *cool*, thanks," said Chelsea. Teenagers never offered change.

Jane closed the door and went to phone Madeline.

"I'm not coming," she told her. "Ziggy is . . . Ziggy isn't well."

"It's this thing going on with Amabella, isn't it?" said Madeline. Jane could hear voices in the background. Some of the other parents were there.

"Yes. You've heard about the petition?" she asked Madeline, trying to keep her voice steady. Madeline must be sick of her: crying over Harry the Hippo, sharing her sordid little sex stories. She probably rued the day that she'd hurt her ankle.

"It's *outrageous*," said Madeline. "I am *incandescent* with rage."

There was a burst of laughter in the background. It sounded like a cocktail party, not a book club. The sound of their laughter made Jane feel stodgy and left out, even though she'd been invited.

"I'd better let you go," said Jane. "Have fun."

"I'll call you," said Madeline. "Don't worry. We'll fix this."

As Jane hung up, there was another knock on the door. It was the woman from downstairs, Chelsea's mother, Irene, holding out the fifty-dollar note. She was a tall, austere woman with short gray hair and intelligent eyes.

"You're not paying her fifty dollars for doing nothing," she said.

Jane took the money gratefully. She'd felt a twinge after she'd given it to Chelsea. Fifty dollars was fifty dollars. "I thought, you know, the inconvenience."

"She's fifteen. She had to walk up a flight of stairs. Is Ziggy OK?"

"We're having some trouble at school," said Jane.

"Oh dear," said Irene.

"Bullying," expounded Jane. She didn't really know Irene all that well, except for their chats in the stairwell.

"Someone is bullying poor little Ziggy?" Irene frowned.

"They say that Ziggy is doing the bullying."

"Oh rubbish," said Irene. "Don't believe it. I taught primary school for twenty-four years. I can pick a bully a mile off. Ziggy is no bully."

"Well, I hope not," said Jane. "I mean, I didn't think so."

"I bet it's the parents making the biggest fuss, isn't it?" Irene gave her a shrewd look. "Parents take far too much *notice* of their children these days. Bring back the good old days of benign indifference, I reckon. If I were you, I'd take all this with a grain of salt. Little kids, little problems. Wait till you've got drugs and sex and social media to worry about."

Jane smiled politely and held up the fifty-dollar note. "Well, thanks. Tell Chelsea I'll book her up for babysitting another night."

She closed the door firmly, mildly aggravated by the "little kids, little problems" comment. As she walked down the hallway she could hear Ziggy still crying: not the angry, demanding cry of a child who wants attention, or the startled cry of a child who has hurt himself. This was a grown-up type of crying: involuntary, soft, sad weeping.

Jane walked into his bedroom and stood for a moment in the doorway, watching him lying facedown on the bed, his shoulders shaking and his little hands clutching at the fabric of his *Star Wars* quilt. She felt something hard and powerful within her. Right this moment she didn't care if Ziggy had hurt Amabella or not, or if he'd inherited some evil secret tendency for violence from his biological father, and anyway, who said the tendency for violence came from his father, because if Renata were standing in front of her right now, Jane would hit her. She would hit her with pleasure. She would hit her so hard that her expensive-looking glasses would fly off her face. Maybe she'd even crush those glasses beneath her heel like the quintessential bully. And if that made her a helicopter parent, then who the fuck cares?

"Ziggy?" She sat down on the bed next to him and rubbed his back.

He lifted his tear-stained face.

"Let's go visit Grandma and Grandpa. We'll take our pajamas and stay the night there."

He sniffed. A little shudder of grief ran through his body.

"And let's eat chips and chocolates and treats all the way there."

Samantha: I know I've been laughing and making jokes and whatever, so you probably think I'm a heartless bitch, but it's like a defense mechanism or something. I mean, this is a tragedy. The funeral was just . . . When that darling little boy put the letter on the coffin? I can't even. I just lost it. We all lost it.

Thea: Very distressing. It reminded me of Princess Diana's funeral, when little Prince Harry left the note saying "Mummy." Not that we're talking about the royal family here, obviously.

44.

It didn't take Celeste long to realize that this was going to be the sort of book club where the book was secondary to the proceedings. She felt a mild disappointment. She'd been looking forward to talking *about* the book. She'd even, embarrassingly, *prepared* for book club, like a good little lawyer, marking up a few pages with Post-it notes and writing a few pithy comments in the margins.

She slid her book off her lap and slipped it into her bag before anyone noticed and started teasing her about it. The teasing would be fond and good-humored, but she no longer had the resilience for teasing. Marriage to Perry meant she was always ready to justify her actions, constantly monitoring what she'd just said or done, while simultaneously feeling defensive about the defensiveness, her thoughts and feelings twisting into impenetrable knots, so that sometimes, like right now, sitting in a room with normal people, all the things she couldn't say rose in her throat and for a moment she couldn't breathe.

What would these people think if they knew there was someone like her sitting across from them, passing them the sushi? These were polite, nonsmoking people who joined book clubs and renovated and spoke nicely. Husbands and wives didn't hit each other in these sorts of congenial little social circles.

The reason no one was talking about the book was because everyone was talking about the petition to have Ziggy suspended. Some people hadn't heard about it yet, and the people who did know had the enjoyable task of passing on the shocking development. Everyone contributed what information they had been able to offer.

Celeste made agreeable murmurs as the conversation flew, presided over by a flushed, animated, almost feverish Madeline.

"Apparently Amabella hasn't actually said that it is Ziggy. Renata is just assuming it is because of what happened on orientation day."

"I heard there were bite marks, which *is* pretty horrifying at this age."

"There was a biter at Lily's day care. She'd come home black-and-blue. I must admit I wanted to murder the little brat who did it, but her mother was so nice. She was in a state over it."

"That's the thing. It's actually worse if your child is the one doing the bullying."

"I mean, we're talking about children here!"

"My question is, why aren't the teachers seeing this?"

"Can't Renata just *make* Amabella say who is responsible? She's five years old!"

"I guess when you're talking about a gifted child—"

"Oh, I didn't know, is Ziggy gifted?"

"Not Ziggy. Annabella. She's definitely gifted."

"It's Amabella, not Annabella."

"Is that one of those made-up names?"

"Oh, no, no. It's French! Haven't you heard Renata talk about it?"

"Well, that kid has a lifetime ahead of her of people getting her name wrong."

"Harrison plays with Ziggy every day. He's never had any problems."

"A petition! It's just ridiculous. It's petty. This quiche is great, by the way, Madeline, did you make it?"

"I heated it up."

"Well, it's like when Renata handed out those invitations to everyone in the class except Ziggy. I thought that was unconscionable."

"I mean, can a public school expel a child? Is it even possible? Don't the public schools have to take everyone?"

"My husband thinks we've all gone too soft. He says we're too ready to label kids bullies these days when they're just being kids."

"He might have a point."

"Although biting and choking—"

"Mmmm. If it were my child—"

"You wouldn't do a *petition*."

"Well, no."

"Renata has pots of money. Why doesn't she send Amabella off to private school? Then she won't have to deal with the riffraff."

"I like Ziggy. I like Jane too. It can't be easy doing everything on her own."

"*Is* there a father, does anyone know?"

"Should we talk about the book?" This was Madeline, finally remembering she was hosting a book club.

"I guess we should."

"Who has actually signed this petition so far?"

"I don't know. I bet Harper has signed it."

"Harper *started* the petition."

"Doesn't Renata work with Harper's husband or something? Or wait, am I mixed up, is it your husband, Celeste?"

All eyes were suddenly upon Celeste, as if they'd been given an invisible signal. She gripped the stem of her wineglass.

"Renata and Perry are in the same industry," said Celeste. "They just know of each other."

"We haven't met Perry yet, have we?" said Samantha. "He's a man of mystery."

"He travels a lot," said Celeste. "He's in Genova at the moment."

No, it was Geneva. Definitely Geneva.

There was still a strange lull in the conversation. An expectant air. Had she spoken oddly?

She felt as if everyone was waiting for more from her.

"You'll meet him at that trivia night," she said. Perry, unlike many men, *loved* costume parties. He'd been keen when she'd checked his schedule and saw that he'd be home for it.

"You'll need a pearl necklace like Audrey wears in *Breakfast at Tiffany's*," he'd told her. "I'll get you one from Swiss Pearls in Geneva."

"No," she said. "Please don't."

You were meant to wear cheap costume jewelry when you went to a costume party school trivia night, not a necklace worth more than the money they needed to raise for SMART Boards.

He'd buy her exactly the right necklace. He loved jewelry. It would cost as much as a car, and it would be exquisite, and when Madeline saw it she'd be delirious and Celeste would long to unclasp it from her neck and hand it over. "Buy one for Madeline too," she had wanted to say, and he would have if she had asked, with pleasure, but of course Madeline would never accept such a gift. Yet it seemed ridiculous that she couldn't hand over something that would give Madeline such genuine happiness.

"Is everyone going to the trivia night?" she said brightly. "It sounds like fun!"

Samantha: Have you seen photos from the trivia night? Celeste looked *breathtaking*. People were staring. Apparently that pearl necklace was the real McCoy. But you know what? I was looking at some of the photos and there's something sad about her face, a look in her eyes, as if she'd seen a ghost. It's almost like she knew something terrible was going to happen that night.

45.

That was fun. Maybe next time we'll actually remember to talk about the book," said Madeline.

Celeste was the last one there and was efficiently scraping plates and putting them into Madeline's dishwasher.

"Stop that!" said Madeline. "You always do that!"

Celeste had a talent for the silent, unobtrusive tidy-up. Any time Madeline had Celeste over, her kitchen would be left pristine, bench tops gleaming.

"Sit down and have a cup of tea with me before you go," she told Celeste. "Look, I've got some of Jane's latest lot of muffins. I was too selfish to share them with the book club."

Celeste's eyes brightened. She went to sit down, but then she awkwardly half stood and said, "Where's Ed? He might want the house back to himself."

"What? Don't worry about *Ed*. He's still snoring away in Chloe's bed," said Madeline. "Anyway, who cares? It's my house too."

Celeste smiled weakly and sat down. "It's awful about poor Jane," she said as Madeline put one of Jane's muffins in front of her.

"At least we know that nobody here tonight will be signing that stupid petition," said Madeline. "When everyone was talking

I just kept thinking about what Jane went through. She told you the story about Ziggy's father, didn't she?"

It was a formality; Jane had told her that she'd told Celeste as well. She wondered for a guilty moment if it was gossipy to mention it, but it was OK, because it was Celeste. Her appetite for gossip was healthy; she wasn't one of those mothers always ravenously searching it out.

"Yes," said Celeste. She bit into the muffin. "Creep."

"I Googled him," confessed Madeline. This was really why she'd brought it up. She felt guilty about it and she wanted the release of confession. Or she wanted to burden Celeste with the same knowledge, which was probably worse.

"Who?" said Celeste.

"The father. Ziggy's father. I know I shouldn't have."

"But how?" Celeste frowned. "Did she tell you his name? I don't think she even mentioned it to me."

"She said his name was Saxon Banks," said Madeline. "You know, like Mr. Banks in *Mary Poppins*. Jane said he sang a *Mary Poppins* song to her. That's why his name stuck in my head. Are you OK? Did it go down the wrong way?"

Celeste banged her chest with her fist and coughed. Her color was high.

"I'll get you some water," said Madeline.

"Did you say Saxon Banks?" asked Celeste hoarsely. She cleared her throat and said it again, slower. "Saxon Banks?"

"Yes," said Madeline. "Why?" Understanding hit her. "Oh my God. You don't know him, do you?"

"Perry has a cousin called Saxon Banks," said Celeste. "He's a . . ." She paused. Her eyes widened. "A *property developer*. Jane said that man was a property developer."

"It's an unusual name," said Madeline. She was trying not to sound breathlessly thrilled by this horrible coincidence. Of course, it was not exciting that Perry was related to Saxon Banks. This was not an "it's such a small world!" coincidence. This was awful. But there was an irresistible breathless pleasure in it and, like the awful petition, it was a welcome distraction from her increasingly embittered, almost crazed feelings about Abigail.

"He has three daughters," said Celeste. She looked off into the distance as she collected her thoughts.

"I know," said Madeline guiltily. "Ziggy's half sisters." She went to get her iPad from the kitchen bench and brought it back to the table.

"And he's devoted to his wife," said Celeste as Madeline pulled up the page again. "He's lovely! Warm, funny. I can't even imagine him being unfaithful. Let alone being so . . . cruel."

Madeline pushed the iPad over to Celeste. "Is that him?"

Celeste looked at the picture. "Yes." She put a thumb and finger on the screen and enlarged the picture. "I'm probably just imagining it, but I think I can see a resemblance to Ziggy."

"Around the eyes?" said Madeline. "I know. I thought so too."

There was silence. Celeste stared at the iPad screen. Her fingers drummed on the table. "I *like* him!" She looked up at Madeline. There was an expression of shame on her face, as though she were feeling somehow responsible. "I've always really liked him."

"Jane did say he was charming," said Madeline.

"Yes, but . . ." Celeste sat back and pushed the iPad away from her. "I don't know what to do. I mean, do I have a responsibility now? To, I don't know, to *do* something about this? It's so . . . tricky. If he'd actually raped her, I'd want him charged, but—"

"He sort of raped her," said Madeline. "It was like a rape. Or an assault. I don't know. It was something."

"Yes but—"

"I know," said Madeline. "I know. You can't send someone to jail for being vile."

"We don't know for sure," said Celeste after a moment, her eyes on the photo. "She might have misheard his name, or—"

"There might be another Saxon Banks," said Madeline. "Who doesn't show up on Google. Not *everyone* shows up on the Internet."

"Exactly," said Celeste with too much enthusiasm. They both knew it was probably him. He ticked all the boxes. What were the chances of there being two men of around the same age named Saxon Banks in property development?

"Is Perry close to him?" asked Madeline.

"We don't see him so much now we've all got children, and he lives interstate," said Celeste. "But when Perry and Saxon were growing up they were very close. Their mothers are identical twins."

"That's where your twins come from, then," said Madeline.

"Well we always assumed that," said Celeste vaguely. "But then I found out that's only for fraternal twins, not identical twins, so my boys were just a random . . ." Her voice lapsed. "Oh, God. What happens when I see Saxon next? There was some talk of there being a big family reunion in Western Australia next year. And should I tell Perry? Is there any point in telling Perry? It would just upset him, right? And there's nothing we can do about it, is there? There really is nothing we can do."

"If it were me," said Madeline, "I'd tell myself that I'd keep it a secret from Ed, and then I'd probably just blurt it out."

"It might make him angry," said Celeste. She gave Madeline a strangely furtive, almost childish look.

"With his bastard cousin? I should think so."

"I meant with me." Celeste pulled on the cuff of her shirt.

"With you? You mean he might feel defensive on his cousin's behalf?" said Madeline. She thought, *So what? Let him be defensive.* "I guess he might be," she added.

"And it would be . . . very awkward," said Celeste. "Like when Perry meets Jane at school events, knowing what he'd know."

"Yes, so maybe you do have to keep it a secret from him, Celeste," said Madeline solemnly, knowing as she spoke that if it were Ed she'd be yelling at him the moment he walked in the front door. *Do you know what your terrible cousin did to my friend!*

"And keep it a secret from Jane?" winced Celeste.

"Absolutely," said Madeline. "I think." She chewed the inside of her mouth. "Don't you think so?"

Jane would be hurt and angry if she were ever to find out, but how would it benefit her to know? It wasn't like she wanted Ziggy to have some sort of relationship with this man.

"Yes, I think so," said Celeste. "Anyway, the fact is, we don't know for *sure* that it's him."

"We don't," agreed Madeline. It was obviously important to Celeste that this point was reiterated. It was their defense, their excuse.

"I'm terrible at keeping secrets," confessed Madeline.

"Really?" Celeste gave her a twisted sort of grimace. "I'm quite good at it."

46.

Celeste drove home from book club thinking about the last time she'd seen Saxon and his wife, Eleni. It was at a wedding in Adelaide just before she got pregnant with the boys, a huge wedding for one of Perry's multitude of cousins.

By chance, she and Perry had pulled up in the reception center parking lot right next to them. They hadn't seen one another at the church, and Perry and Saxon had jumped straight from their cars to give each other bear hugs and manly slaps on the back. Both Perry and Saxon were teary. There was real affection between the two of them. Celeste and Eleni were both shivering in sleeveless cocktail dresses, and they were all looking forward to a drink after sitting through the long wedding ceremony in a cold, damp church.

"The food is meant to be excellent here," Saxon had said, rubbing his hands together, and they'd all been walking up the path into the warmth when Eleni stopped. She'd left her phone sitting on a pew in the church. It was a one-hour return trip.

"You stay. I'll go," said Eleni, but Saxon just rolled his eyes and said, "No you won't, my love."

Perry and Saxon had ended up driving back together to get the phone, while Celeste and Eleni went inside and enjoyed champagne in front of a roaring fire. "Oh dear, I feel just terrible,"

Eleni had said cheerfully as she beckoned over a waiter to refill her glass.

No you won't, my love.

How could a man who reacted with such rueful, chivalrous good humor to a really annoying inconvenience be the same person who treated a nineteen-year-old girl with such cruelty?

But she should know better than anyone that of course that was possible. Perry would have gone back to get the phone for her too.

Did the two men share some sort of genetic mental disorder? Mental illnesses ran in families, and Perry and Saxon were the sons of identical twins. Genetically speaking they weren't just cousins, they were half brothers.

Or had their mothers somehow broken them? Jean and Eileen were sweet elfin women with identical babyish voices, tinkly laughs and good cheekbones; the sort of women who seemed so femininely submissive and were anything but. The sort of women who attracted the sort of successful men who spent their days telling people what to do, and then went home and did exactly as they were told by their wives.

Perhaps that was the problem. Celeste and Eleni lacked that peculiar combination of sweetness and power. They were just ordinary girls. They couldn't live up to the maternal role models established by Jean and Eileen for their sons.

And so Saxon and Perry both had developed these unfortunate . . . glitches.

But what Saxon had done to Jane was far, far worse than anything Perry had ever done.

Perry had a bad temper. That was all. He was hotheaded. Volatile. The stress of his job and the exhaustion and upheaval of all that international travel made him snap. It didn't make it right. Of course not. But it was *understandable*. It wasn't malevolent. It wasn't evil. It was poor Eleni who was unknowingly married to an evil man.

Did she have a responsibility to tell Eleni what her husband had done? Did she have a responsibility to the tipsy, impressionable young girls Saxon might still be picking up in bars?

But they didn't even know for sure it was him.

Celeste drove her car into her driveway, flicking the switch for the triple-car garage and seeing their lavish panoramic view: the twinkling lights of homes around the bay, the mighty black presence of the ocean. The garage door opened like a curtain revealing a lit-up stage, and her car purred on in without her having to lift her foot off the accelerator.

She turned the key. Silence.

There was no garage in that other pretend life she was planning. There was an underground parking lot for the apartment block, but the spaces looked tiny, with big concrete posts. She'd have to reverse into her spot. She already knew that she'd smash a taillight. She was a terrible parker.

She pulled up the sleeve of her shirt and looked at the bruises on her arm.

Yes, Celeste, stay with a man who does this to you, because of the great parking.

She opened her car door.

At least he wasn't as bad as his cousin.

47.

"What is this petition-writing woman's name?" said Jane's father.

"Why? What are we going to do to her, Dad?" said Dane. "Break her knees?"

"I'd bloody like to," said Jane's father. He held a tiny jigsaw piece up to the light and squinted at it. "Anyway, what sort of name is *Ama*bella? Silly sort of a name. What's wrong with *Anna*bella?"

"You have got a grandson called Ziggy," pointed out Dane.

"Hey," said Jane to her brother. "It was your idea."

Jane was at her parents' place, sitting at the kitchen table, drinking tea, eating biscuits and doing a jigsaw puzzle. Ziggy was asleep in Jane's old bedroom. She was going to give him the day off school tomorrow, so they would stay the night and just hang around here in the morning. Renata and her friends would be happy.

Perhaps, thought Jane as she looked at her mother's 1980s apricot-and-cream kitchen, she would never go back to Pirriwee. This was where she belonged. It had been a kind of madness moving so far away in the first place. Almost a sickness. Her motives had been warped and weird, and this was her punishment.

Here, Jane felt bathed in familiarity: the mugs, the old brown teapot, the tablecloth, the smell of home, and of course, the puzzle. Always the puzzles. Her family had been addicted to jigsaw puzzles for as long as Jane could remember. The kitchen table was never used for eating, only for the latest puzzle. Tonight they were beginning a new one Jane's father had ordered online. It was a two-thousand-piece puzzle of an Impressionist painting. Lots of hazy swirls of color.

"Maybe I should move back over this way," she said, seeing how it felt, and as she spoke she thought for some reason of Blue Blues, the smell of coffee, the sapphire-blue shimmer of the sea, and Tom's wink as he handed over her takeout coffee, as if they were both in on a secret joke. She thought of Madeline holding up the roll of cardboard like a baton as she walked up the stairs of her apartment, and Celeste's bobbing ponytail as they went on their morning walks around the headland, beneath the towering Norfolk pines.

She thought of the summer afternoons earlier in the year when she and Ziggy had walked straight from school to the beach, Ziggy taking off his school shoes and socks on the sand, peeling off his shorts and shirt and running straight into the ocean in his underpants, while she chased him with a tube of sunscreen and he laughed with joy as the white froth of a wave broke around him.

Recently, thanks to Madeline, she'd picked up two new lucrative local clients within walking distance of her flat: Pirriwee Perfect Meats and Tom O'Brien's Smash Repairs. Their paperwork didn't smell. (In fact, Tom O'Brien's receipts smelled of potpourri.)

She realized with a shock that some of the happiest moments of her life had taken place over the last few months.

"But we actually do love living there," she said. "Ziggy loves school too—well, he normally does."

She remembered his tears earlier tonight. She couldn't keep sending him to school with children who told him they weren't allowed to play with him.

"If you want to stay, you stay," said her father. "You can't let that woman bully you into leaving the school. Why doesn't *she* leave?"

"I cannot believe that Ziggy would be bullying her daughter," said Jane's mother, her eyes on the jigsaw pieces she was sliding rapidly back and forth on the table.

"The point is that *she* believes it," said Jane. She tried to slot a piece into the bottom right-hand corner of the puzzle. "And now the other parents believe it too. And, I don't know, I can't say for sure that he didn't do something."

"That piece doesn't go there," said her mother. "Well, I can say for sure that Ziggy hasn't done anything. He simply hasn't got it in him. Jane, that piece does *not* go there, it's part of the lady's hat. What was I saying? Oh yes, Ziggy, I mean, my gosh, look at *you*, for example, you were the shyest little thing in school, wouldn't say boo to anyone. And of course, Poppy had the sweetest nature—"

"Mum, Poppy's nature isn't relevant!" Jane gave up on the puzzle piece and threw it down. Her frustration manifested itself in a sudden burst of anger and irritability that she directed at her poor defenseless mother. "For heaven's sake, Ziggy is not Poppy reincarnated! Poppy didn't even believe in reincarnation! And the fact is, we don't know what personality traits Ziggy might have inherited from his father, because Ziggy's father was, his father was . . ."

She stopped herself just in time. *Idiot.*

There was a sudden stillness around the table. Dane looked up from where he'd been reaching across the table to slot in a puzzle piece.

"Darling, what are you saying?" Jane's mother removed a crumb from the corner of her mouth with her fingernail. "Are you saying he . . . Did he hurt you?"

Jane looked around the table. Dane met her eyes with a question. Her mother tapped two fingers rapidly against her mouth. Her father's jaw was clenched. There was an expression something like terror in his eyes.

"Of course not," she said. When someone you loved was depending on your lie, it was perfectly easy. "Sorry! God, no. I didn't mean *that*. I just meant that Ziggy's biological father was basically a stranger. I mean, he seemed perfectly nice, but we don't know anything about him, and I know that's shameful—"

"I think we've all gotten over the shock of your hussy-like behavior by now, Jane," said Dane deliberately. He wasn't falling for the lie, she could tell. He didn't need to believe it as badly as her parents did.

"We certainly have," said Jane's mother. "And I don't care what sort of personality traits Ziggy's biological father had, I know my grandson, and he is not and never will be a bully."

"Absolutely not," agreed Jane's father. His shoulders sagged. He took a sip of his tea and picked up another jigsaw piece.

"And just because you don't believe in reincarnation, missy"—Jane's mother pointed at her—"doesn't mean you can't be reincarnated!"

Jonathan: When I first saw the playground at Pirriwee Public I thought it was amazing. All those secret little hideaways. But now I see that had its downside. All sorts of things were going on at that school out of sight and the teachers were clueless.

48.

Madeline stood in her living room and wondered what to do.

Ed and the kids were asleep, and thanks to Celeste, all the cleaning up after book club was done. She should go to bed, but she didn't feel tired enough. Tomorrow was Friday, and Friday mornings were hectic because she had to drive Abigail to her math tutor before school, and Fred did chess club and Chloe—

She stopped.

She didn't need to get Abigail to her math tutor by seven-thirty a.m. That was no longer her responsibility. Nathan or Bonnie would have to take Abigail. She kept forgetting her services as Abigail's mother were no longer required. Her life was theoretically easier with only two children to get out of the house each day, but each time she remembered a task relating to Abigail that was no longer hers, she felt that sharp sense of loss.

Her whole body jangled with anger she couldn't release.

She picked up Fred's toy lightsaber from where he'd conveniently left it on the floor for someone to trip over tomorrow morning. She turned on the switch so it burned red and green and sliced it through the air like Darth Vader, taking down each of her enemies.

Damn you to hell for stealing my daughter, Nathan.

Damn you to hell for helping him, Bonnie.

Damn you to hell, Renata, for that nasty petition.

Damn you to hell, Miss Barnes, for letting poor little Amabella get secretly bullied in the first place.

She felt bad for damning poor dimpled Miss Barnes to hell and quickly moved on with her list.

Damn you to hell, Saxon Banks, for what you did to Jane, you nasty, nasty man. She swung the lightsaber so enthusiastically over her head that it clanged against the hanging light and sent it swinging back and forth.

Madeline dropped the lightsaber on the couch and reached up to hold the light fixture steady.

Right. No more playing with the lightsaber. She could just imagine Ed's face if she'd broken a light fixture pretending to be Darth Vader.

She went back into the kitchen and picked up the iPad from where she'd left it after showing Celeste the pictures of Saxon Banks. She would play some nice soothing Plants vs. Zombies. It was important to keep her skills up-to-date. She liked hearing Fred say, "Mum, that's awesome!" when he looked over her shoulder and saw she'd gone up a level and gotten a new fancy weapon for taking on the zombies.

First she'd have another quick look at Abigail's Facebook and Instagram accounts. When Abigail was living at home Madeline had dutifully checked in every now and then on her daughter's online presence, just to be a good responsible modern mother. But now she did it addictively. It was like she was stalking her own daughter, pathetically seeking out bits of information about her life.

Abigail had changed her profile picture. It was a full-length photo of her facing the camera, doing a yoga pose, hands folded in prayer, one skinny leg propped on the other knee, her hair falling over one shoulder. She looked beautiful. Happy. Radiant, even.

Only the most selfish of mothers could feel resentful toward Bonnie for introducing her daughter to something that made her so obviously happy.

Madeline must be the most selfish of mothers.

Perhaps Madeline should take up yoga so she and Abigail would have something in common? But every time she tried yoga she found herself silently chanting her own mantra: *I'm so boooored, I'm so boooored.*

She scrolled down the comments from Abigail's friends. They were all supportive, but then she stopped on one from Abigail's friend Freya, who Madeline had never liked all that much. One of those toxic friends. Freya had written: *Is this the shot you're going to use on your "project"? Or not sexy/slutty enough?*

"Sexy/slutty"? Madeline's nostrils flared. What was the little witch Freya talking about? What "project" required Abigail to be sexy/slutty? It sounded like a project that needed to be stopped.

This was the thing with the murky world of the Internet. You swam along through cyberspace, merrily picking up this and that, and next thing you knew you'd stumbled upon something unsavory and ugly. She thought of how she'd felt seeing the face of Saxon Banks on her computer screen. This was what happened when you spied.

Abigail had replied to Freya's comment: *Shhhhhh!!! Top secret!!!!*

The reply had been sent five minutes ago. Madeline looked at the time. It was nearly midnight! She always insisted that Abigail had an early night before math tutoring, because otherwise she had to be dragged out of bed and the tutoring money would be wasted if Abigail was too tired to concentrate.

She sent her a private message: *Hey! What are you doing up so late? You've got tutoring tomorrow! Go to bed! Mum xxx.*

She noticed that her heart was beating after she pressed Send. As if she'd broken a rule. But she was Abigail's mother! She still had the right to tell her to go to bed.

Abigail answered immediately: *Dad has canceled the tutor. He's going to tutor me instead. Go to bed yourself! x*

"He *what?*" said Madeline to the computer screen. "He fucking *what?*"

Nathan had canceled the math tutor. He'd made a unilateral decision about Abigail's education. The very same man who had missed school plays and parent-teacher interviews and athletics carnivals and preparing a trembly little five-year-old for show-and-tell every Monday morning and projects on big sheets of cardboard and projects that needed to be submitted for the first time online with log-in instructions that didn't make any sense and homework forgotten until late the night before and covering books with contact paper and exam nerves and the meeting with that lovely teacher with the crazy jewelry who said all those years ago that Abigail would probably always struggle with math so *give her all the support she needs.*

How *DARE* he?

She dialed Nathan's number without a moment's thought, trembling with righteous rage. There was no way she could wait till the morning. She needed to yell at him now, right now, before her head exploded.

He answered with slurred, sleepy surprise: "Hello?"

"You canceled Abigail's math tutor? You just canceled without even checking with me first!?"

There was silence.

"Nathan?" said Madeline sharply.

She heard him clear his throat. "Maddie." He sounded wide awake now. "Did you seriously ring me at midnight to talk to me about Abigail's math tutor?"

It was an entirely different tone of voice than the one he normally used. For years her interactions with Nathan had reminded her of dealing with an unctuous, eager-to-please salesman working on commission only. Now that he had Abigail, he thought he was her equal. He didn't need to be apologetic anymore. He could be irritable. He could be like a regular ex-husband.

"We're all asleep," he continued. "Could it seriously not have waited until tomorrow morning? Skye and Bonnie are both very light—"

"You're not all asleep!" said Madeline. "Your fourteen-year-old daughter is wide awake and on the Internet! Is there any supervision in that house? Do you have *any* idea what she's doing right now?"

Madeline could hear the soft, melodious tones of Bonnie saying something sweet and understanding in the background.

"I'll go check on her," said Nathan. He sounded more conciliatory now. "I thought she was asleep. And look, she wasn't getting anywhere with that math tutor. He's just a kid. I can do a better job than him. But you're right, of course I should have talked to you about it. I *meant* to talk to you about it. It just slipped my mind."

"That tutor was making real progress with her," said Madeline.

She and Abigail had tried out two other tutors first before they'd gotten Sebastian. The kid got such good results, he had a waiting list of students. Madeline had begged him to squeeze in Abigail.

"No, he wasn't," said Nathan. "But let's talk about it when I'm not half-asleep."

"Fabulous. Look forward to it. Will you be letting me know of any other changes you've made to Abigail's schedule? Just curious."

"I'm hanging up now," said Nathan.

He hung up.

Madeline threw her mobile phone so hard against the wall it bounced back, landing faceup on the carpet, right at her feet, so she could see the shattered screen, like the sharp reprimand of an adult to a child.

> **Stu:** Look, I didn't think poor old Nathan was a bad bloke. I saw him a bit about the school. The place is overrun by women, and half the time they're all so busy rabbiting away to each other, it's hard to get a word in edgewise. So I'd always made a point of talking to the other dads. I remember one morning Nathan and I were having a good old natter about something when Madeline comes stalking by on her high heels and, jeez Louise—if looks could kill!

> **Gabrielle:** I couldn't stand to live in the same suburb as *my* ex-husband. If our kids attended the same school, I'd

probably end up murdering him. I don't know how they thought that arrangement could work. It was just crazy.

Bonnie: It was not crazy. We wanted to be as close as possible to Abigail, and then we happened to find the perfect house in the area. What's crazy about that?

49.

Five Days Before the Trivia Night

I t was Monday morning just before the bell rang, and Jane was on her way back from the school library where she'd returned two books Ziggy had forgotten to take back. She'd left him happily swinging along the monkey bars with the twins and Chloe. At least Madeline and Celeste weren't banning their children from playing with Ziggy.

After she dropped the books off, Jane was staying on at school to help out listening to the children practice their reading. She and Lily's dad, Stu, were the Monday-morning parent volunteers.

As she came out of the library she could see two of the Blond Bobs standing outside the music room, very deep in important, loudly confidential conversation.

She heard one of them say, "Which one is the mother?"

The other one said, "She sort of flies under the radar. She's *really* young. Renata thought she was the nanny."

"Wait, wait! I know the one! She wears her hair like this, right?" The Blond Bob pulled back her blond locks in an exaggeratedly tight ponytail, and at that moment her eyes met Jane's and widened. She dropped her hands like a child caught misbehaving.

The other woman, who was facing away from Jane, continued talking. "Yes! That's her! Well, apparently her kid, this *Ziggy*, has been *secretly* bullying poor little Amabella. I'm talking really vicious stuff— What?"

The first Blond Bob made frantic head-jerking movements.

"What's wrong? Oh!"

The woman turned her head and saw Jane. Her face turned pink.

"Good morning!" she said. Normally someone so high on the school parent hierarchy would nod vaguely and graciously at Jane as she walked by, a royal nod for a commoner.

"Hi," said Jane.

The woman was holding a clipboard up to her chest. She suddenly dropped her arm by her side so that the clipboard hung behind her legs, exactly like a child hiding a stolen treat behind his back.

It's the petition, thought Jane. It wasn't just kindergarten parents signing it. They were getting parents in other years to sign it. Parents who didn't even know her or Ziggy or anything about it.

Jane kept walking past the women. Her hand was on the glass doors leading back out into the playground when she stopped. There was a roaring, ascending feeling in her body, like a plane taking off. It was the disdainful way that woman had used Ziggy's name. It was Saxon Banks, his breath tickling her ear: *Never had an original thought in your life, have you?*

She turned. She walked back to the women and stood directly in front of them. The women took tiny steps backward, their eyes comically round. The three of them were almost exactly the same height. They were all mothers. But the Blond Bobs had husbands and houses and absolute certainty about their places in the world.

"My son has never hurt anyone," said Jane, and all of a sudden she knew it was true. He was Ziggy Chapman. He was nothing whatsoever to do with Saxon Banks. He was nothing to do with Poppy. He wasn't even anything to do with her. He was just *Ziggy*, and she didn't know everything about Ziggy, but she knew this.

"Oh, darling, we've all been there! We *sympathize*! This is just a terrible situation," began the Blond Bob with the clipboard. "How much screen time do you let him have? I've found cutting down on screen time really—"

"He's never hurt anyone," repeated Jane.

She turned and walked away.

> **Thea:** So, the week before the trivia night, Jane accosted Trish and Fiona when they were in the middle of a private conversation. They said her behavior was just bizarre, to the point where they even wondered if she had some . . . *mental health issues.*

Jane walked into the playground feeling a strange sense of calm. Perhaps she needed to learn from Madeline's example. No more avoiding confrontation. March up to your critics and bloody well tell them what you think.

A Year 1 girl strolled alongside her. "I'm having a sausage roll for lunch today."

"Lucky you," said Jane. This was one of her favorite parts of walking around the school playground: the way children chatted so artlessly, launching into whatever happened to be on their minds at the time.

"I wasn't meant to be having a sausage roll, because it's not Friday, but this morning my little brother got stung by a bee, and he was screaming, and my sister broke a glass, and my mum said,

'I'm losing my mind!'" The little girl put her hands over her head to demonstrate. "And then Mum said I could buy my lunch at the canteen as a special treat, but no juice, but I could still have a gingerbread man, but not the chocolate sort. Bees die after they sting you, did you know that?"

"I did," said Jane. "That's the very last thing they do."

"Jane!" Miss Barnes approached, carrying a laundry basket full of dress-up clothes. "Thank you for coming today!"

"Um. You're welcome?" said Jane. She'd been doing this every Monday morning since the beginning of the year.

"I mean, in light of, you know, everything." Miss Barnes winced and shifted the laundry basket onto her hip. She stepped closer to Jane and lowered her voice. "I haven't heard anything else about this petition. Mrs. Lipmann has been telling the parents involved that she wants it stopped. Also, she's assigned me a teacher's aide to do nothing else but observe the children, and in particular Amabella and Ziggy."

"That's great," said Jane. "But I'm pretty sure the petition is still circulating."

She could feel eyes on her and Miss Barnes from all corners of the playground. It felt like every parent was secretly observing their conversation. This must be what it felt like to be famous.

Miss Barnes sighed. "I noticed you kept Ziggy home on Friday. I hope you're not feeling intimidated by these tactics."

"Some parents are telling their children they're not allowed to play with him," said Jane.

"For goodness' sake."

"Yeah, so I've started a petition too," said Jane. "I want all those kids who won't play with Ziggy suspended."

For a moment Miss Barnes looked horrified. Then she threw back her head and laughed.

Harper: It's all very well, the school saying they were taking the situation seriously, but then you see Jane and Miss Barnes standing in the playground laughing their heads off! To be frank, that got me riled up. That was the same morning as the assault, and yes, I am going to use the word "assault."

Samantha: *Assault.* Give me a break.

50.

Parent reading was done outside in the playground. Today Jane was in Turtle Corner, named because of the giant concrete turtle sitting in the middle of a sandy play area. There was room for an adult and a child to sit comfortably together on the turtle's neck, and Miss Barnes had provided two cushions and a blanket to put across their knees.

Jane loved listening to the children read: watching them frown as they sounded out a word, their triumphant expressions when they untangled the syllables, their sudden bursts of laughter over the story and their random, offbeat observations about the story. Sitting on a turtle with the sun on her face, the sand at her feet and the sea glittering on the horizon made her feel as if she were on holiday. Pirriwee Public was a magical little school, almost a dream school, and the thought of pulling Ziggy out and having to start again somewhere else without a Turtle Corner or a Miss Barnes filled her with regret and resentment.

"Beautiful reading, Max!" she said, double-checking as she did that it was indeed Max and not Josh who had just finished reading *Monkey's Birthday Surprise*. Madeline had told her that the trick to differentiating Celeste's boys was to look for the strawberry-shaped birthmark on Max's forehead. "I think to myself, Marked Max," said Madeline.

"You used *great* expression, Max," said Jane, although she wasn't sure that he had. The parents had been told to try to find something specific to compliment after each child read.

"Yep," said Max coolly. He slid off the turtle's neck and sat down cross-legged on the sand and began digging.

"Max," said Jane.

Max sighed theatrically, sprang to his feet and suddenly ran back toward his classroom, his arms and legs pumping comically, like a cartoon character running for his life. The twins both ran faster than Jane would have thought possible for five-year-olds.

Jane checked his name off her list and looked up to see who Miss Barnes was sending out next. It was Amabella. Max nearly collided with her as she walked through the playground toward Jane, her curly head lowered, her book in her hand.

"Hi, Amabella!" Jane called out cheerily. *Your mother and her friends are petitioning to have Ziggy suspended because they think he's hurting you, honey! So do you think you could tell me what's really going on?*

She'd become fond of Amabella since she'd been doing the reading this year. She was a quiet little girl with a serious, angelic face, and it was impossible not to like her. She and Jane had had some interesting conversations about the books that they read together.

Of course she would not say a word to Amabella about what was going on with Ziggy. That would be inappropriate. That would be wrong.

Of course she wouldn't.

Samantha: Don't get me wrong, I love Miss Barnes, and
anyone who spends her days wrangling five-year-olds

deserves a medal, but I do think letting Amabella read to Jane that day might not have been the most sensible thing in the world.

Miss Barnes: That was a mistake. I'm human. I make mistakes. It's called human error. These parents seem to think I'm a machine and they can demand a refund every time a teacher makes a mistake. And look, I don't want to say anything bad about Jane—but she was in the wrong that day too.

Amabella was reading to Jane from a book about the solar system. It was the highest-level book for kindergarten children, and as usual Amabella read it fluently, with impeccable expression. The only way that Jane felt she could add any value for Amabella was by interrupting and asking her some questions raised by the book, but today Jane was finding it difficult to muster any interest in the solar system. All she could think about was Ziggy.

"What do you think it would be like to live on Mars?" she said finally.

Amabella lifted her head. "It would be impossible because you can't breathe the atmosphere, there's too much carbon dioxide and it's too cold."

"Right," said Jane, although she'd actually have to Google it to be sure. It was possible that Amabella was already smarter than she was.

"Also, it would be lonely," said Amabella after a moment.

Why would a smart little girl like Amabella not say the truth? If it was Ziggy, why wouldn't she just say it? Why not tell on him? It was so strange. Children were normally such tattletales.

"Sweetheart, you know I'm Ziggy's mum, right?" she asked.

Amabella nodded in a "duh" sort of a way.

"Has Ziggy been hurting you? Because if he has, I want to know about it, and I promise I will make sure he never *ever* does anything like that again."

Amabella's eyes filled with instant tears. Her bottom lip quivered. She dropped her head.

"Amabella," said Jane. "Was it Ziggy?"

Amabella said something Jane didn't catch.

"What's that?" said Jane.

"It wasn't . . ." began Amabella, but then her face crumpled. She began to cry in earnest.

"It *wasn't* Ziggy?" said Jane, filled with desperate hope. She felt an urge to shake Amabella, to demand the child just say the truth. "Is that what you said, it wasn't him?"

"Amabella! Amabella, *sweetie!*" Harper stood at the edge of the sandpit, holding a box of oranges for the canteen. She had a white scarf tied so tightly around her neck, it looked like she was being garroted, an effect enhanced by the fact that her long, droopy face was now purpling with rage. "Whatever is the matter?"

She dumped the box at her feet and walked across the sand to them.

"Amabella!" she said. "What's going on?"

It was like Jane wasn't there, or as though she were another child.

"Everything is fine, Harper," said Jane coldly. She put her arm around Amabella and pointed behind Harper. "Your oranges are going everywhere." Turtle Corner was at the top of a small slope, and Harper's box had tipped on one side. A cascade of oranges slid down the playground toward where Stu was listening to another kindergarten child read near the Starfish Wall.

Harper's eyes stayed fixed on Amabella, ignoring Jane in such a pointed, deliberate way, it was almost laughable, except for the fact that it was also breathtakingly rude.

"Come with me, Amabella." Harper held out her hand.

Amabella sniffed. Her nose was running into her mouth in that heedless, disgusting way of five-year-olds.

"I am right here, Harper!" said Jane as she pulled a packet of tissues from her jacket pocket. This was infuriating. If she'd had just another minute with Amabella she might have been able to get some information out of her. She held the tissue over Amabella's nose. "Blow, Amabella."

Amabella obediently blew. Harper finally looked at Jane. "You have obviously been upsetting her! What have you been saying to her?"

"Nothing!" said Jane furiously, and her guilt over her desire to shake Amabella only made her angrier still. "Why don't you go collect a few more signatures for your nasty little petition?"

Harper's voice rose to a shout. "Oh yes, good idea, and leave you here to keep bullying a defenseless little girl! Like mother, like son!"

Jane stood up from the turtle and kicked at the sand with her boot, just barely managing to stop herself from kicking it in Harper's face. "Don't you dare talk about my son!"

"Don't you *kick* me!" yelled Harper.

"I didn't kick you!" yelled back Jane, surprising herself with the volume of her voice.

"What on earth . . . ?" It was Stu, dressed in his blue plumber's overalls, his hands full of the oranges he was rescuing from the playground. The little boy who had been reading with him was standing next to him, an orange in each hand, his eyes saucer-like at the sight of two mothers yelling.

At that moment there was a high-pitched yelp as Carol Quigley, hurrying back from the music room with her spray-and-wipe bottle held aloft, slipped over a stray orange and fell slapstick-style on her bottom.

Carol: I had a very badly bruised tailbone, in fact.

51.

Gabrielle: Next thing I hear, Harper is accusing Jane of assaulting her in Turtle Corner, which seems unlikely.

Stu: Harper carried on like a pork chop. She didn't look like she'd been assaulted. I don't know. I'd just gotten a call about a blown water main. I didn't have time to deal with two mothers fighting it out in the sandpit.

Thea: And that's when some of the parents decided to report matters to the Department of Education.

Jonathan: . . . which obviously freaked poor Mrs. Lipmann out. I think it was her birthday too. Poor woman.

Mrs. Lipmann: I will say this: We couldn't possibly have suspended Ziggy Chapman. The only time he'd even been accused of bullying was at the orientation day, when he wasn't even a student. After that it was all just conjecture on the part of the parents. I have no idea if it was my birthday. That is of no relevance.

Miss Barnes: Those parents were crazy. How could we possibly have suspended Ziggy? He was a model student. No behavioral issues. I never had to put him on the Sad Chair. In fact, I can't remember even giving him a red dot! And he certainly *never* got a yellow card. Let alone a white one.

The Day Before the Trivia Night

Madeline worked on Fridays, which meant that she mostly missed the Friday-morning school assembly. Ed normally made an appearance if one of the kids was performing or receiving a merit award. Today, however, Chloe had begged Madeline to come because the kindergarten class was reciting "The Dentist and the Crocodile" and Chloe had a line to say all on her own.

Also, Fred's class was performing on their recorders for the first time. They were going to play "Happy Birthday to You" to Mrs. Lipmann, which would be a painful experience for all concerned. (There was a general feeling around the school that Mrs. Lipmann might be turning sixty, but no one could confirm or deny.)

Madeline had decided to go to the assembly and then work late next Monday afternoon, something she didn't used to be able to do on a Monday because she took Abigail to basketball practice while Ed took the little kids to their swimming lesson.

"Abigail probably doesn't need to go to basketball training anymore," she said to Ed as they got out of the car with their take-out coffees. After they'd dropped the children off they'd zipped down to Blue Blues, where Tom was doing a roaring trade from all the Pirriwee Public parents in need of caffeine to get through a recorder performance at the assembly. "Maybe Nathan is coaching her now."

Ed chuckled warily, probably worried she was about to launch into another rant about the cancellation of the math tutor. Her husband was a patient man, but she had noticed a glazed look on his face as she'd talked, admittedly for quite a long time, about Abigail's difficulty with algebra and the fact that Nathan had never been there to help Abigail with her math homework and therefore had no idea how outrageously bad she was at it, and yes it was true that Nathan had always been good at math, but that didn't mean he could *teach* it, and so on and so forth.

"Joy e-mailed this morning," said Ed as he locked the car. Joy was the editor of the local paper. "She wants me to do a piece on what's going on at the school."

"What? The trivia night?" said Madeline disinterestedly. Ed often wrote short articles about school fund-raising events for the local paper. She could see Perry and Celeste crossing the street to go into the school. They were holding hands, loved-up gorgeous couple that they were, Perry walking slightly ahead, as if he were protecting Celeste from the traffic.

"No," said Ed carefully. "The bullying. The petition. Joy says 'bullying' is one of those hot-button issues."

"You can't write about that!" Madeline stopped abruptly in the middle of the road.

"Get out of the road, you bloody idiot." Ed grabbed her elbow as a car came whizzing up from the beach. "One day I'm going to be writing a story about a tragedy on this road."

"Don't write it, Ed," said Madeline. "That's so bad for the school's reputation."

"I am still a journalist, you know," said Ed.

It had been three years since Ed had given up a stressful, high-grade job with longer hours and much better pay at the *Australian* so that Madeline could go back to work and the two of them could evenly share parenting duties, and he'd never once complained about the intrinsically sedate nature of work at a local paper, cheerfully going off to surf carnivals and fetes and one-hundred-year birthday celebrations at the local nursing home. (The sea air seemed to preserve its residents.) This was the first time he'd ever hinted at the possibility that he wasn't entirely satisfied.

"It's a valid story," said Ed.

"It's not a valid story!" said Madeline. "You *know* it's not a valid story!"

"What's not a valid story? Gidday, Ed. Madeline, nice to see you." They had caught up with Perry and Celeste. Perry was in a beautifully cut suit and tie; bespoke, Italian, worth more than Ed's entire wardrobe, Madeline guessed, including the wardrobe. She managed to caress the silky fabric of his sleeve with her fingertips as Perry leaned over to kiss her and she breathed in the scent of his aftershave.

She wondered what it would be like to be married to a man who dressed so well. If it were Madeline, she would take such pleasure in all those lovely textures and colors, the softness of the ties, the crispness of the shirts. Of course, Celeste, who didn't have much interest in clothes, probably didn't even register the difference between Perry and rumpled, unshaven Ed, with his old musty-smelling, olive-green fleece over his T-shirt. Watching Ed and Perry talk, though, she felt an unexpected surge of affection for Ed, even though she'd just that minute been feeling aggravated with him. It was something to do with the open, interested way he listened to Perry, and his graying, stubbled chin, in contrast with Perry's shiny-smooth jaw.

Yes. She'd much rather kiss Ed. So that was lucky.

"Are we late? We dropped the boys off first at kiss-and-drop because there was no parking," said Celeste in her flustered, worried way. "The boys are so excited about Perry being here to see them perform this poem."

"We're not late," said Madeline. She wondered if Celeste had said anything to Perry yet about his cousin possibly being Ziggy's father. She would have told Ed by now.

"Have you seen Jane?" asked Celeste, as if she'd read her mind. Perry and Ed had walked ahead of them.

"Have you told him . . . ?" Madeline lowered her voice and inclined her head at Perry's back.

"No!" hissed Celeste. She looked almost terrified.

"Anyway, Jane isn't here," said Madeline. "Remember, she's got the thing with the thing." Celeste looked blank. Madeline lowered her voice. "You know. The appointment." Jane had sworn them to secrecy about the appointment she'd made for Ziggy to see the psychologist. "If people hear I'm taking him to a psychologist, they'll think it's proof that he's doing something wrong."

"Oh yes, of course." Celeste tapped a finger to her forehead. "I forgot."

Perry slowed down so that Madeline and Celeste could catch up with them.

"So Ed has just been telling me about this bullying controversy," said Perry. "Is this Renata Klein's daughter? The poor little girl who is being bullied?" He said to Madeline, "I sort of know Renata through work."

"Really?" said Madeline, although she already knew this from Celeste; it always seemed a safer policy not to let husbands know just how much information their wives shared.

"So should I sign this petition if Renata asks me?" asked Perry.

Madeline drew herself up, ready to go into battle for Jane, but Celeste spoke first. "Perry," she said, "if you sign that petition I will leave you."

Madeline laughed with uneasy surprise. It was obviously meant to be a joke, but there was something wrong with Celeste's delivery. She sounded perfectly serious.

"That's telling you, mate!" said Ed.

"It sure is," said Perry, and he put his arm around Celeste and pressed his lips to her head. "The boss has spoken."

But Celeste still didn't smile.

To: ALL PARENTS

From: YOUR SOCIAL COMMITTEE

The much anticipated AUDREY AND ELVIS TRIVIA NIGHT kicks off tomorrow in the school assembly hall at seven p.m.! Put your thinking caps on and be ready for a night of fun and merriment! THANK YOU to Year 2 dad Brett Larson, who will be our MC for the night. Brett has been busy preparing some tricky mind-benders to keep us on our toes!

Fingers crossed the weather forecast will be wrong (90 percent chance of rain—but, hey, what do they know?) and we'll be able to enjoy cocktails and canapés on our beautiful balcony before the night begins.

THANK YOU also to all our generous local sponsors! Raffle prizes include a FAB MEAT TRAY kindly donated by our friends at the wonderful Pirriwee Perfect Meats, a scrumptious BREAKFAST FOR TWO at BLUE BLUES (we love you, TOM!) and a SHAMPOO AND BLOW-DRY at HAIRWAY TO HEAVEN! WOW!

Remember, all money raised goes to buy SMART Boards for the education of our little folk!

Hugs! from your friendly Social Committee,

Fiona, Grace, Edwina, Rowena, Harper, Holly and Helen!

xxxxxxx

P.S. Mrs. Lipmann reminds us all to be mindful of our neighbors and to keep noise levels to a minimum when we're leaving.

52.

Samantha: I was watching the kindy kids do a poem at school assembly the day before the trivia night and I noticed all the Renata supporters were on one side and all the Madeline supporters were on the other side, just like at a wedding. I had a little chuckle to myself.

Pirriwee Public School assemblies always took far too long to start and finish, but the one thing you couldn't complain about was the location. The school assembly hall was on the second floor of the building and had a huge balcony that ran all the way along the side, with big glass sliding doors that revealed a glorious view out to sea. Today all the glass doors were slid open, allowing the crisp autumn air to flow through. (The hall did get a bit stuffy when all the doors were closed, with all the farting children, perfumed Blond Bobs and their lavishly cologned husbands.)

Madeline looked out at the view and tried to think happy thoughts. She felt ever so slightly snappy, which meant that tomorrow would be her peak day for PMS. Nobody better cross her at trivia night.

"Hi, Madeline," said Bonnie. "Hi, Ed."

She sat down on the empty aisle seat next to Madeline, bringing with her a nose-tickling scent of patchouli.

Madeline felt Ed's hand come down and rest unobtrusively, comfortingly on her knee.

"Hi, Bonnie," said Madeline wearily, looking over her shoulder. Was this really the only empty chair in the place? "How are you?"

"Very well," said Bonnie. She pulled her single plait over her white, hippie-like shoulder with its little scattering of dark moles. Even Bonnie's *shoulder* felt alien to Madeline.

"Aren't you *cold*?" shivered Madeline. Bonnie was wearing a sleeveless top and yoga pants.

"I just taught a Bikram yoga class," said Bonnie.

"That's the sweaty one, right?" said Madeline. "You don't look sweaty."

"I showered," said Bonnie. "But my core body temperature is still quite high."

"You'll catch a chill," said Madeline.

"No I won't," said Bonnie.

"You will," said Madeline. She could sense Ed on her left trying not to laugh.

She changed the subject while she still had the last word. "Nathan not here?"

"He had to work," answered Bonnie. "I told him he probably wouldn't miss much. Skye is so terrified of performing, she'll probably hide behind the other kids." She smiled at Madeline. "Not like your Chloe."

"Not like my Chloe," agreed Madeline.

At least you can never take Chloe away from me, the way you've taken Abigail.

It seemed quite outrageous to her that this *stranger* knew what her daughter had for breakfast this morning and yet Madeline did not. Even though she'd known Bonnie for years now, even though they'd had a hundred civil conversations, she still didn't seem like a real person. She felt like a caricature to Madeline. It was impossible to imagine her doing anything normal. Was she ever grumpy? Did she ever yell? Fall about laughing? Eat too much? Drink too much? Call out for someone to bring her toilet paper? Lose her car keys? Was she ever just a human being? Did she ever stop talking in that creepy, singsong yoga teacher voice?

"I'm sorry that Nathan didn't tell you about canceling the math tutor," said Bonnie.

Not here, you idiot. Let's not talk about family business with sharp-eared mothers all around us.

"I said to Nathan we have to get better with our communication skills," continued Bonnie. "This is all a process."

"Right," said Madeline. Ed fractionally increased the pressure of his hand on her knee. Madeline looked over toward him, and to Perry and Celeste on the other side, to see if she could naturally become involved in conversation with someone else, but Perry and Celeste were looking at something on Celeste's phone, and the two of them were laughing, their heads close together like young dating teenagers. That strangeness between them over the signing of the petition had obviously been nothing.

She looked back to the front of the hall, where there was still a hubbub of noisy activity, with kids being asked to sit down please, and teachers fiddling with sound equipment, and the Blond Bobs hurrying about looking very involved and important as they did each Friday morning.

"Abigail is really developing a social conscience," said Bonnie. "It's amazing to see. Did you know she has some sort of secret charity project she's working on?"

"Just as long as her social conscience doesn't get in the way of school marks," said Madeline in a clipped tone, firmly establishing herself as the awful, misanthropic parent. "She wants to do physiotherapy. I've been talking to Samantha about it. Lily's mum. Samantha says Abigail needs math."

"Actually, I don't think she wants to do physiotherapy anymore," said Bonnie. "She seems to be developing an interest in social work. I think she'd make a wonderful social worker."

"She'd make a terrible social worker!" snapped Madeline. "She's not tough enough. She'd kill herself trying to help people and she'd get too involved with their lives—and my God, that would just be so *wrong* a career choice for Abigail."

"Do you think?" said Bonnie dreamily. "Oh, well, there's no rush to make any decisions right now, is there? She'll probably change her mind a dozen times before then."

Madeline could hear herself making little puffing noises through her lips, as if she were in labor. Bonnie was trying to turn Abigail into somebody that she wasn't, that she couldn't be. There would be nothing left of the real Abigail. Madeline's daughter would be a stranger to her.

Mrs. Lipmann walked gracefully onto the stage and stood silently in front of the microphone, her hands clasped, smiling benignly as she waited for her royal presence to be noticed. A Blond Bob rushed onto the stage and did something important to the microphone before rushing off again. Meanwhile a Year 6 teacher began clapping a catchy, rhythmic beat that had magical, hypnotic powers over the children, immediately causing them to stop talking, look to the front and begin clapping in the same rhythm. (It didn't work at home. Madeline had tried.)

"Oh!" said Bonnie, as the clapping rose in volume and Mrs.

Lipmann lifted her hands for silence. She leaned over and spoke in Madeline's ear, her breath sweet and minty. "I nearly forgot. We'd love to have you and Ed and the children over to celebrate Abigail's fifteenth birthday next Tuesday! I know Abigail would just love to have all her family together. Would that be too awkward, do you think?"

Awkward? Are you kidding, Bonnie, that would be wonderful, glorious! Madeline would be a *guest* at her daughter's fifteenth-birthday dinner. Not the host. A guest. Nathan would offer her drinks. When they left, Abigail wouldn't come in the car with them. She'd stay there. Abigail would stay there because that was her home.

"Lovely! What shall I bring?" she whispered back, while she put one hand on Ed's arm and squeezed hard. It turned out that a conversation with Bonnie was just like being in labor: The pain could always get much, much worse.

53.

iggy is a lovely little boy," said the psychologist. "Very articulate and confident and kind." She smiled at Jane. "He expressed concern over my health. He's the first client this week who has even noticed I have a cold."

The psychologist blew her nose noisily as if to demonstrate that she did indeed have a cold. Jane watched impatiently. She wasn't as nice as Ziggy. She couldn't care less about the psychologist's cold.

"So, er, you don't think he's a secret psychotic bully?" said Jane with a little smile to show that she was sort of joking, except of course she wasn't. That's why they were here. That's why she was paying the huge fee.

They both looked at Ziggy, who was playing in a glassed-off room adjoining the psychologist's office where he presumably couldn't hear them. As they watched, Ziggy picked up a stuffed doll, a toy for a much younger child. *Imagine if Ziggy suddenly punches the doll,* thought Jane. *That would be pretty conclusive. Child pretends to care about psychologist's cold and then beats up toys.* But Ziggy just looked at the doll, then put it back down, not noticing that he'd missed the corner of the table and it had slid to the floor, proving only that he was pathologically messy.

"I don't," said the psychologist. She was silent for a moment, her nose twitching.

"You're going to tell me what he said, right?" said Jane. "You don't have any client/patient confidentiality thing, do you?"

"Achoo!" The psychologist sneezed a massive sneeze.

"Bless you," said Jane impatiently.

"Patient confidentiality only starts to apply when they get to about fourteen," said the psychologist sniffily, "which is just when they're telling you all sorts of stuff you'd really quite like to share with their parents, know what I mean? They're having *sex*, they're taking *drugs*, and so on and so forth!"

Yes, yes, little people, little problems.

"Jane, I don't think Ziggy is a bully," said the psychologist. She steepled her fingers and touched her fingertips to the outside of her red nostrils. "I brought up the incident you mentioned at the orientation day, and he was very clear that it wasn't him. I'd be very surprised if he's lying. If he's lying, then he's the most accomplished liar I've ever seen. And frankly, Ziggy does not show any of the classic signs of a bullying personality. He's not narcissistic. He most certainly demonstrates empathy and sensitivity."

Tears of relief blocked Jane's nose.

"Unless he's a psychopath, of course," said the psychologist cheerfully.

What the fuck?

"In which case he could be faking empathy. Psychopaths are often very charming. But——" She sneezed again. "Oh, dear," she said, wiping her nose. "Thought I was getting better."

"But," prompted Jane, aware that she was demonstrating no empathy whatsoever.

"But I don't think so," said the psychologist. "I don't think he's a psychopath. I'd definitely like to see him for another appointment. Soon. I think he's suffering from a lot of anxiety. I believe there was a lot that he didn't share with me today. I wouldn't be at all surprised to learn that Ziggy himself was being bullied at school."

"Ziggy?" said Jane. "Being bullied?"

She felt a rush of instant heat, as though she had a fever. Energy thrummed through her body.

"I might be wrong," said the psychologist, sniffing. "But I wouldn't be surprised. My guess is that it's verbal. Perhaps a smart kid has found his weak spot." She took a tissue from the box on her desk. She made a little *tch* sound. "Also, Ziggy and I talked about his father."

"His father?" Jane reeled. "But what—"

"He's very anxious about his father," said the psychologist. "He thinks he might be a Stormtrooper, or possibly Jabba the Hutt, or, worst-case scenario"—the psychologist couldn't hold back a broad grin—"Darth Vader."

"You're not serious," said Jane. She was somewhat mortified. It was Madeline's Fred who had gotten Ziggy into *Star Wars*. "*He's* not serious."

"Children often get caught halfway between reality and fantasy," said the psychologist. "He's only five. Anything is possible in a five-year-old's world. He still believes in Santa Claus and the Tooth Fairy. Why shouldn't Darth Vader be his father? But I think it's more that he has somehow picked up the idea that his father is someone . . . frightening and mysterious."

"I thought I'd done a better job than this," said Jane.

"I asked if he'd talked to you much about his father, and he said yes, but he knows it upsets you. He was very firm with me. He didn't want me upsetting you." She looked down at her notes and up again. "He said, 'Be careful if you're talking to Mummy about my daddy, because she gets a funny look on her face.'"

Jane pressed the flat of her hand to her chest.

"You OK?" said the psychologist.

"Do I have a funny look on my face?" asked Jane.

"A little bit," said the psychologist. She leaned forward and gave Jane a woman-to-woman look of understanding as if they were chatting in a bar. "I take it Ziggy's father was not exactly a good guy?"

"Not exactly," said Jane.

54.

erry drove Celeste back home after the assembly.

"Do you have time to stop for a coffee?" asked Celeste.

"I'd better not," said Perry. "Busy day."

She looked at his profile. He seemed fine, his thoughts focused on the day ahead. She knew he'd enjoyed seeing his first school assembly, being one of the school dads, wearing his corporate uniform in a noncorporate world. He liked the daddy role, relished it even, talking with Ed in that gently ironic, this-is-all-a-bit-of-a-laugh dad-type way.

They'd all laughed at the boys careering about the stage, wearing the big green crocodile suit. Max had the head and Josh had the tail; sometimes the crocodile seemed in danger of being torn in two as they headed in opposite directions. Before they left the school, Perry had taken a photo of the boys wearing the suit on the balcony outside the hall, the ocean in the background. Then he'd asked Ed to take a photo of all four of them: the boys peering out from underneath the costume, Perry and Celeste crouched down next to them. It would already be on Facebook. Celeste had seen him fiddling with his phone as they'd walked back to the car. What would it say? *Two stars are born! The boys rocked it as a scary croc!* Something like that.

"See you at the trivia night!" everyone had called to one another as they'd left that day.

Yes, he was in a good mood. Things should be OK. There hadn't been any tension since he'd gotten back from his last trip.

But she'd seen the lightning-quick flash of rage when she'd made her comment about leaving him if he signed the petition to have Ziggy suspended. She'd meant it to sound like a joke, but she knew it hadn't come across that way, and that would have embarrassed him in front of Madeline and Ed, who he liked and admired.

What had come over her? It must be the apartment. It was almost completely furnished now, and as a result, the possibility of leaving was always present, the question being constantly asked: *Will I or won't I? Of course I will, I must. Of course I won't.* Yesterday morning when she was there she'd even made up the beds with fresh linen, taking a strange, soothing pleasure in the task, turning down the sheets just so, making each bed look inviting, making it possible. But then in the middle of the night last night, she'd woken in her own bed, Perry's arm heavy across her waist, the ceiling fan turning lazily the way Perry liked it, and she'd thought suddenly of those made-up beds and she'd been as appalled as if she'd remembered a crime. What a betrayal of her husband! She'd rented and furnished another apartment. What a *crazy*, secretive, malicious and self-indulgent thing to do.

Maybe she'd threatened Perry that she'd leave him because she wanted to confess what she'd done; she couldn't bear the burden of her secret.

Of course, it was also because the thought of Perry, or anyone, signing that petition filled her with rage, but *especially* Perry. He owed a debt to Jane. A family debt because of what his cousin had done. (*May have done,* she kept reminding herself. They didn't know for sure. What if Jane had misheard the name? It could have been *Stephen* Banks, not Saxon Banks at all.)

Ziggy might be Perry's cousin's child. He owed him at least his loyalty.

Jane was Celeste's friend, and even if she weren't, no five-year-old deserved to have a community begin a witch hunt against him.

Perry didn't take the car into the garage, pulling up outside the house in the driveway. Celeste assumed that meant he wasn't coming in.

"I'll see you tonight," she said, leaning over to kiss him.

"Actually, I need to come in to get something from my desk," said Perry. He opened the car door.

She felt it then. It was like a smell or a change in the electrical charge in the air. It was something to do with the set of his shoulders, the blank, shiny look in his eyes and the dryness in her throat.

He opened the door for her and let her in first, with a courtly gesture.

"Perry," she said quickly, as she turned around and he closed the door, but then he grabbed her by the hair, twisting it behind her and pulling so hard, so astonishingly hard, that pain radiated through her scalp and her eyes filled with instant, involuntary tears.

"If you ever, ever embarrass me like that again, I will kill you,

I will fucking kill you." He tightened his grip. "How dare you. How *dare* you."

He let go.

"I'm sorry," she said. "I'm so sorry."

But she mustn't have said it right, because he stepped forward slowly and took her face in his hands the way he did when he was about to tenderly kiss her.

"Not good enough," he said, and he slammed her head against the wall.

The cold deliberateness of it was as shocking and surreal as the first time he'd hit her. The pain felt intensely personal, like a broken heart.

The world swam as though she were drunk.

She slid to the floor.

She retched once, twice, but she wasn't sick. She only ever retched. She was never sick.

She heard his footsteps walking away, down the hallway, and she curled up on the floor, her knees near her chest, her hands interlaced over the back of her cruelly throbbing head. She thought of the boys when they hurt themselves, the way they sobbed: *It hurts, Mummy, it hurts so much.*

"Sit up," said Perry. "Honey. Sit up."

He crouched down next to her, pulled her up into a sitting position and gently laid an ice pack wrapped in a tea towel on the back of her head.

As the blessed coldness began to seep through, she turned her head and studied his face through blurry eyes. It was dead white, with purplish crescents under his eyes. His features were dragged downward, as though he were being ravaged by some terrible disease. He sobbed once. A grotesque, despairing sound, like an animal caught in a trap.

She let herself fall forward against his shoulder, and they rocked together on their glossy black walnut floor beneath their soaring cathedral ceiling.

55.

adeline had often said that living and working in Pirriwee was like living in a country village. Mostly she adored that sense of community—except, of course, on those days when PMS had her in its malicious grip, and she longed to walk through the shopping village without people smiling and waving and being so goddamned nice. Everyone was connected to everyone in Pirriwee, often in multiple ways, through the school or the surf club, the kids' sporting teams, the gym, the hairdresser and so on.

It meant that when she sat at her desk in her tiny, crammed office in the Pirriwee Theatre and made a quick call to the Pirriwee local paper to see if she could get a last-minute quarter-page ad in next week's paper (they urgently needed more numbers for the preschoolers' drama class to help bring in some cash), she wasn't just calling Lorraine, the advertising representative. She was calling *Lorraine*, who had a daughter, Petra, in the same year as Abigail, and a son in Year 4 at Pirriwee Public, and was married to Alex, who owned the local bottle shop and played in an over-forty soccer club with Ed.

It wouldn't be a quick call, because she and Lorraine hadn't talked for a while. She realized this as the phone was ringing, and nearly hung up and sent an e-mail instead—she had a lot to do today and she was already running late from going to the assembly—but still, just a quick chat with Lorraine would be nice, and she did want to hear what Lorraine had heard about the petition and so on, but then again, Lorraine did go *on* sometimes, and—

"Lorraine Edgely!"

Too late. "Hi, Lorraine," said Madeline. "It's Madeline."

"Darling!" Lorraine should really work for the theater, not the local paper. She had that flamboyant theater-talk down pat.

"How are you?"

"Oh my God, we should have coffee! We must have coffee! There's so much to talk about," said Lorraine. She lowered her voice so much, it became muffled. Lorraine worked in a busy open-plan office. "I have gossip hot off the press. I have sizzling-hot gossip."

"Give it to me now," said Madeline happily, settling back and resting her feet. "Right this minute."

"OK, here's a hint," said Lorraine. *"Parlez-vous anglais?"*

"Yes, I do speak English," said Madeline.

"That's all I can say in French," said Lorraine. "So this is a French matter."

"A French matter?" said Madeline confusedly.

"Yes, and um, and it relates to our mutual friend Renata."

"Is this something to do with the petition?" said Madeline. "Because I hope you haven't signed it, Lorraine. Amabella hasn't even said that it *is* Ziggy who has been hurting her, and the school is monitoring the class now every single day."

"Yeah, I thought a petition was a bit dramatic, although I did hear the child's mother made Amabella cry and then kicked Harper in the sandpit, so I guess there are two sides to every story—but no, this is nothing to do with the petition, Madeline, I'm talking about a *French* matter."

"The nanny," said Madeline with a flash of inspiration. "Is that who you mean? Juliette? What about her? Apparently, this bullying had been going on for ages and that Juliette didn't even—"

"Yes, yes, that's who I mean, but forget the petition! It's, ah, how can I say this? It's related to our mutual friend's husband."

"And the nanny," said Madeline.

"Exactly," said Lorraine.

"I don't under— *No.*" Madeline put her feet back on the floor and sat up straight. "You're not serious? *Geoff* and the *nanny?*" It was impossible not to feel a rush of pleasure at the tabloid-type shock of it. Rule-following, righteous, bird-watching, paunchy Geoff and the young French nanny. It was such an appallingly delicious cliché. "They're having an affair?"

"Yup. Just like Romeo and Juliet, except it's, you know, Geoff and Juliette," said Lorraine, who had apparently given up hope of trying to keep the details of her conversation secret from her colleagues.

Madeline felt a slightly sick feeling, as if she'd scoffed down something sickly sweet and bad for her. "That's awful. That's horrendous." She wished Renata ill, but she didn't wish her this. The only woman who deserved a philandering husband was a philandering wife. "Does Renata know?"

"Apparently not," said Lorraine. "But it's confirmed. Geoff told Andrew Faraday at squash, and Andrew told Shane, who told Alex. Men are such shocking gossips."

"Someone has to tell her," said Madeline.

"Well, it won't be me," said Lorraine. "Shoot the messenger and all that."

"It can't be *me*," said Madeline. "I'm the last person she should hear it from."

"Just don't tell anyone," said Lorraine. "I promised Alex I wouldn't tell a soul."

"Right," said Madeline. No doubt this juicy piece of gossip was hurtling its way like a pinball across the peninsula, bouncing from friend to friend, husband to wife, and would soon enough hit poor Renata smack in the face, just when the poor woman thought the most stressful thing going on in her life was her daughter being bullied at school.

"Apparently little Juliette wants to take him to meet 'er parents in France," said Lorraine, putting on a French accent. "Ooh la la."

"Oh, enough, Lorraine!" said Madeline sharply. "It's not funny. I don't want to hear anymore." It was completely unfair, seeing as she'd relished receiving the gossip in the first place.

"Sorry, darling," said Lorraine unperturbed. "What can I do for you, anyway?"

Madeline made the booking, and Lorraine handled it with her usual efficiency, and Madeline wished she'd just sent her an e-mail.

"So I'll see you Saturday night," said Lorraine.

"Saturday night? Oh, of course, the trivia night," said Madeline. She spoke warmly to make up for her earlier sharpness. "Looking forward to it. I've got a new dress."

"I bet you have," said Lorraine. "I'm going as Elvis. No rules that say the women have to go as Audrey and the men have to go as Elvis."

Madeline laughed, feeling fond of Lorraine again, whose big, loud, raucous laugh would set the tone for a fun night.

"I'll see you then," said Lorraine. "Oh, hey! What's this charity thing that Abigail is doing?"

"I'm not sure exactly," said Madeline. "She's raising money for Amnesty International doing something. Maybe a raffle? Actually, I should tell her she needs to get a permit to run a raffle."

"Mmmm," said Lorraine.

"What?" said Madeline.

"Mmmm."

"What?" Madeline swung her swivel chair around and her elbow knocked a manila folder off the corner of her desk. She caught it in time. "What's going on?"

"I don't know," said Lorraine. "Petra just mentioned something about this project Abigail was doing, and I got the feeling there was something, I don't know, a bit off about it. Petra was giggling, being all irritating and silly, and making these obscure references about some of the other girls not approving of what Abigail was doing, but *Petra* approved, which is no great endorsement. Sorry. I'm being a bit vague. Just that my mother instincts went a little, you know, wah, wah, wah." She made a sound like a car alarm.

Madeline remembered now that strange comment that somebody had made on Abigail's Facebook page. She'd forgotten all about it because she'd been distracted by her rage over the cancellation of the math tutor.

"I'll find out," she said. "Thanks for the heads-up."

"It's probably nothing. *Au revoir,* darl." Lorraine hung up.

Madeline picked up her phone and sent Abigail a text: *Call me as soon as you get this. Mum x.*

She'd be in class now, and the kids weren't meant to look at their phones until school hours were over.

Patience, she told herself as she put her hands back on the keyboard. *Right. What next?* The posters to promote next month's

King Lear. Nobody in Pirriwee wanted to see *King Lear* lurching madly about the stage. They wanted contemporary comedy. They had enough Shakespearean drama in their own lives in the school playground and on the soccer field. But Madeline's boss insisted. Ticket sales would be sluggish, and she'd subtly blame Madeline's marketing. It happened every year.

She looked at the phone again. Abigail would probably make her wait till later tonight before she finally called.

"How sharper than a serpent's tooth it is to have a thankless child, *Abigail*," she said to the silent phone. (She could quote great chunks of *King Lear*, thanks to having to listen to the cast rehearsing so often.)

The phone rang, making her jump. It was Nathan.

"Don't get upset," he said.

56.

Violent relationships tend to become more violent over time.

Had she read it in some of that folder of paperwork, or was it something Susi had said in that cool, nonjudgmental voice of hers?

Celeste lay on her side in bed, hugging her pillow to her and looking out the window where Perry had pulled back the curtain so she could see the sea.

"We'll be able to lie in bed and see the ocean!" he'd crowed when they'd first looked at this house, and the real estate agent had shrewdly said, "I'll leave you to look on your own," because, of course, the house spoke for itself. Perry had been like a kid that day, an excited kid running through a new house, not a man about to spend millions on a "prestige ocean-view property." His excitement almost frightened her; it was too raw and optimistic. She'd been right to be superstitious. They were surely heading for a fall. She was fourteen weeks pregnant at the time, nauseated and bloated, with a permanent metallic taste in her mouth, and she was refusing to believe in this pregnancy—but Perry was high on hope, as if the new house would somehow guarantee the pregnancy would work, because "What a life! What a life for children, living this close to the beach!" That was before he'd ever even raised his voice to her, when the idea of his hitting her would have been impossible, inconceivable, laughable.

She was still so shocked.

It was just so very, very . . . surprising.

She'd tried so hard to convey the depth of her shock to Susi, but something told her that all of Susi's clients felt the same way. ("But no, you see, for *us*, it's really surprising!" she wanted to say.)

"More tea?"

Perry stood at the bedroom door. He was still in his work clothes, but he'd taken off his jacket and tie and rolled the sleeves of his shirt up above his elbows. "I have to go into the office this afternoon, but I'll work from home this morning to make sure you're OK," he'd said after he'd helped her off the hallway floor, as if she'd slipped and hurt herself, or been suddenly overcome by a dizzy spell. He'd called Madeline, without asking Celeste, and asked if she would mind picking the boys up from school today. "Celeste is sick," she'd heard him say, and the concern and compassion in his voice were so real, so genuine, it was as though he really did believe that she'd suddenly been felled by a mysterious illness. Maybe he did believe it.

"No thanks," she said.

She looked at his handsome, caring face, blinked and saw his face up close to hers, jeering, "Not good enough," before he slammed her head against the wall.

So surprising.

Dr. Jekyll and Mr. Hyde.

Which one was the baddie? She didn't know. She closed her eyes. The ice pack had helped, but the pain had settled at a certain level and stayed that way, as if it were always going to be there: a tender, throbbing circle. When she put her fingertips to it, she expected it to feel like a pulpy tomato.

"OK, well. Sing out if you need anything."

She almost laughed.

"I will," she said.

He left, and she closed her eyes. She'd *embarrassed* him. Would he feel embarrassed if she really did leave? Would he feel humiliated if the world knew that his Facebook posts didn't tell the whole story?

"You need to take precautions. The most dangerous time for a battered woman is after she ends the relationship," Susi had told Celeste more than once at their last session, as though she were looking for a response that Celeste wasn't giving her.

Celeste had never taken that seriously. For her it was always about making the decision to leave, to stay or to go, as though going would be the end of her story.

She was delusional. She was a fool.

If his anger had burned just a notch higher today, then he would have hit her head once more against the wall. He would have hit harder. He could have killed her, and then he would have sunk to his knees and cradled her body, keening and shouting and feeling really very upset and sorry for himself—but so what? She'd be dead. He could never make it up to her. Her boys would have no mother, and Perry was a wonderful father, but he didn't give them enough fruit and he always forgot to clean their teeth and she wanted to see them grown up.

If she left he would probably kill her.

If she stayed, and they remained on this trajectory together, he would probably, eventually, find something to be angry enough about that he would kill her.

There was no way out. An apartment with neatly made beds was no escape plan. It was a joke.

It was just so very *surprising* that the good-looking, worried man who had just offered her a cup of tea, and was right now working at his computer down the hallway, and who would come running if she called him, and who loved her with all of his strange heart, would in all probability one day kill her.

57.

"Abigail has built a website," said Nathan.

"OK," said Madeline. She had stood up from her desk, as if she had to leave for somewhere, right now. The school? The hospital? Jail? What could be so momentous about a website?

"It's to raise funds for Amnesty International," said Nathan. "It's very professionally put together. I've been helping her with this Web design course she's doing at school, but obviously, I didn't . . . um . . . yes, well I didn't foresee this."

"I don't get it. What's the problem?" said Madeline sharply. It wasn't like Nathan to see a problem when there wasn't one. He was more likely to miss a problem that was staring him in the face.

Nathan cleared his throat. He spoke in a strangled voice. "It's not the end of the world, but it's certainly not ideal."

"Nathan!" Madeline stamped her foot in frustration.

"Fine," said Nathan. He spoke in a rush: "Abigail is auctioning off her virginity to the highest bidder as a way of raising awareness for child marriage and sex slavery. She says, um, 'If the world stands by while a seven-year-old is sold for sex, then the world shouldn't blink an eye if a privileged white fourteen-year-old girl sells herself for sex.' All the money raised will go to Amnesty International. She can't spell 'privileged.'"

Madeline sank back down in her chair. Oh, calamity.

"Give me the address," said Madeline. "Is the site live? Are you telling me the site is actually live right now?"

"Yes," said Nathan. "I think it went up yesterday morning. Don't look at it. Please don't look at it. The problem is that she hasn't set it up so she can moderate comments, and naturally, the Internet trolls are in a feeding frenzy."

"Give me the address right now."

"No."

"Nathan, you give me the address right now!" She stomped her foot again, almost in tears of frustration.

"It's www.buymyvirginitytostopchildmarriageandsexslavery .com."

"Fabulous," said Madeline as she typed in the address with shaky hands. "That's going to attract a wonderful class of chari- table person. Our daughter is an idiot. We raised an idiot. Oh, wait, you didn't raise her. I raised her. I've raised an idiot." She paused. "Oh God."

"You're looking at it?" said Nathan.

"Yes," said Madeline. It was a professional-looking website, which made it worse for some reason, more real, more official, as if the right for some stranger to purchase Abigail's virginity had been officially endorsed. The home page featured the photo of Abigail doing her yoga pose that Madeline had seen on her Face- book page. Viewed in the context of "buy my virginity," the photo took on a sinister sexuality: the hair falling over her shoulder, the long, skinny limbs, the small, perfect breasts. Men were looking at her daughter's photo on their computer screens and thinking about having sex with her.

"I think I'm going to be sick," said Madeline.

"I know," said Nathan.

Madeline took a breath and clicked through the site with her professional marketing and PR eye. Along with the photo of Abigail, there were also images from the Amnesty International website about child marriage and sex slavery; Abigail had presumably helped herself without asking permission. The copy was good. Straightforward. Persuasive. Emotional without being over-the-top. Apart from the typo in the word "privileged" and the fact that the entire premise was horrifyingly flawed, it was hugely impressive for a fourteen-year-old.

"Is this even legal?" she said after a moment. "It must be illegal for an underage child to sell her virginity."

"It would be illegal for someone to buy it," said Nathan. She could tell he was speaking through gritted teeth.

For a moment Madeline felt disoriented as she realized that she was talking to *Nathan*. She must have subconsciously felt as though she were dealing with Ed, because she'd never before had to discuss a tricky parenting problem with Nathan. She set the rules and Nathan followed them. They weren't a team.

But the thought simultaneously occurred to her that if it were Ed, it wouldn't be the same. Ed would be horrified at the thought of a man buying Abigail's virginity, of course he would, but he wouldn't be experiencing the visceral agony that Nathan was feeling. If it were Chloe, yes. But there was that subtle distance in Ed's relationship with Abigail, the distance Madeline had always denied and yet Abigail had always felt.

She clicked on the section for "bids and donations." Abigail had set it up so that people could leave comments and register their "bids."

The words swam in front of her:

How much for a gang bang?

You can suck my cock for $20! Any time, any place.

Hey, pretty little girl, I'll fuck that tight little cunt of yours for free.

Madeline pushed herself back away from her desk, the taste of bile in her mouth. "How do we shut this website down right now? Do you know how to shut it down?"

She was pleased to note that she hadn't lost control, that she was speaking as if this were a work crisis: a leaflet that needed reprinting, a mistake on the theater website. Nathan was tech savvy. He must know what to do. But as she clicked off the comments page and saw the photo of Abigail again, her innocent, ridiculous, misguided daughter—vile men were thinking and saying vile things about her *little girl*—her anger rose volcanically from the pit of her stomach and burst from her mouth.

"How the hell did this happen? Why weren't you and Bonnie watching what she was doing? You fix it! Fix it now!"

Harper: Has anyone told you about Madeline's daughter's little drama? I mean, I hate to say it, but as I said to Renata at the time, she was over at my place for dinner I think, I said, "Now, that wouldn't happen at a private school." I'm not saying there's anything *wrong* with public high schools per se, I just think your children are more likely to interact with, you know, a better class of person.

Samantha: That Harper is so up herself. Of course it could have happened at a private school. And Abigail's intentions were so noble! It's just that fourteen-year-old

girls are stupid. Poor Madeline. She blamed Nathan and
Bonnie, although I don't know if that was fair.

Bonnie: Yes, Madeline did blame us. I accept that. Abigail was in my care at the time. But that had absolutely
nothing to do with . . . with the tragedy. Nothing at all.

58.

After their visit to the psychologist, Jane drove Ziggy down to the beach to have some morning tea at Blue Blues before she took him back to school.

"The special today is apple pancakes with lemon-spiced butter," said Tom. "I think you should try some. On the house."

"On the house?" frowned Ziggy.

"For free," explained Jane. She looked up at Tom. "But I think we should pay."

Tom was always giving her free food. It was starting to get embarrassing. She wondered if he had somehow gotten the impression she was poverty-stricken.

"We'll work that out later," Tom said with a little wave of his hand, which meant that he wouldn't accept any money from her, no matter how hard she tried.

He disappeared into the kitchen.

She and Ziggy both turned their faces to look at the ocean. There was a brisk breeze blowing and the sea looked playful, with white wavelets dancing across the horizon. Jane breathed in the wonderful scents of Blue Blues and felt an intensely nostalgic feeling, as if the decision had already been made and she and Ziggy were definitely going to move.

The lease on her apartment was up for renewal in two weeks'

time. They could move somewhere brand-new, put him into a new school, start afresh with their reputations unsullied. Even if the psychologist was right and Ziggy really was experiencing bullying himself, there was no way that Jane could make the school consider that a possibility. It would be like a strategic move, as if she were countersuing. *Accuse me of damages and I'll accuse you right back.* Anyway, how could they possibly stay at a school where parents were signing a petition for them to leave? Everything had become too complicated now. People probably thought she'd attacked Harper in the sandpit and bullied Amabella. She *had* made Amabella cry, and she felt terrible about that. The only solution was to go. That was the right thing to do. The right thing for both of them.

Perhaps it had been inevitable that her time at Pirriwee would end so disastrously. Her real, unadmitted reasons for coming here were so peculiar, so messed up and downright weird, that she couldn't even let herself properly articulate them.

But perhaps coming here actually had been a strange necessary step in some process, because something had healed in the last few months. Even while she'd been suffering the confusion and worry over Ziggy and the other mothers, her feelings for Saxon Banks had undergone a subtle change. She felt she could see him with clear eyes now. Saxon Banks was not a monster. He was just a man. Just your basic nasty thug. They were a dime a dozen. It was preferable not to sleep with them. But she had. And that was that. Ziggy was here. Perhaps only Saxon Banks had sufficiently thuggish-enough sperm to get past her fertility issues. Perhaps he really was the only man in the world who could have given her a baby, and perhaps she could now find a fair, balanced way to talk about him so that Ziggy stopped thinking his father was some kind of sinister supervillain.

"Ziggy," she said, "would you like us to move to another school where you could make brand-new friends?"

"Nope," said Ziggy. He seemed in a cheeky, quirky, flip mood right now. Not at all anxious. Did that psychologist know what she was talking about?

What did Madeline always say? "Children are so weird and random."

"Oh," said Jane. "Why not? You were very upset the other day when those children said they weren't—you know—allowed to play with you."

"Yeah," said Ziggy cheerfully. "But I've got lots of other friends who are allowed to play with me, like Chloe and Fred. Even though Fred is in Year 2, he's still my friend, because we both like *Star Wars*. And I've got other friends too. Like Harrison and Amabella and Henry."

"Did you say *Amabella*?" said Jane. He'd never actually mentioned playing with Amabella before, which was part of the reason it had seemed so unlikely that he'd been bullying her. She thought they traveled in different circles, so to speak.

"Amabella likes *Star Wars* too," said Ziggy. "She knows all this stuff because she's a really super-good reader. So we don't really *play*, but sometimes if I'm a bit tired of running we sit together under the Sea Dragon Tree and talk about *Star Wars* stuff."

"Amabella Klein? Amabella in kindergarten?" checked Jane.

"Yeah, Amabella! Except the teachers won't let us talk anymore," sighed Ziggy.

"Well, that's because Amabella's parents think you've been hurting her," said Jane with a touch of exasperation.

"It's not me who hurt her," said Ziggy, half sliding off his chair in that profoundly annoying way of little boys. (She'd been relieved to see Fred doing exactly the same thing.)

"Sit up," said Jane sharply.

He sat up and sighed again. "I'm hungry. Do you think my pancakes are coming soon?" He craned his neck to look back toward the kitchen.

Jane surveyed him. The words he'd just said registered properly. *It's not me who hurt her.*

"Ziggy," she said. Had she asked him this question before? Had *anyone* asked him this question? Or had they all just said over and over, "Was it you, Ziggy? Was it you?"

"What?" he said.

"Do *you* know who has been hurting Amabella?"

It happened instantly. His face closed down. "I don't want to talk about it." His lower lip trembled.

"But just tell me, sweetheart, do you know?"

"I promised," said Ziggy softly.

Jane leaned forward. "You promised what?"

"I promised Amabella I wouldn't tell anyone ever. She said if I told anyone she would probably get killed dead."

"Killed dead," repeated Jane.

"Yes!" said Ziggy passionately. His eyes filled with tears.

Jane tapped her fingers. She knew he wanted to tell her.

"What if," she said slowly, "what if you wrote down the name?"

Ziggy frowned. He blinked and brushed away the tears.

"Because then you're not breaking your promise to Amabella. That's not like telling me. And *I promise you* that Amabella will not get killed dead."

"Mmmm." Ziggy considered this.

Jane pulled a notebook and pen from her bag and pushed it toward him. "Can you spell it? Or just have a go at spelling it."

That's what they were taught at school; to "have a go" with their writing.

Ziggy took the pen, and then he turned around, distracted by the café door opening. Two people came inside: a woman with a blond bob and an unremarkable businessman. (Graying middle-aged men in suits all looked pretty much the same to Jane.)

"That's Emily J's mum," said Ziggy.

Harper. Jane felt her face flush as she remembered the mortifying incident in the sandpit, where Harper had accused her of assault. There had been a strained call from Mrs. Lipmann that night, advising Jane that a parent had made an official complaint against her and suggesting that she "lay low, so to speak, until this difficult matter was resolved."

Harper glanced her way, and Jane felt her heart race, as if with a terrible fear. *For God's sake, she's not going to kill you,* she thought. It was so strange to be in a state of intense conflict with a person she barely knew. Jane had spent most of her grown-up life side-stepping confrontations. It was mystifying to her that Madeline could *enjoy* this sort of thing and actually seek it out. This was awful: embarrassing, awkward and distressing.

Harper's husband tapped one finger smartly on the bell on the counter—*ding!*—to summon Tom from the kitchen. The café wasn't busy. There was a woman with a toddler in the far right-hand corner and a couple of men in paint-splattered blue overalls eating egg and bacon rolls.

Jane saw Harper nudge her husband and speak in his ear. He looked over at Jane and Ziggy.

Oh God. He was coming over.

He had one of those big, firm beer bellies he carried proudly, as if it were a badge of honor.

"Hi there," he said to Jane, holding out his hand. "Jane, is it? I'm Graeme. Emily's dad."

Jane shook his hand. He squeezed just hard enough to let her know that he was making the decision not to squeeze any harder. "Hello," she said. "This is Ziggy."

"Gidday, mate." Graeme's eyes flickered toward Ziggy and then straight back again.

"Please leave it, Graeme," said Harper, who had come to stand next to him. She studiously ignored Jane and Ziggy; it was like at school in the sandpit when she'd played that freaky "avoid eye contact at all costs" game.

"Listen, *Jane*," said Graeme. "Obviously I don't want to say too much in front of your son here, but I understand you're embroiled in some sort of dispute with the school and I don't know the ins and outs of all that, and frankly I'm not that interested, but let me tell you this, *Jane*."

He placed both palms on the table and leaned over her. It was such a calculated, intimidating move, it was almost comical. Jane lifted her chin. She needed to swallow, but she didn't want him to see her gulping nervously. She could see the deep lines around his eyes. A tiny mole next to his nose. He was doing that ugly teeth-jutting thing that a certain type of shirtless, tattooed man did when he was yelling at reporters on tabloid television.

"We decided not to get the police involved this time, but if I hear that you go near my wife again I'll be taking out a restraining order against you, quick-smart, *Jane*, because I will not stand for this. I'm a partner in a law firm and I will bring the full weight of the law down on your—"

"You need to leave now."

It was Tom, carrying a plate of pancakes. He placed the plate on Jane's table and cupped one hand gently over the back of Ziggy's head.

"Oh, Tom, I'm sorry we just . . ." fluttered Harper. The mothers of Pirriwee were addicted to Tom's coffee and treated him as a beloved drug dealer.

Graeme straightened and pulled once on his tie. "All OK here, mate."

"No," said Tom. "It's not. I won't have you harassing my customers. I'd like you to leave right now." Tom's teeth weren't jutting, but his jaw was clenched.

Graeme tapped his closed fist, knuckles down, on Jane's table. "Look, legally, mate, I don't think you actually have the right to—"

"I don't want legal advice," said Tom. "I am asking you to leave."

"Tom, I'm so sorry," said Harper. "We certainly didn't mean—"

"I'm sure I'll see you both another time," said Tom. He went to the door and held it open. "Just not today."

"Fine," said Graeme. He turned and pointed a finger an inch away from Jane's nose. "Remember what I said, young lady, because—"

"Get out before I throw you out," said Tom, dangerously quiet.

Graeme straightened. He looked at Tom.

"You just lost yourself a customer," he said as he followed his wife out the door.

"I certainly hope so," said Tom.

He let the door go and turned and looked back at his customers. "Sorry about that."

One of the men in overalls clapped. "Good on ya, mate!" The woman with the toddler stared curiously at Jane. Ziggy twisted around in his seat to look out the glass windows at Harper and Graeme hurrying off down the boardwalk, then he shrugged, picked up his fork and began to eat his pancakes with gusto.

Tom came over to Jane and crouched down beside her, his arm on the back of her chair.

"You OK?"

Jane took a deep, shaky breath. Tom smelled sweet and clean. He always had that distinctive fresh, clean smell because he surfed twice a day, followed by a long, hot shower. (She knew this because he'd once told her that he stood under the hot water, replaying all the best waves he'd just caught.) It occurred to Jane that she loved Tom, just as she loved Madeline and Celeste, and that it would break her heart to leave Pirriwee, but that it was impossible to stay. She'd made real friends here, but she'd also made real enemies. There was no future for her here.

"I'm OK," she said. "Thank you. Thank you for that."

"Excuse me! Oh dear, I'm sorry!" The toddler had just spilled his babycino all over the floor and was crying.

Tom put his hand on Jane's arm. "Don't let Ziggy eat all those pancakes." He stood and went over to help the woman, saying, "It's OK, little buddy, I'm going to get you another one."

Jane picked up her fork and took a mouthful of the apple pancakes. She closed her eyes. "Mmmm." Tom was going to make some lucky man extremely happy one day.

"I wrote it down," said Ziggy.

"Wrote what down?" Jane used her fork to cut another edge of the pancake. She was trying not to think of Harper's husband. The way he'd leaned over her. His intimidation tactics were absurd, but they'd also worked. She'd felt intimidated. And now she felt ashamed. Had she deserved it? Because she'd kicked at Harper in the sandpit? But she hadn't actually kicked *Harper*! She was positive she hadn't actually made contact. But still. She'd let her temper get the better of her. She'd behaved badly, and Harper had gone home upset, and she had a loving, overprotective husband who had felt angry on her behalf.

"The *name*," said Ziggy. He pushed the notepad at her. "The name of the kid who does stuff to Amabella."

> **Samantha:** So apparently Harper's husband won't let her go into Blue Blues anymore. I said, "Harper, it's not 1950! Your husband can't forbid you to go into a café!" But she said he'd see it as a betrayal. Bugger that. I'd betray Stu for Tom's coffee. Jeez. I'd murder for it! I'm not the murderer, though, if that's what you're thinking. I don't think coffee was involved.

Jane put down her fork and pulled the notebook toward her. Ziggy had scrawled four letters across the page. Some were enormous. Some were tiny.

M a K s

"Maks," said Jane. "There's no one called——" She stopped. Oh, calamity. "Do you mean *Max*?"

Ziggy nodded. "The mean twin."

59.

It's two o'clock. I'm going for my meeting now," said Perry. "Madeline is picking up the kids. I'm going to be back by four, so just stick them in front of the TV until I'm home. How are you feeling?"

Celeste looked up at him.

It was a kind of lunacy, really. The way he could behave like this. As if she were in bed with a bad migraine. As if this had nothing to do with him. The more time that passed, the less anguished he looked. His guilt slowly seeped away. His body metabolized it, like alcohol. And she colluded in his lunacy. She went along with it. She was behaving as if she were ill. She was letting him take care of her.

They were both crazy.

"I'm all right," she said.

He'd just given her a strong painkiller. She normally resisted analgesics because she was so susceptible to them, but the pain in her head had finally become more than she could stand. Within minutes the pain had begun to melt away, but everything else was melting as well. She could feel her limbs becoming heavy and somnolent. The walls of the bedroom seemed to soften, and her thoughts became languid, as if she were sunbathing on a hot summer's day.

"When you were little," she said.

"Yes?" Perry sat beside her and held her hand.

"That year," she said. "That year when you were bullied."

He smiled. "When I was a fat little kid wearing glasses."

"It was bad, wasn't it?" she said. "You laugh about it, but it was a really bad year."

He squeezed her hand. "Yes. It was bad. It was very bad."

What was her point? She couldn't turn it into words. Something to do with the frustrated anger of a terrorized eight-year-old and how she always wondered if that's what this was all about. Each time Perry felt disrespected or humiliated, Celeste bore the brunt of a fat little boy's violent, suppressed rage. Except that now he was a six-foot man.

"It was Saxon who helped you in the end, wasn't it?" she said. Her words were melting too. She could hear it.

"Saxon knocked out the ringleader's front tooth," said Perry. He chuckled. "Never got picked on again."

"Right," said Celeste. Saxon Banks. Perry's hero. Jane's tormentor. Ziggy's father.

Ever since the night of the book club, Saxon had been in the back of her mind. She and Jane had something in common: They had both been hurt by these men. These handsome, successful, cruel cousins. Celeste felt responsible for what Saxon had done to Jane. She was so young and vulnerable. If only *Celeste* had been there to protect her. She had experience. She could hit and scratch when necessary.

There was some connection she was trying to make. A fleeting thought she couldn't catch, like something half glimpsed in her peripheral vision. It had been bugging her for a while.

What was Saxon's excuse for behaving the way he did? He

hadn't been bullied as a child as far as Celeste knew. So did that mean Perry's behavior wasn't anything to do with the year he was bullied? It was a family trait they shared?

"But you're not as bad as him," she mumbled. Wasn't that the only point? Yes. That was key. That was key to everything.

"What?" Perry looked bemused.

"You wouldn't do that,"

"Wouldn't do what?" said Perry.

"So sleepy," said Celeste.

"I know," said Perry. "Go to sleep now, honey." He pulled the sheets up under her chin and pushed her hair off her face. "I'll be back soon."

As she succumbed to sleep she thought she heard him whisper in her ear, "I'm so sorry," but she might have already been dreaming.

60.

I can't bloody shut it down," said Nathan. "If I could have shut
it down, don't you think I would have? Before I called you? It's
a public website held on a server *that's not inside the house*. I
can't just flick a switch. I need her log-in details. I need her password."

"Miss Polly had a dolly!" shouted Madeline. "That's the password.
She's got the same password for everything. Go shut it down!"

She'd always known Abigail's passwords for her social media
accounts. That was the deal so Madeline could check in any time,
along with the understanding that Madeline was allowed to silently creep into Abigail's bedroom at random moments like a cat
burglar and look over her shoulder at the computer screen for as
long as it took Abigail to notice she was standing there, which
often took a while, because Madeline had a special talent for
creeping. It drove Abigail crazy and made her jump out of her skin
each time she finally sensed Madeline's presence, but Madeline
didn't care, that was good parenting in this day and age, you spied
on your children, and *that* was why this would never have happened if Abigail had been at home where she belonged.

"I've tried 'Miss Polly had a dolly,'" said Nathan heavily. "It's
not that."

"You mustn't be doing it right. It's all lowercase, no spaces. It's *always*—"

"I told her just the other day that she shouldn't have the same password for everything," said Nathan. "She must have listened to me."

"Right," said Madeline. Her anger had cooled and solidified into something mammoth and glacial. "Good one. Good advice. Great fathering."

"It's because of identity theft—"

"Whatever! Be quiet, let me think." She tapped two fingers rapidly against her mouth. "Have you got a pen?"

"Of course I've got a pen."

"Try 'Huckleberry.'"

"Why Huckleberry?"

"It was her first pet. A puppy. We had her for two weeks. She got run over. Abigail was devastated. You were— Where were you? Bali? Vanuatu? Who knows? Don't ask questions. Just listen."

She listed off twenty potential passwords in quick succession: bands, TV characters, authors and random things like "chocolate" and "I hate Mum."

"It won't be that," said Nathan.

Madeline ignored him. She was filled with despair at the impossibility of the task. It could be anything, any combination of letters and numbers.

"Are you sure there is no other way to do this?" she said.

"I was thinking I could try to redirect the domain name," said Nathan, "but then I still need to log in to her account. The world revolves around log-ins. I guess some IT genius might be able to hack into the site, it's just a Google-hosting account, but that would take time. We'll get it down eventually, but obviously the fastest way is for her to do it herself."

"Yes," said Madeline. She'd already pulled her car keys from her bag. "I'm going to get her out of school early."

"You, I mean, *we*, we just have to *tell* her to take it down." Madeline could hear the keyboard clattering as he tried the different passwords. "We're her parents. We have to tell her there will be, er, *consequences* if she doesn't listen to us."

It was sort of hilarious hearing Nathan using modern parenting terminology like "consequences."

"Right, and that's going to be so easy," said Madeline. "She's fourteen, she thinks she's saving the world and she's as stubborn as a mule."

"We'll tell her she's grounded!" said Nathan excitedly, obviously remembering that's what parents did to teenagers on American sitcoms.

"She'd love that. She'll see herself as a martyr to the cause."

"But I mean, for God's sake, surely she's not *serious*," said Nathan. "She's not really planning to actually go through with this. To have sex with some stranger? I just can't . . . She's never even had a boyfriend, has she?"

"As far as I know, she hasn't even kissed a boy," said Madeline, and she wanted to cry, because she knew exactly what Abigail would say in response to that: *Those little girls haven't kissed any boys either.*

She squeezed the keys tight in her hand. "I'd better rush. I've only just got time before I pick up the little kids."

She remembered then that Perry had called earlier to ask if

she'd pick up the twins because Celeste was sick. Her left eyelid began to twitch.

"Madeline," said Nathan, "don't yell at her, will you? Because——"

"Are you kidding? Of course I'm going to yell at her!" yelled Madeline. "She's selling her virginity on the Internet!"

61.

Jane drove Ziggy up to the school after their morning tea at Blue Blues.

"Will you tell Max to stop hurting Amabella?" he said to her as she parked the car.

"A grown-up will talk to him," said Jane as she turned the key in the ignition. "Probably not *me*. Maybe Miss Barnes."

She was trying to work out the best way to handle this. Should she march straight into the principal's office right this minute? She'd prefer to speak with Miss Barnes, who would be more likely to believe that this wasn't a case of Ziggy simply deflecting the blame by pointing the finger at someone else. Also, Miss Barnes knew that Jane and Celeste were friends. She would know this was potentially awkward.

But Miss Barnes was teaching right now. She couldn't drag her out of the classroom. She would have to e-mail her and ask her to call.

But she wanted to tell someone *now*. Perhaps she *should* go straight to Mrs. Lipmann?

It wasn't like Amabella was in mortal danger. Apparently the teacher's aide never took her eyes off her. Jane's impatience simply reflected her own desire to tattle. *It wasn't my son! It was her son!*

And what about poor Celeste? Should she call her first and warn her? Was that what a good friend would do? Maybe it was. There was something awful and underhanded about going behind her back. She couldn't bear it if this affected their friendship.

"Come on, Mummy," said Ziggy impatiently. "Why are you just sitting there staring at nothing?"

Jane undid her seat belt and turned around to face Ziggy. "You did the right thing telling me about Max, Ziggy."

"I didn't tell you!" Ziggy, who had already unbuckled his belt and had his hand on the car-door handle ready to jump out, flung himself back around to face her. He was outraged, horrified.

"Sorry, sorry!" said Jane. "No, of course you didn't tell me. Definitely not."

"Because I promised Amabella I would never ever tell anyone." Ziggy pushed his body between the driver's seat and the passenger seat so his anxious little face was right next to hers. She could see a smear of sticky sauce above his lip from Tom's pancakes.

"That's right. You kept your promise." Jane licked her finger and tried to use it to clean his face.

"I kept my promise." Ziggy ducked away from her finger. "I'm good at keeping promises."

"So you remember at the orientation day?" Jane gave up on cleaning his face. "When Amabella said that it was you who hurt her? Why did Amabella say it was you?"

"Max said if she told on him he would do it again when no grown-ups were looking," said Ziggy. "So Amabella pointed at me." He shrugged impatiently, as if he were becoming bored with the whole subject. "She said sorry about that. I said it was OK."

"You're a very nice boy, Ziggy," said Jane. *And you're not a psychopath! (*Max *is a psychopath.)*

"Yup."

"And I love you."

"Can we go into school now?" Ziggy put his hand back on the car-door handle.

"Absolutely."

As they walked down the path toward the school, Ziggy skipped ahead, his backpack bouncing on his back, as if he didn't have a care in the world.

Jane's heart lifted at the sight of him and hurried to keep up. He hadn't been anxious because he was being bullied. He'd been anxious because he'd been bravely and foolishly carrying a secret. Even when Mrs. Lipmann had accused him, her brave little soldier hadn't cracked. He'd stood firm for Amabella. Ziggy wasn't a bully. He was a *hero*.

He was also pretty dumb for not telling on Max straightaway and because he seriously seemed to think writing down a name didn't count as telling, but he was five, and he was a kid in desperate need of a loophole.

Ziggy picked up a stick lying on the pavement and waved it over his head.

"Put down the stick, Ziggy!" she called. He tossed the stick and made a sharp right turn at the grassy alleyway leading past Mrs. Ponder's house and into the school.

Jane kicked the stick off the path and followed him. What could Max have said to make a clever little girl like Amabella think that she had to keep his behavior a secret? Had he really told her he would "kill her dead"? And had Amabella genuinely believed that was a possibility?

She considered what she knew about Max. Apart from Max's birthmark, she couldn't differentiate between Celeste's boys.

She'd thought their personalities were identical too. To her, Max and Josh were like cute, naughty little puppies. With their boundless energy and big cheeky grins, they'd always seemed like such uncomplicated children, unlike Ziggy, who was so often unreadable and brooding. Celeste's boys seemed like the sort of children who needed to be fed and bathed and run about: physically exhausting, but not mentally draining; the way a secretive little boy like Ziggy could be.

How would Celeste react when she found out what Max had done? Jane couldn't imagine. She knew exactly how Madeline would react (crazily, loudly), but she had never seen Celeste really angry with her boys; of course she got frustrated and impatient, but she never shouted. Celeste so often seemed jumpy and preoccupied, startled by the existence of her children when they suddenly ran at her.

"Good morning! Did you sleep in this morning?" It was Mrs. Ponder, calling out from her front yard where she was watering the garden.

"We had an appointment," explained Jane.

"So tell me, love, are you dressing up as Audrey or Elvis tomorrow night?" Mrs. Ponder gave her a sparky, teasing grin.

For a moment Jane couldn't think what she was talking about. "Audrey or Elvis? Oh! The trivia night." She'd forgotten all about it. Madeline had organized a table ages ago, but that was before all the recent events: the petition, the sandpit assault. "I'm not sure if—"

"Oh, I was teasing, love! Of course you'll go as Audrey. You've got just the figure for it. Actually you'd look lovely with one of those short, boyish haircuts. What do they call it? A pixie cut!"

"Oh," said Jane. She pulled on her ponytail. "Thanks."

"Speaking of hair, darling"—Mrs. Ponder leaned forward confidentially—"Ziggy is having a good old scratch there."

Mrs. Ponder said "Ziggy" like it was a hilarious nickname.

Jane looked at Ziggy. He was vigorously scratching his head with one hand while he crouched down to examine something important he'd seen in the grass.

"Yes," she said politely. *So what?*

"Have you checked?" said Mrs. Ponder.

"Checked for what?" Jane wondered if she was being particularly obtuse today.

"Nits," said Mrs. Ponder. "You know, head lice."

"Oh!" Jane clapped her hand to her mouth. "No! Do you think— Oh! I don't— I can't— Oh!"

Mrs. Ponder chuckled. "Didn't you ever have them as a child? They've been around for thousands of years."

"No! I remember one time there was an outbreak at my school, but I must have missed out. I don't like anything creepy-crawly." She shuddered. "Oh God."

"Well, I've had plenty of experience with the little buggers. All us nurses got them during the war. It's nothing whatsoever to do with cleanliness or hygiene, if that's what you're thinking. They're just downright annoying, that's all. Come here, Ziggy!"

Ziggy ambled over. Mrs. Ponder broke off a small stick from a rosebush and used it to comb through Ziggy's hair. "Nits!" she said with satisfaction in a nice, clear, loud, carrying voice, at the exact moment that Thea came hurrying by, carrying a lunch box. "He's *crawling* with them."

Thea: Harriett had forgotten her lunch box, and I was rushing into school to drop it off to her—I had a million things to do that day—when what do I hear? Ziggy is crawling with nits! Yes, she took the child home, but if it weren't for Mrs. Ponder, she would have brought him into school! And why is she asking an old lady to check her child's hair in the first place?

62.

Whatever," said Abigail.

"No. Don't say 'whatever.' This is not a 'whatever'-type situation. This is grown-up stuff, Abigail. This is serious." Madeline gripped the steering wheel so hard, she could feel a slick of sweat beneath her palms.

It was incredible, but she hadn't yelled yet. She'd gone to the high school and told Abigail's principal that there was a family emergency and she needed to bring Abigail home. Obviously the school hadn't yet discovered Abigail's website. "Abigail is doing very well," her principal had said, all gracious smiles. "She's very creative."

"She certainly is that," said Madeline, and had managed not to throw back her head and cackle like a hysterical witch.

It had taken a Herculean effort, but she hadn't said a word when they'd gotten in the car. She hadn't screamed, "What were you thinking?" She'd waited for Abigail to speak. (It seemed important, strategically.) Abigail finally spoke up, defensively, her eyes on the dashboard: "So what's this family emergency?"

Madeline said, very calmly, as calmly as Ed, "Well, Abigail, people are writing about having sex with my fourteen-year-old daughter on the Internet."

Abigail had flinched and muttered, "I knew it."

Madeline had thought the involuntary flinch meant that it was going to be fine; Abigail was probably already regretting it. She'd gotten in too far out of her depth and was looking for a way out. She *wanted* her parents to order her to take it down.

"Darling, I understand exactly what you were trying to do," she'd said. "You're doing a publicity campaign with a 'hook.' That's great. It's clever. But in this case the hook is too sensational. You're not achieving what you want to achieve. People aren't thinking about the human rights violations; all they're thinking about is a fourteen-year-old auctioning off her virginity."

"I don't care," said Abigail. "I want to raise money. I want to raise awareness. I want to *do* something. I don't want to say, 'Oh, that's terrible,' and then do nothing."

"Yes, but you're not going to raise money or awareness! You're raising awareness of yourself! 'Abigail Mackenzie, the fourteen-year-old who tried to auction her virginity.' Nobody will care or even remember that you were doing it for charity. You're creating an online footprint for all future employers."

That's when Abigail said, ridiculously, "Whatever."

As if this were all a matter of opinion.

"So tell me, Abigail. Are you planning to go *through* with this? You do know you're below the age of consent? You're fourteen years old. You're too young to be having sex." Madeline's voice shook.

"So are those little girls, Mum!" said Abigail. Her voice shook.

She had too much imagination. Too much empathy. That's what Madeline had been trying to explain to Bonnie at assembly that morning. Those little girls were completely real to Abigail, and of course, they *were* real, there was real pain in the world, right this very moment people were suffering unimaginable atrocities and you couldn't close your heart completely, but you couldn't leave it wide open either, because otherwise how could you possibly live your life, when through pure, random luck you got to live in paradise? You had to register the existence of evil, do the little that you could, and then close your mind and think about new shoes.

"So we'll do something about it," said Madeline. "We'll work together on some sort of awareness-building campaign. We'll get Ed involved! He knows journalists—"

"No," said Abigail flatly. "You'll say all this but then you won't really do anything. You'll get busy and then you'll forget all about it."

"I promise," began Madeline. She knew there was truth in this.

"No," said Abigail.

"This is not actually negotiable," said Madeline. "You are still a child. I will get the police involved if necessary. The website is coming down, Abigail."

"Well, I'm not taking it down," said Abigail. "And I'm not giving Dad the password even if you torture me."

"Oh, for God's sake, don't be so ridiculous. Now you sound like a five-year-old," said Madeline, regretting the words even while they were coming out of her mouth.

They were pulling into the kiss-and-drop zone at the primary school. Madeline could see Renata's shiny black BMW directly in front of her. The windows were too dark to see who was driving—presumably Renata's slatternly French nanny. She imagined Renata's face if she found out that Madeline's daughter was auctioning off her virginity. She'd feel sympathy. Renata wasn't a bad person.

But she'd also feel just a hint of satisfaction, the same way Madeline had when she'd heard about the affair.

Madeline prided herself on not caring what other people thought, but she cared about Renata thinking less of her daughter.

"So you're planning to go through with this? You're going to sleep with some stranger?" said Madeline. She inched the car forward and tried to wave to Chloe, but she didn't see her because she was busy talking animatedly to Lily, who looked faintly bored. Chloe's skirt was hitched up by her backpack so that the entire car line could see her Minnie Mouse underpants. Madeline would normally have found that cute and funny, but at the moment it seemed somehow sinister and wrong, and she wished one of the teachers would notice and fix it.

"Better than sleeping with some Year 12 guy while we're both drunk," said Abigail with her face turned to the window.

Madeline saw Celeste's twins being separated by a teacher. They both had red, angry little faces. She remembered with a start that she was picking them up today. She was so distracted, she could easily have forgotten.

The car line wasn't moving because whoever was at the front of the line was having some long conversation with a teacher, as expressly forbidden by the Pirriwee Primary Kiss-and-Drop/Pickup Policy. It was probably a Blond Bob, because rules obviously didn't apply to them.

"But, my God, Abigail, are you thinking about the reality of this? The logistics? How will it actually work? Where is this going to happen? Are you going to meet this person at a hotel? Are you going to ask me for a lift? 'Oh, Mum, I'm just off to lose my virginity, better stop at a drugstore to buy some condoms'?"

She looked at Abigail's profile. She had her head dropped and one hand shielding her eyes. Madeline could see her lip trembling. Of course she hadn't thought it through. She was fourteen.

"And have you thought through what it would be like to have sex with a stranger? To have some horrible man touching you—"

Abigail dropped her hand and turned her head. "Stop it, Mum!" she shouted.

"You're in la-la land, Abigail. Are you thinking some handsome George Clooney type will take you to his villa, tenderly take your virginity and then write out a generous check to Amnesty International? Because it won't be like that. It will be vile and painful—"

"It's vile and painful for those little girls!" cried Abigail, tears sliding down her face.

"But I'm not their mother!" shouted Madeline, and she slammed straight into the back of Renata's BMW.

> **Harper:** Look, I don't want to be the one casting aspersions, but Madeline deliberately *rammed* Renata's car the day before the trivia night.

63.

J   ust don't spread the word I'm doing this." Mrs. Ponder's
         daughter leaned down and spoke quietly in Jane's ear be-
         neath the cover of roaring hair dryers. "Otherwise I'll have
all the posh mothers coming in here wanting me to delouse their
precious little kids."

At first Mrs. Ponder had told Jane to go to the drugstore to
pick up a lice treatment. "It's easy," she said. "You just comb
through the hair and pick the little bloodsuckers . . ." She stopped
as she considered the expression on Jane's face. "Tell you what,"
she said. "I'll see if Lucy can fit you in today."

Mrs. Ponder's daughter Lucy ran Hairway to Heaven, the very
popular hairdressing salon in Pirriwee, in between the newsagent
and the butcher. Jane had never been in the salon before. Apparently Lucy and her team were responsible for all the blond bobs
on the Pirriwee Peninsula.

As Lucy fastened a cape around Ziggy's neck, Jane looked
around surreptitiously for any parents she might know, but she
didn't recognize anyone.

"Shall I give him a trim while I'm here?" asked Lucy.

"Sure, thanks," said Jane.

Lucy glanced at Jane. "Mum wants me to cut your hair too.
She wants me to give you a pixie cut."

Jane tightened her ponytail. "I don't really bother with my hair that much."

"At the very least you'd better let me have a check of your hair," said Lucy. "You might need a treatment yourself. Lice don't fly, but they do trapeze from head to head, like *leetle lice acrobats*." She put on a Mexican accent and Ziggy chuckled appreciatively.

"Oh, God," said Jane. Her scalp felt instantly itchy.

Lucy considered Jane. She narrowed her eyes. "Have you ever seen the movie *Sliding Doors*? Where Gwyneth Paltrow gets her hair all cut off and it looks fantastic?"

"Sure," said Jane. "Every girl loves that part."

"So does every hairdresser," said Lucy. "It's like a dream job." She kept looking at Jane for a few seconds longer, then she turned back to face Ziggy and put her hands on his shoulders. She grinned at his reflection. "You're not going to recognize your mum once I've finished with her."

> **Samantha:** I didn't recognize Jane when I first saw her at the trivia night. She had this amazing new haircut and she was wearing black capri pants with a white shirt with the collar up and ballet flats. Oh dear. Poor little Jane. She looked so happy at the start of the night!

64.

Celeste really did look ill, thought Madeline as she shepherded the twins in the door. She was wearing a man's white T-shirt and checked pajama pants and her face was dead white.

"Gosh, is it some sort of virus, do you think? It came on so fast!" said Madeline. "You looked perfectly fine at assembly this morning!"

Celeste gave a strange little laugh and put a hand to the back of her head. "Yes, it came out of nowhere."

"Why don't I just take the boys back to my place for a while? Perry can pick them up from there on his way home," said Madeline. She looked back at her car in the driveway. The smashed headlight stared at her reproachfully and expensively. She'd left Abigail crying in the front seat and Fred and Chloe squabbling in the back (and she'd also noticed Fred giving his head a good, vicious scratch, and she knew from horrible experience exactly what that probably meant; it would be just absolutely marvelous if she also had to deal with a nit outbreak right now).

"No, no, that's nice of you, but I'm fine," said Celeste. "I let them have unlimited screen time on Friday afternoons. They'll just be ignoring me anyway. Thank you so much for picking them up."

"Do you think you'll be OK for the trivia night tomorrow?" asked Madeline.

"Oh, I'm sure I'll be fine," said Celeste. "Perry is looking forward to it."

"All right, well, I'd better go," said Madeline. "Abigail and I were shouting at each other in the car line and I ran into the back of Renata's car."

"No!" Celeste put her hand to her face.

"Yes, I was shouting because Abigail is auctioning off her virginity online in a bid to stop child marriage," continued Madeline. Celeste was the first person she'd been able to tell; she was desperate to talk about it.

"She's *what?*"

"It's all for a good cause," said Madeline with mock nonchalance. "So I'm fine with it, of course."

"Oh, Madeline." Celeste put her hand on her arm, and Madeline felt like she might cry.

"Take a look," said Madeline. "The address is www.buymyvirginitytostopchildmarriageandsexslavery.com. Abigail refuses to take it down, even while people are writing the most disgusting things about her."

Celeste winced. "I guess it's better than prostituting herself to finance a drug addiction?"

"There is that," said Madeline.

"She's making one of those grand symbolic gestures, isn't she?" mused Celeste. She pressed one hand to the back of her head again. "Like when that American woman swam the Bering Strait between the US and the USSR during the Cold War."

"What *are* you talking about?"

"It was in the eighties. I was at school at the time," said Celeste.

"I remember thinking that it seemed so silly and pointless to swim across icy waters, but apparently it did have an effect, you know?"

"So you think I should go ahead and let her sell her virginity? Is this virus making you delirious?"

Celeste blinked. She seemed to sway a little on her feet and put out a hand to the wall to steady herself. "No. Of course not." She closed her eyes briefly. "I just think you should be proud of her."

"Mmmm," said Madeline. "Well I think you should go and lie back down." She kissed Celeste's cool cheek good-bye. "Hope you feel better soon, and when you do, you might want to check your kids for nits."

65.

Eight Hours Before the Trivia Night

It had been raining steadily all morning, and as Jane drove back into Pirriwee it got so heavy she had to turn up the radio and put the wipers on fast, panicky mode.

She was on her way back from dropping Ziggy off at her parents' house, where he was going to stay the night so that Jane could go to the trivia night. It was an arrangement they'd made a couple of months back when the invitations for the trivia night had first come out and Madeline had gotten all excited about planning fancy dress costumes and putting together a table with the right mix of accumulated knowledge.

Apparently her ex-husband was known for his pub trivia skills ("Nathan has spent a lot of time in pubs, you see") and it was very important to Madeline that their table beat his. "And obviously it would be nice to beat Renata's table," said Madeline. "Or anyone with a gifted and talented child, because I know they all secretly think their children inherited their genius brains from them."

Madeline had said that she herself was hopeless at trivia, and Ed didn't know anything that happened after 1989. "My job will be to bring you drinks and rub your shoulders," she'd said.

With all the dramas going on over the last week, Jane had told her parents she wouldn't go. Why put herself through it? Besides, it would be a kindness not to go. The petition organizers would see it as a good opportunity to collect more signatures. If she went, some poor person might find themselves in the embarrassing predicament of asking her if she'd like to sign a petition to have her own child suspended.

But this morning, after an excellent night's sleep, she'd woken to the sound of rain and a strange sense of optimism.

Nothing was sorted yet, but it would be.

Miss Barnes had e-mailed back, and they'd arranged a time to meet before school on Monday morning. After the hairdresser yesterday, Jane had texted Celeste and asked her if she wanted to meet for coffee, but Celeste had replied that she was sick in bed. Jane was in two minds about whether to try to tell her about Max before Monday. (The poor girl was sick. She didn't need to hear bad news.) Perhaps it wasn't necessary. Celeste was too nice to let it affect their friendship. It would all be fine. The petition would discreetly disappear. Maybe, once the news got out, some parents might even apologize to Jane. (She would be gracious.) It wasn't beyond the realm of possibility, was it? She didn't want to hand her bad-mother title over to poor Celeste, but people would react differently when they knew it was Celeste's child who was the bully. There wouldn't be a petition for Max to be suspended. Rich, beautiful people weren't asked to leave anywhere. It was going to be distressing for Celeste and Perry, but Max would get the help he needed. It would all blow over. A storm in a teacup.

She could stay in Pirriwee and keep working at Blue Blues and drinking Tom's coffee. Everything would be fine.

She knew she was prone to these bouts of crazy optimism. If a strange voice said "Ms. Chapman?" on the phone, Jane's first thought was often something ridiculous and impossible, like, *Maybe I've won a car!* (Even though she never entered competitions.) She'd always quite liked this particular quirk of her personality, even when her insane optimism proved to be once again unfounded, as it invariably did.

"I think I'm going to go to the trivia night after all," she'd told her mother on the phone.

"Good for you," her mother had said. "You hold your head high."

(Jane's mother had whooped when she'd heard Ziggy's revelation about Max. "I knew all along it wasn't Ziggy!" she'd cried, but so exuberantly it was obvious she must have harbored some secret doubts.)

Ziggy and Jane's parents were going to spend the afternoon working on a brand-new *Star Wars* jigsaw, in the hope of finally passing the jigsaw passion to Ziggy. Tomorrow morning Dane was going to take him to an indoor rock-climbing center, then bring him back later in the afternoon.

"Have some time to yourself," said Jane's mother. "Relax. You deserve it."

Jane was planning to catch up on laundry, pay some bills online and do a clean-out of Ziggy's room without him there to untidy as she tidied. But as she got closer to the beach, she decided to stop at Blue Blues. It would be warm and cozy. Tom would have his little potbelly stove going. Blue Blues, she realized, had begun to feel like home.

She pulled up in a non-metered spot down near the boardwalk. There were no cars about. Everyone was indoors. All the Saturday-morning sports would have been canceled. Jane looked at the passenger-seat floor where she normally kept a fold-up umbrella and realized it was back at the apartment. Rain splattered so hard on her windshield, it was as though someone were pouring buckets of water. It looked like very determined, very wet and cold rain, the sort that would make her gasp.

She put a hand to her head, considering. At least she didn't have as much hair to get wet. That was the other thing that was responsible for her good mood. Her new haircut.

She pulled down the rearview mirror to study her face.

"I love it," she'd told Mrs. Ponder's daughter yesterday afternoon. "I absolutely love it."

"You tell everyone you see I gave you that cut," said Lucy.

Jane couldn't believe how the short cut had transformed her face, giving her cheekbones and enlarging her eyes. The new darker color did something good to her skin.

For the first time since before that night in the hotel, when those words had wormed their malevolent way into her head, she looked at herself in the mirror and felt uncomplicated pleasure. In fact she couldn't *stop* looking at herself, sheepishly grinning and turning her head from side to side.

It was embarrassing just how much genuine happiness she was gaining from something so superficial. But maybe it was natural? Normal even? Maybe it was OK to enjoy her appearance. Maybe she didn't need to analyze it any further than that, or to think about Saxon Banks and society's obsession with beauty and youth and thinness and Photoshopped models setting unrealistic expectations and how a woman's self-worth shouldn't rest on her looks, it was what was on the inside that mattered, and blahdy, blah, blah . . . Enough! Today she had a new haircut and it suited her and that made her happy.

("Oh!" said her mother when she'd seen her walk in the door, and she'd clamped her hand over her mouth and looked like she might burst into tears. "You don't like it?" said Jane, putting a self-conscious hand to her head, suddenly doubting herself, and her mother had said, "Jane, you silly girl, you look *gorgeous*.")

Jane put her hand on the keys in the ignition. She should go back home. It was ridiculous to go out in the rain.

But she had such an irrational craving for Blue Blues and everything about it: the smell, the warmth, the coffee. Also she wanted Tom to see her new haircut. Gay men noticed haircuts.

She took a deep breath, opened the car door and ran.

66.

Celeste woke late to the sound of rain and classical music. The house smelled of bacon and eggs. It meant that Perry was downstairs in the kitchen with both boys sitting up on the island bench in their pajamas, legs swinging, crazy-happy faces. They adored cooking with their father.

Once, she'd read an article about how every relationship had its own "love account." Doing something kind for your partner was like a deposit. A negative comment was a withdrawal. The trick was to keep your account in credit. Slamming your wife's head against a wall was a very large withdrawal. Getting up early with the kids and making bacon and eggs was a deposit.

She pulled herself upright and felt the back of her head. It still felt tender, but it was OK. It was amazing how fast the healing and forgetting process had begun again. The cycle was endless.

Tonight was the trivia night. She and Perry would dress up as Audrey Hepburn and Elvis Presley. Perry had ordered his Elvis outfit online from a premium costume supplier in London. If Prince Harry wanted to dress up as Elvis, he would probably get his outfit there. Everyone else would be wearing polyester and props from the two-dollar shop.

Tomorrow Perry was flying to Hawaii. It was a junket, he'd admitted. He'd asked her a few months back if she'd wanted to go with him, and for a moment she'd seriously considered it, as that might be the answer. A tropical holiday! Cocktails and spa treatments. Away from the stress of day-to-day life! What could go wrong? (Things could go wrong. He had hit her once in a five-star hotel because she'd teased him about his mispronunciation of the word "menial." She would never forget the horrified humiliation on his face when he realized he'd been mispronouncing a word his whole life.)

While he was in Hawaii she would move herself and the boys into the McMahons Point apartment. She would make an appointment with a family lawyer. That would be easy. The legal world wasn't scary to her. She knew lots of people. It would be fine. It would be awful, of course, but it would be fine. He wasn't going to *kill* her. She was always so dramatic after they had an argument. It seemed especially silly to use a word like "kill" while her supposed "killer" was downstairs frying eggs with her children.

It would be terrible for a while, but then it would be fine. The boys could still make breakfast with Daddy when they had their weekends with him.

Yesterday was the last time he would hurt her.

It was over.

"Mummy, we've made breakfast for you!" The boys came running in, scrabbling up on the bed next to her like eager little crabs.

Perry appeared at the door with a plate balanced high on his bunched-together fingertips like a waiter in a fine-dining establishment.

"Yum!" said Celeste.

67.

I know what to do," said Ed.

"No you don't," said Madeline.

They were sitting at the living room table, listening to the rain and gloomily eating Jane's muffins. (It was terrible the way she kept *giving* them to Madeline, as if she were on a mission to urgently expand Madeline's waistline.)

Abigail was in her bedroom, lying on the sofa bed they'd moved in to replace her beautiful four-poster bed. She had headphones on and was lying on her side with her knees up to her chest.

The website was still up. Abigail's virginity was still available for purchase anywhere in the world.

Madeline had a grimy, exposed feeling, as if the eyes of the world were peering in her windows, as though strange men were right now silently creeping down her hallway to leer and sneer at her daughter.

Last night Nathan had come over and he and Madeline had sat with Abigail for more than two hours: begging, reasoning, cajoling, yelling, crying. It had been Nathan who cried, finally, with frustration, and Abigail had been visibly shocked, but the ridiculous child still would not budge. She would not give them the password. She would not take it down. She might or might not go ahead with the auction, but that wasn't really the point, she'd said; they needed to stop "obsessing over the sex part." She was leaving the website up to raise awareness of the issue and because she was "the only voice those little girls have."

The *egocentricity* of the child, as if international aid organizations were sitting around twiddling their thumbs while little Abigail Mackenzie on the Pirriwee Peninsula was the only one taking decisive action. Abigail said she couldn't care less about the horrible sexual comments. Those people were nothing to her. That was completely irrelevant. People were always writing mean stuff on the Internet.

"Don't suggest calling the police," said Madeline to Ed now. "I really don't—"

"We contact the Australian office of Amnesty International," said Ed. "They don't want their name associated with something like this. If the organization that really does represent the rights of these children tells her to take it down, she'll listen."

Madeline pointed her finger at him. "That's good. That might actually work."

There were bangs and crashes from down the hallway. Fred and Chloe did not respond well to being stuck indoors on a rainy day.

"Give it back!" screamed Chloe.

"No way!" shouted Fred.

They came running into the room, both of them gripping a sheet of scrap paper.

"Please don't tell me you're fighting over that piece of paper," said Ed.

"He's not sharing!" screamed Chloe. "*Sharing* is *caring!*"

"You get what you get and you don't get upset!" screamed Fred.

In normal circumstances that would have made Madeline laugh.

"It's my paper airplane," said Fred.

"I drew the passengers!"

"You did not!"

"Well, you can stop all your stressing." Madeline turned to see Abigail leaning against the doorjamb.

"What?" Madeline said.

Abigail said something that she couldn't hear over the yelling of Fred and Chloe.

"Bloody hell!" Madeline snatched the piece of paper from Fred's hand and tore it in half, handing them a piece each.

"Now get out of my sight!" she roared. They ran.

"I've taken down the website," said Abigail with a world-weary sigh.

"You have? Why?" Madeline resisted the urge to throw her arms above her head and run around in circles like Fred did when he kicked a goal.

Abigail handed her a printout of an e-mail. "I got this."

Ed and Madeline read it together.

To: Abigail Mackenzie

From: Larry Fitzgerald

Subject: Auction Bid

Dear Miss Mackenzie,

My name is Larry Fitzgerald and it's a pleasure to make your acquaintance. You probably don't hear from many eighty-three-year-

old gentlemen living on the other side of the world in Sioux Falls,
South Dakota. My darling wife and I visited Australia many years
ago, in 1987, before you were born. We had the pleasure of seeing the
Sydney Opera House. (I'm an architect, since retired, and it had
always been a dream of mine to see the Opera House.) The people of
Australia were so kind and warm to us. Sadly, my beautiful wife passed
away last year. I miss her every day. Miss Mackenzie, when I came
across your website, I was moved by your obvious passion and your
desire to bring attention to the plight of these children. I would not
like to purchase your virginity; however I would like to make a bid.
This is what I propose: If you close your auction immediately, I will
make an immediate donation of $100,000 to Amnesty International.
(I will, of course, send you a receipt.) I have spent many years
campaigning against the abuse of human rights, and I do so admire
what you are trying to achieve, but you are a child yourself, Miss
Mackenzie, and I cannot in good conscience stand by and see you take
this project to fruition. I look forward to hearing whether my bid is
successful.

Yours sincerely,
Larry Fitzgerald

Madeline and Ed looked at each other and over at Abigail.

"I thought one hundred thousand dollars was quite a big donation," said Abigail. She was standing at the open fridge as she talked,
pulling out containers, opening lids and peering into them. "And
that Amnesty could probably do something, you know, pretty good
with that money."

"I'm sure they could," said Ed neutrally.

"I've written back to him and told him I've taken it down,"

said Abigail. "If he doesn't send back the receipt I'm going to put it straight back up."

"Oh, naturally," murmured Ed. "He's got to follow through."

Madeline grinned at Ed and then back at Abigail. You could see the relief coursing through her daughter's young body; her bare feet were doing a little dance as she stood at the refrigerator. Abigail had put herself in a corner, and the wonderful Larry Fitzgerald of South Dakota had given her an out.

"Is this spaghetti Bolognese?" said Abigail, holding up a Tupperware container. "I'm starving."

"I thought you were vegan now," said Madeline.

"Not when I'm staying here," said Abigail, taking the container over to the microwave. "It's too hard to be vegan here."

"So tell me," said Madeline. "What was your password?"

"I can just change it again," said Abigail.

"I know."

"You'll never guess," said Abigail.

"I know that," said Madeline. "Your father and I tried everything."

"No," said Abigail. "That's it. That's my password. 'You'll never guess.'"

"Clever," said Madeline.

"Thanks." Abigail dimpled at her.

The microwave dinged, and Abigail opened the door and took out the container.

"You know that there are going to have to be, er, consequences for all this," said Madeline. "When your father and I expressly ask you to do something, you can't just ignore us."

"Yup," said Abigail cheerfully. "Do what you've got to do, Mum."

Ed cleared his throat, but Madeline shook her head at him.

"Can I eat this in the family room while I watch TV?" Abigail lifted the steaming plate.

"Sure," said Madeline.

Abigail virtually skipped off.

Ed leaned back in his chair with his hands crossed behind his head. "Crisis averted."

"All thanks to Mr. Larry Fitzgerald." Madeline picked up the e-mail printout. "How lucky was . . ."

She paused and tapped a finger to her lips. Just how lucky was that?

68.

There was a CLOSED sign on the door of Blue Blues. Jane pressed her palms to the glass door and felt bereft. She couldn't remember ever seeing a CLOSED sign at Blue Blues before.

She'd just gotten herself completely, ridiculously, extravagantly soaked for nothing.

She dropped her hands from the door and swore. Right. Well. She'd go home and have a shower. If only the hot water at her apartment lasted for more than two minutes and twenty-seven seconds. Two minutes and twenty-seven seconds was not long enough to get yourself warm; it was just long enough to be cruel.

She turned to go back to the car.

"Jane!"

The door swung open.

Tom was wearing a long-sleeved white T-shirt and jeans. He looked extremely dry and warm and delicious. (In her mind Tom was always associated with good coffee and good food, so she had a Pavlovian response just looking at him.)

"You're closed," said Jane dolefully. "You're never closed."

Tom put his dry hand on her wet arm and pulled her inside. "I'm open for you."

Jane looked down at herself. Her shoes were filled with water.

She made squelching noises as she walked. Water rolled down her face like tears.

"I'm sorry," she said. "I didn't have an umbrella, and I thought if I just ran really fast—"

"Don't worry about it. Happens all the time. People walk through fire and flood for my coffee," said Tom. "Come out back and I'll get you some dry clothes. I decided I might as well close up and watch TV. I haven't had a customer in hours. Where's my man Ziggy?"

"Mum and Dad are babysitting so I can go to the school trivia night," said Jane. "Wild night out."

"It probably will be," said Tom. "Pirriwee parents like a drink or two. I'm going, did you know? Madeline has gotten me on your table."

Jane followed him through the café, leaving wet footprints, and to the door marked PRIVATE. She knew that Tom lived at the back of the café, but she'd never been past the private door.

"Ooh," she said as Tom opened the door for her. "Exciting!"

"Yes," said Tom. "You're a lucky, lucky girl."

She looked around her and saw that his studio apartment was just like an extension of the café—the same polished floorboards and rough white walls, bookshelves filled with secondhand books. The only differences were the surfboard and guitar leaning against the wall, the stack of CDs and stereo.

"I can't believe it," said Jane.

"What?" asked Tom.

"You're into jigsaws," she breathed, pointing at a half-finished jigsaw on the table. She looked at the box. It was a proper hard-core (as her brother would have said), two-thousand-piece jigsaw featuring a black-and-white photo of wartime Paris.

"We jigsaw," said Jane. "My family. We're kind of obsessed."

"I like to always have one on the go," said Tom. "I find them sort of meditative."

"Exactly," said Jane.

"Tell you what," said Tom. "I'll give you some clothes, and you can have some pumpkin soup with me and help me jigsaw."

He pulled some tracksuit pants and a hooded sweatshirt from a chest of drawers, and she went into his bathroom and put her soaked clothes, right down to her underwear, into his sink. The dry clothes smelled like Tom and Blue Blues.

"I feel like Charlie Chaplin," she said, with the sleeves hanging below her wrists and pulling up the waist of the tracksuit pants.

"Here," said Tom, and he neatly folded up the sleeves of the shirt above her wrists. Jane submitted like a child. She felt unaccountably happy. Cherished.

She sat down at the table and Tom brought them over bowls of pumpkin soup swirled with sour cream and buttered sourdough bread.

"I feel like you're always feeding me," said Jane.

"You need feeding," said Tom. "Eat up."

She took a mouthful of the sweet, spicy soup.

"I know what's different about you!" said Tom suddenly. "You've had all your hair cut off! It looks great."

Jane laughed. "I was thinking on the way here that a gay man would notice straightaway that I'd had a haircut." She picked up a piece of the puzzle and found a spot for it. It felt like being at home, eating and doing a puzzle. "Sorry. I know that's a terrible cliché."

"Um," said Tom.

"What?" said Jane. She looked up at him. "That's where it

goes. Look. It's the corner of the tank. This soup is incredible. Why don't you have it on the menu?"

"I'm not gay," said Tom.

"Oh yes you are," said Jane merrily. She assumed he was making a bad sort of joke.

"No," said Tom. "No, I'm not."

"What?"

"I know I do jigsaws and make amazing pumpkin soup, but I'm actually straight."

"Oh!" said Jane. She could feel her face turning crimson. "I'm sorry. I thought . . . I didn't think, I knew! How did I know? Someone told me. *Madeline* told me ages ago. But I remember it! She told me this whole story about how you broke up with your boyfriend and you took it really bad and you just spent hours crying and surfing . . ."

Tom grinned. "Tom O'Brien," he said. "That's who she was talking about."

"Tom O'Brien, the smash-repair guy?" Tom O'Brien was big and burly with a black bushy beard. She had never even properly registered the fact that the two Toms had the same name, they were so different.

"It's perfectly understandable," said Tom. "It would seem more likely that Tom the barista was gay than Tom the giant smash-repairer. He's happy now, by the way, in love with someone new."

"Huh," said Jane. She considered. "His receipts did smell really nice."

Tom snorted.

"I hope I didn't, um, offend you," said Jane.

She hadn't fully closed the bathroom door when she'd gotten dressed. She'd left it partly ajar, the way she would have if Tom had been a girl, so that they could keep talking. She wasn't wearing any underwear. She had talked to him so *freely*. She'd always been so free with him. If she'd known he was straight she would have kept a part of herself safe. She'd let herself feel attracted to him because he was gay, so it didn't count.

"Of course not," said Tom.

Their eyes met. His face, so dear and familiar to her now after all these months, felt suddenly strange. He was blushing. They were both blushing. Her stomach dropped as if she were at the top of a roller coaster. Oh, *calamity*.

"I think that piece goes in the corner there," said Tom.

Jane looked at the jigsaw piece and slotted it into place. She hoped the tremor in her fingers looked like clumsiness.

"You're right," she said.

Carol: I saw Jane having a very, shall we say, *intimate* conversation with one of the fathers at the trivia night. Their faces were this close, and I'm pretty sure he had his hand on her knee. I was a little shocked, to be frank.

Gabrielle: It wasn't a school dad. It was just *Tom*! The barista! And he's gay!

69.

Half an Hour Before the Trivia Night

You look *so* beautiful, Mummy," said Josh.

He stood at the bedroom door, staring at Celeste. She was wearing a sleeveless black dress, long white gloves, and the pearl necklace Perry had bought for her in Switzerland. Celeste had even put her hair up in a passable Audrey Hepburn–style beehive bun and had just that moment found a vintage diamond comb. She looked pretty nice. Madeline would be pleased with her.

"Thank you, Joshie," said Celeste, more touched than she could remember ever being from a compliment. "Give me a cuddle."

He ran to her, and she sat on the end of the bed and let him snuggle into her. He'd never been as snuggly as Max, so when he needed a hug she made sure to take her time. She pressed her lips to his hair. She'd taken more painkillers, even though she wasn't sure if she really needed them, and was feeling detached and floaty.

"Mummy," said Josh.

"Hmmm?"

"I need to tell you a secret."

"Hmmmm. What's that?" She closed her eyes and hugged him closer.

"I don't want to tell you," said Josh.

"You don't have to tell me," said Celeste dreamily.

"But it makes me feel sad," said Josh.

"What makes you feel sad?" Celeste lifted her head and made herself focus.

"OK, so Max isn't hurting Amabella anymore," said Josh. "But then, yesterday, he pushed Skye down the stairs near the library again, and I said he shouldn't do that, and we had a big fight because I said I was going to tell."

Max pushed Skye.

Skye. Bonnie and Nathan's anxious, waif-like little girl. Max had pushed Skye down the stairs *again*. The thought of her son hurting that fragile child made Celeste feel instantly sick.

"But why?" she said. "Why would he do that?" The back of her head had begun to ache.

"Dunno," shrugged Josh. "He just does."

"Wait a moment," said Celeste. Her mobile phone was ringing somewhere downstairs. She pressed a fingertip to her forehead. Her head felt fuzzy. "Did you say, 'Max isn't hurting Amabella anymore'? What are you talking about? What do you mean?"

"I'll answer it!" called out Perry.

Josh was impatient with her. "No, no, Mummy. *Listen!* He doesn't go near Amabella anymore. It's *Skye*. He's being mean to Skye. When no one is looking except me."

"Mummy!" Max came running in. His face was ecstatic. "I think my tooth is wobbly!" He put his finger in his mouth. He looked so cute. So sweet and innocent. His face still had that baby-roundness. He was desperate to lose a tooth because he was obsessed with the idea of the Tooth Fairy.

When the boys turned three, Josh asked for a digger and Max asked for a baby doll. She and Perry had enjoyed watching him cradle the doll, singing it soft little lullabies, and Celeste had loved the fact that Perry didn't mind at all that their son was behaving in such a nonmasculine way. Of course, he'd soon dropped dolls for lightsabers, but he was still her cuddly son, the most loving of the boys.

And now he was staking out the quiet little girls in the class and hurting them. Her son was a bully. "How does the abuse affect your children?" Susi had asked. "It doesn't," she'd said.

"Oh, *Max*," she said.

"Feel it!" said Max. "I'm not making it up! It's definitely loose!" He looked up at his father as Perry came into the room. "You look funny, Daddy! Hey, Daddy, look at my tooth! Look, look!"

Perry was barely recognizable in his perfectly fitted shiny black wig, gold aviator glasses and, of course, the iconic white Elvis jumpsuit with glittering gemstones. He held Celeste's mobile phone in his hand.

"Wow! It's really loose this time?" he said. "Let me see!"

He put the phone down on the bed next to Celeste and Josh and got down on his knees in front of Max, pushing his glasses down over his nose so he could see.

"I have a message for you," he said, glancing at Celeste. He put his finger on Max's lower lip. "Let me see, buddy. From Mindy."

"Mindy?" said Celeste vaguely. "I don't know anyone called Mindy." She was thinking about Jane and Ziggy. The petition that should have Max's name on it. She needed to tell the school. Should she call Miss Barnes right now? Should she call Jane?

"Your property manager," said Perry.

Celeste's stomach plunged. She let Josh wriggle off her lap.

"I bet your tooth isn't loose!" he said to his brother.

"Maybe a little loose," said Perry. He ruffled Max's hair and straightened his glasses. "They're putting new smoke alarms in your apartment and want to know if they can get access Monday morning. Mindy wondered if nine a.m. was OK with you." He grabbed both boys by their waists and lifted them up on his hips, where they clung comfortably like monkeys, their faces joyous. Perry tilted his head at Celeste. A white-toothed Elvis smile. "Does that suit you, honey?"

The doorbell rang.

70.

Stu: As soon as you walked in the door you were handed one of these girly-looking pink fizzy cocktails.

Samantha: They were *divine*. Only problem was the Year 6 teachers made some sort of miscalculation with quantities, so each drink was worth about three shots. These are the people teaching our kids math, by the way.

Gabrielle: I was starving because I'd been saving all my calories for that night. I had half a cocktail and—hooeee!

Jackie: I go to a lot of corporate events with big-drinking highfliers, but let me tell you, I've never seen a group of people get so drunk so fast as they did at this school trivia night.

Thea: The caterer's car broke down, so everyone was hungry and drinking these very strong alcoholic drinks. I thought to myself, *This is a recipe for* disaster.

Miss Barnes: It's not a good look for teachers to get drunk at school functions so I always sit on one drink, but that cocktail! Like, I'm not even sure exactly what I was saying to people.

Mrs. Lipmann: We are currently reviewing our procedures in relation to the serving of alcohol at school events.

The Trivia Night

Cocktail?" A blond Audrey Hepburn held out a tray.

Jane took the proffered pink drink and looked about the school assembly hall. All the Blond Bobs must have had a meeting to ensure they all wore identical pearl chokers, little black dresses and updos. Perhaps Mrs. Ponder's daughter had offered a group discount.

"Are you new to the school?" asked the Blond Bob. "I don't think I know your face."

"I'm a kindy mum," said Jane. "I've been here since the beginning of the year. Gosh, this drink is *good*."

"Yes, the Year 6 teachers invented it. They're calling it 'Not on a School Night' or something." The Blond Bob did a double take. "Oh! I do know you! You've had a haircut. It's, er, Jane, isn't it?"

Yep. That's me. The mother of the bully. Except he's actually not.

The Blond Bob dropped her like a hot potato. "Have a great night!" she said. "There's a seating plan over that way." She waved a dismissive hand in no particular direction.

Jane wandered into the crowd, past groups of animated Elvises and giggling Audreys, all of them tossing back the pink cocktails. She looked around for Tom, because she knew he'd enjoy joining her in analyzing exactly what was in it to make it taste so good.

Tom is straight. The thought kept disappearing and then popping up in her head like a jack-in-the-box. Boing! *Tom is not gay!* Boing! *Tom is not gay!* Boing!

It was hilarious and wonderful and terrifying.

She came face-to-face with Madeline, a vision in pink: pink dress, pink bag and pink drink in her hand.

"Jane!" Madeline's hot-pink silk cocktail dress was studded with green rhinestones and had a huge pink-satin bow tied around her waist. Almost every other woman in the room was in black, but Madeline, of course, knew exactly how to stand out in a crowd.

"You look gorgeous," said Jane. "Is that Chloe's tiara you're wearing?"

Madeline touched the tiara with its pink plastic stones. "Yes, I had to pay her an exorbitant rental fee for it. But you're the one who looks gorgeous!" She took Jane's arm and spun her around in a slow circle. "Your hair! You never told me you were getting it cut! It's perfect! Did Lucy Ponder do that for you? And the outfit! It's so cute!"

She turned Jane back around to face her and put a hand over her mouth. "Jane! You're wearing red *lipstick*! I'm just so, so . . ." Her voice trembled with emotion. "I'm just so *happy* to see you wearing *lipstick*!"

"How many of those pretty pink drinks have you had?" asked Jane. She had another long sip of her own.

"This is only my second," said Madeline. "I have terrible, ghastly PMS. I may kill someone before the night is out. But! All is good! All is great! Abigail closed her website down. Oh, wait, you don't even know about the website, do you? So much has happened! *So* many calamitous catastrophes! And wait! How was yes-terday? The appointment with the you-know-who?"

"What website did Abigail close down?" said Jane. She took another long draw on her straw and watched the pink liquid dis-appear. It was going straight to her head. She felt marvelously, gloriously happy. "The appointment with the psychologist went well." She lowered her voice. "Ziggy isn't the one who bullied Amabella."

"Of course he isn't," said Madeline.

"I think I've finished this already!" said Jane.

"Do you think they even have alcohol in them?" said Madeline. "They taste like something fizzy and fun from childhood. They taste like a summer afternoon, like a first kiss, like a—"

"Ziggy has nits," said Jane.

"So do Chloe and Fred," said Madeline gloomily.

"Oh, and I've got so much to tell you too. Yesterday, Harper's husband got all Tony Soprano on me. He said if I went near Harper again he'd bring the full weight of the law down on me. He's a partner in a law firm, apparently."

"*Graeme?*" said Madeline. "He does tax law, for heaven's sake."

"Tom threw them out of the coffee shop."

"Seriously?" Madeline looked thrilled.

"With my bare hands." Jane spun around to see Tom standing in front of her, wearing jeans and a plaid button-down shirt. He was holding one of the ubiquitous pink drinks.

"*Tom!*" said Jane as ecstatically as if he were a returned soldier. She took an involuntary step closer to him, and then stepped back fast when her arm brushed against his.

"You both look beautiful," said Tom, but his eyes were on Jane.

"You don't look anything like Elvis," said Madeline disapprovingly.

"I don't do costumes," said Tom. He pulled self-consciously on his nicely ironed shirt. "Sorry." The shirt didn't really suit him. He looked far better in the black T-shirts he wore at the café. The thought of Tom standing bare-chested in his little studio apartment, conscientiously ironing his unflattering shirt, filled Jane with tenderness and lust.

"Hey, can you taste mint in this?" said Tom to Jane.

"That's it!" said Jane. "So it's just strawberry puree, champagne—"

"—and I'm thinking vodka," said Tom. He took another sip. "Maybe quite a lot of vodka."

"Do you think?" said Jane. Her eyes were on his lips. She'd always known Tom was good-looking, but she'd never analyzed why. It was possibly his lips. He had beautiful, almost feminine lips. This really was a very sad day for the gay community.

"Aha!" said Madeline. *"Aha!"*

"What's that?" said Tom.

"Gidday, Tom mate." Ed strolled up next to Madeline and put his arm around her waist. He was in a black and gold Elvis outfit with cape-like sleeves and a huge collar. It was impossible to look at him without laughing.

"How come Tom doesn't have to dress up like a dickhead?" he said. He grinned at Jane. "Stop laughing, Jane. You look smashing, by the way. Have you done something different to your hair?"

Madeline grinned idiotically at Jane and Tom, her head turning back and forth like she was at a tennis match.

"Look, darling," she said to Ed. *"Tom* and *Jane."*

"Yes," said Ed. "I see them. I just spoke to them, in fact."

"It's so *obvious*!" said Madeline, all shiny-eyed, one hand to her heart. "I can't believe I never——"

To Jane's immense relief, she stopped, her eyes over their shoulders. "Look who's here. The king and queen of the prom."

71.

Perry didn't speak as they drove the short distance to the school. They were still going. Celeste couldn't quite believe they were still going, but then again, of *course* they were going. They never canceled. Sometimes she had to change what she'd planned to wear, sometimes she had to have an excuse ready, but the show must go on.

Perry had already posted a Facebook photo of them in their costumes. It would make them look like good-humored, funny, fun people who didn't take themselves too seriously and cared about their school and their local community. It perfectly complemented other more glamorous posts about overseas trips and expensive cultural events. A school trivia night was just the thing for their brand.

She looked straight ahead at the briskly working windshield wipers. The windshield was just like the never-ending cycles of her mind. Confusion. Clear. Confusion. Clear. Confusion. Clear.

She watched his hands on the steering wheel. Capable hands. Tender hands. Vicious hands. He was just a man in an Elvis costume driving her to a school event. He was a man who had just discovered that his wife was planning to leave him. A hurt man. A betrayed man. An angry man. But just a man.

Confusion. Clear. Confusion. Clear.

When Gwen had arrived to babysit the boys, Perry had turned on the charm as though something vital depended on it. She was cool with Perry at first but it turned out that Elvis was Gwen's weak spot. She launched into a story about how she'd been one of the "golden girls" when Elvis's gold Cadillac toured Australia, until Perry cut in smoothly, like a gentleman stealing a woman away at a dance.

The rain eased as they drove into the school's street. The street was jammed with cars, but there was a space waiting for Perry near the school entrance, as if he'd prebooked it. He always got a parking spot. Lights turned green for him. The dollar obediently went up or down for him. Perhaps that's why he got so angry when things didn't go right.

He turned off the ignition.

Neither of them moved or spoke. Celeste saw one of the kindergarten mothers hurrying past the car in a long dress that forced her to take little steps. She was carrying a child's polka-dotted umbrella. *Gabrielle,* thought Celeste. The one who talked endlessly about her weight.

Celeste turned to look at Perry.

"Max has been bullying Amabella. Renata's little girl."

Perry kept looking straight ahead. "How do you know?"

"Josh told me," said Celeste. "Just before we left. Ziggy has been taking the blame for it."

Ziggy. Your cousin's child.

"He's the one the parents are petitioning to have suspended." She closed her eyes briefly as she thought of Perry slamming her head against the wall. "It should be a petition to have *Max* suspended. Not Ziggy."

Perry turned to look at her. He looked like a stranger with his black wig. The blackness made his eyes appear brilliant blue.

"We'll talk to the teachers," he said.

"*I'll* talk to his teacher," said Celeste. "You won't be here, re-member?"

"Right," said Perry. "Well, I'll talk to Max tomorrow, before I go to the airport."

"What will you say?" said Celeste.

"I don't know."

There was a huge heavy block of pain lodged beneath her chest. Was this a heart attack? Was this fury? Was this a broken heart? Was this the weight of her responsibility?

"Will you tell him that's not the way to treat a woman?" she said, and it was like jumping off a cliff. Never a word. Not like that. She'd broken an unbreakable rule. Was it because he looked like Elvis Presley and none of this was real, or was it because he knew about the apartment now and everything was more real than ever before?

Perry's face changed, cracked open. "The boys have never—"

"They *have*," cried Celeste. She'd pretended so very hard for so very long and there was nobody here except the two of them. "The night before the party last year, Max got out of bed, he was standing right there at the doorway—"

"Yes OK," said Perry.

"And there was that time in the kitchen, when you, when I—"

He put his hand out. "OK, OK."

She stopped.

After a moment he said, "So you've leased an apartment?"

"Yes," said Celeste.

"When are you leaving?"

"Next week," she said. "I think next week."

"With the boys?"

This is when you should feel fear, she thought. This is not the way Susi said it should be done. Scenarios. Plans. Escape routes. She was not treading carefully, but she'd tried to tread carefully for years and she knew it never made the slightest difference anyway.

"Of course with the boys."

He took a sharp intake of breath as if he'd experienced a sudden pain. He put his face in his hands and leaned forward so that his forehead was pressed to the top of the steering wheel, and his whole body shook as if with convulsions.

Celeste stared, and for a moment she couldn't work out what he was doing. Was he sick? Was he laughing? Her stomach tightened and she put her hand on the car door, but then he lifted his head and turned to her.

His face was streaked with tears. His Elvis wig was askew. He looked unhinged.

"I'll get help," he said. "I promise you I'll get help."

"You won't," she said quietly. The rain was softening. She could see other Audreys and Elvises hurrying along the street, huddled under umbrellas, and hear their shouts and laughter.

"I will." His eyes brightened. "Last year I got a referral from Dr. Hunter to see a psychiatrist." There was a note of triumph in his voice as he remembered this.

"You told Dr. Hunter about . . . us?" Their family GP was a kindly, courtly grandfather.

"I told him I thought I was suffering from anxiety," said Perry. He saw the expression on her face.

"Well, Dr. Hunter *knows* us!" he said defensively. "But I *was* going to see a psychiatrist. I was going to tell him. I just never got around to it, and then I just kept thinking I could fix it myself."

She couldn't think less of him for this. She knew the way your mind could go round and round in endless pointless circles.

"I think the referral is out of date now. But I'll get another one. I just get so . . . When I get angry . . . I don't know what *happens* to me. It's like a madness. Like this unstoppable . . . and I never ever actually make the decision to . . . It just happens, and every time, I can't believe it, and I think, I will never, ever, let that happen again, and then yesterday. Celeste, I feel sick about yesterday."

The car windows were fogging up. Celeste ran her palm over her side window, making a porthole to see out. Perry was speaking as if he genuinely believed this was the first time he'd said this sort of thing, as if it were brand-new information.

"We can't bring the boys up like this."

She looked out at the rainy, dark street, which was filled with shouting, laughing, blue-hatted children each school morning.

She realized with a tiny shock that if it weren't for Josh's revelation tonight about Max's behavior, she probably *still* wouldn't have left. She would have convinced herself that she'd been over-dramatic, that yesterday hadn't been that bad, that any man would have been angry if they'd been humiliated the way she'd humiliated Perry in front of Madeline and Ed.

The boys had always been her reason to stay, but now for the first time they were her reason to leave. She'd allowed violence to become a normal part of their life. Over the last five years Celeste herself had developed a kind of imperviousness and acceptance of violence that allowed her to hit back and sometimes even hit first. She scratched, she kicked, she slapped. As if it were normal. She hated it, but she did it. If she stayed, *that was the legacy she was giving her boys.*

She turned away from the window and looked at Perry. "It's over," she said. "You must know it's over."

He flinched. She saw him prepare to fight, to strategize, to win. He never lost.

"I'll cancel this next trip," he said. "I'll *resign.* I'll do nothing for the next six months but work on us—not on us, on *me.* For the next— Jesus fucking Christ!"

He jumped back, his eyes on something, past Celeste's shoulder. She turned and gasped. There was a face pressed gargoyle-like against the window.

Perry pressed a button and Celeste's window slid down. It was Renata, smiling brightly as she leaned down into the car, a gauzy wrap about her shoulders clutched in one hand. Her husband stood next to her, sheltering her from the rain with a huge black umbrella.

"Sorry! Didn't mean to startle you! Do you need to share our umbrella? You two look *fabulous!*"

72.

It was like watching movie stars arrive, thought Madeline. There was something about the way Perry and Celeste held themselves, as if they were walking onto a stage; their posture was too good, their faces were camera-ready. They were wearing similar outfits to many of the guests, but it was like Perry and Celeste weren't in costume; it was as though the *real* Elvis and Audrey had arrived. Every woman wearing a black *Breakfast at Tiffany's* dress touched a hand to her inferior pearl necklace. Every man in a white Elvis suit sucked in his stomach. The levels of pink fizzy drinks went down, down, down.

"Wow. Celeste looks so beautiful."

Madeline turned to see Bonnie standing next to her.

Like Tom, Bonnie obviously didn't do costumes. Her hair was in its normal single plait over one shoulder. No makeup. She looked like a homeless person on a special night out: long-sleeved top of some faded thin fabric falling off one shoulder (all her clothes fell off one shoulder in that irritating way; Madeline longed to grab her and straighten everything up), long shapeless skirt, old leather belt around her waist, lots of that weird skull-and-bones, crazy gypsy-lady jewelry, if you could call it jewelry.

If Abigail were here, she would look at her mother and her stepmother, and it would be Bonnie whose outfit she would admire, it would be Bonnie she chose to emulate. And that was *fine*, because no teenager wanted to look like her mother, Madeline knew that, but why couldn't Abigail admire some random, drug-addicted celebrity? Why did it have to be bloody Bonnie?

"How are you, Bonnie?" she said.

She watched Tom and Jane melt away into the crowd. Someone was asking Tom for a soy latte to much hilarity (poor Tom), but Tom didn't seem bothered; his eyes kept returning to Jane, as Jane's did to him. Watching their obvious mutual attraction had made Madeline feel as if she were witnessing some beautiful, extraordinary, but everyday event, like the hatching of a newborn chick. But now she was making conversation with her ex-husband's wife, and although the alcohol was numbing her nicely, she could feel the subterranean rumbling of her PMS.

"Who is looking after Skye?" she said to Bonnie. "I'm sorry!" She tapped her forehead. "We should have offered to have Skye over to our place! Abigail is looking after Chloe and Fred for us. She could have babysat all her siblings at once."

Bonnie smiled warily. "Skye is with my mother."

"Abigail could have given them all a tutorial on website design," said Madeline at the same time.

Bonnie's smile disappeared. "Madeline, listen, about that—"

"Oh, Skye is with your mother!" continued Madeline. "Lovely! Abigail has a 'special connection' with your mother, doesn't she?"

She was being a bitch. She was a terrible, awful person. She needed to find someone who would let her say all sorts of horrible, bitchy things and not judge her for it or pass them on. Where was Celeste? Celeste was great for that. She watched Bonnie drain her glass. A Blond Bob came by carrying a tray of more pink drinks. Madeline took two more drinks, for herself and Bonnie.

"When are we starting the trivia competition?" she said to the Blond Bob. "We're all getting too drunk to concentrate."

The Blond Bob looked predictably harried. "I know! We're way off schedule. We're meant to have finished the canapés by now, but the caterer is stuck in a huge traffic jam on Pirriwee Road." She blew a lock of blond hair out of her eyes. "And Brett Larson is the MC and he's stuck in the same traffic jam."

"Ed will be MC!" said Madeline blithely. "He's a great MC." She looked about for Ed and saw him approaching Renata's husband, all handshakes and backslaps. *Great choice, darling. Are you aware your wife ran into his wife's car yesterday afternoon, resulting in a public scream-ing match?* Ed probably thought he was talking to Gareth the golfer, not Geoff the bird-watcher, and was currently asking Geoff if he'd been on the course much lately.

"Thanks anyway, but Brett has all the trivia questions. He's been working on them for months. He's got this whole multi-media presentation planned," said the Blond Bob. "Just bear with us!" She moved off with her tray of drinks.

"These cocktails are going straight to my head," said Bonnie.

Madeline was only half listening. She was watching Renata nod coolly at Ed and turn quickly to talk to someone else. She remembered suddenly the hot gossip she'd heard yesterday about Renata's husband being in love with the French nanny. That news had gone straight out of her head when she'd found out about Abigail's website. Now she felt bad for yelling back when Renata yelled at her for running into her car.

Bonnie swayed a little. "I don't drink much these days, so I guess I have a very low tolerance—"

"Excuse me, Bonnie," said Madeline. "I need to go collect my husband. He seems to be in a very animated conversation with an adulterer. I don't want him picking up any ideas."

Bonnie swung her head to see who was talking to Ed.

"Don't worry," said Madeline. "*Your* husband isn't the adulterer! Nathan is always monogamous right up until he deserts you with a newborn baby. Oh, but wait, he didn't desert *you* with a newborn baby. That was just me!"

Bugger niceness. It was overrated. The Madeline of tomorrow was going to regret every word she said tonight, but the Madeline of right now was exhilarated by the removal of all those pesky inhibitions. How wonderful to let the words just come slip-sliding out of her mouth.

"Where is my delightful ex-husband anyway?" said Madeline. "I haven't seen him yet tonight. I can't tell you how *great* it is to know that I can go to the school trivia night and know that I'll run into Nathan."

Bonnie fiddled with the end of her plait and looked at Madeline with slightly unfocused eyes. "Nathan left you fifteen years ago," she said. There was something in her voice that Madeline had never heard before. A roughness, as though something had been rubbed off. How interesting! *Yes, please do show me another side of yourself, Bonnie!*

"He did a terrible, terrible thing. He will never forgive himself for it," said Bonnie. "But it might be time *you* thought about forgiving *him*, Madeline. The health benefits of forgiveness are really quite extraordinary."

Madeline inwardly rolled her eyes. Maybe she outwardly did as well. She'd thought for a minute that she was about to see the real Bonnie, but she was just speaking her normal airy-fairy, no-substance rubbish.

Bonnie looked at her earnestly. "I've had personal experience—"

There were sudden squeals of delight from a group of people behind Bonnie. Someone cried, "I'm so happy for you!" A woman stepped back, causing Bonnie to lurch forward so that her cocktail spilled right down Madeline's pink dress.

> **Gabrielle:** It was an accident. Davina was hugging Rowena. She'd just made some sort of announcement. I think she'd reached her goal weight.

> **Jackie:** Rowena had just announced she'd bought a Thermonix. Or a Vitamix. I wouldn't know. I have an actual life. So of course Davina hugged her. *Because she'd bought a new kitchen appliance.* I'm not making this stuff up.

> **Melissa:** No, no, we were talking about the latest nit outbreak, and Rowena asked Davina if she'd checked her own hair, and then someone's husband pretended he could see something crawling through Davina's hair. The poor girl went crazy and collided with Bonnie.

> **Harper:** What? No! Bonnie *threw* her drink at Madeline. I saw it!

73.

The trivia night had been going for over an hour now without food or trivia. Jane had a sense of gentle undulating movement, as though she were on a ship. The room was becoming warmer. It had been cold earlier and the heat was on too high. Faces were turning pink. The rain picked up again and pounded on the roof, so people had to raise their voices to be heard over the roar. The room rippled with laughter. A rumor circulated that someone had ordered in pizza. Women began to pull emergency snacks from handbags.

Jane watched as a large Elvis offered to donate five hundred dollars to the school in return for Samantha's salt and vinegar chips.

"Sure," said Samantha, but her husband, Stu, swept the chips out of her hand before the deal could be struck. "Sorry, mate, I need these more than the kids need SMART Boards."

Ed said to Madeline, "Why don't you have snacks in your bag? What sort of woman are you?"

"This is a clutch!" Madeline brandished her tiny sequined bag. "Stop that, Bonnie. I'm fine!" She swatted at Bonnie, who was following her about, dabbing at her dress with a handful of paper towels.

Two Audreys and an Elvis argued loudly and passionately about standardized testing.

"There is no evidence to suggest—"

"They teach to the test! I know for a *fact* they teach to the test!"

Blond Bobs ran this way and that with mobile phones pressed to their ears. "The caterer is just five minutes away!" scolded one when she saw Stu eating his salt and vinegar chips.

"Sorry," said Stu. He held out the pack. "Want one?"

"Oh, all right." She took a chip and hurried off.

"Couldn't organize a root in a brothel." Stu shook his head sadly.

"Shhhhh," hissed Samantha.

"Are school trivia nights always this . . ." Tom couldn't seem to find the right word.

"I don't know," said Jane.

Tom smiled at her. She smiled at him. They seemed to be smiling at each other quite a lot tonight, as if they were both in on the same private joke.

Dear God, please don't let me be imagining this.

"Tom! Where's my large skim cap, please! Ha ha!" Tom widened his eyes fractionally at Jane as he was swept off into another conversation.

"Jane! I've been looking out for you! How are you?" Miss Barnes appeared, totteringly taller than usual in very high heels. She was wearing a giant hat, a pink boa and carrying a parasol. She didn't look anything like Audrey Hepburn as far as Jane could see. She was enunciating her words very slow-ly and care-ful-ly to make sure nobody knew she was tipsy.

"How are you holding up?" she said, as though Jane were recently bereaved, and for a moment Jane struggled to recall her recent bereavement.

Oh, the petition of course. The whole school thought her child was a bully. That. Whatever. *Tom isn't gay!*

"We're meeting before school on Monday morning, right?" said Miss Barnes. "I assume it's about the . . . issue."

She put air quotes around the word "issue."

"Yes," said Jane. "Something I need to tell you. I won't talk about it now." She kept seeing Celeste in the distance with her husband, but she hadn't even gotten to say hello yet.

"I'm dressed as Audrey Hepburn in *My Fair Lady*, by the way," said Miss Barnes resentfully. She gestured at her outfit. "She made other movies besides *Breakfast at Tiffany's*, you know."

"I knew exactly who you were," said Jane.

"Anyway, this bullying thing has gotten out of control," said Miss Barnes. She stopped enunciating and let her words flow in a slurred, sloppy rush. "Every *day* I'm getting e-mails from parents concerned about bullying. I think there's a roster. It's constant. 'We need to be sure our children are in a safe environment,' and then some of them do this passive-aggressive thing: 'I know you're under-resourced, Miss Barnes, so do you need more parent helpers? I am available to come in on Wednesday afternoons at one p.m.' And then if I don't answer straightaway, 'Miss Barnes, I have not yet heard back from you regarding my offer,' and of course they fucking cc Mrs. Lipmann on everything."

Miss Barnes sucked on the straw of her empty glass. "Sorry for swearing. Kindergarten teachers shouldn't swear. I never swear in front of the children. Just in case you're thinking of making an official complaint."

"You're off duty," said Jane. "You can say what you want." She took a small step back because Miss Barnes's hat kept banging against Jane's head as she talked. Where was Tom? There he was, surrounded by a cluster of adoring Audreys.

"Off duty? I'm never off duty. Last year my ex-boyfriend and I went to Hawaii and we walked into the foyer of the hotel, and I hear this cute little voice saying, 'Miss Barnes! Miss Barnes!' and my heart sank like a stone. It was the kid who had just given me the most grief over the whole last term and *he was staying at the same hotel*! And I had to pretend to be happy to see him! And play with him in the fucking pool! The parents lay on their deck chairs, smiling benevolently, as if they were doing me a wonderful favor! My boyfriend and I broke up on the holiday and I blame that kid. Do not tell anyone I said that. Those parents are here tonight. Oh my God, promise me you'll never tell anyone I said that."

"I promise," said Jane. "On my life."

"Anyway, what was I saying? Oh, yes, the e-mails. But that's not all. They keep *turning up*!" said Miss Barnes. "The parents! At any time! Renata has taken a leave of absence from work so she can do random checks on Amabella, even though we've got the teacher's aide who does nothing *but* observe Amabella. I mean, fair enough, I never saw what was going on, and I feel bad about that. But it's not just Renata! I'll be in the middle of doing some activity with the kids and suddenly I'll look up and there's a parent at the door, just *watching* me. It's creepy. It's like I'm being stalked."

"It sounds like harassment to me," said Jane. "Oops— Just watch. There you go." She gently pushed Miss Barnes's hat out of her face. "Do you want another drink? You look like you could use another drink."

"I'm at Pirriwee Drugstore on the weekend," said Miss Barnes, "because I've got a terrible urinary tract infection—I'm seeing someone new, anyway, sorry, too much information—and I'm standing at the counter, waiting, and all of a sudden Thea Cunningham is standing at my side, and honestly, I didn't even hear her say hello before she launches into this story of how Violet was so upset after school the other day because Chloe told her that her hair clips didn't match. Well, they *didn't* match. I mean, for God's sake, that's not bullying! That's kids being kids! But oh no, Violet was so wounded by this, and could I please talk to the whole class about speaking nicely to one another, and . . . I'm sorry, I just saw Mrs. Lipmann giving me a death stare. Excuse me. I think I'll just go splash cold water on my face."

Miss Barnes turned so fast, her pink boa swung against Jane's face.

Jane turned around and came face-to-face with Tom again.

"Hold out your hand," he said. "Quickly."

She held out her hand and he gave her a handful of pretzels.

"That big scary-looking Elvis over there found a bag of them in the kitchen," said Tom. He reached to the side of her face and removed something pink from her hair.

"Feather," he said.

"Thanks," said Jane. She ate a pretzel.

"Jane." She felt a cool hand on her arm. It was Celeste.

"Hello, you," said Jane happily. Celeste looked so beautiful tonight; it was a pleasure simply to lay eyes upon her. Why was Jane always so weird about beautiful people? They couldn't help their beauty, and they were so lovely to look at, and Tom had just brought her pretzels and blushed a little when he took the feather out of her hair and he wasn't gay, and these fizzy pink cocktails were glorious, and she loved school trivia nights, they were just so funny and fun.

"Can I talk to you for a minute?" said Celeste.

74.

Shall we go out onto the balcony?" said Celeste to Jane. "Get some air?"

"Sure," said Jane.

Jane seemed so young and carefree tonight, thought Celeste. Like a teenager. The hall felt claustrophobic and overheated. Beads of sweat rolled down Celeste's back. One of her shoes was viciously rubbing away the skin at the back of her heel, leaving a nasty, bloody little blister, like she imagined a bedsore to be. This night would never end. She'd be here forever, assaulted by malicious snatches of conversation.

"So I said, that's unacceptable . . ."

"Completely incompetent, they have a duty of care . . ."

"They're spoiled brats, they eat nothing but junk food, so . . ."

"I said, if you can't control your child then . . ."

Celeste had left Perry talking to Ed about golf. Perry was being charming, seducing everyone with his attentive "no one could be more fascinating than you" gaze, but he was drinking much more than he normally did, and she could see his mood changing direction, almost imperceptibly, like the slow turn of an ocean liner. She could see it in the hardening of his jaw and the glazing of his eyes.

By the time they left for home, the distraught, sobbing man in the car would have vanished. She knew exactly how his thoughts would be twisting and turning, like the roots of an ancient tree. Normally, after a bad "argument" like yesterday, she would be safe for weeks on end, but the discovery of her apartment was a betrayal of Perry. It was disrespectful. It was humiliating. She'd kept a secret from him. By the end of the night, nothing else would matter except her deception. It would be as if it were only that, as if they were a perfectly happily married couple and the wife had done something mystifying and bizarre: She'd set up a secret, elaborate plan to leave him. It *was* mystifying and bizarre. She deserved whatever was going to happen.

There was no one else out on the huge balcony running the length of the hall. It was still raining, and although it was under cover the wind was blowing in a fine mist, making the tiles wet and slippery.

"Maybe this isn't so nice," said Celeste.

"No, it's good," said Jane. "It was getting so noisy in there. Cheers."

She clinked glasses with Celeste and they both drank.

"These cocktails are crazy good," said Jane.

"They're ridiculous," agreed Celeste. She was on her third. All her feelings—even her thumping fear—were nicely coated in fluffy cotton wool.

Jane breathed in deeply. "I think the rain is finally stopping. It smells nice. All salty and fresh." She moved to the balcony edge and put her hand on the wet railing. She looked out at the rainy night. She seemed exhilarated.

It smelled damp and swampy to Celeste.

"I have to tell you something," said Celeste.

Jane raised her eyebrows. "OK?" She was wearing red lipstick, Celeste noticed. Madeline would be thrilled.

"Just before we left tonight, Josh came and told me that it's Max who has been bullying Amabella, not Ziggy. I was horrified. I'm sorry. I'm so, so sorry." She looked up and saw Harper coming out onto the balcony, rummaging in her bag. Harper glanced their way and quickly clip-clopped up the other end, out of earshot, where she lit up a cigarette.

"I know," said Jane.

"You know?" Celeste took a step back and nearly slipped on the tile.

"Ziggy told me yesterday," said Jane. "Apparently Amabella told him and asked him to keep it a secret. Don't worry about it. It's all OK."

"It's not OK! You've had to put up with that terrible petition, and people like her." Celeste nodded her head in Harper's direction. "And poor little *Ziggy* and parents saying their kids couldn't play with him. I'm going to tell Renata tonight, and Miss Barnes and Mrs. Lipmann. I'm going to tell everyone. I might get up and make a public announcement: *You got the wrong kid.*"

"You don't have to do that," said Jane. "It's fine. It will all get sorted out."

"I'm just so terribly sorry," said Celeste again, and her voice shook. She was thinking now of Saxon Banks.

"Hey!" said Jane. She put her hand on Celeste's arm. "It's fine. It will all get sorted out. It's not your fault."

"No, but in a way it is my fault," said Celeste.

"It couldn't possibly be," said Jane firmly.

"Could we join you?"

The glass door slid open. It was Nathan and Bonnie. Bonnie looked as she always did, and Nathan was dressed in a less expensive–looking version of Perry's outfit, except that he'd taken his black wig off and was twirling it about on his fist like a puppet.

Celeste knew she was obliged to dislike Nathan and Bonnie on Madeline's behalf, but it was difficult at times. They both seemed so harmless and eager to please, and Skye was such a sweet little girl.

Oh, God.

She'd forgotten. Josh said Max had pushed Skye down the stairs *again*. He'd moved on to a new victim. She had to say something.

"I found out tonight that my son Max has been bullying some of the little girls in his class. I think he might have pushed your daughter on the stairs, um, more than once," she said. She could feel her cheeks burning. "I'm so sorry, I only just—"

"It's all right," said Bonnie calmly. "Skye told me about it. We discussed some strategies for what to do if this sort of thing happens again."

Strategies, thought Celeste bleakly. *She sounds like Susi, as though Skye were a domestic violence victim.* She watched Harper stub out her cigarette on the wet balcony railing and then carefully wrap it up in tissue, before hurrying off inside, ostentatiously not looking their way.

"We did actually e-mail Miss Barnes today to tell her about it," said Nathan earnestly. "I hope you don't mind, but Skye is painfully shy and has difficulty asserting herself, so we wanted Miss Barnes to keep an eye on things. And of course, it's up to the teacher to sort these things out. I think that's the school policy.

Let the teachers handle it. We would never have approached you about it."

"Oh!" said Celeste. "Well, thank you. Again, I'm just so sorry—"

"No need to be sorry! Gosh! They're kids!" said Nathan. "They've got to learn all this stuff. Don't hit your friends. Stand up for yourself. How to be a grown-up."

"How to be a grown-up," repeated Celeste shakily.

"Still learning myself, of course!" said Nathan.

"It's all part of their emotional and spiritual development," said Bonnie.

"There's some book along those lines, isn't there?" said Jane. "Something like *Everything You Need to Know You Learned in Kindergarten: Don't Be Mean, Play Nicely, Share Your Toys*."

"Sharing is caring," quoted Nathan, and they all laughed at the familiar line.

Detective-Sergeant Adrian Quinlan: Eight people, including the victim, were on the balcony at the time of the incident. We know who they are. They know who they are and they know what they saw. Telling the truth is the most important thing a witness has to do.

75.

Madeline was trapped in a passionate conversation with some Year 2 parents about bathroom renovations. She liked the parents very much, and she knew she'd just bored the husband silly while she and the wife had an intense conversation about the most flattering types of wrap dresses, so she owed it to the poor man to keep listening.

The problem was she really had nothing to say about bathroom renovations, and although she agreed it must have been terrible when they ran out of tiles, and that particular line was discontinued, and they only needed *three more tiles* to finish, she was sure it probably all worked out in the end, and she could see Celeste and Jane out on the balcony, and they were laughing with Bonnie and Nathan, which was unacceptable. Celeste and Jane were *her* friends.

She looked about for someone else to take her place and grabbed Samantha. Her husband was a plumber. She must surely have an interest in bathroom renovations. "You've got to hear this story!" she said. "Can you imagine? They, um, ran out of tiles!"

"Oh no! That exact same thing happened to me!" said Samantha.

Bingo. Madeline left Samantha listening intently and eagerly awaiting her turn to tell her own bathroom renovation disaster story. Good Lord. It was a mystery to her how anyone could find that more interesting than wrap dresses.

As she made her way through the crowd, she passed a group of four Blond Bobs huddled together so close, it was obvious they were sharing something scandalous. She paused to listen:

"The French nanny! That funny-looking girl."

"Didn't Renata fire her?"

"Yes, because she totally missed the fact that Amabella was being bullied by that Ziggy kid."

"What's happening with the petition, by the way?"

"We're going to submit it to Mrs. Lipmann on Monday."

"Have you seen the mother tonight? She's had her hair cut. She's flitting about like she hasn't got a care in the world. If *my* kid were a bully, I wouldn't be out showing my face, that's for sure. I'd be at home, with my child, giving him the attention he obviously needs."

"Needs a good smack, is what he needs."

"I hear she was bringing him to school with nits yesterday."

"I am just gobsmacked that the school let it go on for as long as it did. In this day and age, when there is so much *information* about bullying—"

"Right, right, but the point is, Renata's nanny is having an affair with Geoff."

"Why would she want to have an affair with *Geoff*?"

"I know it for a *fact*."

Madeline felt enraged on Jane's behalf, and strangely enough on behalf of Renata too—even though Renata had presumably approved the petition.

"You are awful people," she said loudly. The Blond Bobs looked up. Their eyes and mouths were little ovals of surprise. "You are awful, awful people."

She kept walking without waiting to hear their reactions. As she slid back the door to go out onto the balcony, she found Renata behind her.

"Just getting some fresh air," said Renata. "It's getting so stuffy in here."

"Yes," said Madeline. "And it looks like it's stopped raining." They stepped out together into the night air. "I've contacted my insurance company, by the way. About the car."

Renata winced. "I'm sorry I made such a fuss yesterday."

"Well, I'm sorry for running into you. I was busy yelling at Abigail."

"I got a fright," said Renata. "When I get frightened, I lash out. It's a flaw." They walked over toward the group near the railing.

"Really?" said Madeline. "How terrible for you. I have a very placid personality myself."

Renata snorted.

"Maddie!" said Nathan. "Haven't seen you yet tonight. How are you? I hear my wife spilled her drink all over you."

He must be a bit drunk too, thought Madeline. He wouldn't normally refer to Bonnie as his "wife" in front of her.

"Luckily it was a pink drink, so it matched my dress," said Madeline.

"I've been celebrating the happy ending to our daughter's little drama," said Nathan. "Here's to Larry Fitzgerald of South Dakota, hey?" He lifted his drink.

"Mmmm," said Madeline. Her eyes were on Celeste. "I have

this funny feeling that 'Larry Fitzgerald' might actually live closer than we think."

"Eh?" said Nathan. "What are you talking about?"

"Are you talking about Abigail's website?" said Celeste. "Did she close it down?"

Her delivery was absolutely perfect, thought Madeline, and that's what gave it away. Most of the time Celeste looked evasive, as though she had something to hide. Right now she looked completely composed and poised, and her eyes held Madeline's. When most people lied, they avoided eye contact; when Celeste lied, she held it.

"You're Larry Fitzgerald of South Dakota, aren't you?" said Madeline to Celeste. "I knew it! Well, I didn't know it for sure, but I had a feeling. It was all too convenient."

"I have absolutely no idea what you're talking about," said Celeste evenly.

Nathan turned to Celeste. "You gave one hundred thousand dollars to Amnesty? To help us? My God."

"You really shouldn't have," said Madeline. "You shouldn't have done that. How can we ever repay you?"

"Goodness," said Renata. "What is this all about?"

"I don't know what you're talking about," said Celeste to Madeline. "But don't forget you saved Max's life, so that's a debt that really can't be repaid."

There were some raised voices from inside the hall.

"I wonder what's going on?" said Nathan.

"Oh, I might have started some little fires," said Renata with a tiny smirk. "My husband isn't the only one who thinks he's in love with our nanny. Juliette found much to distract her in Pirriwee. What's the French word for it? *Polyamour*. I found out she had an eye for a certain type of man. Or I should say a certain type of bank account."

"Renata," said Celeste. "I found out tonight that—"

"Don't," said Jane.

"—my son Max was the one who was hurting Amabella," said Celeste.

"*Your* son?" said Renata. "But are you sure? Because on orientation day Amabella pointed out Ziggy."

"I'm quite sure," said Celeste. "She picked out Ziggy at random because she was frightened of Max."

"But . . ." Renata couldn't seem to get her head around it. "You're sure?"

"I'm quite sure," said Celeste. "And I'm sorry."

Renata put a hand to her mouth. "Amabella didn't want me to invite the twins to her *A* party," she said. "She made such a fuss about it, and I just ignored her. I thought she was being silly."

She looked at Jane. Jane looked steadily back. She really did look wonderful tonight, thought Madeline with satisfaction, and she realized that the constant gum-chewing had stopped sometime over the last few weeks without her noticing.

"I owe you a very big apology," said Renata.

"You do," said Jane.

"And Ziggy," said Renata. "I owe you and your son an apology. I am so sorry. I will . . . Well, I don't know what I'll do."

"I accept," said Jane. She lifted her glass. "I accept your apology."

The glass door slid open yet again, and Ed and Perry appeared.

"Things are getting a bit out of hand in there," said Ed. He grabbed some bar stools that had been lined up near the door and brought them over. "Shall we make ourselves comfortable? Hello,

Renata. I'm very sorry about my wife's lead foot on the accelerator yesterday."

Perry brought some stools over as well.

"Perry," said Renata. Madeline noticed she wasn't quite as obsequious toward Perry now that she knew his son had been bullying her daughter. In fact, there was a definite edge to her voice. "Nice to see you in the country."

"Thanks, Renata. Nice to see you too."

Nathan held out his hand. "Perry, is it? I don't think we've met. I'm Nathan. I understand we're very much in your debt."

"Really?" said Perry. "How is that?"

Oh Jesus, Nathan, thought Madeline. *Shut up. He doesn't know. I bet he doesn't know.*

"Perry, this is Bonnie," interrupted Celeste. "And this is Jane. She's Ziggy's mother."

Madeline met Celeste's eyes. She knew they were both thinking about Perry's cousin. The secret hung in the air between them like an evil amorphous cloud.

"Pleasure to meet you both." Perry shook their hands and with courtly gestures offered seats to the women.

"Apparently you and your wife donated one hundred thousand dollars to Amnesty International to help our daughter out of a spot," gabbled on Nathan. He was twirling his Elvis wig around in his hand, and it suddenly flew off and over the balcony and into the darkness. "Oh shit!" He looked over the balcony. "I'll lose my deposit at the shop."

Perry removed his own black Elvis wig. "They do get a bit itchy after a while," he said. He ruffled his hair with his fingertips so he looked boyishly rumpled and sat himself up on a bar stool, his back to the balcony. He looked very tall up on the bar stool, with the sky clearing behind him, clouds backlit by the moonlight from an emerging full moon, like a magical gold disc. Somehow they'd formed a semicircle around Perry, as though he were their leader.

"What's this about donating one hundred thousand dollars?" he said. "Is this another one of my wife's secrets? She's a surprisingly secretive woman, my wife. Very secretive. Just look at that Mona Lisa expression of hers."

Madeline looked at Celeste. She was sitting on her bar stool with her long legs crossed, her hands folded in her lap. She was completely still. She looked like she was carved out of stone, a sculpture of a beautiful woman. She'd turned slightly so she was looking away from Perry. Was she breathing? Was she all right? Madeline felt her heart speed up. Something was falling into place. Pieces of a puzzle forming a picture. Answers to questions she didn't know she had.

The perfect marriage. The perfect life. Except Celeste was always so flustered. A little fidgety. A little edgy.

"She also seems to think we have unlimited financial resources," said Perry. "Doesn't earn a cent herself, but sure knows how to spend it."

"Hey *now*," said Renata sharply, as if she were remonstrating a child.

"I think we've already met," said Jane to Perry.

Nobody heard her except for Madeline. Jane had remained standing while everyone else perched up on their bar stools. She looked tiny in the middle of them, like a child addressing Perry. She had to tip back her head. Her eyes were very big.

She cleared her throat and spoke again. "I think we've already met."

Perry glanced at her. "Really? Are you sure?" He inclined his head charmingly. "I'm sorry. I don't recall."

"I'm sure," said Jane. "Except you said your name was Saxon Banks."

76.

At first his face was completely neutral: friendly, this-is-of-no-relevance-to-me polite. He didn't recognize her. *I wouldn't know her from a bar of soap!* The cheery phrase popped inappropriately into her head. Something her mum would say.

But when she said "Saxon Banks" there was a flicker, not because he recognized her, he still had no idea, couldn't even be bothered to go to the effort of dredging up the appropriate memory, but because he understood who she must be, what she represented. She was one of many.

He'd lied about his name. It had never occurred to her that he would do that. As if your name could not be fabricated, even though you could fabricate your personality, fabricate your attention.

"I kept thinking I might run into you," she said to him.

Perry?" said Celeste.

Perry turned to her.

His face was naked again, like in the car, as though something had been ripped away. Ever since Madeline had first mentioned Saxon's name on the night of the book club, there had been something niggling at Celeste, a memory from before the children were born, before Perry hit her for the first time.

That memory slid into place now. Fully intact. As though it had just been waiting for her to retrieve it.

It was Perry's cousin's wedding. The one where Saxon and Perry had driven all the way back to the church to collect Eleni's mobile phone. They were sitting at a round table. White starched table-cloth. Giant bows tied around the chairs. Light hitting the wine-glasses. Saxon and Perry were telling stories. Stories of a shared suburban childhood: homemade billy carts and the time Saxon saved Perry from the bullies at school and what about the time when Perry brazenly stole a banana paddle pop from the freezer at the fish and chip shop and the big scary Greek man grabbed him by the scruff of his neck in one big beefy hand and said, "What's your name?" and Perry said, "Saxon Banks." The fish and chip shop owner called Saxon's mother and said, "Your son stole from me," and Sax-on's mother said, "My son is right here," and hung up on him.

So funny. So cheeky. How they'd laughed while they drank their champagne.

"It didn't mean anything," said Perry to Celeste.

There was a hollow roaring sensation in her ears, as though she were deep underwater.

Jane watched Perry turn away from her to look at his wife, instantly dismissing her without even bothering to remember or acknowledge her. She'd never really existed to him. She was of no consequence in his life. He was married to a beautiful woman. Jane was pornography. Jane was the adult movie that didn't ap-pear on his hotel bill. Jane was Internet porn, where every fetish can be fulfilled. You have a fetish for humiliating fat girls? Enter your credit card number and click right here.

"That's why I moved to Pirriwee," said Jane. "Just in case you were here."

The glass bubble elevator. The muffled, dimly lit hotel room.

She remembered how she'd looked around the room—casually, pleasurably—for more evidence of the sort of man he was, more evidence of his money and style, more evidence to indicate that this would be a delightfully lavish one-night stand. There wasn't much to see. A closed laptop. An upright overnight bag standing neatly in the corner. Next to the laptop there was a real estate leaflet. FOR SALE. A picture of an ocean view. LUXURY FAMILY HOME OVERLOOKING THE GLORIOUS PIRRIWEE PENINSULA.

"Are you buying this house?" she'd said.

"Probably," he answered. He was pouring her champagne.

"Do you have kids?" she asked, recklessly, stupidly. "It seems like a good house for children." She never asked about a wife. No ring. There was no ring.

"No kids," he said. "One day, I'd like kids."

She'd seen something on his face: a sadness, a desperate sort of yearning, and she had thought, in all her idiotic naivety, that she knew exactly what that sadness indicated. He'd just been through a break-up! Of course he had. *He was just like her*, nursing a broken heart. He was desperate to find the right woman and start a family, and maybe she was even moronic enough to think, as he smiled his devastatingly attractive smile and handed her the champagne glass, that *she* might turn out to be that woman. Stranger things had happened!

And then stranger things did happen.

Over the years that followed, she reacted viscerally to the

words "Pirriwee Peninsula" in conversation or in print. She changed the subject. She turned the page.

Then one day, without warning, she did the exact opposite. She told Ziggy they were going to the beach and they drove to the glorious Pirriwee Peninsula, and all the way there she tried to pretend that she didn't even remember that real estate leaflet, even as she remembered it, over and over.

They played on the beach and she looked over his shoulder for a man coming out of the surf with a white-toothed smile. She listened for the sound of a wife calling out the name "Saxon."

What did she want?

Revenge? Recognition? To show him she was skinny now? To hit him, to hurt him, to report him? To say all the things she should have said instead of her bovine "bye"? To somehow let him know that he hadn't gotten away with it, even though of course he had?

She wanted him to see Ziggy.

She wanted him to marvel at his beautiful, serious, intense little boy.

It made no sense. It was such a stupid, strange, weird and wrong desire, she refused to properly acknowledge it and sometimes she flatly denied it.

Because how would this moment of magical fatherly marveling possibly work? "Oh, hi there! Remember me? I had a son! Here he is! No, no, of *course* I don't want a relationship with you, but I do just want you to stand for a moment and marvel over your son. He loves pumpkin. He's always loved pumpkin! Isn't that incredible? What kid loves pumpkin? He's shy and brave and he has excellent balance. So there you go. You're a bastard and a prick and I hate you, but just look for a moment at your son, because isn't it the strangest thing? Ten minutes of depravity created something perfect."

She told herself she'd taken Ziggy to Pirriwee for the day and seen a flat for lease and "on a whim" she decided to move here. She pretended it so fiercely she almost believed it, and as the months went by and it seemed less and less likely that Saxon Banks lived here at all, it had become the truth. She stopped looking for him.

When she told Madeline the story about the night at the hotel with Saxon, it hadn't even occurred to her to tell her that he was part of the reason she'd moved to Pirriwee. It was preposterous and embarrassing. "You *wanted* to run into him?" Madeline would have said, trying her best to understand. "You *wanted* to see that man?" How could Jane explain that she did and she didn't want to see him? Anyway, she'd forgotten all about that real estate brochure! She *had* moved to Pirriwee on a whim.

And Saxon clearly wasn't here.

But now here he was. Celeste's husband. He must have been married to Celeste at the time he met Jane.

"We had a really hard time getting pregnant with the boys," Celeste had told Jane once on one of their walks. *That* was why he'd looked sad when she had mentioned children.

Jane felt her face flush warm with humiliation in the cool night air.

I t meant nothing," Perry said again to Celeste.

"It meant something to *her*," said Celeste.

It was his shrug that did it. The almost imperceptible shrug that said *Who cares about her?* He thought this was about infidelity.

He thought he'd been caught out in a garden-variety business-executive-goes-on-an-interstate-trip one-night stand. He thought it was nothing to do with Jane.

"I thought you were . . ."

She couldn't speak.

She thought he was kind. She thought he was a good person with a bad temper. She thought that his violence was something private and personal *between them*. She thought he wasn't capable of casual cruelty. He always spoke so nicely to waitresses, even the incompetent ones. She thought she knew him.

"Let's talk about this at home," said Perry. "Let's not make a spectacle of ourselves."

"You're not looking at her," whispered Celeste. "You're not even looking at her."

She threw the contents of her half-full glass of champagne cocktail straight in his face.

The champagne splashed across his face.

Perry's right hand rose instantly, instinctively, gracefully. It was as though he were an athlete catching a ball, except he didn't catch anything.

He hit Celeste with the back of his hand.

His hand curved in a perfect, practiced, brutal arc that flung back her head and sent her body flying across the balcony where she fell, clumsily and hard on her side.

The air rushed from Madeline's lungs.

Ed sprang to his feet so fast, his bar stool tipped over. "Whoa! Whoa there!"

Madeline rushed to Celeste's side and dropped to her knees. "My God, my God, are you—"

"I'm fine," said Celeste. She pressed her hand to her face and half sat up. "I'm perfectly fine."

Madeline looked back at the little circle of people on the balcony. Ed stood with his arms held wide, one hand up like a stop sign directed at Perry, the other held protectively in front of Celeste.

Jane's glass had slipped from her fingers and shattered at her feet.

Renata rummaged through her handbag. "I'm calling the police," she said. "I'm calling the police right now. That's assault. I just witnessed you assaulting your wife."

Nathan had his hand on Bonnie's elbow. As Madeline watched, she shook his hand free. She was blazing with passion as though lit from within.

"You've done that before," she said to Perry.

Perry ignored Bonnie. His eyes were on Renata, who had her phone to her ear. "OK, let's not get ahead of ourselves," he said.

"That's why your son has been hurting little girls," said Bonnie. It was that same rough-edged voice Madeline had heard her use earlier in the night, except it was even more pronounced now. She sounded so . . . well, she sounded like she came from the "wrong side of town," as Madeline's mother would say.

She sounded like a drinker. A smoker. A fighter. She sounded real. It was strangely exhilarating to hear that guttural, angry voice coming out of Bonnie's mouth. "Because he's seen what you do. Your little boy has seen you do that, hasn't he?"

Perry exhaled. "Look, I don't know what you're implying. My children haven't 'seen' anything."

"Your children see!" screamed Bonnie. Her face was ugly with rage. "We see! We fucking *see!*"

She shoved him, both her small hands flat on his chest.

He fell.

77.

If Perry had been just a few inches shorter.

If the balcony railing had been just a few inches higher.

If the bar stool had been at a slightly different angle.

If it hadn't been raining.

If he hadn't been drinking.

Afterward Madeline could not stop thinking of all the ways it could have happened differently.

But it happened the way that it happened.

Celeste saw the expression on Perry's face when Bonnie screamed at him. It was the same mildly amused face as when Celeste lost her temper with him. He liked it when women got angry with him. He liked getting a reaction. He thought it was cute.

She saw his hand grab for the railing and slip.

She saw him flip back, his legs high, like he was romping on the bed with the boys.

And then he was gone without making a sound.

An empty space where he'd been.

It all happened too fast. Jane's mind was dull with shock. As she groped for comprehension she became aware that there was a commotion going on inside the hall: yells, bangs, thuds.

"Jesus Christ Almighty!" said Ed. He leaned over the balcony railing, both hands gripping the edge as he peered over, his gold Elvis cape stretched out behind him like foolish little wings.

Bonnie had sunk down on to her haunches, her body curved into a ball, her hands clasped tightly over the back of her head as though she were waiting for a bomb to explode.

"No, no, no, no." Nathan took little agitated steps, dancing around his wife, bending to touch her back and then straightening up and pressing his hands to his temples.

Ed spun around. "I'll go see if he's—"

"Ed!" said Renata. She'd dropped the hand holding her mobile phone to her side. The balcony light reflected off her glasses.

"Call an ambulance!" barked Ed.

"Yes," said Renata. "I am. I will. But um . . . I didn't see what happened. I didn't see him fall."

"What?" said Ed.

Madeline was still on her knees next to Celeste. Jane saw Madeline look straight past Ed at her ex-husband. Nathan's hair was all sweaty from the wig and stuck to his forehead. He looked at Madeline with distraught, pleading eyes. Madeline looked back at Celeste, who was staring catatonically at the place where Perry had been sitting.

"I don't think I saw either," said Madeline.

"Madeline," said Ed. He pulled angrily at his costume, as if he longed to tear it off. The glitter was coming off onto his hands, turning his palms gold. "Do not—"

"I was looking the other way," said Madeline. Her voice was stronger. She got to her feet, holding her tiny clutch bag in front of her, her back straight and her chin high, as if she were about to walk into a ballroom. "I was looking inside. I didn't see."

Jane cleared her throat.

She thought of the way Saxon—Perry—had said, "It didn't mean anything." She looked at Bonnie, cowering near an up-turned bar stool. She felt hot liquid anger suddenly cool and harden into something powerful and immovable.

"So was I," she said. "I didn't see anything either."

"Stop this." Ed glanced at her and back at Madeline. "All of you stop it."

Celeste reached for Madeline's hand and pulled herself grace-fully to her feet. She straightened her dress and pressed one hand to her face, where Perry had hit her. She looked for a moment at the curled-up form of Bonnie.

"I didn't see a thing," she said, and her voice sounded almost conversational.

"Celeste." Ed's face crumpled as though in terror. He pressed his hands hard against his temples, and then dropped them. His forehead sparkled gold.

Celeste walked to the edge of the balcony and put her hands on the railing. She looked back at Renata and said, "Call the am-bulance now."

Then she began to scream.

It was easy after all those years of pretending. Celeste was a fine actress.

But then she thought of her children and she didn't need to pretend anymore.

Stu: All hell had broken loose by this stage. Two blokes were fighting over some French chick, and next thing this four-foot weasel is laying into me because I'd said his wife couldn't organize a root in a brothel and I'd offended her honor or something. I mean, jeez Louise, it's just an expression.

Thea: It's true the argument over standardized testing got a little heated. I have four children, so I do lay claim to some expertise in the matter.

Harper: Thea was shouting like a fishwife.

Jonathan: I was with some Year 4 parents and we got into an argument over the legality and morality of that damned petition. There were some raised voices. Maybe some shoving. Look, I'm not proud of any of this.

Jackie: Give me a vicious corporate takeover any day.

Gabrielle: I was considering cannibalism by this time. Carol looked delicious.

Carol: I was cleaning the kitchen when I heard the most terrible bloodcurdling scream.

Samantha: Ed came running for the stairs and he was shouting something about Perry White falling off the balcony and would someone for the love of God call an ambulance. I looked over at the balcony and saw two Year 5 dads go crashing out through the open door.

"There's been an accident," Renata was saying into her mobile phone. She had one finger plugged into her ear so she could hear the person on the other end over the sound of Celeste's screams. "A man has fallen. From a balcony."

"It was him?" Madeline took Jane's arm and pulled her close. "It was *Perry* who—"

Jane stared at the perfect pink cupid's bow of Madeline's lipstick. Two perfect peaks. "Do you think he's—"

She never got to finish her sentence because that's when the two grappling white-satin Elvises, their arms wrapped tightly around each other's backs as if in a passionate embrace, slammed violently into Jane and Madeline, sending them flying in opposite directions.

As Jane fell, she put one hand to save herself and felt something snap with sickening wrongness near her shoulder as she landed hard on her side.

The tiles of the balcony were wet against Jane's cheek. Celeste's screams mingled with the far-off sounds of ambulances and the soft sound of Bonnie sobbing. Jane could taste blood in her mouth. She closed her eyes.

Oh, calamity.

> **Bonnie:** The fighting spilled out onto the balcony, and that's when poor Madeline and Jane got so badly injured. I didn't see Perry White fall. I . . . Would you excuse me for just a moment, Sarah? Wait, it is Sarah, isn't it? Not Susan. My mind went blank. Sorry, Sarah. Sarah. A lovely name. It means "princess," I think. Listen, Sarah, I need to pick up my daughter now.

78.

Detective-Sergeant Adrian Quinlan: We're looking at any available CCTV footage, photos taken on the night and mobile phone footage. Obviously we'll be studying the forensic evidence when it becomes available. We're currently in the process of interviewing every one of the one hundred and thirty-two parents who attended the event. Rest assured, we *will* find out the truth about exactly what took place last night, and I'll charge the bloody lot of them if I have to.

The Morning After the Trivia Night

I don't think I can do it," said Ed quietly. He was sitting on a chair next to Madeline's hospital bed. She had a private room, but Ed kept looking nervously over his shoulder. He looked like he was seasick.

"I'm not asking you to do anything," said Madeline. "If you want to tell, tell."

"*Tell.* For God's sake." Ed rolled his eyes. "This isn't snitching to the teacher! This is breaking the law. This is lying under . . . Are you OK? Are you in pain?"

Madeline closed her eyes and winced. Her ankle was broken. It happened when the two Year 5 dads crashed into her and Jane.

At first she thought she wouldn't fall, but then, it seemed like it happened in slow motion, one of her legs slid behind the other one on the wet balcony as though she were doing a fancy dance move. It was her good ankle too, not the one that kept rolling. She had to lie there on the wet balcony last night in excruciating pain for what seemed like hours while Celeste screamed that awful, endless scream, and Bonnie sobbed, and Nathan swore and Jane lay on her side with blood on her face and Renata yelled at the fighting Year 5 dads to "grow up, for God's sake!"

Madeline was scheduled for surgery this afternoon. She would be in a cast for four to six weeks, and after that there would be physiotherapy. It would be a long time before she'd be in stilettos again.

She wasn't the only one who had ended up in the hospital. As Madeline understood it, the final tally this morning of injuries from the trivia night were one broken ankle (Madeline's contribution), one broken collarbone (poor Jane), a broken nose (Renata's husband, Geoff—less than he deserved), three cracked ribs (Harper's husband, Graeme, who had also been sleeping with the French nanny), three black eyes, two nasty cuts requiring stitches and ninety-four splitting headaches.

And one death.

Madeline's head swirled with a violent merry-go-round of images from the previous night. Jane, with her bright red lipstick, standing in front of Perry and saying, "You said your name was Saxon Banks." At first Madeline had thought Jane had the two men mixed up, that Perry must resemble his cousin, until Perry said, "It didn't mean anything." The look on Celeste's face after Perry hit her. No surprise at all. Just embarrassment.

What sort of an obtuse, self-absorbed friend had Madeline been to have missed something like that? Just because Celeste didn't walk around nursing black eyes and split lips didn't mean there hadn't been clues, if she'd just bothered to notice them. Had Celeste ever tried to confide in her? Madeline had probably been rattling on about eye cream or something equally superficial and hadn't given her the opportunity. She'd probably *interrupted* her! Ed was always calling her out on that. "Let me finish," he'd say, holding up a hand. Just three little words. *Perry hits me.* And Madeline had never given her friend the three seconds it took to say them. Meanwhile Celeste had listened while Madeline had talked endlessly about everything from how much she hated the under-seven soccer coordinator to her feelings about Abigail's relationship with her father.

"She brought around a vegetarian lasagna for us today," said Ed.

"Who?" said Madeline. Regret was making her nauseous.

"Bonnie! For God's sake, Bonnie. The woman we're apparently protecting. She was just bizarrely normal, as if nothing happened. She's completely nuts. She's already been talking this morning to a 'very nice journalist called Sarah.' God knows what she's been saying."

"It was an accident," said Madeline.

She remembered Bonnie's face disfigured with rage as she screamed at Perry. That strange guttural voice. *We see! We fucking see!*

"I know it was an accident," said Ed. "So why don't we just say the truth? Tell the police exactly what happened? I don't get it. You don't even like her."

"That's not relevant," said Madeline.

"It was Renata who started it," said Ed. "And then everyone else jumped on board. 'I didn't see. I didn't see.' We didn't
even know if the man was dead or alive and we were already
planning the cover-up! I mean, Jesus, does Renata even *know*
Bonnie?"

Madeline thought she understood why Renata had said what
she'd said. It was because Perry had cheated on Celeste, like Geoff
cheated on Renata. Madeline had seen the expression on Renata's
face when Perry said, "It didn't mean anything." At that moment
Renata had wanted to shove Perry off the balcony herself. Bonnie
just got there first.

If Renata hadn't said, "I didn't see him fall," then perhaps
Madeline's mind wouldn't have moved fast enough to even consider the consequences for Bonnie, but as soon as Renata said
what she did, Madeline had thought of Bonnie's daughter. That
fluttery thing Skye did with her eyelashes, the way she always hid
behind her mother's skirt. If ever there was a child who needed
her mother, it was Skye.

And maybe it was more than that.

Maybe it was actually an unspoken instant agreement between
the four women on the balcony: *No woman should pay for the accidental death of that particular man.* Maybe it was an involuntary,
atavistic response to thousands of years of violence against women.
Maybe it was for every rape, every brutal backhanded slap, every
other Perry that had come before this one.

"Bonnie has a little girl," said Madeline.

"Perry had two little boys—so what?" said Ed. He looked off
to a space above Madeline's bed. His face was haggard in the harsh
single light. She could see the old man he'd one day be. "I just
don't know if I can live with this, Madeline."

He was the first one to get to Perry. He was the one who saw the broken, twisted body of a man who had just moments before been talking and laughing with him about golf handicaps. It was too much to ask of him. She knew this.

"Perry was not a good person," said Madeline. "He's the one who did those things to Jane. Did you get that? He's Ziggy's father."

"*That's* not relevant," said Ed.

"It's up to you," said Madeline. Ed was right. Of course he was right, he was always right, but sometimes doing the wrong thing was also right.

"Do you think she meant to kill him?" she asked.

"I don't," said Ed. "But so what? I'm not judge and jury. It's not my job to—"

"Do you think she'll do it again? Do you think she's a danger to society?"

"No, but again, so what?" He gave her a look of genuine anguish. "I just don't think I can knowingly lie in a police investigation."

"Haven't you already?" She knew he'd spoken to the police briefly last night before he came to the hospital, as she'd been taken off in one of the three ambulances that had pulled up in the kiss-and-drop zone out in front of the school.

"Not officially," said Ed. "Some officer wrote down a few notes and I said . . . God, I don't really know what I said, I was drunk. I didn't mention Bonnie, I know that, but at one o'clock this afternoon I've agreed to go down to the police station and give an *official* witness statement. They'll tape it, Madeline. They'll have two officers sitting in a room, looking at me while I knowingly lie. I'll have to sign an affidavit. That makes me an accessory—"

"Hey there." It was Nathan, charging into the room holding a big bunch of flowers and smiling a big wide celebrity smile, as if he were a motivational speaker walking onto a stage.

Ed jumped. "Jesus Christ, Nathan, you scared the life out of me."

"Sorry, mate," said Nathan. "How are you, Maddie?"

"I'm fine," said Madeline. There was something unsettling about having your husband and your ex-husband standing next to each other, looking down at you while you lay in bed. It was weird. She wished they would both leave.

"There you go! Poor girl!" Nathan dumped the flowers on her lap. "I hear you're going to be on crutches for quite a while."

"Yes, well—"

"Abigail has already said she's moving back home to help you."

"Oh," said Madeline. "Oh." She fingered the pink petals of the flowers. "Well, I'll talk to her about it. I'll be perfectly fine. She doesn't need to look after me."

"No, but I think she wants to move back home," said Nathan. "She's looking for an excuse."

Madeline and Ed looked at each other. Ed shrugged.

"I always thought the novelty would wear off," said Nathan. "She missed her mum. We're not her real life."

"Right."

"So. I should get going," said Ed.

"Could you stay for a moment, mate?" said Nathan. The big positive-thinking smile had gone, and now he looked like the man in the wrong at a car accident. "I wouldn't mind talking to the two of you for a bit—about, um, about what happened last night."

Ed grimaced, but he pulled over a nearby chair and placed it next to his, gesturing for Nathan to sit.

"Oh, thanks, *thanks*, mate." Nathan looked pathetically grateful as he sat down.

There was a long pause.

Ed cleared his throat.

"Bonnie's father was violent," said Nathan without preamble. "Very violent. I don't think I even know half the stuff he did. Not to Bonnie. To her mum. But Bonnie and her little sister saw it all. They had a very tough childhood."

"I'm not sure I should——" began Ed.

"I never met her dad," continued Nathan. "He died of a heart attack before I met Bonnie. Anyway, Bonnie is . . . well, one psychiatrist diagnosed post-traumatic stress. She's fine most of the time, but she has very bad nightmares and just, um, some difficulties sometimes."

He looked blankly past Madeline to the wall behind her head. His eyes were blank as he considered all the secrets of what Madeline now realized was his complicated marriage.

"You don't have to tell us any of this," said Madeline.

"She's a good person, Maddie," said Nathan desperately. He wasn't looking at Ed. His eyes were fixed on Madeline. He was calling on their history. He was calling on past memories and past love. Even though he'd walked out on her, he was asking her to forget all that and remember the days when they were obsessed with each other, when they woke up smiling goofily at each other. It was crazy, but she knew that's what he was asking. He was asking twenty-year-old Madeline for a favor.

"She's a wonderful mother," said Nathan. "The best mother.

And I can promise you, she never ever meant for Perry to *fall*. I think it was just that when she saw him hit Celeste like that . . ."

"Something snapped," said Madeline. She saw Perry's hand swinging back in its graceful, practiced arc. She heard Bonnie's guttural voice. It occurred to her that there were so many levels of evil in the world. Small evils like her own malicious words. Like not inviting a child to a party. Bigger evils like walking out on your wife and newborn baby or sleeping with your child's nanny. And then there was the sort of evil of which Madeline had no experience: cruelty in hotel rooms and violence in suburban homes and little girls being sold like merchandise, shattering innocent hearts.

"I know you don't owe me anything," said Nathan, "because obviously what I did to you when Abigail was a baby was completely unforgivable and—"

"Nathan," interrupted Madeline. It was crazy and it made no sense because she did not forgive him, and she chose to never forgive him, and he would drive her to distraction for the rest of her life, and one day he'd walk Abigail down the aisle and Madeline would be grinding her teeth the whole way, but he was still family, he still belonged on her piece of cardboard showing her family tree.

How could she possibly explain to Ed that she didn't particularly like Bonnie, or understand her, but that it turned out she was prepared to lie for her in the same way that she would automatically lie for Ed, her children, her mother? It turned out, as strange and improbable as it seemed, that Bonnie was family too.

"We're not going to say anything to the police," said Madeline. "We didn't see what happened. We didn't see a thing."

Ed stood with a sudden backward scrape of his chair and left the room without looking back.

Detective-Sergeant Adrian Quinlan: Someone is not telling the truth about what happened on that balcony.

79.

The policeman looked like a nice young soccer dad, but there was something cool and knowing about his tired green eyes. He was sitting next to Jane's hospital bed with a pen poised over his yellow notepad.

"Let me get this straight: You were standing on the balcony but you were looking back inside?"

"Yes," said Jane. "Because of all the noise. People were throwing things."

"And then you heard Celeste White scream?"

"I think so," said Jane. "It's all so confusing. Everything is muddled. Those champagne cocktails."

"Yes," sighed the policeman. "Those champagne cocktails. I've heard a lot about them."

"Everyone was very drunk," said Jane.

"Where were you standing in relation to Perry White?"

"Um, I think sort of off to one side." The last nurse had said that someone would be taking her for an X-ray soon. Her parents were on their way with Ziggy. She looked at the door of her room and wished for someone, anyone, to come and save her from this conversation.

"And what was *your* relationship with Perry? Were you friends?"

Jane thought of the moment when he took off his wig and became Saxon Banks. She never got to tell him that he had a son called Ziggy who liked pumpkin. She never got an apology. Was *that* what she'd come to Pirriwee for? Because she wanted his remorse? She actually thought she'd get his remorse?

She closed her eyes. "We only met for the first time last night. I'd only just been introduced to him."

"I think you're lying," said the policeman. He put down his notepad. Jane flinched at his sudden change of tone. His voice had the implacability, the weight and violence of a swinging hammer. "Are you lying?"

80.

There's someone here who wants to see you," said Celeste's mother.

Celeste looked up from the couch where she was sitting with the boys on either side of her, watching cartoons. She didn't want to move from her position. The boys were comforting, warm, heavy weights against her body.

She didn't know what the children were thinking. They'd cried when she'd told them about their father, but she wondered if they were crying because Perry had promised to take them fishing at the rock pool this morning and now that wasn't happening. She suspected that right now their little minds were as blank and stunned as hers and that the bright flickering colors of the cartoon characters were the only thing that felt real.

"It's not another journalist, is it?" she said.

"Her name is Bonnie," said her mother. "She says she's one of the school mums and she'd just like to talk to you for a few minutes. She says it's important. She brought this." Her mother lifted a casserole dish. "She says it's a vegetarian lasagna." Her mother lifted an eyebrow to indicate her opinion of a *vegetarian* lasagna.

Celeste stood, gently lifting the boys and letting them fall on their sides on the couch. They made little murmurs of protest but didn't move their eyes from the television.

Bonnie was waiting for her in the living room, standing very still, looking out to the ocean with her long blond plait falling down the center of her yoga-straight back. Celeste stood in the doorway and watched her for a moment. This was the woman responsible for her husband's death.

Bonnie turned slowly and smiled sadly. "Celeste."

You couldn't imagine this placid, luminous-skinned woman screaming, *"We see! We fucking see!"* You couldn't imagine her swearing.

"Thank you for the lasagna," said Celeste, meaning it. She knew that soon her house would be filled with Perry's grieving family members.

"Well, that's the least . . ." An expression of pure anguish momentarily distorted Bonnie's tranquil face. "The word 'sorry' is hardly adequate for my actions, but I needed to come here to say it."

"It was an accident," said Celeste faintly. "You didn't mean for him to fall."

"Your little boys," said Bonnie. "How are they . . . ?"

"I don't think they really understand anything yet," said Celeste.

"No," said Bonnie. "They wouldn't." She breathed out a long, slow, deliberate breath through her mouth as if she were demonstrating yogic breathing.

"I'm going to the police now," said Bonnie. "I'm going to make a statement and tell them exactly how it happened. You don't need to lie for me."

"I already told them last night I didn't see—"

Bonnie held up her hand. "They'll be back again for a proper witness statement. This time just tell them the truth." She took another long, slow breath. "I was going to lie. I've had a lot of practice, you see. I'm a good liar. When I was growing up I lied all the time. To the police. To social workers. I had to keep big secrets. I even let a journalist interview me this morning, and I was fine, but then, I don't know. I went to pick up my little girl from my mother's place, and when I walked in the front door, I remembered the last time I saw my father hit my mother. I was twenty. A grown-up. I'd gone home for a visit, and it started. Mum did something. I don't remember what. She didn't put enough tomato sauce on his plate. She laughed the wrong way." Bonnie looked directly at Celeste. "You know."

"I know," said Celeste hoarsely. She put her hand on the couch where Perry had once held her head.

"You know what I did? I ran to my old bedroom and I *hid under the bed*." Bonnie gave a little bitter laugh of disbelief. "Because that's what my sister and I always did. I didn't even think. I just ran. And I lay there on my stomach, my heart pounding, looking at that old green shag carpet, waiting for it to be over, and then all of a sudden I thought, 'My God, what am I doing? I'm a grown woman hiding under the bed.' So I got out, and I called the police."

Bonnie pulled her plait over her shoulder and readjusted the elastic at the end. "I don't hide under the bed anymore. I don't keep secrets, and I don't want people to keep secrets for me."

She pushed her plait back over her shoulder. "Anyway, the truth is bound to come out. Madeline and Renata will be able to lie to the police. But definitely not Ed. And not Jane. And probably not even my poor hopeless husband. Nathan will probably be the worst of the lot."

"I would have lied for you," said Celeste. "I can lie."

"I know you can." Bonnie's eyes were bright. "I think you're probably very good at it too."

She stepped forward and put her hand on Celeste's arm. "But you can stop now."

81.

Bonnie is telling the truth.

It was a text message from Celeste.

Madeline fumbled the phone as she dialed Ed's number. It suddenly seemed as though the future of her marriage depended on her reaching him before he went in for his interview.

The phone rang and rang. It was too late.

"What is it?" His voice was curt.

Relief flooded her. "Where are you?"

"I've just parked the car. I'm about to go into the police station."

"Bonnie is confessing," said Madeline. "You don't need to lie for her."

There was silence.

"Ed?" she said. "Did you hear me? You can tell them exactly what you saw. You can tell them the truth."

It sounded like he was crying. He never cried.

"You shouldn't have asked that of me," he said roughly. "That was too much to ask of me. That was for him. You were asking me to do that for your ex-bloody-husband."

"I know," said Madeline. She was crying now too. "I'm sorry. I'm so sorry."

"I was going to do it."

No, you weren't, my darling, she thought as she brushed away her tears with the back of her hand. *No, you weren't.*

Dear Ziggy,

I don't know if you remember this, but last year at kindergarten orientation day I was not very nice to you. I believed that you had hurt my daughter and I now know this was not true. I hope you will forgive me and I hope that your mum will forgive me too. I behaved very badly to you both and I am sorry.

Amabella is having a going-away party before we move to London, and we would be honored if you would attend as our very special guest. The theme is Star Wars. *Amabella said to bring your lightsaber.*

Yours sincerely,

Renata Klein (Amabella's mum)

82.

Four Weeks After the Trivia Night

H as she tried to speak to you?" said Jane to Tom. "That journalist who is interviewing everyone?"

It was midmorning on a beautiful winter day. They stood together on the boardwalk outside Blue Blues. A woman sat at a table near the window, frowning as she transcribed notes onto her laptop from a Dictaphone attached to her ear by a single earplug.

"Sarah?" said Tom. "Yeah. I just give her free muffins and tell her I've got nothing to say. I'm hoping she'll mention the muffins in her story."

"She's been interviewing people since the morning after the trivia night," said Jane. "Ed thinks she's trying to get a book deal. Apparently even Bonnie spoke to her before she was charged. She must have reams of stuff."

Tom waved to the journalist, and she waved back, lifting her coffee in a salute.

"Let's go," said Tom.

They were taking some sandwiches around to the headland for an early lunch. Jane's sling for her broken collarbone had come off yesterday. The doctor had told her she could start doing some gentle exercise.

"Are you sure Maggie can handle the café?" asked Jane, referring to Tom's only part-time employee.

"Sure. Her coffee is better than mine," said Tom.

"No, it's not," said Jane loyally.

They walked up the stairs where Jane used to meet Celeste for their walks after school drop-off. She thought of Celeste hurrying to meet her, flustered and worried because she was late again, oblivious to a middle-aged jogger who had nearly run into a tree trying to get a second look at her.

She had barely seen Celeste since the funeral.

The worst part of the funeral had been those little boys, with their blond hair slicked to the side, their good white dress shirts and little black pants, their serious faces. There was the letter that Max had written to his father and placed on top of the coffin. "Daddy" in uneven scrawling letters with a picture of two stick figures.

The school had tried to support the parents of the kindergarten class as they decided whether or not to send their children to the funeral. An e-mail had gone out with helpful links to articles written by psychologists: "Should I Let My Child Attend a Funeral?"

The parents who didn't let their children go were hopeful that those kids who did attend would have nightmares and be just a little bit scarred for life, at least enough to affect their university entrance results. The parents who did let their children go were hopeful their kids would have learned valuable lessons about the circle of life and supporting friends in their hour of need and would probably be more "resilient," which would stand them well in their teenage years, making them less likely to commit suicide or become drug addicts.

Jane had let Ziggy go because he wanted to go, and also because it was his father's funeral, even though he didn't know it, and there would be no second chance to let him attend his father's funeral.

Would she tell him one day? *Do you remember when you were little you went to your first funeral?* But he would try to attach some sort of meaning to it. He would look for something that Jane finally understood wasn't there. For the last five years she'd been searching fruitlessly for meaning in a drunken, nasty act of infidelity, and there was no meaning.

The church had been packed with Perry's grief-stricken family. Perry's sister (*Ziggy's aunt,* Jane had told herself as she sat in the back of the church with the other school parents who didn't really know Perry) had put together a little movie to commemorate Perry's life. It was so professionally done, it felt like a real movie, and it had the effect of making Perry's life seem more vibrant, rich and substantial than the lives currently being lived by the congregation. There were crisp, clear photos of him as a fair-haired chubby baby, a plump little boy, a suddenly handsome teenager, a gorgeous groom kissing his gorgeous wife, a proud new father of twins with a baby in each arm. There were video clips of him rap-dancing with the twins, blowing out candles, skiing with the boys between his legs.

The sound track was beautiful and perfectly synchronized for maximum emotional impact, so that by the end even school parents who barely knew Perry were sobbing violently, and one man accidentally clapped.

Ever since the funeral, Jane kept remembering that movie. It seemed irrefutable evidence that Perry was a good man. A good husband and father. Her memories of him in the hotel room and on the balcony—the casual violence with which he'd treated Celeste—felt flimsy and unlikely. The man with two little boys on his knees, laughing in slow motion at someone off-camera, could not possibly have done those things.

Forcing herself to remember what she knew to be true about Perry seemed pointless and pedantic, almost maliciously so. It was better manners to remember that nice movie.

Jane hadn't seen Celeste cry at the funeral. Her eyes were puffy and bloodshot, but Jane hadn't seen her cry. She looked like she was clenching her teeth, like she was waiting something out, for some awful pain to pass. The only time it looked like she might have broken down into tears was when Jane had seen her outside the church, comforting a tall, good-looking man who could barely walk he seemed so weighed down by his grief.

Jane thought she heard Celeste say, "Oh, *Saxon*," as she took his arm, but perhaps that was her mind playing tricks on her.

"Are you going to speak to her?" asked Tom as they reached the top of the stairs.

"To Celeste?" said Jane. They hadn't spoken, or at least not properly. Celeste's mother was staying with her, helping her with the boys, and Jane knew that Perry's family was also taking up a lot of her time. Jane felt as though she and Celeste would never talk about Perry. On one hand there was far too much to say, and on the other, there was nothing. Madeline said that Celeste was moving to an apartment in McMahons Point. The big beautiful house was going on the market.

"Not Celeste." Tom gave her an odd look. "To that journalist."

"Oh," said Jane. "God, no. No, I haven't. I won't. Ed said I should say no thank you when she calls in a firm, polite voice and hang up fast, the same way you do with a telemarketer. He said people get this strange idea that they have to talk to journalists, and of course you don't. They're not like the police."

She had no desire to talk to the journalist. Too many secrets. Just thinking about the policeman interviewing her in the hospital made her feel breathless. Thank God Bonnie had decided to confess.

"Are you feeling OK?" Tom stopped and put his hand on her arm. "I'm not walking too fast?"

"I'm fine. Just out of condition."

"We'll get you back to your normal athletic self."

She flicked his chest with her fingertip. "Shut up."

He smiled. She couldn't see his eyes because he was wearing sunglasses.

What were they now? Very dear friends who were more like siblings? Flirty friends who knew they would never take it any further? She honestly couldn't tell. Their attraction at the trivia night had been like a tiny perfect blossom that needed tender nurturing, or at least a drunken first kiss up against a wall in the school car park. But then everything that happened, happened. Their little seedling got stomped on by a big, black boot: death and blood and broken bones and police and a story she hadn't yet told him about Ziggy's father. They couldn't seem to get back on track now. Their rhythm was all off.

Last week they'd been out together on a date-like night to the movies and dinner. It had been perfectly nice, perfectly comfortable. They were already such good friends from all the hours they'd talked when she worked in Blue Blues. But nothing had happened. They hadn't even gotten close.

It appeared that Tom and Jane were destined for friendship. It was mildly disappointing, but not devastating. Friends could last a lifetime. The statistics were better than for relationships.

This morning she'd gotten a text from her friend's cousin,

asking if she wanted to get together for that drink. She'd texted back *Yes please.*

They walked to the park bench with the plaque dedicating it to VICTOR BERG, WHO LOVED TO WALK AROUND THIS HEAD-LAND. *Those we love don't go away, they sit beside us every day.* It always made Jane think of Poppy, who was born the same year as Victor.

"How's Ziggy?" asked Tom as they sat down and went to open their sandwiches.

"He's good," said Jane. She looked out at the expanse of blue. "Great."

Ziggy had made friends with a new boy at school who had just moved back to Australia after living in Singapore for two years. Ziggy and Lucas were suddenly inseparable. Lucas's parents, a couple in their forties, had invited Jane and Ziggy over for dinner. There were plans to set Jane up with Lucas's uncle.

Tom suddenly put his hand on Jane's arm. "Oh my God."

"What?" said Jane. He was looking out to sea as if he'd seen something.

"I think I'm getting a message." He put a finger to his temple. "Yes! Yes, I am. It's from Victor!"

"Victor?"

"Victor Berg, who loved to walk around this headland!" said Tom impatiently. He jabbed a finger at the plaque. "Vic, mate, what is it?"

"God, you're a dork," said Jane affectionately.

Tom looked at Jane. "Vic says if I don't hurry up and kiss this girl, I'm a bloody fool."

"Oh!" said Jane. She felt a rush of goose bumps. Her stomach lurched with elation as if she'd won a prize. She'd been trying to comfort herself with little lies. My God, of *course* she'd been disappointed that nothing was happening. She'd been so, so disappointed. "Really? Is that what he's—"

But he was already kissing her, one hand on the side of her face, the other removing the sandwich from her lap and putting it on the seat next to him, and it turned out that little seedling hadn't been crushed after all, and that first kisses didn't necessarily require darkness and alcohol, they could happen in the open air, with the sun warm on your face and everything around you honest and real and true and thank God she hadn't been chewing gum because she would have to have swallowed it quick-smart and she might have missed the fact that Tom tasted exactly the way she always suspected he'd taste: of cinnamon sugar and coffee and the sea.

"I was worried we were destined for friendship," she said when they came up for air.

Tom brushed a lock of hair off her forehead and tucked it behind her ear. "Are you kidding? Besides, I've got enough friends."

83.

Samantha: So we're done then? You've got everything you need? Quite a saga, eh? We're all back to normal now, except all us parents are being extremely *nice* to one another. It's kind of hilarious.

Gabrielle: They've canceled the spring ball. We're sticking to cake stalls now. Just what I need. I've put on five kilos from the stress of all this.

Thea: Renata is moving to London. The marriage is kaput. I would have tried harder myself, but that's just me. I can't help myself, I just have to put my children first.

Harper: Naturally, we'll be visiting Renata in London next year! Once she's settled, of course. She says it might take a while. Yes, I am giving Graeme a second chance. One trashy little nanny isn't going to destroy my marriage. Don't worry. He's paying. Not just with his cracked ribs. We're all off to see *The Lion King* tonight.

Stu: The biggest mystery is this: Why didn't that French bird ever make a move on me?

Jonathan: She actually did make a move on me but that's off the record.

Miss Barnes: I have no idea what happened to the petition. No one spoke of it again after the trivia night.

We're all looking forward to a new term and a fresh start. I thought we might do a special unit on conflict resolution. It seems appropriate.

Jackie: Hopefully the kids can be left alone now to learn to read and write.

Mrs. Lipmann: I think perhaps we've all learned to be a little kinder to one another. And to document everything. *Everything.*

Carol: So apparently Madeline's book club didn't actually have anything to do with erotic fiction at all! It was all a joke! Such prudes they turned out to be! But funnily enough, just yesterday, a friend from church mentioned she belonged to a Christian Erotic Fiction Club. I'm already three chapters into our first book, and I won't lie, it's quite fun and really rather, well, what's the word? *Spicy!*

Detective-Sergeant Adrian Quinlan: I thought it was the wife, to be honest. All my instincts were telling me it was the wife. I would have put money on it. Goes to show you can't always trust your instincts. So there you go. That's it. You must have all you need by now, right? You're turning that off? Because I was wondering, I don't know if this is appropriate, but I wondered if you fancied a dri—

84.

A Year After the Trivia Night

Celeste sat behind a long table with a white tablecloth, waiting for her name to be called. Her heart thumped. Her mouth was dry. She picked up the glass of water in front of her and watched her hand tremble. She quickly put it back down; she wasn't sure if she could get it safely to her mouth without spilling it.

She'd spoken in court a few times recently, but this was different. She didn't want to cry, although Susi had told her it was fine, and understandable, and even likely.

"You'll be speaking about some very personal, very painful experiences," said Susi. "It's a big thing I'm asking of you."

Celeste looked out at the small audience of men and women in suits and ties. Their faces were blank, professional; some of them looked a little bored.

"I always pick someone in the audience," Perry had told her once when they were talking about public speaking. "A friendly-looking face somewhere right in the middle of the crowd, and when I get up, I speak to him or her as if it's just the two of us."

She remembered that she'd been surprised to hear that Perry needed any techniques at all. He always appeared so scrupulously confident and relaxed when he spoke in public, like a charismatic Hollywood star on a talk show. But that was Perry. Looking back it seemed that he'd actually lived his life in a state of perpetual low-level fear: fear of humiliation, fear of losing her, fear of not being loved.

For a moment, she wished he were here to see her speak. She couldn't help thinking that he'd be proud of her, in spite of the subject matter. The real Perry would be proud of her.

Was that delusional? Probably, yes. Delusional thinking was her specialty these days—or perhaps it had always been her specialty.

The hardest thing over the past year had been second-guessing and mistrusting her every passing thought and emotion. Every time she cried over Perry's death it was a betrayal of Jane. It was foolish and misguided and *wrong* to grieve for a man who had done what he'd done. It was wrong to cry over the tears of her sons when there was another little boy who didn't even know that Perry was his father. The right emotions were hatred and fury and regret. That was how she should be feeling, and she was happy when she felt all those things, which she often did, because they were appropriate, rational feelings, but then she'd find herself missing him, and looking forward to when he returned home from his trip, and she'd feel idiotic all over again and remind herself that Perry had cheated on her, probably on multiple occasions.

In her dreams she screamed at him. *How dare you, how dare you?* She hit him over and over. She woke with tears still wet on her face.

"I still love him," she told Susi, as if she were confessing something disgusting.

"You're allowed to still love him."

"I'm going crazy," she told her.

"You're working through it," said Susi, and she listened patiently as Celeste talked through every misdemeanor for which

Perry had punished her, in what must have been excruciating detail—"I know I should have gotten the boys to tidy up the Legos that day, but I was tired"; "I shouldn't have said what I said"; "I shouldn't have done what I did." For some reason she needed to pick endlessly over even the most trivial events over the last five years and try to get it straight in her mind.

"That wasn't fair, was it?" she kept saying to Susi, as if Susi were the referee, as if Perry were there listening to this independent arbiter.

"Do *you* think it was fair?" Susi would say, just like a good therapist should. "Do *you* think you deserved that?"

Celeste watched the man sitting to her right pick up his glass of water. His hand trembled even worse than hers, but he persevered on bringing it to his mouth, even as the ice cubes clinked and water slopped over his hand.

He was a tall, pleasant-looking, thin-faced man in his midthirties, wearing a tie under an ill-fitting red sweater. He must be another counselor, like Susi, but one who suffered a pathological fear of public speaking. Celeste wanted to put her hand on his arm to comfort him, but she didn't want to embarrass him when he, after all, was the professional here.

She looked down and saw where his black trousers had ridden up. He was wearing light brown ankle socks with his well-polished black business shoes. It was the sort of sartorial mishap that would give Madeline a fit. Celeste had let Madeline help choose her a new white silk shirt to wear today, together with a pencil skirt and black court shoes. "No toes," Madeline had said when Celeste had modelled the outfit with her choice of sandals. "Toes are not right for this event."

Celeste had acquiesced. She'd been letting Madeline do a lot of things for her over the past year. "I should have *known*," Madeline had kept saying. "I should have known what you were going through." No matter how many times Celeste assured her that there was no possible way that she could have known, that Celeste would never have *permitted* her to know, Madeline had continued to battle genuine guilt. All Celeste could do was let her be there for her now.

Celeste looked for her friendly face in the audience and settled on a woman in her fifties, with a bright bird-like face, who was nodding along encouragingly as Susi did her introduction.

She reminded Celeste a little of the boys' Year 1 teacher at their new school just around the corner from the flat. Celeste had made an appointment to see her before they started. "They idolized their father, and since his death, they've been having some behavioral issues," Celeste had told her at her first meeting.

"Of course they have," said Mrs. Hooper. She looked like nothing would surprise her. "Let's have a weekly meeting so we can stay on top of this."

Celeste had managed not to throw her arms around her and cry into her nice floral blouse.

The twins had not coped well over the past year. They were so used to Perry being gone for long periods that it took a long time for them to understand that he wasn't ever coming home. They reacted like their father reacted when things went wrong: angrily, violently. Every day they tried to kill each other, and every night they ended up in the same bed, their heads on the same pillow.

Seeing their grief felt like a punishment to Celeste, but a punishment for what? For staying with their father? For *wanting* him to die?

Bonnie did not have to do jail time. She was found guilty of involuntary manslaughter by an unlawful and dangerous act and sentenced to two hundred hours of community service. In handing down his sentence the judge noted that the defendant's moral culpability was at the lower end of the scale for this type of offense. He took into account the fact that Bonnie did not have a criminal record, was clearly remorseful and that, although it was possibly foreseeable that the victim would fall, this was not her intent.

He also took into account the testimony of expert witnesses who proved that the balcony railing was beneath the minimum height requirements of the current building code, that the bar stools were not appropriate for use on the balcony, and that other contributing factors included the weather, the consequent slipperiness of the railing and the intoxication of both the defendant and the victim.

According to Madeline, Bonnie had performed her community service with great pleasure, Abigail by her side the whole time.

There were letters going back and forth from insurance companies and lawyers, but it felt like something between all of them. Celeste had made it clear she wanted no money from the school and that she would be donating back any payouts she received to cover higher insurance premiums as a result of the accident.

The house and the other properties had been sold, and Celeste had moved the boys into the little apartment in McMahons Point and had gone back to work three days a week at a family law firm. She enjoyed the fact that she didn't think about anything else for hours at a time.

Her boys were trust-fund kids, but their trust funds weren't going to define them, and she was determined that Max and Josh would one day be asking, "Do you want fries with that?"

She'd also set up a trust fund of equal value for Ziggy.

"You don't need to do that," Jane had said, when she'd told her, over lunch at a café near Celeste's apartment. She'd looked appalled, almost nauseous. "We don't want his money. Your money, I mean."

"It's Ziggy's money. If Perry knew Ziggy was his son he would have wanted him to be treated exactly the same as Max and Josh," Celeste had told her. "Perry was——"

But then she'd found herself unable to speak, because how could she say to *Jane* that Perry was generous to a fault, and scrupulously fair. Her husband had always been so fair, except for those times when he was monstrously unfair.

But Jane had reached across the café table and taken her hand and said, "I know he was," almost as if she did understand everything that Perry was and wasn't.

Susi stood at the lectern. She looked nice today. She'd cut back on the eye makeup, thank goodness.

"Domestic violence victims often don't look at all like you'd expect them to look," said Susi. "And their stories don't always sound as black-and-white as you'd expect them to sound."

Celeste searched for her friendly face in the audience of emergency department doctors, triage nurses, GPs and counselors.

"Which is why I've asked these two lovely people here today. They've very generously given up their time to share their experiences with you." Susi lifted her hand to encompass Celeste and the man sitting next to her. He had placed one hand on his own thigh to try to stop his leg from jiggling up and down with nerves.

My God, thought Celeste. She blinked back a sudden rush of hot tears. *He's not a counselor. He's someone like me. It happened to him.*

She turned to look at him and he smiled back at her, his eyes darting about like tiny fish.

"Celeste?" said Susi.

Celeste stood. She glanced back at the man in the sweater, and then over to Susi, who nodded encouragingly, and Celeste walked the few steps to stand behind the wooden lectern.

She searched the audience for that nice-looking woman. Yes. There she was, smiling, nodding a little.

Celeste took a breath.

She'd agreed to come here today as a favor for Susi, and because, sure, she wanted to do her bit to make sure health professionals knew when to ask more questions, when not to let things go. She'd been planning to give them the facts, but not to spill her soul. She would keep her dignity. She would keep a little piece of herself safe.

But now she was suddenly filled with a passionate desire to share everything, to say the bare ugly truth, to hold nothing back. Fuck dignity.

She wanted to give that terrified man in the uncool sweater the confidence to share his own bare ugly truth. She wanted to let him know that at least one person here today understood all the mistakes he'd made along the way: the times he'd hit back, the times he'd stayed when he should have left, the times he'd given her another chance, the times he'd deliberately antagonized her, the times he'd let his children see things they shouldn't see. She wanted to tell him that she knew all the perfect little lies he'd told himself for all those years, because she'd told herself the same lies. She wanted to enfold his trembling hands between her own and say, "I understand."

She gripped both sides of the lectern and leaned in close to the

microphone. There was something so simple and yet so complicated that she needed these people to understand.

"This can happen . . ."

She stopped, stepped away slightly from the microphone and
cleared her throat. She saw Susi standing to one side with the
held-breath expression of a parent whose child is performing in
public for the first time; her hands were held slightly aloft, as if
she were ready to run onstage and scoop Celeste to safety.

Celeste put her mouth closer to the microphone, and now her
voice was loud and clear.

"This can happen to anyone."

Acknowledgments

As always, I am so grateful to all the wonderful, talented people at Amy Einhorn Books, with special thanks to the amazing Amy Einhorn herself, as well as Liz Stein and Katie McKee.

Thank you to my agent, Faye Bender, and my publishers and editors around the world, especially Cate Paterson, Celine Kelly, and Maxine Hitchcock.

Thank you so much to Cherie Penney, Marisa Vella, Maree Atkins, Ingrid Bown, and Mark Davidson for generously giving up your time so I could benefit from your various professional fields of expertise.

I have a terrible habit of scavenging through conversations looking for material. Thank you, Mary Hassal, Emily Crocker, and Liz Frizell for allowing me to borrow tiny pieces of your life for fictional purpose. Now seems like a good time to make clear that the parents at the lovely school where my children currently attend are *nothing* like the parents at Pirriwee Public, and are disappointingly well-behaved at school functions.

Thank you to Mum, Dad, Kati, Fiona, Sean, and Nicola, with special thanks to my sister, the brilliant author Jaclyn Moriarty, who always has been and always will be my very first reader.

Thank you to Anna Kuper for making my life so much easier in so many ways.

Thank you to fellow authors and friends Ber Carroll and Dianne Blacklock for turning book tours into girls weekends away. (Ber even manages to make *shopping* fun.) We produce a joint newsletter called *Book Chat*. To subscribe, visit my website at lianemoriarty.com.

Thank you to Adam, George, and Anna for making my world complete. And kind of loud and crazy.

In the end, this novel turned out to be a story about friendship, so I'm dedicating it to my friend Margaret Palisi, with whom I share thirty-five years of memories.

The following books were useful to me in writing this novel: *"Not to People Like Us": Hidden Abuse in Upscale Marriages* by Susan Weitzman (2000) and *Surviving Domestic Violence: Voices of Women Who Broke Free* by Elaine Weiss (2004).

Big Little Lies

Discussion Questions

1. At the beginning of the novel, Madeline is enraged over Ziggy not being invited to Amabella's birthday party. Why do you think Madeline becomes so angry about such a seemingly small injustice? Do you think Madeline is the kind of person who just looks for a fight, or do you think she was justified in feeling so upset? And do you think that by tackling both ends of the spectrum—from school yard bullying and parents behaving badly in the playground to displays of domestic violence in all its incarnations—the author is trying to say something about the bullying that happens out in the open every day?

2. There is a lot of discussion about women and their looks. On the beach Jane's mom shows that she has rather poor body image. Jane observes that women over forty are constantly talking about their age. And Madeline says, "She didn't want to admit, even to herself, just how much the aging of her face really did genuinely depress her. She wanted to be above such superficial concerns. She wanted to be depressed about the state of the world . . ." [p. 86] Do you think this obsession with

looks is specific to women, particularly women of a certain age? Why or why not?

3. There are a lot of scenes in which the characters say they wish they could be violent: Jane says she wants to throw Ziggy into the wall when he has a tirade in the bathtub, that she would hit Renata if she was in front of her, and then she stops just short of kicking Harper. Do you think the author is trying to show the reader Perry's side and have us sympathize with him? Or, rather, that feeling violent is a natural impulse but one that people learn to suppress?

4. When Ziggy has to do his family tree, Madeline comments, "Why try to slot fractured families into neat little boxes in this day and age?" [p. 193] A lot of Madeline's storyline is about the complications that arise from the merging of new modern families. What kind of problems exist among families and extended families now that didn't when you were a child?

5. When Jane recounts what happened the night she got pregnant, she focuses on what the man said rather than on what he did. Why does Jane feel more violated by two words—*fat* and *ugly*—than by the actual assault? Jane seems to think the answer is "Because we live in a beauty-obsessed society where the most important thing a woman can do is make herself attractive to men." [p. 206] Do you agree?

6. The power of secrets is a theme throughout the novel. Jane remembers, "She hadn't told anyone. She'd swallowed it whole and pretended it meant nothing, and therefore it had

come to mean everything." [p. 232] Do you think this is a universal truth, that the more you keep something secret, the more power it takes on?

7. Gwen, the babysitter, seems to be the only one to suspect what is going on with Celeste and Perry. Celeste then realizes she's never heard Gwen talk about a husband or a partner. Do you think the author intended to insinuate that perhaps Gwen had had an abusive husband or partner and that she left him? And in light of what happens at the end with Bonnie, do you think it's only people who have personally experienced abuse who pick up on the signs?

8. At one point Jane thinks she and Ziggy will have to leave Pirriwee because "rich, beautiful people weren't asked to leave anywhere." [p. 383] Do you think different rules apply to rich people? Do you think being rich allowed Perry to get away with things longer than would have been likely if he hadn't had money?

9. Bonnie says, "We see. We fucking *see!*" [p. 447] Were you surprised to learn about Bonnie's history? Were you surprised to discover that all along Max had been seeing what Perry was doing to Celeste?

10. What did you make of the interview snippets to the reporter? Do you think the author used them almost like a Greek chorus to make a point?

11. Madeline muses, "Maybe it was actually an unspoken instant agreement between the four women on the balcony: *No woman*

should pay for the accidental death of that particular man. Maybe it was an involuntary, atavistic response to thousands of years of violence against women. Maybe it was for every rape, every brutal backhanded slap, every other Perry that had come before this one." [p. 456] And then Madeline thinks, "Sometimes doing the wrong thing was also right." [p. 457] Do you agree with this statement? Do you agree with what the women decided to do? Do you think there's a stronger bond between women than there is between men? Were you surprised that women who ostensibly didn't like one another—Madeline and Bonnie, Madeline and Renata—ended up coming together to help one another out?

12. At one point in the book, Susi says that, in Australia, one woman dies every week because of domestic violence. In the United States, more than three women are murdered by their husbands or boyfriends every day. Every nine seconds in the United States a woman is assaulted or beaten. Domestic violence is the leading cause of injury to women—more than that caused by car accidents, muggings, and rapes combined. Are you surprised by these statistics? Why or why not? Clearly, the author chose Celeste—the picture-perfect mom and wife as well as an educated lawyer—to be the victim of domestic violence in order to make a point. Do you think it's plausible that someone like her would fall victim to abuse such as this?

13. Madeline comments that "there were so many levels of evil in the world." [p. 460] Discuss the implications of this statement in light of the novel and the novel's different storylines.

About the Author

Liane Moriarty is the author of seven internationally bestselling novels, *Three Wishes*, *The Last Anniversary*, *What Alice Forgot*, *The Hypnotist's Love Story*, *The Husband's Secret*, *Big Little Lies* and *Truly Madly Guilty*. *The Husband's Secret*, *Big Little Lies* and *Truly Madly Guilty* all reached #1 on the *New York Times* bestsellers list. Liane's books have been translated into more than thirty-five languages and have sold millions of copies worldwide, and most have been optioned for film. Liane lives in Sydney with her husband, son and daughter.

The #1 *New York Times* Bestselling Author
LIANE MORIARTY

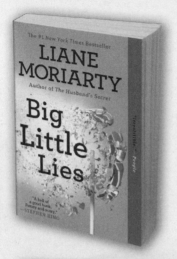

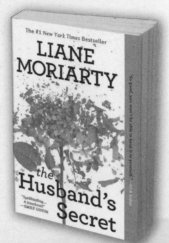

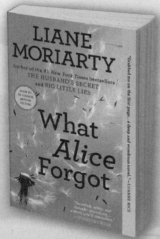

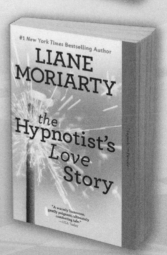

 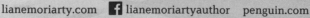